MR DARCY AND THE SUFFRAGETTE

SUFFRAGETTE

Maggie Mooha

PRAISE FOR MAGGIE MOOHA'S BOOKS

Elizabeth in the New World

"JANE AUSTEN FANS! THIS IS FOR YOU!!!!! This is an extremely well written "sequel" to Jane Austen's Pride and Prejudice. A tale of romance, intrigue, passion, exotic locations, heroism, and one of the greatest love stories for the ages!" ~dandelackland

"A breathtakingly original twist and continuation on a cherished Austen classic, Elizabeth in the New World *opens doors to "what-ifs" and imaginative, well thought out scenarios that will leave fans of the original book enthralled and satisfied. A well written, exciting novel that is both daring and unique. I look forward to more from this author!"* ~Sebastian Moran

"This book is a fantastic continuation of the Elizabeth and Darcy story. I'd read before bed and tell myself, "just finish this chapter, then go to sleep." But it was hard, because I couldn't wait to read what would happen next! The characters were very well-developed, and the story compelling. Great ending, too. I can't wait for a sequel so I can continue on their journey." ~Amy Pippins

"I consider this among the outstanding Austen variations that I have read and give it my highest recommendation. This book has it all, an enduring love story amidst historical references to slavery, other social and class changes, and characters who grew in character while loving each other. The depth of emotion is wonderful. This is quite a masterpiece for a first book." ~Donna D. Krug

"This is a romance, all right, but it is also so much more. It's an exposé on the whole class system. I was immediately drawn into the adventure story, and the further I read, the more engrossing the story got. Mooha writes the characters in such a way that you really

care about them. At the conclusion I was literally in tears."
~Madelyn

The Darcys of New Orleans

"As good as the first book. I was not able to stop reading because the story kept my attention. Mooha is a fantastic new author who does her homework on the period and events in history that she writes about. Her characters are three dimensional and the situations feel real. It is a powerful insight into the life and events of the 19th century. For a few hours I was experiencing what it must have been like to be caught in a time when one's personal cultural perspective was fundamentally challenged." ~Lynn

"This book has an exciting, fast-moving plot and it is full of wonderful characters. I loved how the book put me in New Orleans high society of the early 1800s, the balls and dinners and opulence but also the wildness, which was especially fascinating because I got to view it through the Darcys' eyes. It's a book full of love--romantic, maternal, paternal, and most movingly, the strong friendship between Elizabeth and Poppy, the former slave now married to a French American aristocrat and plantation owner. I love the way Maggie Mooha writes!" ~braingirl

"In her two novels, Maggie has given us what we Jane Austen fans longed for....an imaginative pair of sequels. She knows how to capture our interest and emotions in this latest ongoing saga of the Darcy family as they traverse the very real perils of the time period. She does her research and develops her characters thoroughly so their behaviors and reactions are no surprise. The book is a page-turner with some sexy scenes thrown in that Austen may have thought about but wouldn't have dared to write! I do love books with happy endings and this one does not disappoint. Keep on writing, Maggie!" ~Rita Ransom

"Once again the author takes us into the realm of Lizzy and Darcy's tale of epic love. Based on the incredible journey Lizzy and Darcy made in Elizabeth in the New World, *the Darcys travel from England to visit their dear friends who have moved from Grenada to New Orleans. Together with their children Emma and Bennett Fitzwilliam, they enter the strange and unfamiliar world of New Orleans society. The wealthy planters of New Orleans, however, turn the Darcys' English sensibilities virtually upside down! The temptations of the Creole world are strange, yet almost irresistible to young Emma. And Darcy's nemesis Wickham returns once again! A tale of forbidden love, conflict, heroism and sacrifice well worth reading!!"* ~Eileen

In the Eye of the Beholder

"5+ stars! This brilliant book weaves romance into a fascinating history lesson on the Crimean War. It follows the Light Brigade into the Valley of Death and the survivors of the battle into the care of Florence Nightingale, who led a group of nurses tending the British wounded. The heart of this novel is when Eleanor Sherbrooke and Lieutenant Joshua Wentworth both find themselves in Crimea - he as part of the Light Brigade preparing for battle, and she as part of Florence Nightingale's staff trying to save lives but fighting abysmal conditions and lack of supplies.

And then things get worse.

I don't have the words to convey how truly excellent this is. The writing engages the reader from the first page to the last. The overwhelming chaos of war feels all too real. All the obviously well-researched historical figures and details are integral to the plot rather than tangential. The contrast between the superficial, polite London drawing rooms with the ghastly turmoil of war is particularly well done. There's also a clever juxtaposition between the opening chapters, where Eleanor's appearance is unsettling, to Wentworth's experience upon his return to England. All the characters felt real to me, from Eleanor's surprising aunt Sophronia to Wentworth's courageous horse, Merlin. And the romance! The chemistry between Wentworth and Eleanor is apparent from the start, and it increases as the story goes on." ~Debbie B.

"I have read all three of Maggie Mooha's books and I am always impressed by the efforts she has made for historical accuracy in a romance novel. All her characters are well developed and the narratives flow so well to keep the reader engaged. I lent my hard copies to people who do not want to give them back!!! I cannot wait to read her next novel." ~Anne Sustik

"As with her previous novels, Mooha once again writes complex and conversational characters that capture one's heart, vivid descriptions that carry one to another time and place, and fast paced action on every page. "In the Eye of the Beholder" is a gripping portrait of the ugliness of war and a great peek into a historical event that most Americans know little about. Staying up late to finish it by lantern light while tent camping, I felt a little kinship with the lady with the lamp!" ~country doc

"This third book written by Ms Mooha was one I couldn't put down until I finished it! The characters were well-developed, & the story kept my intent interest! Keep some tissues handy, though, because there are some very sad parts that will have you feeling the pain of losing someone dear to you! Keep on writing, Ms Mooha~~ you've got it going on!" ~Karla Allen

www.BOROUGHSPUBLISHINGGROUP.com

PUBLISHER'S NOTE: This is a work of fiction. Names, characters, places and incidents either are the product of the author's imagination or are used fictitiously. Any resemblance to actual events, locales, business establishments or persons, living or dead, is coincidental. Boroughs Publishing Group does not have any control over and does not assume responsibility for author or third-party websites, blogs or critiques or their content.

Mr Darcy and the Suffragette
Copyright © 2023 Maggie Mooha

ISBN: 978-1-957295-24-4

To the suffragettes and all the defenders of women's rights who followed in their footsteps

AUTHOR'S NOTE

For those of you who are sticklers for historical accuracy, I apologize for the tango teas taking place a year and a half before the craze hit in 1913. Artistic license.

I did quite a bit of research for this book, and if you are interested in the *Titanic* sinking, the best book on the subject was one I used extensively and was written by someone who was there. It's called *The Story of the Titanic as Told by Its Survivors* by Jay Winocour. And yes, there were those who swam away from the *Titanic* and survived. Amazing.

As for the suffragette movement, *The Suffragette: The History of the Women's Militant Suffrage Movement* by Sylvia Pankhurst and Emmeline Pankhurst is a bit dry but written by the people who were the leaders of the movement. You'll be surprised at Winston Churchill's attitude in those days.

Of course, I have to give credit to a book called *Shopgirls* by Pamela Cox and Annabel Hobley. It was a real eye-opener.

And finally, a book called *Shopping, Seduction and Mr. Selfridge* by Linda Woodhead. It was the book they based the TV series on. But trust me, they took quite a few liberties with the actual story. (That dishy window dresser from France was a figment of someone's imagination. The man in charge of the fabulous Selfridge window displays was a man from Chicago called Goldsman.)

There are many, many websites I used, and there are too many to mention here.

If you are interested in the Suffrage Pilgrimage, take a look at this webpage: https://blog.nationalarchives.gov.uk/the-1913-suffrage-pilgrimage-peaceful-protest-and-local-disorder/

One of the best things about writing historical fiction is all the interesting things I get to learn along the way.

I hope you enjoyed reading the story as much as I enjoyed writing it.

MR DARCY AND THE SUFFRAGETTE

Chapter 1

Wickham followed the steward to his first-class stateroom, a satisfied smile crossing his lips. The steward, however, didn't smile. He ran a jaundiced eye over Wickham, no doubt noticing his waiter's uniform, and wordlessly slipped the key into the lock and turned it.

It was then he spoke. "Are you sure this is your cabin? Don't you belong below with the rest of us?"

"Not that it is any of your business, but my life prospects have suddenly changed for the better." Wickham, returning the scrutiny, ran his eye over the steward. "I'll call you if I need you, my good man." The steward huffed and turned on his heel.

One of Wickham's life ambitions was to either be a kept man or, saving that, marry money. Tonight, he accomplished the latter. The delicious irony of it was that he completed the task by marrying a nearly penniless girl. He tossed back his head and laughed but snapped his head back at the twinge of pain. His encounter with Darcy the evening before still left its mark on his throat. He ran his fingers inside his collar. Almost a dead man to a man of wealth in the space of two days. *Ah, Wickham, the fates have smiled on you indeed.*

It was past twenty-four hundred hours, and he was finally off duty, ready to commence his wedding night. How many times before had his feet sunk into this lush carpet, while he, bent over a trolley, pushed comestibles to the high and mighty. Now his days as a waiter were over… well, they would be over as soon as this voyage was. He and his bride would return posthaste to London in style and present themselves to the firm of Huntley and Associates, where he would claim his bride's "dowry". Until that fortune was firmly in his grip, he was beholden to the masters of this vessel and would retain his position. It was safer that way. No point in burning one's bridges. Still, what could go wrong?

He turned the knob and entered the stateroom. Oddly, no lights were on. Ah, perhaps the little minx was waiting for him, young and nubile and divested of her clothing, nestled in the four-poster.

"Where are you, my dove?" he purred as his gaze adjusted to the dim light shed through the porthole by the crescent moon. Blinking, he could scarcely believe his eyes. The bed was rumpled but empty. Snapping on the lights, he found the sitting room and the bath empty as well. He noticed it then. Silence. The noise of the throbbing engines that they all lived with from the very outset of the voyage had ceased for the second time. When the noise stopped before, he thought perhaps he had imagined it, but now, he was sure. Why were they stopping, and more to the point, where was his bride?

She must have left him a note or some clue as to her whereabouts. He ran his hands along the sheets of the bed and inspected the mahogany nightstand. Nothing. He looked again in the bath. Towels strewn across the floor, still damp. She had bathed for him. Lovely. He picked one of them up and ran the plush cotton through his fingers. Soft, thick, inviting, and even monogrammed…

"RMS *Titanic.*" He made a mental note to pack one of these towels in his suitcase as a souvenir of the night his fortunes changed. Draping it over the side of the bath, he resolved to go in search of his new wife.

***

Fourteen Months Earlier

"I don't know, Lizzy." Jane let her gloved hand cover her sister's as they jostled along in the train carriage towards the city, and Lizzy relaxed. "You are always so sure of yourself. I just don't know. Perhaps we should have disclosed our plans to Mama and Papa."

"I have talked to Papa. He approves wholeheartedly."

Jane gave a visible start. She touched a wisp of hair that came loose from her pompadour and tucked it under her flowered hat. "Really?"

"Well, perhaps not wholeheartedly. He didn't like the idea at first, of course." Elizabeth tried to gently revise her rather bold statement. "It did take a bit of convincing, and I did tell him that, if we couldn't find a position during our two-week visit, then we would be back to Longbourn like a shot."

Jane shook her head. "Working as a shopgirl in London... how you get Papa to go along with your schemes, I'll never know."

"It's merely a question of economics. He has five daughters and no sons and entailed property. Entailment. It's 1911... the twentieth century. You'd think they would have done away with something so archaic, wouldn't you?" This attempt at changing the subject wasn't working. Elizabeth could read her sister's expression like a book. "You know, you can always go home if you want, but I won't... and that is a fact."

Jane's expression became pained. "Is home so distasteful to you?"

"No, of course not. I just feel... I just feel like a caged tigress: full of energy and nowhere to put it."

"You know, Father said you could further your education..."

Elizabeth squeezed Jane's hand. "Yes, I could, but then what? Marry and have children and—"

"Oh, I want to marry and have children, don't you? Do you think if we follow your plan that we'll never marry or have any children? Oh, Lizzy."

She couldn't help it. Elizabeth had to laugh. "Oh, good gracious, Jane, we're not entering a convent. We are seeking employment. We are going to live on our own, the two of us. We are going to make our own way in the world. Once we have a taste of freedom, who knows? It's going to be wonderful. You'll see."

Jane's expression, which varied between skepticism and outright terror, spoke more to Elizabeth than words. Obviously, Jane didn't share in Lizzy's enthusiasm but was doing what she always did: lending her support to her younger sister. "You can always go home if you don't want to carry on. I can stay in London by myself."

"Absolutely not." Jane put more force in her voice than before. "We will have this adventure together."

Elizabeth had to smile. She patted Jane's hand again. "Besides, we always have the Gardiners to scoop us up if we fall." That last remark seemed to settle Jane a bit and she relaxed back in the seat. Elizabeth joined her. Jane leaned her head on Lizzy's shoulder and whispered, "It will be an adventure, won't it?"

***

Aunt Gardiner was well and truly appalled at Elizabeth's plan. The shopgirls of London had a rather checkered reputation. Elizabeth was sure that it was due to the fact most of these millionaire goods purveyors paid less than a living wage, and a girl needed to eat, one way or another. Elizabeth, though, wasn't about to be shut up in a dormitory, fed gruel, and worked until she dropped. No indeed. She and Jane would start at the top. She and Jane would apply for a position at Selfridges.

She remembered the first day, two years ago, she was taken by the arm by her uncle and shown the wonders of the Selfridge windows at Christmas time. She had never seen anything so magnificent in all her life, not even at the theatre. Not even at a *London* theatre. As they wandered up and down the aisles inside the store, she was treated to wonder after wonder. This place was a fairy land compared to the stuffy little shops in Meryton. It surpassed every store in London as well. This place beckoned to her, and she would be part of it.

Within two days of their arrival at the Gardiners, they were standing in a queue of at least fifty if not a hundred young women vying for positions. Judging from the conversation around them, many had worked in other places before—eating spoilt meat, living in on the store's premises (and supervised at every turn like errant children), paying fines out of their meager wages for minor infractions. Selfridges was an escape from all those things *and* they paid a higher wage. It seemed to Elizabeth that every girl in London stood in that queue.

Soon after they gained admittance to the store, Elizabeth and Jane were busily writing on their applications. A murmur of voices from nearby caught Elizabeth's attention. Several men, all having the look of floor walkers, celluloid collars spotless, murmured and gazed in Jane's direction. Jane was a beauty, and that fact didn't escape their interviewers. A middle-aged man, upright, balding, in a smart, grey gabardine suit, walked over. Jane was still busy scribbling. He cleared his throat and Jane looked up. Unlike a social occasion, the gentleman came directly to the point.

"Have you any experience attending in a shop?" he asked, peering over his pince-nez in Jane's direction.

"No, sir, I am afraid not." She looked over at Elizabeth in desperation.

"We are willing to work hard for this enterprise," Elizabeth said before the floorwalker strode away. "And we do know how to speak to ladies of fashion and discernment." How that had popped into her head, she would never know. As their interrogator harumphed and walked away, Elizabeth observed the others. They eyed Jane.

After the applications were collected, they were told to come back tomorrow. A list of those they would deign to interview would be pinned on the door. Elizabeth's thoughts swung from wild hope to crushing despair. Why would they hire two young ladies from the provinces with no experience in waiting in a shop when they had scores of girls who could walk in tomorrow and know exactly what they were doing?

"Oh, I 'ope they call me," Elizabeth heard one of them say. "I ain't too fond of me present situation. Can't fairly breathe wrong there."

"And if you call any of these old bags 'dearie' see if you don't pay a right great fine for it."

Jane listened to all this banter as well and gave Lizzy a demure smile. When they finally reached the street and were out of earshot of the other girls, she spoke. "I do believe I am catching your enthusiasm for this adventure. We may not have any shopkeeping experience, but we certainly can speak well."

Hope ascended in Lizzy's heart. Selfridges had a reputation to maintain. Most of these girls were working class. Perhaps the education they received, which was not extensive but at least existent, and their growing up in the house of a gentleman might serve them well.

"Well, there is nothing else for it now, dear sister. Let's return to the Gardiners and tell them of our adventures. Perhaps we should bring some sweets for the children."

"Or some treacle tarts," said Jane, her eyes twinkling. There was no end of wonders to be had in London.

Chapter 2

Mr Darcy sat comfortably ensconced in the plush furniture of Mr Bingley's house in town and brushed the non-existent lint from the crisp crease in his trouser leg. "It is not that I think anything is inherently *wrong* with being in trade. After all…" He dared not finish his sentence, but his friend had no such compunction.

"After all, you are friends with the likes of me."

"Oh, really, Bingley." The exasperation was evident. "I do know that the world is changing. I am not such a Luddite as you think."

"I do not think you a Luddite, Mr Darcy…" Caroline Bingley's simpering tones always raised his hackles, but to show anything but civility would not be gentlemanly. "…only discerning."

He was about to, God forbid, agree with Caroline when Bingley interrupted. "I just want you to go to the store. It really is a wonder. I can't believe that you have never been."

"Charles is right, Mr Darcy. It is a wonder."

"For ladies, perhaps…"

"Oh, really, Darcy. Selfridge has installed barber shops, a smoking room, even a firing range for the gentlemen. Please, come along… just to be sociable."

Caroline was undoubtedly batting her eyelids at him, so he dared not look. "All right, I will go, but do not expect me to acquiesce to anything else."

"First steps are always the most difficult." Caroline chimed in again and he had to meet her eye this time. Yes, batting her lashes, as he suspected. He rose from the overstuffed armchair.

"All right then. Lead on."

***

Life was full of irony, was it not? Elizabeth could feel the life drain out of her as she read through the list a second time. Jane had been called back for an interview, but she hadn't. Who had the dream of working at Selfridges? Who convinced her father that, as the two eldest, they could contribute to the waning family fortune? Who wanted to live independently in London, beholden to no one? Not Jane. Jane had come along for company, and now it was Jane who held the brass ring in her hand. Now, here she was in the employment department anteroom at Selfridges as Jane's companion and moral support.

Jane kept her voice to almost a whisper. The oak-panelled waiting room was filled with other prospects. The two of them sat, squeezed together with the other girls on one of the benches that lined the walls. "No, Lizzy. I won't do it. The plan all along was that we were to work together, not me alone."

"It's all right. Really. I will go along to Harrods or Owens or another place and find a position. You'll see."

"But if you do that, you will have to live-in, and our plan to share a room will come to naught. I can't afford a place on my own."

"You can always share with another girl from Selfridges and live with the Gardiners until you make arrangements. It can be done." Lizzy listened to her own words as if someone else spoke them. She wondered if her sister could detect the disappointment and artifice in her tone. She was making a good argument but didn't agree with it herself. Then something occurred to her. "Just think, Jane. If you are employed here and do well, you could make a path for me later." She was about to go on, when the door to the office swung open.

"Miss Jane Bennet, Miss Mabel Cartwright, Miss…" That selfsame gentleman from their application process read the list aloud of those who were granted interviews. Jane threw a panicked glance at Lizzy.

"It's all right. Go on. I will wait for you here."

Jane joined the line of excited young women with the air of someone attending a hanging. Elizabeth hoped her sister would pluck up her courage. This was but a minor setback. They would succeed.

Jane was inside an awfully long time. Elizabeth hoped it was a good sign. After all, how long did it take to say "no"? She had been ruminating on such thoughts when the office door opened again.

"Is there a Miss Elizabeth Bennet here?"

"Yes, yes, I am Elizabeth Bennet."

"Come with me, miss."

***

Jane, indeed, was a loyal sister. She wouldn't take a position if it didn't include Lizzy, so there they were… together. They had only been a week in their new positions as window dressers, and Elizabeth did not flatter herself that her and Jane's talent were the reason they were not stuck behind a counter. They were in window display because they *were* window display. Again, she did not flatter herself. Jane was window display.

At first, it was disconcerting to have people on the street stop and stare at them as they opened the curtained window to evaluate the stage sets they had draped with fur-collared coats over Louis XIV chairs.

"I feel like an animal in the zoo," Jane whispered over to Lizzy as they propped up some spectacular hats—wide brimmed and teaming with ostrich feathers, black silk roses, and yards of ribbon. "I feel that it is I who am on display."

"Oh, you are, silly girl. You're the most beautiful thing in this window."

Jane gave Lizzy a shy smile and set a rather magnificent chapeau on an unseeing, unhearing mannequin head. "Wouldn't you just love a hat like this?"

"And where would I wear it? To the fish-and-chip shop?" They both laughed before the stern voice of Mr Goldsman called from inside the store.

"This is not a vacation at the shore, ladies. Finish and come inside for further instruction. I am going out to look." His flat, American accent gave his words extra emphasis

Lizzy made a face, imitating their supervisor, and Jane had to cover her mouth to suppress a giggle.

"Come here, Jane, and look over the display. See if we can change anything before we are scolded." Lizzy motioned her sister to the corner of the window to get a view of their work.

"I think we've done a masterful job." Jane folded her arms and gazed over the scene with satisfaction. The window rivalled a room in a great house. The walls were made of walnut wainscotting, papered in the latest mode, and hung with mirrors. Antique tables, inlaid with ivory and mother of pearl and draped with fine fabric, displayed the most massive and fabulous hats and coats of the day.

Elizabeth walked across the length of the window and, after crouching down, adjusted the drape of a "casually thrown" exquisite wrap. "There, that's better. I do believe we are mastering this art, don't you?" As she turned to look at Jane, she noticed three people, two men and a woman, so close to the window that, if it wasn't there, they could have reached up and touched the hem of Jane's skirt. One of the young men, slight build, tall, with light brown hair visible beneath his bowler hat, fixated on Jane. He had one of those faces one might describe as angelic, with an open expression that betrayed every thought in his head. The thought Lizzy saw now was that of complete and utter rapture. Jane had captured another heart. "Don't look now, but you have another admirer at your feet."

Jane turned suddenly, and the young man jumped back, jostling his companion. The other man, not quite as tall, with piercing dark eyes and an intense expression, said something Elizabeth could not hear. No doubt, his friend had tread upon his toe. Jane looked down at her admirer and, of course, smiled. He gazed up at her with a beatific expression. They were both entranced for some moments.

His companions, however, were not so entranced. The woman, who seemed to be looking down her nose even as she tilted her head upward, muttered something. The intense young man fell silent but scowled. Lizzy, who always was in the mood for mischief, called out to their supervisor.

"Would you mind if we join you outside, Mr Goldsman? You can show us then if you want anything changed."

"Absolutely. Good idea. Come outside, ladies."

This exchange broke the spell. Jane stared, wide-eyed, at Lizzy. "What are you doing?"

"You want to meet him, don't you? Come along." Elizabeth took Jane by the hand, and they slipped off.

***

"Really, Charles, what do you think you're doing?"

Mr Bingley had his sister by the elbow and hastened her inside.

Mr Darcy smiled in spite of himself. "She really is a beauty, Charles, but wait until she opens her mouth. No doubt a cockney twang will pop out."

"I highly doubt it. There is some quality about her..." Bingley hurried Caroline through the doors, with Darcy close on his heels. They soon reached the interior wall of the window, but the access doors were closed, and there was no one about except other shoppers and the girls behind the counters.

"Damn and blast," Bingley said impatiently under his breath.

"Really, your language." Caroline tossed her head. "You forget yourself… and your manners. We are here to show Mr Darcy about. Have you forgotten?"

Bingley stood turning this way and that. "I'm sorry, what did you say?"

Darcy sighed. "Come along. There must be other wonders here for you to show me."

Caroline was already distracted. "Oh, look at those divine gloves. Come along, gentlemen." As the two men reluctantly followed, they were suddenly affronted by a rather short, but impeccably dressed gentleman with salt-and-pepper hair parted down the middle, and he sported a rather prodigious moustache. He offered his hand to Bingley.

"Charles, how nice to see you. Come to poke about my little shop?" He had an American accent and exuded energy.

"Little shop, indeed. You are comical. Harry, may I introduce my sister, Caroline Bingley and my friend, Mr Darcy. Caroline, Darcy, this is Harry Selfridge."

***

Elizabeth's scheming had come to naught. When they arrived outside to view the window, the trio they had observed only moments before was gone. Jane looked about for a moment, then riveted her attention on the designer, Mr Goldsman. She appeared to give him all her attention, but Elizabeth knew better. She was disappointed that the young man had disappeared.

Mr Goldsman approved their work, as did a throng of onlookers. "I do believe you captured my idea, Miss Bennets. We needn't fiddle with it. Let us look at the next display. We will begin changing that one out tomorrow." He always referred to them as the "Miss Bennets" as if they were a set of bookends. "We'll get a few of the fellas to move the heavier things."

As they returned to the store, a commotion near the glove counter caught Lizzy's attention. So, that's where they got to. The hubbub was caused by Mr Selfridge himself. It appeared to Elizabeth that he knew Jane's admirer quite well. She elbowed her sister. "Looks like you might be seeing more of that young man of yours." She teased everyone, and poor Jane was no exception.

"Oh, stop. He's certainly not 'my young man.'" Jane blushed.

"His two companions seem rather… what's the word I am looking for?"

"Reserved?"

"I was going to say 'pompous."

"Oh, no. You misjudge them, I'm sure. He would never have mean-spirited companions."

Lizzy laughed and that caught the attention of their supervisor. "Are you coming, ladies? I have plans to show you for the window we are dressing tomorrow. My, my, you are distracted today."

***

"So, you see, Mr Darcy, being a member of our board of directors has advantages for us both. For you, generous compensation for your services, and for us, the benefit of your advice and counsel." They were sitting in the Palm Court Restaurant, inside Selfridges, where Mr Selfridge had invited them to lunch. The atmosphere was very informal, which, oddly, didn't put Darcy at his ease as the conversation had taken a wild and interesting turn.

Darcy squinted at Harry Selfridge in disbelief. "Whatever could I contribute to your enterprise? I know nothing of commerce, let alone retail commerce."

"Oh, now, Darcy, don't sell yourself short," Bingley chimed in. Darcy threw him a questioning look. Darcy knew he was being led down the primrose path, but as yet could not put his finger on exactly what it was this Selfridge fellow wanted of him. Bingley also seemed a bit desperate for him to take Selfridge's offer. He could certainly use an additional four thousand pounds a year that Selfridge's salary would afford him. The lot of a landowner and head of a long and distinguished line had not been a happy one of late. For so much money, though, there must be something the two of them were not telling him. Bingley was making alternately encouraging and frantic faces at him.

"Let us just say that a man of distinction such as yourself gives an enterprise such as ours a certain *savoir faire*, if you get my meaning."

Ah-ha. It became abundantly clear. Mr Henry Gordon Selfridge wanted to avail himself of Darcy's influence among his peers in the landed gentry and the aristocracy, his connections, and most of all, of his good name—all for the generous price of four thousand pounds per year.

A generation ago, he would have turned the man down flatly and stormed out of his dining establishment never to return. Now, with tenant farmers, the magnificent but aging manor house, and of course, his future and Georgiana's and, in fact, the future of the Darcy name and all it entailed to consider, he paused. Entwining his fingers and pressing them to his lips, he chose his words carefully.

"I am intrigued with your proposition, Mr Selfridge…"

"Harry, please…."

Ugh, these Americans and their informality. "Harry, then. Can you give me some time to consider your offer?"

Selfridge's face lit up and he literally jumped out of his seat and proffered his hand. "Well, that's good to hear, Darcy. Very good." While still shaking Darcy's hand, he grinned at Bingley. It occurred to him then that this was not an accidental meeting. He was angry with Bingley, but he would not show it now. Selfridge continued. "When you finish your lunch, please feel free to walk about the store, ask the staff any questions you like, come to our meetings, and see how we operate. I'm sure you'll be impressed with the way we do things around here. We make use of our employees' talent. Yes, we do. Now, I have to be going." Selfridge propelled himself out of his seat, his repast half eaten, leaving a stunned Darcy and grinning Bingley behind.

Chapter 3

After their evening meal, Jane and Elizabeth retired to their room. The boarding house was clean, if not opulent, and they were happy to find it. They were not far from the Gardiners, in Cheapside. The other lodgers were also employees of Selfridges, and that is how they found the place—through their fellow workers. Although they loved their aunt, uncle, and the children, it was a relief to get out and be on their own. That, after all, was the whole point.

Besides, the place felt like home. A white tablecloth always covered the long dining table, and Mrs Clarke was a good cook. The fare was simple and plentiful, and room and board did not take all their salaries. The dining room had been papered since the Victorian era, thankfully, and was white with a pattern of climbing roses rather than something dark and dreary. Lizzy pretended it was a garden in the presently bleak winter months. Their room stood on the second floor and looked over the mews, so they were spared the street noise. They shared a cupboard, and a large bed against the outer wall with a window on either side. Mrs Clarke provided them with a desk and two chairs, which fitted in the small space, almost comfortably, and Elizabeth was grateful that they didn't have to sit upon their bed while reading or writing letters. All in all, the place was most satisfactory. They usually took the Underground to work along with most of the rest of London, it seemed to Lizzy. The crush of people was something new to the two of them, but not unpleasant. Yes, all in all, Lizzy was pleased. Jane, however, removed her shoes and lay down on her bed with a sigh.

"Whatever is the matter? Are you ill?" Lizzy looked up from the desk where she penned a letter home to her family.

"Oh, I suppose I'm just being silly. After all, I didn't even speak to the man, or even know his name." Jane peered at Lizzy and scowled. A scowl made her look prettier than ever. "Now, don't you laugh at me."

"I'm not laughing. Really, I'm not. So, do you think this was a case of 'love at first sight'?"

"Oh, you are laughing at me." Jane grinned. "You might as well. I don't know what I'm thinking. I'll probably never see him again. He may even be a foreigner here on holiday. After all, everyone comes to Selfridges."

"A foreigner. Honestly, Jane. Such drama. I saw him talking with Mr Selfridge. He probably resides here in London. I saw the way he looked at you. He will be back, and he will inquire after you. And after a suitable time, perhaps a week or two, you will be married and then you can start having all those children you want." Lizzy laughed.

Jane threw a pillow at her, but it landed at her feet. "Oh, you."

Lizzy turned her attention to the post that had arrived for them today. There was a letter from her mother, addressed in care of the Gardiners. Her uncle must have dropped it off sometime earlier. She dreaded reading it. No doubt, her mother wanted them to come home. She was resolved to stay, but she wasn't sure about Jane.

"There's a letter here from Mother." Lizzy turned and Jane sat up.

"Oh, read it. I'm anxious to hear about the family."

Lizzy tore open the envelope and began to read.

Dear Jane and Lizzy,

Since the Gardiners have not seen fit to install a telephone in their home, I have to resort to writing you a letter, since there is much to

say. I hope you are enjoying your visit with your aunt, uncle, and the
children, but really, it is time for you to come home. I am sure…

Jane got up from her bed and joined Lizzy at the desk. "What did she mean, we are enjoying our visit? You didn't tell her that we are employed and living here, did you?"

Lizzy screwed up her face and looked up at Jane. "Not exactly, no. I thought I would tell her when the time came. You know how she is. Why stir up trouble if there is no need?"

Jane shook her head and then pulled up the extra chair to sit beside her. "Well, you'll have to tell her now, won't you? Oh, Lizzy." Jane sighed. "Read on."

Lizzy turned back to the letter.

"I am sure that you girls have been helpful to your aunt, but by now have worn out your welcome. Besides, I need you home at once. It is vital to the family that you come."

Lizzy looked up at Jane and shook her head. "Now I know where Lydia gets her flare for drama. Vital, indeed. What could be so important?"

"We'll never know if you keep stopping. Read on."

"Your father has a distant cousin, Mr Collins by name. He is a clergyman in a parish in Kent on the grounds of a great house called Rosings. He seems to be well connected and a gentleman. Also, now this is important, girls, he is the relative who will inherit Longbourn."

Lizzy glanced up at Jane. "I don't see what this has to do with us."

Jane gave Lizzie's arm a slight nudge. Lizzy smiled and continued.

"This Mr Collins has hinted in his letter (another one who has no telephone) that he would like to, as he put it, do right by one of you girls. *That can only mean one thing – he intends to marry one of you and keep the house and the farm in the family."*

Lizzie slammed the letter down on the desk and let out a disgusted huff. "How medieval can one be?" She stood up and pretended to be Mr Collins addressing the crowd of sisters standing before him. She pointed with a wave of her hand, "Oh, I don't know. Perhaps Jane? She is the handsomest. Or maybe Miss Elizabeth? She looks sturdy enough. Oh, I don't think I want a wife who spends the day giggling like those two in the corner. What are their names again, Kitty and Lydia? Ah, then there is Miss Mary... perhaps she would lecture me. Can't have that."

Jane laughed. "Stop it. You make him sound so—"

"Stupid? Arrogant? Full of himself?" She began imitating the absent Mr Collins again. "Oh, I'll just look over the stable of fillies you've produced, Mrs Bennet, and pick the one—"

"All right, that will do," Jane said. "You never know. Perhaps he is a nice man and really does mean to do the right thing."

"Don't be fooled. A man like that feels that he has power over all of us and can do as he pleases because he will inherit all that is ours. It is ridiculous. I will write Mother now and tell her exactly where we are, what we are doing, and what she can do with her Mr Collins."

"Perhaps you should take a walk first and compose your thoughts. Or better yet, I will write to Mother and tell her that we can't possibly come home as we are recently employed and have already put up a month's rent at a boarding establishment." Jane peered at Lizzy and seemed to try to offer an encouraging look.

Lizzy motioned to the chair in front of the desk and let out a sigh of resignation. "As usual, you are right. I would write in anger, and that would solve nothing. Finish reading Mother's letter. I don't think I can tonight, and you write to her. I can't trust myself at the moment.

Lizzy sat down on the edge of her bed and removed her shoes as a paper slipped under her door. After fetching it, she held it under the lamp on the desk.

Jane looked over. "What is it? Another letter?"

Frowning, Lizzy dropped the paper on the desk and opened the door to the hallway but could see no one. Returning to the desk, she took up the paper.

"It's a pamphlet or newspaper of some kind. Look at the cover—*Votes for Women*, and there's a drawing of John Burns, actually two of him. Look." She handed the paper over to Jane, who glanced at it, then handed it back.

Jane didn't look happy. "I don't know. Maybe you should just throw it away. It's one of those suffragette papers. They're getting arrested for burning things down. I don't know, Lizzy."

"The way I feel right now, I could burn something down easily." Jane lifted her gaze, alarmed, and Lizzy laughed ruefully. "Don't worry. I don't have the energy to run about creating havoc." She took the pamphlet and, sitting on her bed, switched on the lamp. She glanced up at Jane, who was sitting at the desk, but still staring at her with a worried look. "It's all right. I can't get arrested for reading." She opened the pamphlet and began reading an article by Emmaline Pankhurst.

***

"You ambushed me, Bingley. Ambushed me." Darcy waved a fork in his friend's direction. They were eating dinner in Bingley's townhome in Kensington. Darcy usually called Charles by his first name, but right now, he was perturbed.

"I am sorry you feel that way about it, old boy, but how else would I have arranged a meeting between you two? Would you have met with Harry Selfridge otherwise?"

Darcy dodged the question. "Why is it so important to you that I meet a man like Selfridge?" He turned his attention to the beef Wellington on his plate. Although it was as tender as butter, he sawed away at it furiously.

"You know why. Because I am your friend."

Darcy was silent for a moment. The two of them were alone, save the servants, and he knew Charles would bring up a painful subject once again. He didn't want to think about it, but he *had* to think about it.

"Look, Selfridge and those like him would be thrilled to have you on their board of directors. It gives them prestige, and it is helpful for you financially. I don't see why you are so reluctant to take advantage of these opportunities."

"Is that what you call them? *Opportunities?* To me, it is like selling my good name for money."

Charles sighed and took a sip of his wine. "I don't see it that way at all." He went back to concentrating on his dinner. Darcy broke the silence.

"I feel like I would be taking the money under false pretenses, and worse, I would be expected to always vote with Mr Selfridge at the board meetings."

Bingley sighed. "In that, you are probably correct. If you look at it practically, though, it is *his* company. Why shouldn't he have the final say in how it is run?"

It was interesting that Bingley was using the same argument that was used again and again against the landed gentry. They could make all the life-and-death decisions about their property even though there were tenant farmers, mill workers, servants, groundskeepers, and sometimes entire villages dependent upon them. Now, here was a man of commerce, Harry Selfridge, who, in some ways, was in the same position. Yes, it was Selfridge's company, just as Pemberley was his estate. Yes, they were both lord and master over what was legally theirs. Darcy had been brought up, and so had all the Pemberley inheritors through the generations, with the concept of *noblesse oblige*, which he took very seriously. He knew that many people depended on the fact that he had their welfare in mind as well as his own. Did a man of commerce have such compunctions? Dare he ask Bingley, a man of commerce himself?

"Good lord, Darcy, you've gone awfully quiet."

Darcy sighed.

"What is it, man, speak up. We're friends, are we not?"

"Of course."

"Then speak frankly." Bingley raised his gaze to meet Darcy's. "It's all right. I won't take offence."

Darcy hesitated, but if he couldn't have an honest discussion with his closest friend, then who, by George, could he confide in? "I am not speaking of you, mind, but it would give me sleepless nights were I to feel as though I've sold my consent to a man who may or may not have the welfare of all those depending on him in mind. I have heard many rumours of your Mr Selfridge…"

"Oh, and what might those be?" Was Charles actually amused? The faintest smile crossed his countenance.

"Really, you have heard the same, I expect. That he is a libertine and a gambler. How can I associate my name with his? And he may squander his fortune, bankrupt his enterprise, and leave all his employees in the street."

Bingley slapped both hands on the table with a loud guffaw. "Good lord, you do see the worst in people."

"And you do not scrutinise enough. I believe that you tend to see the good in everyone, no matter their character."

Bingley shook his head. "You say that as if it is a fault rather than a virtue. 'Judge not, lest ye be judged,' eh?"

Darcy didn't have an immediate retort for this comment, which vexed him. He, no doubt, would think of something scathing to say later, and that would vex him more. Bingley raised his wineglass as if in a toast.

"Have some more wine, my friend, and let's forget the entire episode. I was only thinking of your welfare."

Darcy looked off over his friend's shoulder at the exquisite Turner that Bingley bought at auction last year. He loved the painter and his flawless sense of light in a scene. He himself had a small Turner collection and thought of that now. Perhaps he would have to sell his prized possessions in small lots to keep Pemberley running. The tide had turned for the landed gentry, and farming was less profitable year by year.

"My welfare? You needn't concern yourself."

"Now, don't be like that. We've discussed this before. The mill, the tenant farmers, they aren't enough anymore, are they? I am your friend, and I will say it now, and then, if you no longer want to discuss it, I will be silent forever. To maintain your inheritance, you must consider commerce—the stock market, which can be volatile, or consider entering into your own concern, which can also be risky, or serving on the board of directors of some going enterprises such as Selfridges, which is the least painful, I think, or… you can always marry for money."

"Charles. Good lord. Who do you suggest? Some loud and silly American heiress? They are looking for a title, of which I have none." Darcy took up his glass of excellent Bordeaux and sipped. "Besides, have you never heard the old adage *marry for money and you earn every penny*?"

"All right, Darcy, all right. You are your own man, and you will do what you want. My scheming days are over. I introduced you to Selfridge, now you must do the rest, but please, think about his offer. If nothing else, you may learn a great deal about commerce. It is the future, you know." Bingley rang for the servant. "Brandy, old man?"

"Yes, thank you. I believe I need one tonight."

Chapter 4

Jane and Lizzy spent the next day on "flags and scenic work" inside the store. Sometimes, Lizzy would find herself staring at the lovely displays of dresses, blouses, skirts, and heaven forefend, cosmetics. How would she look with a splash of lip rouge or a powdered nose? Jane, her lithe figure shown off even in her high-collared, long-sleeved white blouse and her plain, black, floor-length skirt, was the perfect argument against any of these enhancements as she was flawless as she was. Some others, though, could use a bit of fine-tuning.

What really occupied her mind now, however, was the idea of women's rights and, more specifically, the right to vote. She needed to read more, to find out more about all of it. For instance, could all men vote? If that were true, then she would be angry. Why couldn't a woman such as herself and her sister, working women, women who made their own way in the world, be trusted with a say in the halls of power? The pent-up energy she felt back at Longbourn was now gaining momentum. She had been seeking something, and she thought it was her independence and her employment, but she knew she was still unsatisfied. She needed a cause, and now she'd found one—enfranchisement of women. That was it.

Mr Selfridge was really a visionary. He not only was unpatronizing in letting his employees live off the premises, but he also provided them with a recreation room, a gymnasium, lockers for their belongings, a canteen, and most importantly, a library. That was where Lizzy headed after work. Jane, who was now finding her feet in London, felt perfectly at ease taking the Underground back to Mrs Clarke's.

When she reached the library, Lizzy was surprised at the number of her coworkers perusing the stacks. Many of the books were about business and commerce. Mr Selfridge, as an American, was far more egalitarian than his British counterparts. He claimed, and Elizabeth believed, that anyone could rise from the circumstances of their birth and become what he had become: a successful captain of industry. That was all well and good, but what she was seeking now was books on law and enfranchisement. She needed to know all about the suffragettes.

To her surprise, there were copies of *Votes For Women*, a *Who's Who of Women*, printed by Selfridges, and other publications of the same ilk available on the shelves. She nearly jumped for joy when she saw them. As she stood pulling one after the other out and looking them over, a voice broke in behind her.

"Come here often?" Soft and modulated tones—male. She turned, and a rakishly good-looking fellow in a waiter's uniform smiled at her. His dark hair was parted in the centre but flipped up slightly above his forehead, giving him a boyish look. He leaned jauntily on the long bookcase, crossing one foot over the other in a pose that exuded confidence and ease. Unlike the young man who admired her sister, this one seemed quite worldly. Of course, this was only her first impression.

"Is it your habit to accost young women in the library?" she asked softly, but pointedly.

He did not seem taken aback, even a little. "I accost anyone I find interesting anywhere I choose." He was nothing if not frank. She liked him immediately. She returned his smile and didn't walk away. Emboldened, he went on. "George Wickham, at your service."

"Elizabeth Bennet. I work in—"

"I know where you work. I've seen you in the window with... is that your sister?"

"Yes, Jane. You seem to know about me, but I know nothing about you."

"We could know more about each other if you let me call on you. Perhaps we could take in a music hall performance, or…"

This type of boldness and directness was not what Elizabeth was used to. In fact, it made her a bit uneasy. She heard many stories from the girls at the boardinghouse about young women, alone and without supervision of their families, becoming entangled in, well, things that brought about their ruin. Still, he was so very different from the young men she met at tea in Meryton, and he was very good-looking.

"You're a waiter." Her comment seemed to take some of the wind out of his sails. He cleared his throat.

"That is true. And you are a shopgirl." He smiled disarmingly. "Now that we have that settled… come out with me?"

"Perhaps another time. I am quite busy now, as you can see. Besides, I am not used to going off with strangers." Drawing her attention back to the bookcase, she opened one of the pamphlets and feigned reading. After a short time, she looked up, thinking that he would be discouraged and be gone. He was not. When they made eye contact, he moved closer.

"All right. A group of us are going to a small dance party near the Strand on Sunday afternoon. Please, come with me. You can bring your sister for a chaperone." Raising his right hand, he said, "I swear that my intentions are honourable." He waggled his eyebrows comically. It made her laugh.

She sighed. "All right. I will do this much. I will talk with Jane, and you may find me tomorrow and ask me again. If she is amenable, we will both come."

"Capital. Tomorrow, then. We will talk and get to know each other, and I will no longer be a stranger." With that he gave her another of those rakish smiles and was gone. Yes, this was very different from Meryton.

***

The usual buzzing throng filled the Palm Court Restaurant for luncheon. Wickham smiled to himself as he draped the crisp linen napkin over his arm and proceeded to the next table. Again, he had been asked for by name. It was one of his paramours come to visit again. Matilda Maxwell, married to an absentee husband, wealthy, and voracious in bed, was one of his frequent customers. He had been told, in no uncertain terms, that pleasing the customers was his principal duty, and who was he to shirk? This position, which he was fortunate enough to acquire before the opening of the store two years ago, had served him well. If all went according to plan, he would marry a wealthy spinster, or at least, have himself set up as a "kept man" by an unhappily but exceedingly wealthy married woman. Either way, this was the perfect job for him, and one that he was convinced he would not have to work in for long.

He also had his diversions among the bountiful females of the Selfridge staff. What bliss it was to be a man. These women safeguarded their reputations, if not their virtue, above all else, so he was fairly free to float among them, picking whatever flowers he chose. Some might gossip, but most would not. If they had been warned off him, so be it. There were dozens more to choose from, and he was not that discerning. Any port in a storm, as it were. Elizabeth Bennet was intriguing. She did not succumb to his charms immediately, which presented a challenge. Challenges were an aphrodisiac to him. He would take his time with her. After all, it was not as if he would be lonely in the meantime.

"Would Madame wish to see a menu?" he asked, engaging the most intense version of his "come hither" look.

Mrs Maxwell lifted her gaze to him, softly touching her impressive pompadour as she removed her equally enormous hat. "Oh, I think I have decided what I want already." Her gaze swept over him, top to bottom, lingering just below his waist for a long moment. He could feel a stirring in his loins. Her expression was that of a sly, hungry fox looking over a plump and promising chicken. So be it. He didn't mind the difference in their stations. He was used to that by now and it didn't keep him out of the best houses in London, even though he was usually there after dark and let in by the back door.

"We are featuring a lovely *sole meunière* today, if madame would like to try something new." He licked his lips and didn't take his eyes off hers for a moment. She didn't flinch.

"You know my tastes so well, George," she said. "I am always in the mood for something new." That smouldering expression never left her face for a moment. "Surprise me."

He was so aroused by now, he felt like surprising her by flinging her across the table and taking her right there. It was then he broke their gaze and tried to think of something revolting so as not to allow his twitching member to announce its intentions to the entire restaurant.

He swallowed hard and took a deep breath. "*Sole meunière* it is, and might I suggest a glass of Chablis to accompany?" He dared look at her again and saw that she was quite amused at his predicament. That amusement cooled his ardour... at least for the moment.

"As you suggest, George. How well you know my tastes. That is why I come here so often."

Indeed. That was why she came here. For the food and... service. "Very good, madame. So nice to see you again." He scribbled on his pad and turned heel towards the kitchen. No doubt there would be a very nice tip for him before long.

Chapter 5

"Well, then I will go by myself, but I will go." Lizzy shook herself free from her coat as she and Jane returned home from work. It had been a trying day at the store. There'd been no pleasing Mr Goldsman because he was not pleasing The Chief and so the cumulative displeasure landed with a thud on Jane and herself. Why were men in charge of everything? Even with Mr Selfridge's progressive ideas, women rose only so far in the organization and were many times treated with a kind of condescension bordering on contempt. Since she could do nothing about how things were structured at work, she would do something about it in her private life. There was to be a suffragette meeting in Hyde Park about the upcoming census, and Elizabeth was determined to get involved.

"Don't go. You might be arrested or even beaten." Jane's worried look shown clearly in the bedroom mirror, and Lizzy had to smile.

"It's just a meeting. We aren't marching or boycotting or burning down Parliament."

Jane shook her head. "Please don't talk like that. You know how it upsets me."

Elizabeth turned around and tried to smile reassuringly. "It's just a meeting. Nothing more. The worst they're planning is to do something about the census. How violent can that get? You're such a worrier. I'll be all right. Come along. Let's go for tea. Mrs Clarke has conjured up something that smells delicious."

Jane didn't look convinced but smoothed the few strands of hair that escaped from her low pompadour and followed Lizzy out the door.

***

Heart pounding, Elizabeth stepped off the train at Hyde Park. It suddenly occurred to her that her self-congratulations on being the sister who took the lead in all things might not have been warranted. As she walked towards The Reformers Tree with an ever-increasing crowd of women, she heartily wished she hadn't been so flippant with Jane and persuaded her to come along. It was much easier to be courageous with Jane by her side than it was heading into the unknown alone. What if the police broke up their meeting with billy clubs? What if she was arrested merely for being here? Recalling her own words, she tried reassuring herself that she was just here to listen and observe. If a torch was handed to her as the crowd veered in the direction of Parliament, she would excuse herself. Ha, she made a joke. She didn't really feel any better for it.

Many more women were gathered than she expected. Some were well dressed and obviously well-heeled, but many who hung about in groups near the back of the burgeoning crowd were working women, women who toiled in mills and factories. Their boisterous conversations talked freely about their toil, their children, and the men some of them supported. Lizzy determined that she was somewhere between these two groups, better educated than a mill worker, but not at leisure like those who were born to fortunes.

A flushed and intense young woman, who passed among them in the crowd, thrust a leaflet into Lizzy's hand while entreating, "Boycott the census. If we are not human enough to vote, we are not human enough to be counted." Lizzy's gaze met the young woman's as she took the leaflet. A cheer suddenly went up and Lizzy saw a woman standing on a table who could have been anyone's favourite aunt. She had curly hair fastened in a tight bun beneath a bonnet surrounding her soft features. Her coat was long and black in a heavy thick material that looked like something a soldier would wear on the frontline in cold weather. Didn't matter what she looked like, aunt or soldier: the crowd soon stilled at her words, and Lizzy did too. The woman was none other than Emmeline Pankhurst.

All conversation ceased as Mrs Pankhurst's words rang out, *"Women had always fought for men, and for their children. Now we are ready to fight for our own human rights. We are willing to break laws that we might force men to give us the right to* make *laws."*

A roar erupted from the crowd and Lizzy felt herself swept along with its euphoria. She didn't know what she expected when she decided to attend this meeting, but she could feel something awaken in her, more than inspiration…a vision perhaps? A vision for the future, not only for herself, but for all women who came after them. The sensation was like jolt of electricity, and it was all she could do to concentrate on what was being said.

No women would participate in the census. If the government thought that they didn't count, they wouldn't be counted. A chant bubbled up from the crowd until all were shouting, some jabbing their fists towards the sky. Lizzy never felt more alive.

"No vote—no census. No vote—no census." Someone clasped her hand. "Mary's my name," she said.

Grinning, Lizzy spun around to face her. "Lizzy."

"First time at a meeting?"

Lizzy nodded, and another woman grasped her other hand. "Constance," said the woman. "That's me."

"Lizzy." Someone began singing close by. *"Shout, shout, up with your song, Cry with the wind for the dawn is breaking. March, march, swing you along. Wide blows our banner and hope is waking…"* Lizzy didn't know the words, but Mary and Constance did. She'd learn them. She would learn them for the next meeting and the one after that. She had found the place where she belonged.

***

Lizzy's teacup rattled in her saucer. She shook her head rapidly as if to stir herself into wakefulness. They were on their morning tea break in the employees' canteen at Selfridges, and Lizzy was grateful for every drop of tea.

"I haven't had a chance to ask you about the meeting last night. You came home very late."

"Oh, Jane, it was magnificent. You should have come. I do believe I found my calling last night."

Jane blinked at her. "I thought working at Selfridges was your calling. I do believe you are becoming as fickle as Kitty or Lydia."

Jane was never one to criticize. She was teasing, but her words did sting a bit.

"I do love working at Selfridges. I do. But the suffrage movement is more than employment. It is a mission. Something I can leave behind for all who come after me." As soon as she said it, Lizzy wished she hadn't. "That sounded pompous, didn't it?"

Jane reached across the small table and took Lizzy's hand. "No, it did not. I am proud of you, Lizzy."

Before Lizzy could react, a masculine presence made itself known. "Well, Miss Bennet. So wonderful to see you. May I?" Before she could respond, Mr Wickham pulled up a chair and joined them. "And who is your lovely friend?"

Lizzy rolled her gaze. "My lovely friend is my lovely sister. Jane, meet Mr George Wickham, of the Palm Court Restaurant."

"So very pleased to meet you." George reached down and kissed Jane's hand before she could resist. The startled look on her face nearly caused a case of the giggles in Lizzy, but she refrained. He turned and took Lizzy's hand. "I have come to ask you to accompany me to a little soiree this Sunday afternoon." Lizzy opened her mouth to speak, but George interrupted. "Oh, you may come too, Miss Jane. You can be our chaperone." George turned his attention back to Lizzy and his eyes narrowed into a "come hither" look. He then began to laugh.

"Honestly, Mr Wickham…" Lizzy began.

"Please, call me George."

"George, then. Jane and I will talk it over and let you know tomorrow."

"Splendid. Oh, do say yes. It will be such fun. Dancing and all." With that, he rose quickly from his seat and disappeared.

"So, that is George Wickham." Jane stared open-mouthed at the retreating figure.

"Yes, indeed." Lizzy shook her head. "So, will you come with us? I think it will be such a lark."

Jane shook her head but smiled. "Oh, all right. Tell him I will come. It might be a lark at that."

Chapter 6

The time had come for Wickham to feed the waning flame of passion he had kindled in Mathilda Maxwell. After all, he was not yet bored with her affections, and certainly not ready to give up the shower of gifts she bestowed on him. Lately, from the corner of his eye, he caught her surveying one of the newer and younger members of the waitstaff at the Palm Court. Recognizing her hungry look, he resolved to redirect it back to himself. What better way to do it than to make her just the slightest bit jealous?

He settled himself between the two sisters, Elizabeth and Jane, as they walked arm in arm to the Underground and soon were within walking distance of their destination on the Strand. Using his well-practiced charm, George attempted to draw Jane out. She was relegated to the unenviable post of chaperone on this, George's first outing with Miss Elizabeth Bennet.

"So, your sister convinced you to seek your fortune in London."

"I could not let her travel here alone."

"You are a good and noble sister. I admire that." Jane positively beamed. "There are not many who would uproot their lives for the sake of their sister's dream. You are, indeed, a unique woman."

"I think you flatter me, Mr Wickham. Families do stick together, you know."

He had no reply, and it was just as well. "Ah, ladies. We have arrived."

And arrived they had. The house was whitewashed and lovely, across from a park, and even in these dreary winter months, looked enchanting due to the ancient oaks and manicured gardens.

"My, this is posh. Are you sure you have the correct address, Mr Wickham?" Jane was looking about as if starstruck.

"It belongs to a... friend of mine. She is hosting a tango tea this afternoon."

"What in the world is that?" Lizzy got no answer as they were already at the door and were admitted by a rather severe-looking butler.

"The other guests are in the ballroom," he said, looking down his nose. Wickham took no notice of the butler's disdain as he clutched both women by the arm and propelled them up the staircase, laughing.

***

Lizzy had to admit she was impressed by Mr Wickham and his extraordinary circle of friends. They were introduced to the lady of the house, a Mrs Matilda Maxwell. She was very grand indeed. But where was Mr Maxwell and how did Mr Wickham, a waiter, know such a grand lady? After divesting themselves of hats and wraps, they were seated with the other guests in a large circle of chairs that surrounded a foreign-looking couple, who stood holding hands. Elizabeth didn't know what to make of the scene.

"Good afternoon, ladies and gentlemen," the man began in an accent either Spanish or something South American. He was extraordinary. His all-black attire included trousers that were very tight at the thigh yet flared slightly at the ankle. His shirt was a shiny material, perhaps silk, over which he wore a short waistcoat that didn't button at the front and didn't reach his waist. The woman's dress was orange, her hair done up tightly in a bun at the back of her head. The skirt was scandalous: above her ankle and free flowing like a cape, slit from the bottom up to her thigh. Even her shoes matched the bright orange of her dress and had a heel higher than anything Lizzy had ever seen. "Tonight, we will all learn the tango. It is the dance of my country, The Argentine. Observe."

The male dancer took the lady in his arms, bringing them impossibly close together. In the corner sat a gramophone, and the lady of the house, Mrs Maxwell, waited for a nod from the speaker, then started the record. The music had a distinctly Latin flavour, and the couple began to dance. They promenaded about the room, very close together, the man's knees between the woman's, which caused a few gasps from Lizzy and Jane. The woman held her elbow high and kept her hand behind the man's shoulder, palm flat to the floor. His hand was on her waist, their other hands touching. The dance seemed complicated and needed lots of space in which to move. It was also so much more sensuous than anything Lizzy had ever seen before.

"Lizzy…"

"Hmmm?"

"*Lizzy*…" Jane stage-whispered from close by and it took a while for Lizzy to react. She tore her gaze away from the dancing duo and peered at her sister.

"What?"

"We should go," she mouthed behind Mr Wickham's back. Elizabeth shook her head, but Jane nodded hers.

Before their pantomime could advance any further, the music stopped.

"All right. Gentlemen, please help us clear the floor. You stand on one side of the room. Ladies on the other, and we will begin."

Wickham practically bounded out of his seat and offered a hand to Lizzy and then Jane. As they rose, he and the other gents quickly took their chairs and put them on the side of the ballroom.

"I believe I shall go and sit over there and watch," Jane said, and she followed the gents over to the side.

Lizzy watched her escape to the far end of the ballroom, then went over. "Oh, come along. As long as you are here, you might as well learn the steps." She held out her hand.

"No." Jane smiled sweetly up at her.

"I'm sure that this dance will be the next big thing. You don't want to be left behind." She tried every argument in her head, but Jane wasn't having it and remained as immovable as a seated Buddha.

Lizzy stood still for a moment, not knowing what to do. To her surprise, the young man they had seen a week ago from Selfridges' window was fast approaching. Jane's face lit up before she promptly got to her feet. He bowed slightly to them both.

"I do hope that I am not being too forward, but I would like to introduce myself. Charles Bingley." He extended his hand to Jane first. She was blushing. "And you are?"

"Jane Bennet, and this is my sister, Elizabeth."

"So pleased to meet you." He shook Lizzy's hand and then turned his attention once more to Jane.

Lizzy could see by the way they looked at one another that this was the perfect time to join the other ladies in the dance lesson. She excused herself. As she walked away, she could hear Mr Bingley entreating Jane to be his partner. Within a few minutes, Jane was on the ladies' side of the ballroom, learning the steps to the tango.

"All right, gentlemen, ladies, now take your partner and let us practice. Step, step, step and close. Step, step, step and close." Wickham offered his hand to Lizzy. She took it, ready to be swept into his arms. The lesson, however, began much more mildly. They were instructed to face each other, only touching hands… nothing so clutching and intimate as the couple had demonstrated. Mr Wickham seemed a bit distracted and was watching Jane and Mr Bingley. He turned his attention back to Lizzy.

"Who is that man dancing with your sister? His name wouldn't by chance be Bingley?"

"Yes, it is. Do you know him?"

A rueful smile crossed Mr Wickham's face. "He is a friend of someone I knew long ago." He then began to scan the ballroom and diverted his attention so much so that he trod on Elizabeth's foot.

"Oh, I am sorry. How clumsy of me. Are you all right?"

Lizzy winced and shook her foot slightly. "I do believe I'll live. You seem a bit distracted."

Wickham gave her one of those knowing smiles, almost a smirk. "No, no. I think all is well."

By this time, the men were instructed to encircle the waists of their partners and, with pressure from the hand, pull the women close. Wickham's smile evaporated, and Lizzy felt a heat rise between them.

By the time the afternoon was over, Lizzy was smitten with the tango. George was a superb dancer, and his smouldering looks and warm breath on her neck were exciting. As they jostled home on the Underground, she resolved to learn more about him.

"You are an enigma, Mr Wickham. You are so well-spoken, as if you have been well-educated, and yet you work as a waiter. I am perplexed."

He smiled. "As much as I would like to remain a mystery to you, Miss Bennet, since we are no longer strangers, I feel I can confide in you my whole, sad story."

"Is it so sad, Mr Wickham?"

"Please, call me George. After all, we are friends now." She nodded, and he continued. "I was raised along with a gentleman's son at a great house in the north called Pemberley. My father managed the estate for the master of the house, and the son of the house and myself grew up almost as brothers. The master was a kind man, one might even say egalitarian. Upon his death, he had left instructions for me to obtain a good living for the rest of my days, but the son chose to ignore it."

"What? How could he? You should find a good solicitor and fight him in court."

"I thought of that, but the bequest had only been a suggestion and not written in the will. By the time everything was settled, both our fathers were gone, and the son of the house made all the decisions."

"The man sounds like a bully and a blackguard. I would smear his name to anyone who would listen. Did you hear this, Jane?" Sat opposite, Jane looked up from her seat and leaned forward.

"I'm sorry. Were you talking to me?"

Elizabeth chuckled. "Never mind. I will tell you all when we get home. Just go back to your sweet dreams." Lizzy knew exactly who she was dreaming of. Jane's cheeks glowed.

"I'm sorry, George..." She made a point to use his given name. "Do go on. As I said, I would spread this story all over London and show this man up as the scoundrel that he is."

Wickham nodded sadly. "No, I honour the memory of his father too much to do any such thing. I am making my way in the world, and I believe I'm happy with my lot."

Lizzy patted George's hand. "I think you are quite an admirable fellow. I really do. By the way, what is this nasty fellow's name? I'd like to know, just on the odd chance our paths ever cross."

George looked off wistfully towards the darkened windows of the underground train. "His name is Darcy... Fitzwilliam Darcy."

Chapter 7

It wasn't long before Mr Bingley was a regular customer at Selfridges. He would position himself at a counter whilst Jane was arranging a palm on the floor or hanging a banner from a balcony. After causing Jane a reprimand for "fraternizing with the customers", he kept a respectful distance and didn't speak to her, but Lizzy observed them exchanging glances and knew that Jane was encouraging him. A fortnight later, Jane and Lizzy walked out of the staff entrance of Selfridges after closing, Mr Bingley stood there waiting like a stage door Johnny. After pleasantries were exchanged, he came right to the point, asking both of them to dinner at his house in Kensington.

"I'll send the motor around for you around seven, if that's all right."

It was fortunate he suggested his motorcar since Lizzy didn't think it wise for them to take a bus or the Underground all dressed to the nines—or as dressed to the nines as they could manage. Jane shot her a thrilled expression and then answered.

"Oh, that would be lovely, thank you. Oh..." Jane began to fumble in her handbag. "You'll need our address."

Elizabeth pulled a card out of her bag handily and gave it to him.

"Elizabeth Bennet, Suffragette, 14 Candlewick Street Ward, Cheapside."

As he looked it over, Lizzy waited for his reaction. She didn't want to spoil Jane's budding romance, but it was better he knew of her involvement in the movement.

"I see you have a business card, Miss Elizabeth. How very modern." He tried to keep his expression neutral, but a hint of a smile crossed his face. Perhaps he wasn't taking her very seriously. "So, Friday at seven, then... so looking forward to it." He took Jane's gloved hand and raised it to his lips, and then he was gone.

***

Mr Goldsman was slightly perturbed with Jane on that Friday afternoon. The entire day she was utterly distracted. Lizzy tried to catch Jane's mistakes, but sometimes she just couldn't manage it as she had her own work to see to. By the time they were finished for the day, Jane could hardly contain her excitement. When they finally arrived home, they began their preparations for the evening. At their mother's suggestion, they'd brought along gowns that Lizzy was sure they would never wear in the city, due to their status as young working women. For once, Lizzy was glad to have heeded her mother's advice.

Jane's was a gold affair that showed off her bare shoulders, and was decorated with a lace trim and puff sleeves. Lizzy's was a sapphire blue that her mother insisted set her eyes off beautifully. Her shoulders peeked between a strap and puff sleeves. Her mother insisted the hobble skirts that were all the rage were, in fact, stupid and both gowns flared at the bottom. Jane's auburn hair shown like a perfect halo as she dressed it in front of the mirror. Not a strand was out of place. Lizzy deferred to her ministrations regarding her own coiffure, as her talents lay elsewhere, certainly not in hair dressing. They both had matching hats with ostrich feathers that Jane insisted they buy from their place of employment. After all, they got a discount. Standing before the mirror, Lizzy thought they looked quite lovely.

"I'm glad you insisted on the hats, Jane. At least we won't embarrass ourselves in front of the toffs."

"Oh, Lizzy." Jane shifted her hat slightly to the right. "We could be considered toffs as well. Our father is a gentleman, you might remember."

Lizzy laughed. "We'll see if we are invited into their inner sanctum." She put her arm around her sister's shoulder and gave her a little squeeze. "Don't be too disappointed if the rest of the party doesn't welcome us as much as your Mr Bingley."

Jane sighed. "It's a shame we couldn't invite your Mr Wickham to come along with us."

"He's hardly *my* Mr Wickham. We've been dancing a few times, and he's amusing, but…"

"But you're not in love with him."

"Oh, goodness. You do rush things along. No, hardly. He is intriguing and has a certain charm, don't you think?"

"He seems a bit dangerous to me." Jane straightened her wrap.

Lizzy snickered. "Perhaps that's why I like him."

Before they knew it, the bell sounded, and a driver escorted them into the rear seat of a large, highly polished black motorcar. The driver sat in the semi-open cab, while they were safe in the back enclosed by glass, metal, and cushioned leather seats. Almost the entire boardinghouse were on the steps or leaning out of windows to see them off. It was quite a spectacular scene, and one that Lizzy was equally enjoying and embarrassed by. Still, it was part of the adventure she craved, and now, thanks to Jane, she was having it.

Mr Bingley's house was one of many in a row of white stone attached houses with grand porticoes and black iron gates. As they entered, the butler greeted them and showed them into the drawing room. Most conversation ceased as they entered, and many turned to gape at them. Bingley sprang towards them instantly.

"Oh, Miss Jane and Miss Elizabeth, how good of you to come. You look lovely." The last sentence was said to them both, but Mr Bingley had eyes only for Jane. He led them into the room among the guests. "This is my sister, Miss Caroline Bingley." The young woman's mouth appeared as if she had just bitten into a lemon, but she managed a forced smile as she extended her hand. "And this is my friend, Mr Darcy."

Jane extended her hand and a smile in this man's direction, but Elizabeth was taken aback for a moment. She remembered him and Mr Bingley's sister. They had been outside the window that day at Selfridges. What she remembered most, though, was what Mr Wickham had told her of his reduced circumstances at the hand of a "Mr Darcy".

"Mr Fitzwilliam Darcy?" she asked as she extended her hand to him.

"One and the same. Have you heard of me?" He smiled slightly, but it was his dark, brooding eyes that riveted her attention. What should she say?

"Oh... everyone about town has heard of Mr Darcy." It wasn't very clever, but he seemed pleased with it. There were more introductions made: a Mr and Mrs Hurst. Mrs Hurst was Charles's and Caroline's sister. It promised to be an interesting evening.

With the Pimm's cups finished, it was time to sit at table. Mr Darcy offered his arm to Lizzy, and since all other arms were otherwise occupied, she took it. He was quite gallant and careful of his manners, deferring to her and the other ladies in conversation. The conversation, however, left Jane and herself out for the most part. The group of them all seemed to know the same people and spent their days socializing with others of their class. Mr Bingley, however, seemed to notice Jane's silence and brought up the windows at Selfridges. Lizzy was gratified. That

Mr Darcy fellow was always looking at her so intently that she found it disconcerting and was grateful when his attention was directed elsewhere.

As Jane finished describing the next new masterpieces of window dressing to be unveiled for the Easter season, Caroline Bingley suddenly strung her proverbial bow and fired an arrow at Lizzy. "So tell us, Miss Bennet, have you ever had the chance to meet Emily Pankhurst herself?"

The entire party stopped chatting, in fact, stopped breathing for a stunned moment. All attention turned to Lizzy. She hesitated, gathering her thoughts, and then answered truthfully. "I have heard her speak many times, but unfortunately, have never had the privilege of speaking with her face-to-face. I hope I will someday."

Caroline directed her attention at Mr Darcy for a moment, and then focused back on Lizzy. "You and your sister are not suffragists, are you? Surely not."

"You seem to have answered your own question," Lizzy said handily. "Jane has not yet accompanied me to the meetings. I, however, am indeed a suffragette. In fact, I helped with the recent census protests."

Mr Hurst blinked several times, rousing himself from a Madeira-induced doze. "Well then, you believe women should have the vote. Humph. Poppycock."

"I most certainly do, and why not? Many of us make our own way in the world, just as men do. Many of us are householders, or the primary source of income for a family. Why should a man who sits about at home while his wife works have suffrage and she does not? How fair is that?"

The voices were rising about the table, when in a soothing tone, Mr Darcy addressed her. "I find that the role of men as the leaders in the country and the protectors of women is the natural order of things. Once the rules that have long held the Empire together are questioned, surely, we invite anarchy, don't you think, Miss Bennet?"

His tone, no doubt, was meant to have a calming effect, but it merely sounded arrogant and condescending. If he meant to placate Lizzy, he had taken the wrong tack. She threw a look over at her sister, who merely smiled and nodded slightly. Lizzy had no intention of spoiling what might develop into a very suitable match for Jane, but she couldn't let Mr Darcy's opinion go unchallenged. Leaning slightly towards him, she matched his calm tone. "You speak of men as the protectors of women, Mr Darcy, but from whom are you protecting them?" She didn't wait for a reply. "I will tell you: other men. If men would look upon women as their equals, then society would greatly benefit from it. I doubt equality would breed anarchy."

She could see that she disconcerted him a bit from his expression. No doubt very few, if anyone, ever spoke to him so frankly.

"Really, Miss Bennet, I am surprised at you. Mr Darcy was only defending a way of life we all hold dear." Caroline Bingley arched her eyebrow and sent a withering glance in Lizzy's direction. Mr Darcy looked as if he was about to say something, but then thought better of it. Lizzy held her own.

"As for the society we all hold dear, it is changing whether the upper classes like it or not. And why not? Will the Empire survive if we all cling to the old ways of doing things and never make any progress?" She looked directly at Mr Darcy, whose eyes narrowed. He made no reply.

Bingley sipped at his wine. "Come now. Let us change the subject before it spoils all our digestion." He raised his wineglass. "Let us drink a toast to something we can all agree on... to England."

They all followed his example and drank to their country. Elizabeth stole a look or two at Mr Darcy across the table, who sat rather sullenly, speaking only when spoken to.

Dessert was finally served: a very impressive blancmange in the shape of a horn of plenty and served with preserved cherries. Lizzy wasn't terribly fond of its texture, but her mother served it because she felt it reflected well on their social status. Not wishing to make any more trouble for Jane, she dutifully ate it with ensuing compliments.

After the wine had made the second circuit around the table for the gentlemen, Caroline Bingley suggested that the ladies retire to the drawing room for coffee. Lizzy thought that a bit old-fashioned, but then noticed that she suggested it while looking at Mr Darcy. She was trying to impress him by being rather Victorian. Well, well. If he was impressed by those sorts of shenanigans, it only confirmed the opinion she had of him since hearing of his shameful treatment of Mr Wickham.

Before reaching the drawing room, she excused herself to use the facilities and, on her way, passed the dining room. Mr Darcy, his voice raised, addressed Bingley.

"For goodness's sake, Charles, shopgirls invited to dinner."

"Their father is a gentleman, with land in Hertfordshire. They have the bearing and manners of ladies of breeding. You cannot deny it."

"Certainly, the young lady who has captured your interest does. She is demure and ladylike... but the sister, my God... one of those 'modern' young women, to be sure."

A snort came, a snuffle, and then another voice joined in. It most certainly was Mr Hurst. "Gave you what for, didn't she, Darcy?" The wine had obviously removed any sort of constraints on his behaviour. Mr Hurst's baritone laugh drifted through, but nothing further came from Mr Darcy.

She didn't stay to hear any more, lest she be discovered. *Humph, Mr Darcy. He is exactly as Wickham described him. He and that Caroline Bingley make a perfect couple. They deserve each other.*

Chapter 8

The conversation with Elizabeth at Bingley's dinner party echoed in Darcy's mind for days. He'd find himself comfortably ensconced in a wingback chair at the club, perusing *The Times,* when a column concerning the latest campaign of the Pankhursts and their suffragettes would cause him to begin constructing mock arguments in his head. He could see himself negating every point Miss Bennet would make, but then a creeping doubt would assail him as to the legitimacy of his position and would rob him of the satisfaction of achieving his victory.

Even though his club was social in nature rather than political, the machinations of government of late, including the Constitutional crisis and exacerbated by the social unrest created by the suffragettes, threatened the peace that had always reigned there. Retrieving his pocket watch, he glanced at it…. Nearly four o'clock. He promised to meet Bingley in the bar at four. Sighing, he rose from the comfortable leather and went to meet his friend.

Bingley and a few of his mates were already seated at a table, gin and tonics at the ready. Darcy signalled the barman to add one more drink and took the empty seat. To his chagrin, among the other affable chaps at the table sat Bingley's brother-in-law, Edwin Hurst. Why would Bingley invite such a disagreeable lout to meet them for a drink? Darcy shot a glance of disapproval at Bingley, who promptly shrugged his shoulders.

"Hope you don't mind my intrusion, old boy—" Hurst sounded, by the elided nature of his words, already well lubricated with drink. "—but Louisa insisted on visiting her sister, and Charles here was escaping to the club. Couldn't resist. Perhaps a game of cribbage later if any of you lot are game?"

"I am afraid I am engaged for dinner later, but thanks all the same." Darcy lied but felt justified. He disliked Hurst for several reasons, not the least of which was his indolent ways.

"I might challenge you, Hurst, if you're game for a small wager." A sly look passed over Cedric Abernathy's face as he spoke, which caused a chuckle from some of his companions. Darcy remained silent.

"Always," Hurst said with a laugh, and he downed what was left of his drink, slamming the empty glass on the table a bit too loudly. Yes, he was definitely in his cups.

The conversation drifted comfortably into sport, and then to the subject of forming a rowing team to compete at Henley. Bingley pounced on the idea. "Now, that is splendid, splendid. You can count on me, chaps. I think I'd rather like getting up at the crack of dawn to practice on the river. What about you, Darcy?"

Bingley was always dragging him into one scheme or another, but he was not averse to exercise and was an excellent swimmer. He smiled in spite of himself. "All right, Charles, if you insist. I don't see what harm it would do."

Hurst, who roused himself from his usual torpor, looked at Darcy incredulously and then looked about at the other men at the table. "I don't see the purpose of getting up when it is still dark and frolicking about in the damp. You can exclude me now, my good fellows."

"Now, there's a surprise," said Joseph Quintrell. He was the youngest of the group, and sometimes was a bit indiscreet in his comments. This appeared to be one of those times.

"And what do you mean by that?" Hurst was roused himself and looked rather like an angry walrus.

"I'm sure it was just an idle remark, old boy. No need for temper." Darcy was trying to diffuse the situation. Hurst wasn't having it.

"Don't try to appease me like you did that suffragette the other night, Darcy. I am not some simpering woman who will hang on your every word."

Darcy closed his eyes for a moment to give himself a time to tamp down his temper. The man was drunk. He was also married to Bingley's sister. Darcy needed to choose his words carefully. Before he could speak again, though, Hurst went on. "Not that you did handle her very well, did you, old boy? She got the better of you, didn't she?"

Darcy stood up, all eyes on him. "You're a bit worse for drink, Hurst, so I will wait until you are sober to continue this discussion. But as for that suffragette, her name is Elizabeth Bennet, and even though she is a woman, she is trying to address what she sees as injustice, which is more than I can say for many of us."

Hurst snuffled a bit but said nothing. The rest of the chaps at the table gaped open-mouthed at Darcy. What did he just say? Wherever did that come from?

Cedric Abernathy raised his glass to Darcy. "Here, here." He was grinning from ear to ear. Darcy didn't like the look in his eye. Was he being sarcastic? "A toast, gentlemen, to Mr Pankhurst... I mean, Mr Darcy."

Young Joseph snorted, but the other men were stonily silent. No one else raised a glass. Darcy clenched his teeth and glared at Abernathy.

"See here now." Bingley was on his feet leaning in toward Abernathy, his voice raised. *Good old Bingley. Ready to jump in to defend a friend.* Darcy took a quick glance about the bar. It wasn't full, but those who were there had their attention fixed on their little group. They were making a scene, which Darcy detested. He quickly laid his hand upon Bingley's arm. "Never mind, Charles. We should be going." He inclined his head towards the assembled group. "Gentlemen."

"Come along, Edwin. Louisa will be wondering what became of you." Bingley nudged the back of Hurst's chair, and the man got groggily to his feet.

"What? Going so soon? What about my cribbage?" Hurst didn't resist, however, to Darcy's relief. He took one of Mr Hurst's arms and Bingley took the other. They then piloted the cause of all the commotion outside to a waiting taxi.

When they reached Hurst's townhouse, Bingley trundled his brother-in-law onto the pavement. "I do apologise for..." Bingley said as he quickly leaned into the taxi.

"Think no more of it, Charles. It was nothing and not your fault..." Darcy didn't continue as Bingley's attention was drawn back to Hurst as he shakily mounted the stairs. Darcy shut the door of the taxi and instructed the driver to take him home.

As he leaned back in the worn leather seat, the scene at the club played over in his head. Less than an hour before, almost without his decision to do so, he had leapt to Elizabeth's defence. The same Elizabeth with whom he had been arguing in his head for days. He began to rub his forehead with his fingers. Why was she and her radical ideas constantly crying out for his attention? The taxi jostled to a stop. Perhaps a quiet dinner and a good book might bring him some relief. He resolved to think no more about that infuriating Cedric Abernathy, the idle and loose-tongued Mr Hurst, and certainly think no more of Miss Elizabeth Bennet.

Chapter 9

The incident at the club created no more than a ripple in Darcy's circle: Bingley was captivated by this latest dance craze. What was it? Oh yes, the tango. So far Darcy had resisted his friend's insistence that he join him for lessons. How would he be able to venture into polite society without the knowledge of this dance was Bingley's argument. What polite society would tolerate such a flagrant display of sensualism was his reply. Bingley, of course, took it all with his usual good humour. After several weeks had gone by, he could resist no longer as Bingley invited him to observe their "graduation" from their lessons. He was to be witness to all his friend had learned and accepted an invitation to his first "tango tea". It was just as well. After that defence of Elizabeth and the suffragettes that he made to all and sundry at the club, he needed something to take his mind off women's rights, the vote, and most of all, Elizabeth Bennet.

They met at the home of a fashionable lady of the Bingleys' acquaintance. Again, Caroline was like-minded about the unsuitability of this sensuous dance of the Argentine, which distressed Darcy a bit. He disliked agreeing with Caroline, as she began to appear narrowminded. Could it be that he was becoming broadminded? It must be his friend Bingley's influence. As they disembarked from Charles's Bollée Landaulet, Caroline continued her protestations.

"I don't know, Charles. There are many of our set who think this dance is...well... a bit obscene." Her tone of voice was even, but her face betrayed her distaste.

"Oh, come now. Once it is all the rage, you will claim that you liked it all along." He was teasing her. She made no reply. "Besides, I have a surprise for you two."

The butler greeted them at the door, and the servants soon relieved them of their coats, and the men of their hats. Caroline insisted on wearing hers. They were shown into the ballroom, where Bingley excused himself.

"I really don't know, Mr Darcy. What if someone sees us here?" Caroline Bingley's gaze darted about the ballroom. At that, a few others entered, most of them of their acquaintance. The Applegate heirs were there, as were the older generation of the Fox-Percys. They were soon joined by their hostess, Mathilda Maxwell. Upon the entry of the well-connected, Caroline became more obsequious and, finally, mercifully silent.

"Good afternoon, ladies and gentlemen, and thank you for coming to my little soiree. Once the demonstrations are over, I invite you for tea and cakes, and hope to add you to my list of tango enthusiasts." The lady threw her arms in the air in gusto, almost dislodging her exquisitely executed pompadour. "Let us begin." The gramophone was cranked, and the needle dropped.

The first couple arrived on the dance floor and took up their position, elbows out, the man's hand at his partner's back, just beneath her shoulder, her hand on the back of his neck, their other hands clasped. There was a respectable distance between them. The dance consisted of a great deal of long steps and twirling about. The lady's skirt was split rather far up her leg to accommodate the long, broad steps of the dancers. The dance was slow, and the couple spent much of the time gazing into each other's eyes.

When the tango finished, there was very enthusiastic applause from the Applegate crowd, who appeared to be mesmerised by the performance. It was then Bingley's turn.

To Darcy's surprise, and obviously to Caroline's as well, his partner was the girl from the dinner party and the Selfridge window—Jane Bennet.

They took up a position much like the first couple, and during the dance, Bingley held her close, up to the point of, how can one say it? Intimacy? The young woman seemed to melt into his embrace, their bodies flowing together in perfect harmony. More enthusiastic applause ensued after their performance.

Darcy felt that there had been enough surprises for one day, when George Wickham stepped up next. And damn the scoundrel, the girl in his arms... that outspoken suffragette, Elizabeth Bennet.

He received no recognition from Wickham, who was concentrating on his partner and giving knowing smiles to the hostess. Mathilda Maxwell even winked at him. That gesture told Darcy all he needed to know. That libertine, Wickham, was "entertaining" their hostess. According to the latest gossip, her husband was absent on an expedition to Egypt or somewhere. The dance was about to begin, but Wickham and Elizabeth were not in their starting pose but standing a few feet from one another. As the silken strains of the tango began, they walked in rhythm slowly towards one another, and when they met, he clutched her, bent her head back, as he swept her in a semicircle around him, his hand at the bottom of her back, his face so near her neck he could have kissed it. This was the Argentine tango.

They began with the promenade, which brought them close to Darcy and the rest of the spectators. Wickham's eyes were locked with Elizabeth's. He then let go of one of her hands and she, holding his neck, and he, holding her waist, did a slow, deliberate turn of several steps in front of the group. Wickham's gaze burned into hers as they circled one another like two adversaries and yet again, two lovers. Darcy couldn't take his gaze off them. Just watching produced an odd sensation, like a chill and then a fire. He closed his eyes for a moment and breathed deeply, trying to control his arousal. When he looked up, Wickham clutched her to him once again, and they danced as one graceful yet voracious animal. She matched his kick with her own, and they twirled off to the other side of the hall as the music came to a close.

This time, Caroline was on her feet applauding, as was the rest of the small crowd. The two of them had, indeed, been magnificent.

***

Lizzy knew that George had deviated from the set of steps in a most sensual manner, and when the music finally stopped, she searched his face. Was he in love with her? Was he trying to seduce her? For a long moment after the dance concluded, he held her unbearably close. He had aroused something purely physical in her that she found nearly irresistible. If there had been no other people in the ballroom, she would have kissed him on the spot. He must have read her thoughts, for still holding her close, he brushed his cheek against hers and then whispered, "Thank you for the dance." Another shiver ran through her. Then applause came only from one person.

"Oh, bravo, bravo." George let go of her at once. She turned her head as a woman approached. Matilda Maxwell came over accompanied by a crowd of onlookers. Wickham did a short bow, the smirk Lizzy found hard to tolerate on his face. "You must introduce me to your talented partner, George."

Mrs Maxwell proffered her hand to Elizabeth. She curled her lips into a smile, but her eyes sparked with a glint that could have only been matched by a drawn blade. Elizabeth swallowed and attempted to remain passive.

"This is my colleague and, I hope, friend, Miss Elizabeth Bennet," he said evenly.

"Charmed, I'm sure." Miss Maxwell released her limp grip on Elizabeth's hand and stepped back. "This is Miss Campbell, of the Northumberland Campbells, and George, I believe you know Mr Darcy."

Elizabeth stole a glance at George, the colour draining from his face. He then hardened his look into something she would only give her worst enemy. "We've met." He then, rather rudely, walked off.

An awkward silence followed. Lizzy felt that she ought to say something. "Mr Darcy and I have met."

Mr Darcy must also have felt the discomfort of the situation and began speaking at the same time as her. "Yes, we met over a blancmange."

Lizzy laughed, and he did also, his dark eyes flashing. She felt the tension break. He could be charming… that was a surprise.

"Now that we have all been introduced, shall we have tea together?" Mrs Maxwell gave Lizzy a dismissive glance and said, "Would you be a dear, my girl, and go find our Mr Wickham?"

Mr Darcy arched one eyebrow.

"With pleasure," she said, although she was affronted by Mrs Maxwell's condescending attitude. Never mind. She should find George.

***

Darcy didn't linger long in Mrs Maxwell's company, opting for the garden on the slight chance he'd run into Elizabeth. What exactly he was going to say to her was a mystery, even to himself, but in spite of his better judgment, she had captivated him. It was absurd, really. She was a shopgirl, friendly with that scoundrel George Wickham, an opinionated suffragette, and to be frank about it, not as comely as her sister. Jane held his friend

Bingley spellbound, and he would deal with that later. Now, it was time to speak to Miss Elizabeth Bennet and confirm his suspicions that she was not of his social class, and she would say or do something to reverse this sudden enchantment and set his heart and mind to rights again.

Mrs Maxwell had a small labyrinth hedge planted in her garden, unique to the confined spaces of Kensington. Looking about, he satisfied himself that she had disappeared therein. He came upon her as she rounded a corner.

"Oh, Miss Bennet." They nearly collided, and at first she smiled at him, then her expression hardened. "I wanted to apologise for Mrs Maxwell's rudeness," he blurted.

"Why shouldn't she treat me as a subordinate? I am only a shopgirl, after all."

Now he was confused. She seemed angry with him for something. No doubt that was Wickham's doing. "That is an odd thing to say. I was under the impression that your father was a gentleman with an estate in Hertfordshire."

"An entailed estate, Mr Darcy. It couldn't hold a candle to yours."

She really was being most abrasive. "I am looking for Mr Wickham and can't seem to find him anywhere."

A short silence passed between them, and then she added, "That is your fault, I expect."

Yes, that was it. Wickham had been filling her head with half-truths, if not out-and-out lies. So be it. "If you expect me to offer you an explanation, you will be disappointed."

She shook her head and looked at him intently. "No doubt, you have none."

Her reaction to him was understandable, but it still made him angry... angry and jealous. Jealous of the regard she had for Wickham. "You are a good and loyal friend, Miss Bennet. That much I will give you. I am not one to gossip, nor air family troubles in public. I hope you can respect that."

She arched one eyebrow, even opened her mouth to speak, but apparently thought better of it. They were near a bench in the maze, quite secluded, and he motioned her towards it. "However, I did want to speak to you alone ever since our dinner conversation at the Bingleys'."

There it was, finally. A smile. To his surprise and pleasure, she sat down. "Are we going to have a great shouting match about women's suffrage here, Mr Darcy?"

She was amusing...and intriguing. Why did he find himself so attracted to her? Was it that torrid dance? As she sat down, she pulled the fabric of her slit skirt over her thigh and knee to keep her modesty. He tried not to rivet his attention there.

"You made me think. I don't change my mind easily, as you probably have guessed, but your arguments for women's rights were compelling. They have caused me a few sleepless nights."

Her eyes sparkled with surprise. "Really, Mr Darcy? I am glad. Perhaps you should come along to one of our meetings. There are some men there, and not only the ones who attend only to heckle."

"Perhaps I will. I wanted to ask you, though... do you believe in violence to achieve your ends?"

She sighed and thought for a moment. "I, personally, do not intend to become involved in any acts of violence. I promised my sister."

"Well, that's a relief."

She arched a brow. "But... I also do not think that our goals will be accomplished without it. Men respect violence."

He was silent for a moment, then looked at her. My god, she was a magnificent creature. He was about to reply when their hostess called out into the garden.

"Mr Darcy, Mr Wickham, Miss Bennet, do come in and join us for tea."

He offered Elizabeth his arm and she took it. The same chills and conflicting heat from seeing her dancing rushed through his body again as her gaze met his. "Did I tell you how superbly you tango?"

She smiled again. It bathed him in the warmth of her presence. "No, you didn't. Please do."

Chapter 10

"I'm sorry, what did you say?" Lizzy and Jane rattled along in the back of a bus towards their digs in Cheapside. They had slipped out soon after their obligatory tea. Having work the next day did circumscribe their social life quite a bit. That lovely Mr Bingley offered to drive them home in his motorcar, but his sister insisted on staying on at Mrs Maxwell's, so that was that. George was nowhere to be found, so they arranged their own passage home. Lizzy was relieved. She had much to think of since her meeting in the garden with Mr Darcy.

"My goodness, you're distracted." Jane offered one of her disarming smiles. "I hope you aren't still angry with Mr Wickham, Lizzy. I don't think he really means to be rude. He's one of those men who just doesn't think."

Elizabeth shook her head and had to smile. Jane could make excuses for the devil himself. She never saw the faults in a person, nor did she judge. "Oh, he thinks very carefully. Don't be fooled. In any case, I wasn't thinking of him. I do believe he's found bigger fish than me to fry."

"I wish you wouldn't use terms like that. Your way of expressing yourself has become rather—"

"Brazen?" Elizabeth laughed.

"I was going to say 'bold'. Honestly, Lizzy. I do believe those suffragettes are having an influence on you."

"I certainly hope so..." She was silent a minute. "That Mr Darcy. He actually told me that he changed his mind about women and the vote."

"What's so remarkable about that? You are very persuasive."

"It's remarkable because men rarely change their minds. They might be persuaded to give in, but they rarely change their minds. It speaks well of him, but I can't reconcile what I know of him now, and what George has told me. I suppose that's made me so pensive."

"Perhaps there's more to the story than Mr Wickham told you."

"Undoubtedly." Elizabeth sighed. "Let's think no more about it. You and Mr Bingley did a splendid job on your dance this afternoon. I was proud of you. I think Mr Bingley might have designs on you that go beyond a dance partner." She rolled her eyes and Jane did too.

"We're behaving like schoolgirls... I do like him, though. I think I may be falling in love with him."

"I could see that coming from the first time he saw you in the window at Selfridges. Has he said anything to you?"

"Not yet, but I expect he may. He does seem awfully fond of me. I think his sister likes me too."

"Caroline Bingley? Ha. That harridan."

"Lizzy, you shouldn't say such things. She has always been very solicitous of me."

"Perhaps... through clenched teeth. She tolerates you at best, and she despises me. I have no idea why."

"Oh, I'm sure you're wrong. I believe she thinks that I'm a good match for her brother."

"I truly doubt that, but if he really loves you, it won't matter what she thinks."

Jane began to tug on her gloves. "Families are important, Lizzy. You know that. Still, perhaps it is too early to talk of love."

"Not if we are speaking of love at first sight," Lizzy teased. Before Jane could object, she glanced outside. "Come along. This is our stop."

With that, they wove their way through the crowd onto the damp street and made their way to their cosy room as the mystery of Mr Darcy haunted Lizzy's thoughts.

***

After that fateful "tango tea," George's interest in Lizzy waned to the point of cordiality and nothing more. He never asked her to another tea or to a music hall. He smiled at her, gave her no explanations, and drifted away. She had to admit that the loss of his attention gave her no real pain. He was amusing, but she was not in love with him.

Unfortunately, Jane saw less of Mr Bingley than she had hoped. The summer season, which began in May with the *vernissage* at the Royal Academy, was in full swing, and Charles Bingley seemed to be off to one house party or garden party after another and was often engaged at cricket matches or parties in bungalows along the Thames. They often saw his photo in the society pages of the London papers. Lizzy suspected that this gay social tumult had been arranged for him by his sister so that he could meet a more suitable young lady than this shopgirl, Jane. She said nothing to Jane as that would only add to her distress of not seeing him. Rumour had it that he was looking for an estate, which would establish him in the upper echelons of society. He might be drifting inexorably away from Jane, as his sister was, no doubt, planning. It angered Lizzy, but there was nothing she could do about it.

The two of them, of course, worked setting the tableaus in Selfridges' windows. Summer frocks for the ladies, slim-fitting suits for the men, and straw hats with wide brims filled the displays. The store bustled, and it gave them less time to think of young men as Mr Goldsman took up all their attention, at least, during the day.

As Lizzy and Jane arrived home at the boardinghouse, a letter was waiting for them from their mother. As soon as they reached their room, Lizzy opened it and read it to Jane.

Dear Jane and Lizzy,

Wonderful news. Papa has received an invitation to attend the Henley Regatta. You girls must join us. Perhaps you can get the entire weekend of July 1 and 2 or even the Monday. It would so please your father. We will be attending with Mr Collins, and he is most anxious to make your acquaintance. Do see if you can manage it, won't you?

"What do you make of that?" Lizzy peered over the letter at Jane.

"What do you mean? Papa wants us to join him for the regatta. I think it will be splendid... if we can convince Mr Goldsman—"

"No, Mama wants to trot us out to that Mr Collins person."

"Oh, Lizzy. Does it matter? It's a chance to attend the regatta. I was so hoping that Mr..." Jane frowned and sat on her bed.

"You were hoping that your Mr Bingley would ask you, weren't you? Perhaps he will and you can just tell him *we are already engaged for that event.*" Lizzy did her best to turn up her nose aristocratically, which worked its magic on Jane. She laughed.

"I have been rather a mope these last few weeks, haven't I?"

"If you have, this outing will just do the trick. I think we might persuade Mr Goldsman to give us either the Saturday before our usual Sunday, or the Monday off, but not both. He's been a bit grumpy lately... complaining that our English summers are not warm like they are in Chicago."

"You want to go, then?"

"Of course, I do. I must admit that I miss all of them, even Mama."

"Well, then, it's settled. Read the rest of the letter."

There was news of Mary, Kitty and Lydia, and the usual gossip around Meryton. Lizzy's friend, Charlotte, was also attending the regatta with her parents, Sir William and Lady Lucas. That pleased Lizzy enormously. She and Charlotte were great friends. In fact, she'd tried to persuade Charlotte to join them in London and try their luck at obtaining a position at Selfridges, but Charlotte declined. Ah, well. They would visit in Henley-on-Thames if Mr Goldsman was amenable. Perhaps, they might even see Mr Bingley and Mr Darcy there. Lizzy couldn't imagine why Mr Darcy seemed to pop into her head more often than not. Perhaps it was that conversation in the garden that disconcerted her. She disliked being contradicted in her opinions, especially when she herself was doing the contradicting.

As luck would have it, Mr Goldsman was perfectly happy to let the two of them leave a trifle early on the Friday and then return for work on Tuesday morning. Both Jane and Lizzy acquitted themselves admirably during the store's decorating craze that Mr Selfridge ordered to celebrate the coronation of King George V and Queen Mary. Any passerby might think that Selfridges was a palace, hung with red bunting along the exterior columns, and gold-embroidered medallions depicting the royal emblems. There were twelve-foot-high shields with the coats of arms of the kings of history, gauntlets, flags, and all manner of royal paraphernalia. The window dressing lasted far into the night, and Lizzy and Jane gladly stayed late after closing. When Mr Goldsman asked questions such as "What about this?" or "What about that?" they could answer each time. "We've finished that, sir. All done." The poor man really had no earthly reason not to grant their request. It was not that his nature was so magnanimous, but Mr Selfridge set a tone in the store that rewarded hard work and, unlike all the other employers in the city, really cared whether his employees were happy. Before they knew it, they were on the train to Henley, all decked out in their summer frocks and brimming with excitement.

Unbeknownst to Jane, Lizzy had a stack of *Votes for Women* pamphlets secreted in her travel bag. The regatta, which drew the rich and powerful to the river for sport, would be a perfect place to distribute her suffragette literature. Her poor sister was convinced that Lizzy would end up in prison being force-fed and abused. Lizzy, however, was firmly entrenched in the idea that discretion was the better part of valor. She had no intention of getting arrested.

"Oh, Lizzy, Jane, there you are." Their mother's voice pierced through the throng at the station like a rapier. She was bouncing about, waving and shouting, and she came over, fluttering around them both like a distraught mother hen. "Come along, come along, girls. Your father has hired a motor, and we have rooms at the Cherry Tree Inn."

"Doesn't that sound lovely?" Jane looked at Lizzy, her face awash in smiles.

"It sounds… cosy." Lizzy wasn't sure what they would find there. Perhaps all five of them would be crowded into one room. Still, it was a chance to see the family again after an absence of so many months, and Lizzy welcomed it.

Chapter 11

Darcy was grateful for the regatta, for Charles Bingley's sake if for nothing else. Despite the round of country house parties, gallery openings, and garden parties, a distinct pall had fallen over his friend. Most couldn't see it. His sister seemed almost oblivious to it, encouraging him to attach himself to one female after another, but Charles wasn't having it. Oh, he was pleasant enough in company, but Darcy could see that he was unhappy. He knew that Charles was enamoured of Jane, but in the few times Darcy had observed them together, he concluded that Jane didn't feel the same. Jane was kind to everyone, and Charles misinterpreted that kindness for affection. Darcy chastised himself, for it was no better for him. Time after time his thoughts returned to Elizabeth. She was so outspoken and radiated a kind of strength he usually found appalling in a woman, and yet...Well, the regatta would distract them both, at least temporarily.

As members of the Beefeaters Club rowing team, they spent many an early summer morning training on the Thames. At the beginning, Darcy felt it would be no great feat to master rowing as he himself was in good physical condition and swam often. The training regimen soon knocked him down a few pegs. He discovered muscles he didn't even know he possessed, and he ached all over for the first few weeks. His hands blistered. Still, not one to give up easily, he persisted. Now he was in fine shape, and so were the rest of the crew. His hands were as calloused as any dock worker. Darcy had to admit to himself that he quite enjoyed the change.

They arrived early. Darcy brought along his cousin, Col Fitzwilliam, as he was in town and seemed keen to cheer them along. By midafternoon their team was assembled. Even though the river was crowded, they were determined to practice at least once or twice before their race the next day. Darcy knew that they had no real hope of winning anything, but he was grateful to Bingley for convincing him to compete. He enjoyed the camaraderie even though he would never seek it out himself.

The boat was long and sleek, and so low to the water that any slight mishap would fill their racing shell with water and send them all into the river. Bingley was the coxswain and steered the boat. He was focused and competent and they would at least make a good showing.

"Good luck, boys," Col Fitzwilliam called out as he gave the shell a good push into the water. They struck out slowly, and Bingley swivelled and swerved them through the crowd of tourist boats filled with ladies all dressed in white and their male companions, many of whom wore striped jackets and jaunty straw hats. Darcy and his team were dressed as racers, all in white, short-sleeved shirts and short trousers. As Darcy leaned into his oar, his body surged with power and anticipation. He longed to get out on the open river and pull for all he was worth.

***

On arrival at Henley, Lizzy was pleasantly surprised. Her parents had booked enough rooms for all of them at the Cherry Tree Inn. She and Jane had a room to themselves, and the Lucases were staying there as well. Opening of the regatta began the next day, so they dressed in their white garb and took a trip down to the river to find their boats. The Thames brimmed with overloaded small craft filled with spectators. Their mother, Lady Lucas, Mary, Lydia, and Kitty went aboard a large tourist vessel equipped with a striped sunshade, lemonade, and comestibles. Lizzy wanted to try her hand at rowing their own boat, so Mr Bennet, Sir William, Charlotte, Jane, and herself struck out in a rowboat.

Charlotte and Jane had no interest in rowing, and her father graciously surrendered his own oar to Lizzy with a wink. She knew his was a sedentary life, and the only reason he was in the boat with Sir William and herself was that it gave him an hour or two's respite from her mother and her nerves. Boats crowded the river, and spectators filled the shoreline and beyond. They were five or six craft deep themselves, and therefore she attempted to steer their little boat around the others into a small space of empty river.

"Let us head for open water, shall we?" she asked Sir William. She and he were more often than not at cross purposes, and bumped into a few vessels, much to the chagrin of their seafaring neighbours.

"Heave, Miss Elizabeth," Sir William shouted, and together they struck their oars in the water and pushed forward into the centre of the river with a mighty splash—just as Lizzy noticed a shallow racing shell filled with men hurtling towards them.

"Pull back," Lizzy shouted, but Sir William, instead of reversing the direction of his oar, pulled in the same direction, propelling them straight into the path of the oncoming racer.

"Hard to port," a familiar voice shouted, but it was too late.

A crash of oars came first, then the boats collided. In an instant, the slender racing shell capsized. Lizzy's boat rocked and splashed them with water, but at least they remained upright. The racers, however, were thrown willy-nilly into the water.

"Where's Bingley? He can't swim." Mr Darcy... Elizabeth was sure of his voice now.

A few men clung to the overturned racer, while most treaded water, trying to stay afloat in the current. Those not struggling for their own survival craned their necks back and forth, searching the river. One of them shouted, "Can't see him." Lizzy shot a glance at Jane. Her face was ashen.

"What can we do to help?" Lizzy shouted.

"You've done quite enough already," one of the team clinging to the bottom of the racer threw back.

Darcy swam around the racer, looking frantically for Bingley. "Do you see him?" he shouted, then looked up at their rowboat. He started for a moment when he saw Lizzy.

"We don't." She scanned the river. "What do we do?"

Darcy didn't answer. None of the other men were attempting a rescue, and his frustration was clear.

"Can't one of you help him?" she shouted at them.

"We can't swim," one shouted from close by.

She could swim.

All her sisters could.

"Right." Lizzy pulled her hat off and handed it to Jane. "Hold this." She did, then Lizzy sat down in front of her. "Undo me."

"What?"

"Undo my dress, I'm going to help him."

Lizzy didn't dare look at her father or Sir William.

"Elizabeth Bennet, I forbid it." Her father gripped her arm.

She shook it off. "Jane, undo these clasps or my dress will drag me down."

Jane did as she was told, and Lizzy, free of her dress and corset, in her petticoat and drawers, dove into the river. The shock of the cold water took her breath away for a moment, but she spluttered to the surface to come face-to-face with Mr Darcy.

"I can't see anything. The river's too muddy. It's impossible." His expression contorted with panic. "You go towards the bow; I'll take the stern."

Before Lizzy could reply, he was gone. A cold fear gripped her. The current could easily have pulled Mr Bingley under and swept him down river. Swallowing down her dread, she forced herself to think clearly. There was one other possibility. If he wasn't there, there was little hope for him. Taking a deep breath, she dove under the capsized shell.

The water was nearly opaque, but she could make out the shape of the racing shell above her and flapping white shapes hanging from the underside. After surfacing underneath the shell, she discovered a thin pocket of air trapped under the boat.

Clinging to one of the seats near the bow, there was Mr Bingley. He grasped tightly to the inverted wooden seat and kept trying to bend his head upward to keep it out of the water. With every movement of the boat from the men clinging to it on the surface, the water splashed over his nose and mouth. Coughing and spluttering, he let out a meagre cry for help. Lizzy took a hold of one of the seats behind him to pull herself up as the boat bobbed. Her efforts splashed the muddy water over Bingley's face. He let out a cry.

"It's all right. We found you."

Bingley did not turn his head to look at her. "Thank God, thank God." And then, "Is that you, Miss Bennet?"

"Yes. I'm going to leave you for a moment—"

"No." He croaked out in panic.

"It's all right. I am going to get Mr Darcy, and he'll come and get you. Hang on just a little bit longer."

Bingley kept his neck bent painfully back so that he could keep both his mouth and nose out of the water. His breath came in short, unnerving spurts like a child's did when she'd been crying. "Don't leave me. I'll drown."

"You won't. We'll get you out."

He might have said something further, but Lizzy didn't wait. She swam out from under the racing shell, towards the other side of the boat, thinking that Darcy would surface there. A moment after she emerged, so did Darcy.

"The current must have carried him down. I—"

"No, he's here. Under the boat. He found a pocket of trapped air and is hanging on... near the bow."

Darcy didn't stop to argue with her. He dove straight down towards the bow.

***

It was too good to be true. Bingley was alive. A stupid accident nearly deprived him of the best friend he had in the world. Just as Miss Bennet said, he was near the bow, hanging on to one of the seats, trying to avail himself of an ever-shrinking pocket of air. Darcy popped up in front of him.

"Listen, Bingley, I'm going to pull you out from under the boat..." Bingley let out a moan. He must have been terrified. "I'm going to come up behind you. Listen, when I tell you, take a deep breath. I'll wrap my arm around you and take you under and out. Understand?"

"Yes." His voice was a squeak.

"Whatever you do, don't fight or try to aid me. Just let me help you, all right?"

Darcy had never pulled anyone to safety from the water and wasn't as confident as he was trying to appear to his friend. There were still some men hanging on, their legs in the water. He'd have to avoid them to bring Bingley to safety. He dove under the boat and under Bingley, bumping his head on the craft as he surfaced. "Breathe."

Bingley breathed in and so did Darcy. He wrapped his arm across Bingley's chest, catching him under the arm. Kicking furiously and bending back, he managed to clear the gunnels of the boat and surface quickly. Bingley gulped and sputtered. A great cheer went up from his teammates. A short distance away, a rescue boat plied its way through the water.

Chapter 12

Both Lizzy's boat and the racing shell were being inexorably carried down river. She was greatly relieved to see Mr Darcy and Mr Bingley bob to the surface. Once they were both safe, she swam for her father's boat. When Lizzy reached the side, Jane's face betrayed her anxiety.

"Are you all right, Lizzy? And Mr Bingley? My goodness."

"We are both fine. Right as rain. I'm going to swim for shore. Come and get me there. It will be easier for me to get into the boat." With that, Lizzy swam for the reeds. With strong strokes she covered a fair distance and then, dragging herself up the deserted bank, she realised that she was cold to the bones. Soon their rowboat slipped into shore, and Jane and Charlotte clambered out, dragging with them Lizzy's corset and the rest of her clothing. They worked as a team doing her up as quickly as they could.

Then Jane embraced her so fiercely it nearly knocked her off her feet. "You're a bona fide heroine, Lizzy—" She hung on tight. "—and if you ever do anything like that again, I will strangle you." Then she burst into tears. Lizzy held her sister for a long moment.

"It's all right. Everything is all right." She suddenly felt like laughing but had no idea why. With her dress covering her soaking underclothes, she, Jane, and Charlotte climbed back into the rowboat. Although she was still drenched and chilled, Lizzy felt a good deal safer now she was dressed again. Since they had beached themselves on shore, they were now behind the shell that had drifted farther to the centre of the river and farther downstream. A kerfuffle of men's voices drifted over as the rescue boat dragged Mr Bingley's teammates, himself, and Mr Darcy from the river. The vessel had a wide hull, and because of its design, didn't rock or capsize when hauling people aboard. Elizabeth and her party watched as Mr Darcy, clutching Mr Bingley fast, fought the current. They were soon hauled aboard the rescue boat. Once the shell was securely fastened and all the men were aboard, the rescue vessel turned and began to chug upriver towards the crowd they had just left.

When it passed them, Lizzy watched as someone threw a blanket around Mr Darcy's shoulders. He was dripping wet, his white shirt and short trousers clinging to his body, accentuating every line and curve of muscle. Her breath caught in her throat. He didn't see her or her little crew safely nestled in the reeds. Within a few moments, they were gone, and Lizzy took one of the oars once more as they steered themselves back onto the river and made their way towards the dock. Jane sat close.

"We were so worried about you, Lizzy. You were under water for such a long time. And Mr Bingley. Are you sure he is all right?"

"He is all right now, really. And I wasn't underwater. I was under the boat..." She confided all that had transpired—how Mr Bingley breathed his pocket of air until Lizzy and Darcy could retrieve him.

"I may not have any sons, but I'd put you up against any man, my Lizzy. Heroic, that's what you are." Her father patted her hand, his face glowing with pride.

"Still, Papa, there might be a scandal. I mean, women don't usually fling off their clothes and go swimming in the Thames before God and everyone."

"We will take whatever comes, Lizzy. You did the right thing. I can see that now. Your mother might need a bit of soothing, however. I expect we will never be able to attend the regatta again." Her father did his best to sound wistful, but Lizzy knew better. If he never had to leave his library at Longbourn again, he would be the happiest man alive.

"We will speak no more about it, agreed?" Sir William finally contributed his two-penny worth. "It is our secret, and ours alone who the mysterious 'Lady of the Lake' is."

"Lady of the River, Papa," said Charlotte. "Don't worry, Lizzy. We'll just say you fell in the river whilst standing in the boat and ruined our outing." She grinned and let out a musical laugh.

"Oh, well, thank you very much." Lizzy laughed too.

When they arrived back at the hotel, it was obvious to her mother that something had happened. Elizabeth's clothes were soaked, and she shivered, her hair in disarray.

"Oh, my goodness, Elizabeth, what happened?" The news of Lizzy's swim in her underclothes in front of a team of rowers might have already reached the hotel, but on the slim chance it hadn't, she attempted to avoid a scolding by her mother.

Charlotte gave an uncomfortable laugh. "Elizabeth fell out of the boat, Mrs Bennet. She must have lost her balance." Sir William remained stoic, but he shot a glance at his daughter.

"Oh, Lizzy. I don't know what to do with you. Mr Collins very much would like to meet us and may already be here. He can't see you like this. Go and make yourself presentable at once. Oh, my poor nerves." Her mother began to flutter about whilst Jane, taking a more practical approach, went to run a hot bath for Lizzy.

Grateful, Lizzy left her father to smooth her mother's ruffled feathers and, on reaching the bath, sank gratefully into the hot water. She realised then just how cold she was and let the soothing heat of the water permeate its comfort into her bones. A soft knock came on the door.

"Lizzy, it's Jane. May I come in?"

"Of course."

The door creaked open, and Jane sat down on a small stool near the tub and put her face in her hands. She gave a shudder, then wiped each of her cheeks. "I wanted to see if you were all right."

Jane struggled to hold back tears, and Lizzy frowned. "I'm fine, just a bit cold. Are *you* all right?"

Jane didn't answer immediately, only directed her gaze at the ceiling. "I wanted to thank you for saving him. For a time I thought I'd lost you both." She broke down into tears.

Lizzy didn't know what to say. She quickly changed the subject. "Come along, now. Take that little pitcher there and pour it over my head. I'd like to wash my hair. It smells like bilgewater."

Jane began to laugh through her tears. "How would you even know what bilgewater smells like? All right, let me help you."

The hot waterfall felt delicious, and Lizzy lathered up her hands with German green soap and massaged it through her hair. Jane stayed to help her rinse it off, neither of them speaking.

"I think I'll let you finish your bath in peace." Jane moved towards the door.

"Jane?" Lizzy stopped soaping herself in the tub.

Jane turned to face her.

"I don't know how any of this will turn out. I can't imagine what Mr Bingley's sister will think of me jumping into the river in my underclothes."

"You saved her brother's life. She should be grateful."

"Mr Darcy saved his life."

"No, you did too. I'm so proud of you, Lizzy." The tears threatened again. Lizzy could hear it in her sister's voice. "I love him, you know… Mr Bingley."

"I know. Everything's all right now. Perhaps you should inquire where the team is staying and send him a note."

"Oh, do you think that's wise? We're trying awfully hard not to give you away."

"Craft it carefully so that anyone who reads it won't know a thing. If it's not too intimate... I could take a look at it before you send it off."

Jane blushed, or perhaps it was the heat from the steam in the bathroom. "Stop it, Lizzy. You are wicked... brave and wicked. I'll go and do that at once."

Lizzy was left to reflect on the momentous events of the afternoon, of the rescue of Mr Bingley, of her impending disgrace... of Mr Darcy.

Chapter 13

Darcy finished washing and towelled himself off. After sending his racing togs to the laundry, he dressed in linen trousers and jacket, clean white shirt, and because he was feeling so triumphant, a bow tie. Darcy heard a decisive rapping at the door.

"Seems that I missed all the excitement, eh wot?" Col Fitzwilliam brushed past Darcy into the room. "You are quite the hero, cousin, but I can't say I'm surprised."

"You would have done the same." Darcy didn't quite know how to reply.

"Doubt that. Can't swim, so there you have it." Col Fitzwilliam put his hand on Darcy's shoulder and gave it a squeeze. "Really, good show." Both men had nothing to say, then Darcy cleared his throat and broke the silence.

"Let's go see about Bingley. He must be dried off by now."

They walked down the hall to Bingley's room. After Darcy quietly knocked on the door, no reply came for a long moment. The two men looked at each other and Darcy began to feel uneasy. He was surprised when Bingley opened the door and seemed positively vigorous.

"Oh, my dear fellows, come in, come in." He pulled Darcy through the door. Col Fitzwilliam followed and offered Darcy his hand. Darcy took it. "Thank you, thank you ever so much. I'd like to thank Miss Bennet too. If it wasn't for her, I don't know what would have happened." Bingley turned back towards the mirror and began brushing back his hair.

"And who is Miss Bennet?" Col Fitzwilliam raised his eyebrows and grinned into the mirror.

"You know you can never breathe a word of Elizabeth Bennet's part in your rescue... not a word. You either, Richard." Darcy directed his sharpness at Bingley.

Bingley began to straighten his tie. "What? Whatever do you mean? I want to shout it from the rooftops." Bingley's jubilant expression reflected in the mirror.

"I'm sure there are rumours all over the regatta already of a young woman who shed her clothes in order to dive in the Thames after you."

"Oh, for goodness's sake. She didn't shed all her clothes... and surely, no one will dwell on that." He continued to scrutinise himself in the mirror.

"Charles, look at me." Darcy must have sounded more forceful than he expected as Bingley turned sharply to look at him. "You don't know who the girl was. You never saw her before. Don't tell anyone about her, not even your sister—"

"You mean especially not my sister." That remark elicited a guffaw from Col Fitzwilliam.

Darcy didn't answer, but the expression on his face must have betrayed his concern. "Please, Charles. For my sake, don't let on that you know her... Act as if she was some good-hearted lady whom you've never seen before, saw us in distress and risked her life and reputation to save you."

Bingley sighed. "All right. If you think that's necessary."

"I do... truly. And you, Fitzwilliam."

Col Fitzwilliam rolled his eyes and ran his fingers through his curly, sandy-coloured hair. "Oh, all right, Darcy, if you insist... I know nothing."

Darcy glanced from one man to the other. "All right, then. Let's go and join the others. It will soon be abundantly clear to you why you need to keep Miss Bennet's identity a secret."

Bingley was now dressed in a blue and white striped jacket, and white trousers. He picked up a straw boater on his way out the door. Before they reached it, he stopped short. "Hold on, why did you say a few minutes ago that I shouldn't speak of Miss Bennet *for your sake*? What did you mean by that?"

Darcy cleared his throat. "Did I? Hmm. Probably meant to say *for her sake*."

Bingley smiled knowingly. "Yes, I'm sure that's what you meant to say."

"I do wish the two of you would tell me what is going on." Col Fitzwilliam reached the door and held it open for them.

Moments later, they joined their fellow teammates in the hotel bar, and a buzz of conversation ceased with their entrance before their entire team erupted in cheers. One of the chaps began "For He's a Jolly Good Fellow" and the entire place burst into song. It was most gratifying, but Darcy knew he must also quash anything vile or scandalous about Elizabeth and her part in Bingley's rescue. As the boys began slapping Bingley on the back, Darcy as well, each was handed a glass of whiskey. Finally, the captain of the team, Teddie Dudley, asked the question.

"All right, Bingley. Who was the girl?"

Bingley shot Darcy a look, then shrugged. "I'm sure I don't know." He raised his glass in a toast. "Here's to her, though."

They all raised their glasses to toast the mysterious swimmer, but Dudley didn't look satisfied. "Oh, come along, now. You must know her... or Darcy knows her. Why would she throw herself in the Thames after you?"

Darcy spoke up. "Perhaps she is one of those modern women who believe that they can do anything a man can do. I assure you... I don't know her."

Dudley turned to Bingley. Before he could speak, Fitzwilliam cut him off. "Don't look at me, old chap. I wasn't even there."

Dudley directed his attention back to Darcy. "I think you're right. One of those modern girls. Independent... Probably one of that Pankhurst crowd."

"Now there's a thought." Darcy took another sip of his whiskey.

"Doesn't matter, though. You did the rescuing. The lady just swam about in her underclothes." The team all began to laugh. Darcy was furious, but he took a breath and then spoke.

"I'd like to take all the credit..." He raised his glass to Charles. "But truth be told, I didn't see Bingley under the boat. The lady found him."

One of the other teammates slapped his shoulder. "You're just saying that, the gentleman that you are."

Darcy shook his head and raised his right hand. "On my honour, I'm not exaggerating. You see, gentleman, I was looking down towards the bottom of the river, and the lady had the sense to look up."

The subject was now dropped in lieu of a more pressing one. Would Bingley race tomorrow? Without him, the team would have no hope of competing.

"Well, of course, chaps," Bingley said jauntily. Darcy, however, knew he was putting on a brave face. "I'll race tomorrow, but you must all swear not to drop me in the drink."

They all swore they would not amid laughter and a few more whiskeys. Sometime later, Darcy sought out Bingley in a quiet corner. "Are you sure you are up to it, Charles? I mean—"

"Can't let the chaps down, can I?" Bingley downed what was left in his glass with one gulp.

"No, I suppose not. But I think we've all had enough for today and should retire early so that we're ready for tomorrow. Oh, and by the by, as soon as this is over, I'm going to teach you to swim."

With their departure, the gathering broke up in favour of a good night's sleep. As Darcy, Bingley, and Col Fitzwilliam passed the front desk, the clerk called out.

"Mr Bingley, a letter arrived for you." Bingley took it and a great smile spread across his face on reading it.

"I'll take leave of you chaps. Good night." He left Darcy and Fitzwilliam staring as he leapt up the stairs, the letter clutched in his hand.

***

Although they all retired early, sleep eluded Darcy. He stared up at the ceiling for quite some time, and then found himself walking through a murky glade. Blanket-thick fog rolled past in brownish waves. A knocking sound filtered through, as if someone beat on a hollow log drum or a door to a cavernous room. Then he floated and everything was blurred before a figure appeared ahead with its back to him.

He tried to walk but moved better if he kicked his legs and pushed the fog back with his arms. Up ahead, the figure floated. Male... dressed in racing whites, standing very still, arms out. Darcy was sure he was dead. As he got closer, he recognised Bingley. Darcy struggled and struggled to reach him, but no matter how furious his movements, he made very little headway. Panic seized him. He clawed his way over to Bingley, and when he finally reached him, he clutched his shoulders and turned the body around to face him. Only it wasn't Bingley.

Elizabeth.

Elizabeth was dead in his arms.

He stifled a groan, yet the moment he let go—she opened her eyes.

Darcy sat up in bed, breathing hard, fast. Sweat plastered his nightclothes to his body.

Dreaming. He must have been dreaming.

Sitting still for a time, he let his breathing return to normal and then got out of bed and ran water over a cloth and put it on the back of his neck. He wanted a whiskey but settled for a glass of water. Finding the overstuffed chair that faced the window, he sat down heavily and watched the moon, wondering how Bingley and Elizabeth were sleeping that night. If only the race weren't tomorrow.

Chapter 14

The first competitions were today, and Lizzy looked forward to her family and the Lucases' picnic as they watched the races. Mr Collins was due to appear the day before, but she still hadn't seen any sign of him. With everything that happened yesterday, Lizzy had forgotten about him until her mother, who had the appearance of a cat who had swallowed a canary, reminded her of his visit.

They joined others from the hotel and travelled by cart to the expanse of lawns crowded with spectators having their noon repast. Once they had settled in their spot, folding chairs, small tables, and blankets were spread out on the lawn. Lydia looked at their mother. "Oh, Mama, why can't we picnic on one of those lovely boats with the striped canopies and eat on the river?" She summoned that pout that made Lizzy want to shake her. It did seem to have the desired effect on her parents.

"You know that your sister, Mary, gets seasick with even the slightest movement, dear girl. You saw that yesterday. We would like this outing to be pleasant for everybody. Besides, we don't want our Lizzy falling in the Thames again, do we?"

Her father cleared his throat and shot Elizabeth a knowing look. "We are eating on shore and let us hear no more about it. We will be close to the river soon enough. I'd like to have my luncheon in peace, if you don't mind."

Mary piped up, never taking her nose out of her book. "Too much of water hast thou, poor Ophelia, And therefore I forbid my tears." Lizzy sighed. Any opportunity to quote Shakespeare or the Bible, Mary would do it. She loved her family dearly but appreciated them much more when she was in London and they were in Hertfordshire. It promised to be a long afternoon before the races began.

From her spot on the lawn, Lizzy could see everything. Many other families were gathered for picnics and lawn games. Soon, a horse-drawn carriage arrived filled with other revellers who went in immediate search of a suitable picnic spot. With them, a rather slight man, dressed in dog collar and clerical robes, climbed down from the wagon, waved in their direction, and approached.

"Oh, so there you all are. I have been searching for you for half an hour." He seemed a bit flustered as the rest of Lizzy's party turned to stare at him. "I am Mr Collins, cousin to you, Mr Bennet." He brushed back his hair nervously and extended his hand to Lizzy's father.

It appeared that Mr Collins's designs on them had not dissipated. Lizzy tried to smile, but she knew it appeared forced. It was the best she could do.

"So, you see, Mrs Bennet, Mr Bennet, I do not rejoice in your daughters' misfortune, but have come to make amends as much as I can... even though I do not bear any responsibility for the entailment of your estate, of course. I am an innocent bystander, as it were." He laughed nervously. Lizzy disliked him more and more with every word. He was so pompous and supercilious. "The only way that I feel I can remedy this situation is to make myself known to your daughters, and, in the fullness of time, perhaps one of them might consider becoming my wife."

Lizzy nearly burst out laughing as a gasp of horror came from Lydia. The sound of it mustn't have reached Mr Collins's ears or his ego for he continued. "Perhaps Miss Jane would like to take a stroll about the grounds with me for a short while." Jane looked wide-eyed at Mr Collins, then her mother, then Lizzy. She was about to vacate her rickety folding chair when their mother spoke up. "I believe Jane is nearly engaged, Mr Collins..." This remark caused all of them, Jane especially, to gape at her mother in surprise. "But Elizabeth, I'm sure, would love to walk with you."

Lizzy looked daggers at her mother, who smiled sweetly and motioned for her to stand. And stand she did, taking Mr Collins's arm. Lydia was now audibly snickering into her hankie, which caused the same reaction in Kitty. Mary merely lifted one eyebrow. Her mind working, Elizabeth surmised that Jane must have been waxing rhapsodic about Mr Bingley in her letters home, so her mother, as was her wont, just extrapolated the situation in the direction that she desired. At least Jane was spared Mr Collins's attentions.

"So, Miss Bennet, are you enjoying the regatta?" Before she could answer, he continued. "I have been here before, of course, as a guest of my most prominent parishioner and my patroness, Lady Catherine de Bourgh." His smile widened and his expression took on an expectant look. Elizabeth supposed that she was to be impressed by this news, but she had no idea who this person was.

"Lady Catherine?" she asked. "I am afraid I am not familiar with the name. Is she very prominent in social circles?"

Mr Collins raised his eyebrows. "Of course, of course, she is quite well known... quite. In Huntsford there is not a citizen for miles around who does not benefit from her magnanimity and condescension."

"Ah." What was she to say to that?

"Any wife of mine would be privileged to dine with her on occasion and also with her charming daughter Anne. I, myself, have been there often."

Again, Lizzy supposed that she was expected to be impressed. She didn't know what to say, exactly, so she tried, "That must be wonderful for you."

"Oh, it is, it is. I suppose you may one day visit from Meryton and see for yourself."

"Meryton, Mr Collins? Jane and I live in London."

Now it was Mr Collins's turn to be surprised. "Really? I got the impression from your mother that you girls were all at home."

"Oh, no, sir. Jane and I have been for some months in London working for Mr Selfridge in his store."

Mr Collins stopped in his tracks. "So, you are saying that you and Miss Jane Bennet are... shopgirls?"

Elizabeth tried to hide her amusement, but she could feel her eyes crinkling and she bit her lip to keep from smiling too widely. "Yes, I suppose you could say that is exactly what we are."

Mr Collins took a breath and then resumed his walking. He asked his questions to the air in front of him and would not meet Elizabeth's eye. "And your father... he approves of such...goings-on?"

"What exactly do you think is going on, Mr Collins? My sister and I are employed at a perfectly respectable place of business and live in a perfectly respectable boardinghouse."

Mr Collins mopped his brow with his handkerchief, kept his eyes firmly on the horizon, and stammered over his words. "I-I did not mean to give offence, Miss Elizabeth... really, I did not... It's just that your situation is... how shall I put it? Not what I expected from my conversations with your mother."

This time Elizabeth couldn't suppress a chuckle. "I do not doubt that in the least, Mr Collins. My mother tends to see the world as she would like it to be, rather than what it is." Mr Collins still didn't meet her gaze, so she pressed on. "I suppose she also neglected to mention that I am in the women's suffrage movement."

"A suffragette?" he squeaked. He stared at her. She felt rather sorry for him since he looked as though he might faint. Finally, he spoke. "Oh, I am afraid my patroness, Lady Catherine de

Bourgh, would never approve, never approve. A parson's wife a suffragette? What example would that set for the women in the community? Oh, dear…" He stood muttering to himself for a few moments. Elizabeth decided to take him in hand. She slipped her arm into his, and he started.

"Come along, Mr Collins. Let's go back to the family. I think we both have had enough of this conversation."

He looked at her quite intently for a moment. "I don't suppose you would ever consider giving up your—"

"No," she said. "No, Mr Collins. I would never consider giving up anything."

As Elizabeth approached their party, Mr Collins uncomfortably took his leave. They hadn't spoken a word to one another on the short walk back to the picnic, and Mr Collins nearly ran from her once he could politely escape. Her mother waved and called to her. "Look, Lizzy, we have a guest. This is Col Fitzwilliam; he is a friend of Mr Bingley."

"And Mr Darcy's cousin," Col Fitzwilliam added,

"Oh, how do you do, Colonel Fitzwilliam. However, did you find us?" The appearance of Mr Darcy's cousin made Elizabeth uneasy. Did he know of what happened the day before? Had he come to tease her, to triumph over her, or worse, to thank her in front of her mother and spoil their entire charade of yesterday?

"Mr Bingley had a note from your sister written on the hotel stationary. It was not difficult after that."

"Stop interrogating the poor man, Lizzy. Do have some lunch with us, Colonel."

"Ah, I will have some refreshment, thank you, but my real purpose in coming here is to invite you all to observe the Beefeaters Club race this afternoon from our place on the shoreline. You will have a very good view from there. It won't be too crowded, as it is reserved."

Mrs Bennet rolled her gaze appreciatively. "Reserved, how nice. Of course, we will join you, Colonel. Mary…Mary, put down that book and go join your sisters at badminton. The colonel can take your seat."

Mary looked up over her book at her mother stoically, reluctantly put it down, and went to join Kitty and Lydia, who were squealing over a flying shuttlecock.

"Mr Bennet, Mr Bennet," her mother called to her father, who was seated at a small table by himself, where a newspaper hid him from view. Occasionally, a piece of cold chicken would disappear behind the paper. "Come and join us. A friend of Mr Bingley is here to invite us to the races this afternoon." Lizzy's father folded his newspaper in half and approached Col Fitzwilliam. After shaking hands, he pointed out something in the paper that might be of interest not only to the colonel but to the entire party.

"Have you seen this article in the Henley Standard, Colonel? Perhaps you might be interested, Mr Collins. Charlotte, Sir William. Listen to this." He began to read.

"Who is the mysterious Lady Diver? Yesterday, a boating accident involving the Beefeaters Club of London and a small recreational boat nearly ended in tragedy. The boat's coxswain, a Mr Bingley of London, was trapped under the racing shell and nearly drowned. Unable to find Mr Bingley once their racing boat capsised, a mysterious woman, believed to be aboard the other vessel involved, divested herself of her clothes and dived in the Thames to aid in the rescue. A Mr Darcy of Pemberley eventually found the coxswain under the racing shell, holding on for his life and breathing a small pocket of trapped air. He was soon pulled out of the water to safety. The lady rescuer swam ashore, but by accounts of eyewitnesses, someone called out to her using the name Izzy, believed to be a sobriquet for the name Isabel. She was subsequently picked up by her party in a rowboat and disappeared into the crowd. If anyone knows who this mysterious lady is, please contact this newspaper at ... etcetera, etcetera, etcetera."

By the time her father had finished, all in their party were riveted, even her sisters at their badminton game.

"Maybe they are talking about you, Lizzy. Your name is almost like Izzy." Lydia leaned on her racket and scrutinised her.

"Oh, good gracious, Lydia. You do try to make a drama out of everything." Elizabeth poured a glass of lemonade for Col Fitzwilliam and glared at her sister.

"If it was Lizzy, she'd tell everyone. Wouldn't you, Lizzy?" Kitty piped in.

"Of course, I would. If I did something heroic, I'd want everyone to know, and why not?"

"Oh, Lizzy, stop. You are embarrassing Mr Collins." Her mother tightened her lips as Lizzy's father turned his attention to Col Fitzwilliam.

"Not racing with your cousin today?"

Lydia, who never could concentrate on any one thing for very long, looked off around her and sighed. A group of young men in racing whites wandered nearby and her gaze fixed upon them.

"Let's go play again, Kitty, you too, Mary. Perhaps we could get those racers over there to play with us." Lydia and Kitty ran off in the direction of the racing team, and Mary dragged along behind. Elizabeth tried her best to concentrate on what Col Fitzwilliam was saying but needed to reassure herself that Lydia had well and truly directed her attention in another direction. Col Fitzwilliam stopped speaking and looked expectantly at Elizabeth.

"Oh, I do beg your pardon, Colonel. What were you saying?"

***

The next two hours passed pleasantly enough for Lizzy, and she was content to lie about on her side on a blanket. Col Fitzwilliam was affable and remained with them, conversing easily with her, her father, and Sir William, as well as Jane and Charlotte. Mr

Collins pontificated and seemed very pleased with himself while doing so. After their conversation on women's suffrage, he never again met Lizzy's eye, though. Her other sisters and their newly acquired companions made a terrific noise from time to time playing their game, and Lizzy resisted their entreaties to join in. Eventually, the young men wandered off to participate in the races.

As the time for the Beefeaters race neared, Lizzy and her family followed Col Fitzwilliam's lead and left on foot for the river. The colonel offered Elizabeth his arm, and together they walked a little ahead of the rest of the party.

"I know your secret," he said once they were out of earshot of the rest of the group.

Elizabeth raised an eyebrow. "Oh, do you, Colonel. And what is that, pray tell?"

"My cousin and Mr Bingley told me, under strictest confidence, of course, that it was you who jumped in the Thames yesterday to save Mr Bingley."

Elizabeth didn't look him in the eye. "Is that so?"

"Don't worry. You have nothing to fear from me. I am the soul of discretion. I must tell you, though, that Mr Bingley is very grateful for your help. He is well aware that, if you hadn't found him, he would not be racing today."

"He is racing? I can scarcely believe it."

"He's the coxswain and steers the boat. If he did not race today, none of them would."

"That is very brave of him, I'm sure... and very foolish."

"Stiff upper lip and all that." The colonel smiled disarmingly at Elizabeth. She was beginning to like him very much. "Besides, it's not the only foolish thing he's ever done."

"Oh?" Elizabeth was intrigued.

"Yes, it seems that he's gotten himself entangled with some shopgirl in the city. Can't let some gold digger turn his head, wot?"

Elizabeth was speechless. He was talking of Jane, wonderful, loving, sweet Jane who had nothing but good intentions and genuine affection for Charles Bingley. It made her blood boil, but she wouldn't let on.

"Oh, really. Do go on."

"My cousin, Darcy, and his sister put an end to that quickly enough, keeping Charles busy all summer and introducing him to women more suitable for his station. Good plan, I say."

"Yes, it sounds like your cousin really did his friend a favour. I'm sure there are plenty of girls who are attracted to a man chiefly because of his wealth."

"You have no idea. Bingley is lucky to have a friend like my cousin to look after his interests... and, it seems, his life."

They fell into silence until Lydia ran up and edged herself between them. "Why do you two have your heads together? Are you telling secrets?" She laughed mischievously.

"I'm telling the colonel all your secrets, Lydia. He is scandalised."

"Oh, that's wonderful. I'll walk with him now, Lizzy. Mama wants you to go and walk with Mr Collins."

Elizabeth gladly left her sister to the gallant colonel and fell back with the rest of the party. Mr Collins seemed to have lost all interest in her and her sisters and contentedly chatted with the Lucases. Elizabeth glanced at her mother, who indicated with a shake of her head that she should join Charlotte, her parents... and Mr Collins. Elizabeth did, but didn't join into the conversation to any great degree. She was roiling inside. How could a man like Mr Darcy, who at one moment seemed so gracious and brave even, be so cruel as to interfere with his friend's budding romance with her sister Jane? She was angry. Angry with Darcy for his meanness and snobbish attitude, and with herself for being so attracted to him.

***

When they got to the spot where they would observe the afternoon races, the conflict in Elizabeth's head had become so severe that she felt she couldn't stay there anymore. To make herself cheer for that awful Mr Darcy would be more than she could bear.

"I am not feeling well, Mama," she whispered to her mother as they settled along the bank. "I have a headache. I think I'll go back to the hotel.

"And miss the races? Really, Lizzy. Mr Collins will be so disappointed."

"I very much doubt that." Lizzy looked over towards the Lucas family where Mr Collins sat firmly ensconced. Her mother followed her gaze. Mrs Bennet closed her eyes and sighed. Lizzy entreated her mother again, "Really, Mama, I need to go."

Her mother softened her expression. "I'm not surprised you are ill after dunking yourself in the river yesterday. All right, Lizzy. I'll have your father take you back to the hotel."

"No, Mama. That is not necessary. He is having such a good time. Remember, Jane and I travel all over London alone. I will be fine getting back to the hotel."

The announcer began his litany of the race participants through his megaphone and the noise of the crowd abated.

"All right, go on now. We will see you later."

Lizzy took her leave. She didn't return to the hotel, however. Not just yet. Winding her way to the walkway along the bank and disappearing into the crowd, she spied a pair she had hoped to find there. "Mary, Constance, hello."

Smiling widely, they beckoned to her. Joining them, she pulled leaflets from her Chelsea bag.

"Votes for women. Here, sir, madam. Please take one. Votes for women."

Chapter 15

The roar of the crowd abated somewhat by the time Darcy and his Beefeaters Club team crossed the finish line, being the fourth boat across, but they made a good showing. More to the point, he couldn't wait to share his near triumph with Elizabeth. He so wanted to talk to her about the events of the previous day. To tell her how much he admired her. He knew that the difference in their families, their fortunes, their social standing was an obstacle to any future together, but it was no use. He couldn't get her out of his mind. He had to speak to her.

When they reached the stands, there was much excitement from all their most loyal supporters. Caroline rushed to embrace Bingley, but he looked right over her shoulder and locked his gaze with Jane Bennet. As soon as Caroline freed him from her embrace, he jostled his way through the crowd and took both of Jane's hands in his. It was no use. He was smitten and there was nothing Darcy or Charles's sister could do about it.

"Oh, Mr Darcy. You did so well. Congratulations." Caroline looked at him so expectantly that it made him uncomfortable.

"Thank you very much, Caroline. I do think we did all right, considering…"

Col Fitzwilliam came to the rescue, slapping him on the back. "Considering? You did very well, very well indeed. Now, let's go have a drink to celebrate." He offered Caroline his arm, and Darcy shot him a look of gratitude. Col Fitzwilliam winked at him. Darcy searched the crowd but couldn't see Elizabeth anywhere. Not having been introduced to anyone in her family but Jane, he approached her and Bingley.

"I beg your pardon, Charles, Miss Bennet, but where is Miss Elizabeth?"

Jane looked about. "I'm sure I don't know. Perhaps Mama would." Taking a few steps through the crowd, she took an older woman in an enormous hat decorated with ostrich feathers by the arm and led her back to Darcy and Bingley.

"Mama, I would like to introduce you to Mr Darcy, he is a friend of Mr Bingley's. Mr Darcy, my mother, Mrs Bennet."

Darcy inclined his head. "Pleased to meet you, I'm sure."

Before her mother had a chance to utter another word, which appeared as though she might, Jane intervened. "Mama, Mr Darcy is looking for Elizabeth."

"Oh, Lizzy? She had a headache and went back to the hotel I believe." She then began to chuckle. "You would not believe it if I told you, Mr Darcy, but our clumsy daughter managed to fall into the river yesterday. I believe she might have caught a chill..." Mrs Bennet then began to look around, her gaze stopping at a small group nearer the river. "And I was so hoping that she and Mr Collins would have a chance to know each other better. Oh, Mr Collins. Come here, please and meet Mr Darcy." Her voice carried over the crowd.

Darcy hoped against hope it was not *that* Mr Collins. In a few seconds, it was revealed that indeed it was.

"Oh, Mr Darcy. How nice to see you here. I thought that was you in the boat. Very good show if you will permit me to say."

Before Darcy could reply, he went on, addressing Mrs Bennet. "Mr Darcy and I know each other quite well. Mr Darcy is the nephew of Lady Catherine de Bourgh, who is a patroness of my little parish. She condescends to let me preside over services at her chapel at Rosings. What a grand lady. You are so fortunate, Mr Darcy."

"Yes, fortunate." It was all he could think of to say. Being Lady Catherine's nephew had never made him feel fortunate, but this little toady couldn't stop singing her praises. He continued to do so for some minutes, stopping all other conversation. When he finally took a breath, Darcy found it an opportunity.

"So nice to see you again, Mr Collins. If you'll excuse me... Mrs Bennet, Charles, Miss Bennet..." Darcy didn't wait for any objections to his departure but took the opportunity of a lull in the conversation to escape. He knew the hotel in which the Bennets were staying, having seen the note from Jane, and resolved to go there immediately.

Darcy did not want to disturb Elizabeth, but by the same token, longed to see her again. On one hand, her actions the previous day were shocking by any standards. Divesting herself of her dress in public and plunging into the Thames... he was scandalised. At least part of him was scandalised. On the other hand, what she did was admirable, even heroic. If it wasn't for her, he wouldn't have found Bingley in time. He was sure of it. Her disregard for convention also meant a disregard for the consequences of her actions on her own reputation. Perhaps none of these thoughts occurred to her, as they always would to him. Perhaps she just saw someone in trouble and jumped in to help, leaving the consequences to be pondered after the fact. Either way, she had worked some sort of magic on him. All of the qualities he had convinced himself he wanted in a woman, in a wife, had been blown from his brain by the explosion that was Elizabeth Bennet. He must speak with her.

He climbed into his motorcar and was at the Cherry Tree Inn within a quarter of an hour. Inquiring after Miss Bennet, he was met with disappointment.

"No, sir. None of the Bennet family is here. They are picnicking and then attending the regatta. Perhaps you could try in the evening."

"Are you quite sure? Miss Elizabeth Bennet is supposed to be here."

The desk clerk turned around to peruse the small boxes of room keys. "I'm afraid not, sir. Their key is here."

Where could she be? And, more importantly if she was not ill, why did she miss the race?

Chapter 16

"You are awfully quiet." Jane nudged Lizzy as the train rocked soothingly on their way back to London.

"Just thinking."

"I'm so sorry you were ill and missed Mr Bingley's race. It was so exciting."

"I'm sure it was. Did you have a chance to speak with him?"

"Yes, I'm afraid I quite monopolised him after the race. He seemed very happy to see me."

"He is mad for you, Jane. Mad."

Jane's eyes twinkled. "I love him. I can't help myself. There is no one in the world for me but him."

"Not even Mr Collins?" Lizzy gave Jane an arched look, then burst out laughing.

"Well... I believe Mama has that gentleman reserved for you."

"I don't think Mr Collins and I are suited somehow. Perhaps Mary will want him and save the Bennet dynasty." She rolled her eyes.

"They might make a good match. He would talk and she wouldn't listen."

Elizabeth scoffed softly. "I do believe some of my outspoken habits are rubbing off on you."

It was times like these that Elizabeth was so grateful to have Jane at her side. She was always there to lighten her mood, or look after her, and most especially, to be her loyal friend. Even

Charlotte, of whom Lizzy was very fond, didn't follow her to the ends of the earth as Jane did. Well, Jane followed her to London, which less than a year ago did seem like the ends of the earth.

They continued their work with Mr Goldsman. Mr Selfridge, always attuned to the fashions and trends from the continent, had them decorate an entire run of windows promoting the Ballets Russe, which Diaghilev just brought to London. Today, she and Jane worked creating the stage set of the ballet, *Giselle,* in a curtained sanctuary in one of the south windows when a call came their way.

"Come out, Miss Bennets. Come out and see," Mr Goldsman called through the hidden entrance to the window. Lizzy threw Jane a look, and they quickly left their cocoon and stepped onto the retail floor just in time to see The Chief with none other than Anna Pavlova on his arm, enrobed in sable from head to toe. She floated next to him like some sort of fairy queen, much to the delight of both customers and staff alike. It was days like these that Lizzy lived for. Having her work helped her forget the mercurial Mr Darcy, who seemed so pompous and arrogant one moment, and so loyal and heroic in another. He thought himself so much above her and her family, there was no use thinking of him at all.

As summer slipped into autumn, Mr Bingley spent considerably less time in London. Jane received missives from him quite often, but he was off for one shooting weekend or house party after another, and their only communication was through letters or an occasional telephone call.

After a particularly gruelling day at the store, Elizabeth climbed the stairs to their room. All she had in mind was removing her hat and shoes and having a quick lie-down before dinner. Jane stayed downstairs a moment to have a chat with Mrs Clarke and retrieve the post.

Just as she was about to drift off, Lizzy heard the door open and a swish of skirts. "Oh, you're asleep." Jane's voice floated through.

"Nearly." Lizzy forced her eyes open and propped herself up on her elbows. "What is it?"

"Post for you... from somewhere called Pemberley."

Lizzy was awake now and stretched out her hand. She tore open the envelope and retrieved a letter on fine paper bearing a watermark and letterhead. The signature confirmed her suspicions. It was from Mr Darcy. Lizzy held it for a moment lost in thought. How dare he write to her when he plotted against her sister to keep her from the man she loved? How dare he?

"Aren't you going to read it?" Lizzy looked up at Jane's beaming face.

"You've received another letter from Mr Bingley, haven't you?"

Jane said nothing, but her smile widened. "He hasn't forgotten me, even though he is always in a whirl of social engagements."

"Of course, he hasn't. Nothing will keep you apart. You'll see."

Jane looked at her quizzically. "What you mean 'nothing will keep us apart'?"

Lizzy chastised herself for her slip of the tongue. She dared not reveal the machinations of Mr Darcy and Miss Bingley. It would break Jane's heart. Besides, apparently, nothing they were doing prevented Mr Bingley from writing to Jane nearly every day.

"Oh, nothing. I only mean that... being absent from you for so long has done nothing to cool his ardour, has it?"

"No, I don't think it has. Go on now. Read your letter and I will read mine." Jane could contain herself no longer, and slicing open the envelope with the letter opener, she settled herself at their small desk and began to read.

Lizzy steeled herself against what Mr Darcy might have to say to her and began his letter.

25 October 1911

My Dear Miss Bennet,

I am sorry that it has taken me so long to write to you since the accident at Henley, but urgent business at my estate has occupied my attention until now. I wanted to thank you personally for all you did to save my friend, Charles Bingley. It would have been an unspeakable tragedy for his family and for me if anything had happened to him. Your bravery and self-sacrifice have left a lasting impression on me.

My cousin, Colonel Fitzwilliam, also spoke highly of you, and enjoyed his conversation with you and your father at Henley. I ask you, though, why did you not attend the gathering after the races? I looked for you there and even sought you at your hotel, but no one knew what had become of you.

Elizabeth stopped reading for a moment. He'd looked for her at the hotel? The man was full of surprises. Perhaps it would have been better to have had it out with him, then and there, about his treatment of Jane. Ah well. It was too late for that now.

I trust you are well, and still doing your work with Selfridges and with the suffragettes. I have taken a keen interest in politics since meeting you. I admit that you have had a profound influence on my life, far greater than I can explain to you in a letter. In fact, there are several things I want to discuss with you in person.

The next time I am in town, I would like to call upon you, if I may. I close now and wish you and your family continued health and happiness.

Sincerely,
Fitzwilliam Darcy

How extraordinary. He asked her questions and by doing so, no doubt expected her to write to him with an answer. And what in the world did he want to discuss with her? No matter. She didn't want anything to do with a man who was so full of pride in his birth and position that he saw nothing wrong in hurting someone as sweet and kind-hearted as Jane. On the other hand, he did prove to be a good and brave friend when Mr Bingley was in danger. The man was full of contradictions. Jane's voice interrupted her thoughts.

"Your letter. Who was it from?"

"Mr Darcy."

"Mr Darcy? What did he have to say?"

Lizzy hesitated for a moment. "Oh, only that he thanks me for helping him save your Mr Bingley."

Jane sighed. "If only I was sure that he was *my* Mr Bingley."

Lizzy said nothing, but Jane's remark hardened her resentment of Mr Darcy and his meddling ways. She would not write to him. If he wanted to, he could come to her.

Chapter 17

As the rain and cold weather battered the streets, Lizzy threw herself into her work and the suffrage movement. The prime minister had introduced a bill giving all males, no matter their landowning status, the right to vote. While Elizabeth believed in giving everyone the right to vote, whether they owned land or not, she agreed with the Pankhursts that this was a slap in the face to their movement. They had been pressing to give landowning women the right to vote, and now this bill seemed to solidify suffrage into the hands of only men. Something had to be done. Lizzy was prepared to do it.

After attending a rousing meeting of the WSPU to find out what *could* be done, Elizabeth shook off the rain from her woollen coat in the dark, thinking Jane might be asleep. But the light turned on, and there was Jane, still dressed and sitting on her bed, holding a letter. She looked unnerved.

"Thank goodness you're home." Jane got up and handed the letter to Elizabeth.

"What's the matter? What's happened? Is someone ill?" It wasn't a telegram, so there was little likelihood that someone died, but still, Jane looked shaken.

"It's from Mama. Bad news, I'm afraid. I don't know what we are supposed to do." She spoke as Lizzy opened the envelope and started to read.

Dear Jane and Lizzy,

I hope you are doing well and that you are in good standing in your positions.

"Good standing in our positions? Whatever does that mean and what a way to begin a letter," said Lizzy.

"I know, I know. Read on."

"I will come right to the point, girls, your sister Lydia needs your help. She has involved herself with a young man who is most unsuitable, and she needs to leave Meryton for a while. I don't say that she has disgraced herself, but that is not long off in my estimation. Your father and I are in agreement. You two will get her a position at Selfridges and she will live with you for a time. The occupation will do her good and you two can supervise her.

"Oh, no." Lizzy sighed and dropped her hands to her side. "This is too much. Do they think that we're great friends with Mr Selfridge and all we must do is ask? What if there's no position? What if she makes trouble at the store and the two of us lose our own positions in the process? No, no, we must tell Mama to find another way to—"

"It's too late, Lizzy. She's coming on the evening train tomorrow."

Lizzy sat heavily on the bed, the letter dangling from her hand. Lydia. What were they to do with Lydia?

The next evening, Lizzy stood with Jane at King's Cross Station in the early evening to meet Lydia's train. On reading further into her mother's letter, Lizzy found that her father must have intervened and involved the Gardiners. He, at least, had sense enough to know that Jane and herself had no hope of arranging accommodation and employment in one day. They met their uncle at the station and were greatly relieved.

"So, our little Lydia is coming to stay for a while. How nice." He was always a pleasant man, and Elizabeth liked him very much.

"I'm afraid the Bennet sisters impose on you too much, uncle." Jane couldn't meet his eyes. The entire situation upset her as much as Lizzy.

"Nonsense, nonsense. We love having her. Your mother wrote that the two of you are going to make enquiries at Selfridges for her."

"We will make enquiries, but I cannot guarantee Mama the outcome she prefers." Elizabeth didn't want to mislead him into thinking that they had some magic plan to obtain employment for their flighty sister.

"No matter. We will keep her for a visit. The children will keep her occupied and there is much to do about the house. Perhaps your aunt will teach her to cook."

Elizabeth looked at Jane after that remark and could see that it finally brought a smile to her face. "I would very much like to see that. Oh, here is the train."

***

From Lydia's demeanour, Elizabeth knew she was not best pleased to be shipped off to London to stay with her uncle, or her sisters for that matter. Lydia's bags were duly deposited in the attic bedroom at the Gardiners'. It was rather makeshift and small, with a sloping ceiling and one dormer that provided much-needed light. Lizzy was grateful that her uncle gave Lydia a room of her own rather than having her share with her younger cousins. He and her aunt really were most accommodating.

The rest of the family had adjourned below with Jane for tea and cake, but Lizzy insisted on talking to Lydia. After all, she was due an explanation to this extraordinary turn of events, and she could hardly rely on her mother for accurate information… or any information, for that matter. Lizzy imagined that her face must have looked like thunder as she turned to follow Lydia up the stairway, for Jane clasped her by the arm and wordlessly told Lizzy to be patient with Lydia. Lizzy nodded, pressed her lips together, and resolved to hear Lydia out.

Lydia sat pouting and bouncing disconsolately on the bed. "This is like a prison cell. I don't know why Mama and Papa are being so mean."

"You have a room to yourself in a crowded household. You should be grateful." From Lydia's pose, arms crossed, head tilted toward the ceiling, Lizzy knew immediately that she had taken the wrong tack. *Patience... patience.* She pulled a chair from under the dormer and sat opposite Lydia, taking both her hands. "Perhaps you should tell me what happened. I know nothing of the situation except that Mama said there was some man involved."

Lydia finally raised her gaze to meet Lizzy's. They were so narrow; it was almost frightening. "Oh, that. I don't know why they were so upset. We didn't *do* anything, not really."

Lydia jumped up off the bed and leaned her head on the narrow, sloping ceiling, and proceeded to gaze out the window. Lizzy knew that ploy. Lydia didn't want to look her in the eye.

"What didn't you do?"

A bit of sighing and huffing ensued. "Martin is a little bit older than me... an officer in the marines." Lydia turned suddenly and flashed Lizzy a dazzling smile. "He was so handsome, Lizzy. Just so handsome. Then, just because he took me out on a picnic in his motorcar without telling Mama and Papa where we were going... Oh, it was so humiliating."

Lydia turned dramatically back to resting against the window.

"Something must have happened, or you wouldn't be here. You haven't told me anything."

Lydia glared back at her. "When they couldn't find me at home, Papa went to the barracks to ask after Martin. Papa told his commanding officer that he ran off with me and had an entire patrol of marines interrupt our picnic...which, by the by, was going splendidly. I had my first entire glass of wine... and, well... other things."

Lizzy's face must have betrayed her feelings of... shock—horror?—because Lydia burst into a gale of giggles. "Oh you should see your face. I told you nothing happened... not really."

"Oh, Lydia. No wonder Mama and Papa wanted you to leave Meryton for a time. This could have been... It could have been the ruin of you. Really, you need to learn to be more discreet."

"I knew you would be on their side. I just knew it." Lydia abandoned her stance at the window and threw herself on the bed.

"I'm not on their side. I know it isn't fair that men can do as they please and women bear the consequences, but that is the way things are right now. You must learn to... judge more carefully...You are very young and older men will take advantage..."

"You just don't understand. We were in love... at least I think we were. He said he was going to marry me... eventually."

Lizzy sighed. "Oh, Lydia." What more could she say? It would fall to Jane and herself to keep a close watch on their wilful and impulsive younger sister.

Chapter 18

Lydia had been to Selfridges once before, but it was some time ago, and Jane convinced Elizabeth that a tour of their place of work might awaken some enthusiasm in Lydia. Her Aunt Gardiner was more than happy to oblige. Elizabeth spoke with Mr Goldsman about Lydia, and he in turn with Mr Aubrey, and she was soon offered a position behind the counter at the front of the store in cosmetics. Jane had also spoken to Mrs Clarke and a cot was moved into their already small room, in place of the writing desk and chairs. It would have to do until either one of the larger rooms was vacated or they found another place to stay that could accommodate all three of them.

When Lydia heard that she would be working in cosmetics, she was over the moon. "I shall wear lip rouge every day," she said to Lizzy and Jane.

"You will wear what the head of department tells you to wear. You know that you also have to attend class four nights per week." Elizabeth straightened the errant strands of her coif. She could still use the mirror that was now over Lydia's cot.

"What? Why?"

"Anyone under the age of eighteen that works for Mr Selfridge has to attend classes."

Lydia crossed her arms and pouted. Elizabeth shook her head. "You know that your display does absolutely nothing for Jane and me. Mama and Papa aren't here to witness your tantrums."

Lydia looked up at her, uncrossed her arms, and sighed. "You know you can win prizes if you do well. Sometimes they even have parties." Jane sat next to her and put her arm around her shoulders.

"Parties? Oh, that does sound jolly, but I don't suppose they have parties very often."

"No, probably not, but you can make new friends there. There will be lots of people your age taking the same courses." Jane was trying to cajole her. After all, what were they to do with her if she rebelled?

"I suppose I'll try it since you and Lizzy have made such a great effort for me. London might be fun."

Lizzy sent a skeptical look Jane's way. *Oh, Lydia. Wait. The new adventure of work has just begun.*

***

Having set some of the more pressing problems at the estate to rights, Darcy returned to town. He had been ruminating on many things, not the least of which was the offer of a seat on the board that Harry Gordon Selfridge made to him so many months before. Times, indeed, were changing. The installation of plumbing, electricity, telephone, and other modern and expensive conveniences along with upkeep of the manor and its lands all took money. He refused to let his estate, his inheritance, go to wrack and ruin, even parts of it. There had always been a policy of letting select members of the public into the house to see some of what he considered the public rooms, but now he followed the example of many of his aristocratic friends of employing a tour guide and charging the public for a look. That change proved to be a godsend, as the money paid some of the daily upkeep and allowed him to keep more of his staff. Still, four thousand a year from Selfridge would do him good, and the work would not be onerous. He could simply give his proxy to Selfridge and be done with it, or he could put some effort into his position and learn something of the life of commerce from one of the age's great innovators. Harry Selfridge disliked long meetings with a passion, so Darcy needn't fear he would be trapped for hours in a stuffy room filled with cigar smoke and men who couldn't stay on the subject. Bingley was right once again. He should avail himself of the opportunity.

He had to admit that there was another, perhaps more pressing reason to visit the store. He couldn't get Elizabeth out of his thoughts. After meeting her rowdy family, taking into consideration that she and her sister were employed for wages, that she brought with her no wealth save her fine mind and strength of character (which might be more of a liability than an asset), that she was a handsome woman, but no great beauty, his logical side told him that she would be a completely unsuitable wife for him. An American heiress, the daughter of a patrician family, even Bingley's sister Caroline made more sense, but no, his heart wanted what it wanted, and it wanted Elizabeth Bennet. As he walked through the door on Oxford Street, he wondered if part of the reason he was saying yes to Selfridge was a chance to see her again.

Darcy arrived at the store and marvelled at the changes that had been made since his last visit. A lovely scent wafted from the store the minute he opened the door. Counter upon counter of perfumes, soaps, and ladies' cosmetics were now set up to greet customers upon entering. His heart beat a little faster. Perhaps he would see Elizabeth today. As he passed a counter laid out with lip rouge and face powder, a young girl behind the counter smiled his way.

He stopped in his tracks.

That face. She looked so familiar. Had he seen her before? He couldn't imagine where.

"Ah, Mr Darcy, how nice of you to come early."

The familiar voice assailed him from behind, and Darcy turned to find Mr Selfridge extending his hand.

"Come, come." Selfridge smiled at him. "I am making my morning rounds. We can talk as we go, and you can get a feel for the business." He looked over the cosmetic counter.

"Miss Bennet, how are your evening classes coming along?"

That was it—she was one of Elizabeth's sisters. He must have seen her at the regatta.

"I believe I am doing very well, thank you, Mr Selfridge."

"Splendid. Splendid. Glad to hear it. Carry on."

Elizabeth's sister had powder on her face, rouge on her cheeks, and her lips were a vivid shade of red. She wore the cosmetics that she was selling: a good sales tactic. A girl of her youth needed no enhancements, but wearing them might convince a more matronly customer that these augmentations on display might restore her youthful beauty. This Selfridge fellow was a clever one, to be sure.

After their walk about the store, which took the better part of an hour, they concluded their business in a matter of moments. Selfridge was not so crude, even being an American, as to write out a check and hand it to Darcy. He would have the money discreetly deposited in Darcy's account. Before Darcy knew it, he was riding the lift down to the main floor. On that short trip, he resolved to talk to Elizabeth about a matter of utmost importance to his happiness.

***

Elizabeth and Jane worked inside a curtained window facing Oxford Street. They were hanging and draping furs, ermine, mink, and of course, sable. Jane looked about and then clutched a lovely sable stole in her arms and rubbed it against her cheek.

"Could you imagine owning such a thing?"

"No, I really can't. They are lovely, though. So soft." Lizzy ran her hand over a floor-length mink, all black with an ermine collar. "I'm sure it would keep out the damp."

"Oh, Lizzy. I'm sure the last thing that women who receive such a gift are thinking of is keeping out the damp."

Elizabeth laughed. "Maybe so, but that's what I'd be thinking about." She arranged a tremendous black hat with a veil, looking like a small dirigible: all festooned with white ostrich feathers, on a stand nearby. "This hat would arrive five minutes before its wearer. Could you imagine this on the Underground? One would need a whole car entirely to oneself."

"Women who wear that never set foot in the Underground."

"True enough."

"Ladies." Mr Goldsman popped his head in a few minutes later to peruse the progress. "Isn't it time you visited the canteen for a cup of tea?"

"We are nearly finished," Jane said, and Mr Goldsmith disappeared, the door closing again.

Jane opened the hidden door that separated the display window from the floor, and who should come through it but Mr Darcy.

"Oh." Jane stepped back, caught off guard for a moment. She soon recovered herself. "Hello, Mr Darcy. What a surprise. Lizzy, I will see you in the canteen." She made her escape with the alacrity of Harry Houdini.

"Jane," Elizabeth called. Too late. She was gone. It was just as well. Lizzy had waited a long time to tell this Mr Darcy what she thought of him and his high and mighty attitude, his treatment of Mr Wickham, and most of all, for breaking Jane's heart regarding Mr Bingley. "Hello, Mr Darcy." She turned her back on him and pulled a sable stole over a Greek balustrade so that it cascaded and puddled on the floor.

"Miss Bennet, I must speak to you."

She wouldn't look back at him. "Well, speak. We are quite alone." She busied herself with the stole, and from behind her, a chair dragged across the floor.

"If you would sit down, Miss Bennet... please."

Now she raised her eyes to his. He appeared to be nervous or in pain or both. No matter. She would sit and listen to what he had to say. He stood behind the chair so she couldn't see his expression, and thankfully, he couldn't see hers.

He hesitated. He cleared his throat. Finally, he spoke. "I have tried to talk sense to myself and convince myself that my head should rule my heart, but it is no use. Miss Elizabeth, I love you... I can't get you out of my mind. I want you to be my wife. There, I've said it."

Elizabeth couldn't believe her ears. What was he saying? And how, in God's name, was he saying it? He, who objected to the fact that she and her sister were employed... objected to Jane as too lowly for his friend Bingley, who was himself in trade... he now professed to love her? It made no sense.

"What do you mean that your head should rule your heart?" She turned in the chair to look up at him, and then stood so that they were face-to-face. He didn't flinch.

"You must understand that I have many obligations of rank and family... that marriage with a woman who would bring her own fortune would be more suitable... that your family is hardly of an aristocratic bent... that you and your sister are employed for wages... that—"

"All right, all right. Enough. I've heard enough. I will be frank with you, Mr Darcy. I am surprised by this declaration... and shocked at what followed. How can you possibly expect me to... what? Fall into your arms after you so meticulously insulted both me and my family?"

"So, you object to my being honest and frank, is that it?" The colour rose in his face. The softness in his eyes disappeared and anger replaced it. "You who are so frank on every occasion whether it is seemly or not? I can't believe that my mode of expression is what has caused you to be so rude to me."

"Rude? Rude to you? I have heard nothing but disparaging remarks about my family, of my profession, my lowly social status…"

He seemed quite taken aback. She could see it in his face. "You have to admit, though, that I have softened my views somewhat since meeting you." He tempered both his voice and his expression. "I thought… after we saved Bingley together, that we—"

"Stop." She didn't let him finish. The entirety of that day flashed before her, how it ended… how Col Fitzwilliam bragged about how his cousin was so clever. "How could you ever believe that I would think well of you, could ever love you, after you deliberately set out to ruin the happiness of my sister?"

He stepped back, the colour draining from his face. He hesitated, then squared his shoulders. "I admit to that. I won't deny it. I could not believe, at the beginning, that your sister really loved Charles and not his money."

"And what of me? Aren't you worried that I might accept your proposal because I am interested in your money?"

"In that regard, I have shown more concern for my friend than I have for myself."

She stared at him. Any slight cracks in the façade of her dislike of him were filling in with impenetrable cement. She didn't stop to take a breath. "Be that as it may, your treatment of poor Mr Wickham—"

"Mr Wickham. You should not speak of something of which you know nothing."

"Know nothing? You forget that Mr Wickham has revealed all to me. How you deprived him of his due, of his living. You are a bully, Mr Darcy."

"So, this is what you think of me."

"It is what I thought of you from the start. Your snobbish, archaic attitudes... your disdain for those of us who work for a living... your use of the power and privilege that was handed to you from birth to make the lives of others miserable. I knew from the beginning that you would be the last man on earth whom I would consider marrying."

He stood silently for a moment, all the ire and combative energy gone from his posture and his face. "Well, that is quite enough. You need not say more. I am sorry now, for ever having brought up the subject and feel quite humiliated in revealing my feelings to you." He turned to go and try to negotiate the hidden door in the display window. When he got it to open, he turned and looked at her, a sagging defeat emanating from him. "I am sorry that I took up your teatime, Miss Bennet. Be well. I wish you happiness." With that, he passed through the door and was gone.

Elizabeth waited a moment or two, then head swimming and heart racing, she ran to the door and opened it. He'd disappeared.

What had just happened? Tears streamed down her face. Wiping them away, they reappeared. She needed to be alone somewhere to try to digest what had just occurred. Mr Darcy wanted to marry *her*. He was capable of such heroism, as he displayed by saving his friend's life, but at the same time, he'd nearly ruined Jane's and admitted it. No explanation of what happened with Mr Wickham. No apology. Yet, here was this man, a snob and a nob to be sure, but he was in love with her, and had been for a long time. She needed time to think. She sat down in the chair he moved for her and wrapped herself in ermine. It was suddenly cold.

Chapter 19

"Lizzy, are you still in here? I didn't see you in the canteen for tea. Whatever is the matter?"

Elizabeth quickly brushed away her tears and, replacing the ermine in its spot, rose to meet Jane. She tried to force a smile, but it was no use.

"Where is Mr Darcy? What's happened?"

Elizabeth took a deep breath. What would she say about Mr Darcy... about his proposal... about her reasons for her refusal? Nothing in the world would induce her to hurt her feelings. "It's nothing. We'd better get on. Mr Goldsman...."

"Mr Goldsman can wait a moment. Tell me what happened."

"Something extraordinary. He asked me to marry him." Jane's face was a picture. It nearly made Lizzy laugh. "Yes, it was a surprise to me too."

Jane took Lizzy's hand. "You refused him, didn't you? Hence the tears."

The last thing in the world Lizzy wanted now was sympathy. She was a whirl of emotions, and the kind and understanding look on Jane's face was undoing her attempt at controlling the maelstrom. All Lizzy could do was nod.

The door to the display window opened and startled them both. It was Mr Goldsman. "Miss Bennets, we are finished here. Let us adjourn to our next endeavour, shall we?"

As Lizzy and Jane withdrew and followed their superior to the next window display, Jane leaned in and whispered to Lizzy, "You can tell me all at home. It will be all right. You'll see."

Elizabeth wasn't sure that everything would be all right. Mr Darcy stirred in her a great cauldron of emotions. Could one of them be love?

***

Elizabeth didn't have time to dwell upon Mr Darcy or his proposal. She told Jane nearly everything, focusing on Mr Darcy's arrogance and his treatment of Mr Wickham as her reasons for refusing him. She made no mention of Mr Darcy's interference on "behalf" of Mr Bingley. That was best left unsaid.

In the ensuing days, her work at Selfridges, with the suffragettes, and minding Lydia gave her little time to think of Mr Darcy. She and Jane divided the four days that Lydia was required for class after work between them. Sometimes they would stay after hours and do more work in the store, sometimes they would go and have a fish and chips meal and walk in the park, but with the winter weather coming on, that became less and less common. The one thing that neither of them did was let Lydia come home alone.

Tonight, it was Elizabeth's turn to stay late and collect Lydia. Lizzy looked up at the clock and sucked in a breath.

"Lord." She was late and rushed down to the staff entrance.

Lizzy's heart fell.

George Wickham stood leaning jauntily against a wall, still dressed in his waiter's uniform. Huddled in a little too close and smiling, Lydia didn't take her eyes off him for a second. The two of them didn't even notice her approach until she laid a gentle hand on Lydia's shoulder.

"Oh, Lizzy. There you are." Lydia jumped and glanced back.

George had one of those expressions that schoolboys have when caught putting salt in their schoolmaster's tea. He got hold of himself quickly and assumed a casual air. "Oh, do you two know each other?"

Lydia giggled. "I should think so. This is my sister, Elizabeth, silly."

"So, your name is Lydia Bennet. Why didn't you tell me?"

"You didn't ask." Little Lydia practically purred. Elizabeth was seething, but she would hold her tongue. It would do no good to create a scene. It would only inflame Lydia's will.

"You heard me speak of Mr Wickham, Lydia, surely?"

"Oh, I suppose so, but this gentleman just told me his name was George. You should have introduced us." She batted her eyes at George. Elizabeth could see why her mother was having difficulty keeping Lydia from dangerous situations. She just jumped in with both feet if there was an attractive man about.

"Since you two need no introduction, I will not make any. Come along, Lydia. Mrs Clarke won't keep tea for you forever. Mr Wickham—"

"Yes, I must be going too. So nice to see you, Elizabeth. We really should go dancing again. I miss it."

Elizabeth said nothing. George touched the brim of his hat and was gone. Elizabeth kept her own counsel on the walk to the Tube, but once they had their tickets and were aboard, she began to quiz her sister. "How did you meet Mr Wickham?" She refused to use his Christian name.

"Oh, I've seen him standing about when we get out of class. He is usually talking with one or another of the other girls, but I have given him a look from time to time."

"Lydia, you didn't. What are you thinking? You are not playing about in Meryton where everyone knows you and there are those who will look after you. You are in London and must be careful."

"You know him. I heard you two. You went dancing with him."

"That's true, but that was some time ago. And we didn't meet behind the store. Really, Lydia…"

"Oh, Lizzy. You sound like an old maid. I was just talking to him. I knew you were coming soon. Either you or Jane come right away. You both worry too much."

No matter how much Elizabeth tried to explain the dangers of talking to strange men, Lydia didn't seem to hear. Finally, she stopped wasting her breath, and for the rest of the Tube ride home, her thoughts returned to Mr Darcy.

***

Lizzy had little time to think of Mr Darcy at all as the suffragette movement began to intensify. The Manhood Suffrage Bill introduced by Mr Asquith gave the right to vote to all men, regardless of their being landowners or not. It looked again as though the government was asserting that voting was the exclusive prevue of men. It enraged Lizzy and all of her sisters in the movement.

When she attended her next meeting, she was handed a toffee hammer. The next step was clear. The Women's Social and Political Union members were all to go on a window smashing campaign in Kensington. Elizabeth could feel the weight of the instrument in her handbag as she took the bus home to their rooms in Cheapside. Whether she had the nerve to do it or not remained to be seen. Damage to property was a lot different to handing out leaflets. But she believed in the cause. She knew that when they appealed to the consciences of those in power, they achieved nothing. These men only seemed to listen after they were faced with wholesale destruction. She wasn't prepared to burn down buildings or assault anyone but admitted to herself that she might feel a great deal of satisfaction breaking a few windows.

They scheduled the protest for a Sunday. Elizabeth didn't want Jane or, God forbid, Lydia to know of her plans. They were off to the Cambridge Circus Cinematograph Theatre, which ordinarily, Elizabeth would have enjoyed, but she had plans of a more momentous nature. By the time she arrived at the meeting place in Kensington, many of the women were already gathered. Elizabeth kept her sash of purple, white, and green carefully folded around her toffee hammer in her bag. She had to admit, excitement electrified her.

"Are you ready, fellow warriors?" a voice shouted out from the crowd. Mrs Pankhurst? Elizabeth couldn't see from where she was standing. No matter.

"I do hope I don't get arrested," one of her companions muttered to no one in particular. "Thomas will be so annoyed." Elizabeth suppressed a laugh, and then it suddenly occurred to her: neither of her sisters knew of her plans, and if she was arrested, what would happen? The crowd began to move into the business district, away from the Underground station and towards the department stores. With a sudden rush of movement, the crowd surged forward, and Elizabeth was bourn along with her companions. Shattering glass assailed her ears. The energy of women shouting, "Votes for Women," accompanied by explosions of shattering glass filled her with courage and determination. She ran up the street and, wielding her hammer, took aim. A plate of window glass shattered under her stroke. It was divine—until the clanging of police bells hurtled towards them.

The women in her section of the crowd began to scatter, but the leaders up ahead continued with their destruction. It was as if they wanted to be arrested, and perhaps they did. She began to run towards the still-rampaging fulcrum of the suffragette destruction machine, when a middle-aged woman came running in her direction, opposite the charging crowd. Elizabeth looked around and realised she was the only one in her group still running forward.

The woman caught her by the arm. "Live to fight another day, dearie."

Lizzy looked into the woman's eyes and took her advice. After turning into a lane behind one of the stores, they hunkered down behind some scattered boxes and refuse barrels until they could no longer hear the screaming, breaking glass, and pattering footfalls. The older woman winked at her and motioned for her to stand up. They edged their way to the entrance of the lane, and Elizabeth's companion peeked around the corner.

"You there, stop." A gruff voice split the air, and the woman disappeared around the corner. As Lizzy inched her way towards the spot where her fellow suffragette disappeared, two bobbies grabbed her roughly by each arm. She was dropped into a horse-drawn police van a moment later. The door slammed and she took her place, then the door opened again, and her erstwhile companion was shoved inside and sat down next to Lizzy and her suffragette comrades. After they pulled up outside the Holborn Police Station and the doors clanged open, officers herded them into a cell to await processing amongst the angered shouts of many other females who were already in custody.

"Here we go again, ladies." The woman offered Lizzy a nod as they tried to find space in the crowded cell. "I'm Bessie."

"Elizabeth." She nodded back, then glanced about. The cell was made for one person, but there were at least a dozen packed inside. The stone walls dripped, and the only light came from a barred, filthy window high above their heads. Lizzy jumped as the iron door clanged shut once more. There was a filthy bucket in the corner, which Lizzy assumed was their toilet facilities. The small cell offered nowhere to sit. "I have to get out of here or I'll lose my situation." Amongst the chatter, her own voice startled her. It was, surprisingly, chatter. Some, like her, were on the verge of tears or weeping outright, but most of the women seemed to take their imprisonment in stride. Their composure instilled a bit of calm in Lizzy.

"They usually release us once the fine is paid. Of course, they may charge us, and that will mean a court appearance." Bessie patted Lizzy's hand. "If your people know you are here and have the means to pay your fine, you have nothing to worry about."

There was so much to worry about. Jane and Lydia didn't know where she was, and they would be frantic. At least Jane would. Missing her start time at Selfridges would mean immediate dismissal. The rules at the store were harsh but fair, and Elizabeth would abide by them. She had no choice. Jane and Lydia would have to wire their father for the fine or the bail money, and that would set off a rippling eruption in her entire family, not to mention ruining all their reputations. A Bennet sister in prison. What if they tortured her? Would she be expected to further the cause with a hunger strike? This downward spiralling vortex of thoughts must have shown as Bessie put her arm around her and squeezed.

"Not to worry. Not to worry. This is your first time enjoying His Majesty's hospitality. If you stay with us, it won't be the last. Whatever happens, you did what you did for a noble cause, and you should never be ashamed of that. It is the gaolers who are the villains, not us. Hm?" Bessie bent her head to look at Lizzy, and her words did invigorate her a bit. "Here, give me your particulars, and I will contact your people. I will be out in a thrice."

Bessie was as good as her word. She didn't spend more than two hours in the sordid cell. Someone came for her directly. As she watched her go, Lizzy was reminded of an old campaigner shaking off the horrors of one battle and readying herself for the next. Lizzy straightened her shoulders. She was a soldier for the cause, that's what she was, and she would bear whatever came with fortitude.

As the darkness fell, so did Elizabeth's spirits. She might well be here overnight; even if Bessie did try to contact Jane, she and Lydia would be at the cinema and perhaps be out for a quick dinner. They may not be home for hours. Then her sisters would have to wire their father. He might even want to come to London himself, and that would take time. She would never get out of here before tomorrow morning, she was sure of it, and then, she would lose her precious position at Selfridges. She would lose her dream. A small space opened against the wall as others were released. She leaned on it.

"Miss Elizabeth Bennet? Is there an Elizabeth Bennet here?" The police sergeant, hatless, clean-shaven except for a black moustache, called into the cell.

"I am Elizabeth Bennet."

"Come along, miss."

The relief that swept over Elizabeth was palpable. She could feel it as if recovering from a near-fatal illness. Standing at the desk, which was higher than her head, she was given back her handbag. She opened it and found the toffee hammer missing.

"Looking for this, miss?" The desk sergeant held up her toffee hammer. "You ain't gettin' it back."

"I was looking to see if the bus fare that I brought with me was still there." Her archness returned to her now that the danger had passed. She regretted her tone immediately.

"You think us coppers would steal a lady's money?"

She thought it prudent not to answer. "Do I have a ticket or something for a court appearance?"

"No, you're free t' go. Fine's been paid." He shuffled some papers on his desk.

"Really? Did my sister pay the fine?"

"Your sister, ha. It was some nob. Now, move along. We've got others waiting."

Another bobby took her gingerly by the elbow, but she twisted away from him and made for the door. Stepping onto the street, she looked about for a sign of her benefactor, but there was no one to be seen.

Reaching the Tube, she rummaged in her bag for the fare, when she noticed a letter that had not been there before. Stepping aside and leaning against the tile wall, she looked at the handwriting. Her name was printed on the front of the envelope, but on the back, in rather more hasty writing, was a quick note.

I have written this letter and struggled with myself as to whether to post it. Your present difficulty strengthened my resolve to put it into your hands.

Fitzwilliam Darcy

Upon reading his name, her heart leapt to her throat. Clutching the letter, she paid her fare and got on the Underground train. The Sunday crowd was thin, and she obtained a seat. After sitting down, she held the letter in her hand a few moments, reading the message on the back. It must have been Mr Darcy who paid her fine and, no doubt, called upon his formidable sphere of influence to have charges against her dropped. She had to admit she was grateful for that. She tore open the envelope.

My Dear Miss Elizabeth,

Please read further. I promise not to reopen a painful subject but wish to clarify some points raised in our latest, rather heated, discussion.

You accused me of interfering with your sister's happiness. I plead guilty to that charge, but you must believe that I did not know it would affect your sister in such a profound way. In observing her, she seemed not to bestow on Charles any more affection than she bestowed on anyone else. Perhaps it is her open and sweet nature that gives the appearance of such magnanimity, but I took it to mean that she did not care for my friend very deeply. That was my mistake, and I admit it. My friend, Charles, also has a nature very like your sister's, and I set myself up as his protector. I think, from now on, I might mind my own affairs, and let him mind his.

Another point that you brought up is the pride I have in my place in society. I do believe that is natural, since my birthright not only conveys on me a great privilege, but it also lays at my feet great responsibility. From what I have seen of your family, although briefly, I hate to say, my opinion is less than favourable. Your younger sisters seem to run wild because of neglect on your father's side and encouragement on your mother's. Only you and Jane seem to have emerged from this rather free and easy rearing with any modicum of decorum. It pains me to say it, but there you have it. I know I only observed them during the regatta when you disappeared, but it was enough time for me to form my opinion.

Elizabeth laid the letter down for a moment and let the words seep in. He was a proud man to be sure, and brutally honest. She had to admit to herself that he hit the mark accurately when it came to her family. Still, it raised her ire once again, for after all, she could say anything she liked about her family, but no one outside of it should dare attack it. She would defend it as a mother wolf would her pups. She took up reading once more.

Finally, I feel compelled to address your accusation that I have ill-treated Mr Wickham. I know he goes about saying he was cheated and ill-used by me and, after I have explained our circumstances, I leave it for you to judge. Mr Wickham is, as you might know, the son of our estate manager, and we grew up together. I had great affection for his father, and for George as well. Both of our fathers died within a year of one another, and my father gave instruction, but not so far as writing it in his will, that his estate should pay for George's education with the idea that he would train for the clergy. By the time he reached his late teens, he told me he had no interest at all in the church and begged me to let him study law. I, therefore, gave him a considerable stipend, more than what my father had designated for seminary, and he left for university.

After some months of hearing nothing from him, I took it upon myself to visit him and found that he had been sent down within a month of his arriving and was living a dissolute life somewhere in London, using the stipend I had provided. I returned home and did not hear from him for a period of some years.

Now comes the most painful part of my narrative. I have a younger sister, Georgiana, who is seven years my junior. One summer she was invited by a close family friend to visit the Japanese-British Exhibition in the city. Trusting in the character of the family, I allowed her to go. By chance or by design, Mr Wickham also attended the exhibition and sought out my sister. Being young (only fifteen) and vulnerable to his charms, he convinced her to elope with him. I am sure that Mr Wickham's only interest in my sister was her considerable fortune. You can imagine the state I was in when I discovered the plan and soon intervened to stop it. Wickham disappeared again, and not wishing to drag my sister's name through the mire, I did not pursue him. So, you can see, I am powerless to answer any charges he lays against me as I seek to protect my sister's good name.

I hope you believe me and my version of events. I have tried to be honest and forthright with you, as I hope I am in all things, even if they be unpleasant. My cousin, Col Fitzwilliam, is in my confidence and can verify all details of what I have told you, and you are free to consult him if you wish. I thought that explaining everything in a letter might be the best way to broach these subjects, since I can lay out my explanation coolly and without interruption.

Please know that I wish you all success in your endeavours at Selfridges and with the WSPU. The more I learn of that organization, the more I come to see their point of view. Thank you for introducing me to the cause.

Yours Sincerely,
Fitzwilliam Darcy

Chapter 20

The train eased into the station and Elizabeth looked up. She'd been so engrossed in her letter that she missed the St. Paul's stop and needed to get off the train and backtrack. Her mind was whirling. Had she really misjudged Mr Darcy so badly? He seemed a man of a persuadable mind, and she had thought so almost from the beginning. Her prejudice against him was fuelled by his superior attitude due to his "birthright," as he called it, and cemented into place by Mr Wickham and, of course, Mr Darcy's interference with her sister's happiness. She then remembered their shared crisis when Mr Bingley nearly drowned. It was then she felt him to be a good and courageous man. Oh, there were too many thoughts for her to sort them all out now. She ran round to the other side of the station and got on a returning train for home.

"Oh, Lizzy. Oh, thank God." Jane threw her arms around Elizabeth as she entered Mrs Clarke's rooming house. She and Lydia must have been waiting in the parlour for her. Mr Bingley stood at Jane's side.

"Humph. And you say *I'm* a lot of trouble." Lydia stood with her arms crossed, glaring at Lizzy. Jane didn't break her embrace but called out enough for Lydia to hear.

"Oh, do be quiet."

Elizabeth smiled at Bingley as Jane let her go. "Do I have you to thank for my rescue?"

"I'm afraid not. Well, perhaps partially. Seems like one good turn deserves another." She smiled at the reference to Bingley's rescue in the river. "Your sister called me on the telephone, and I, in turn, called Darcy. He is the one with the level head, you know."

"So, it was he who went to the police station after me."

"Quite so. He did all the calling about that needed to be done as well. I'm afraid I have no head for such things."

"Did they beat you, Lizzie? Was it awful?" The concern inherent in the question didn't match the glee in Lydia's eyes.

"No. They didn't beat me, but I wouldn't like to repeat the experience. I'm afraid I am a disgrace... getting arrested." Lizzy kept an eye on Mr Bingley. She wanted to assess how much damage she had done to his affection for Jane in light of her "unsuitable" family. After all, his friend, Mr Darcy, had a sharp eye for such things.

"Oh, not at all, Miss Elizabeth. I quite admire you... standing up for your principles in the face of danger and all that. Well done, I say."

That was good news. Jane's face absolutely glowed as he spoke. At that moment, Elizabeth could hardly believe that Mr Darcy could dissuade his friend's affections for her sister in any way.

"Now that the excitement is over, I must be off. Caroline has arranged for me to look over an estate to let somewhere in Hertfordshire." Bingley spoke with such a mischievous look in his eye, Elizabeth had to laugh.

"Hertfordshire? Is it near Meryton?" Jane barely maintained her usual demure demeanour.

"Why, I think it is. It's a place called Netherfield." He grinned broadly at her and raised his eyebrows in anticipation of her reaction.

She slapped him playfully on the sleeve. "Oh, you. How wonderful."

"We shall see. We shall see. I don't think Caroline has made the very obvious connection yet. She doesn't often attend to what other people are saying." Retrieving his watch from his waistcoat pocket, he repeated, "I really must be off." He took both Jane's hands in his and then kissed one of them. "So glad to see you safe and sound, Miss Elizabeth… Miss Lydia." He dandily placed his bowler hat on his head and took his leave.

"Wait until Mama and Papa hear about this." Lydia bounded over. "Finally, I have something to write about besides work."

Jane took her roughly by the elbow and turned her so that they were face-to-face. "You will do no such thing, Lydia Bennet. What happens to Elizabeth and me is our own business and none of yours."

Lydia easily twisted away. "Ha. But you and Lizzy interfere in my business all the time. You act like you are my mother and father."

"That is because we are charged with your welfare by our mother and father. Besides…" Lizzy broke off as she noticed that one of the other tenants was making her way down the staircase, as Mrs Clarke would be starting tea soon. "Come along. We'll finish this discussion in our room. I need to change before supper. I'm starving."

Lydia looked like she was about to speak, but then clapped her mouth shut and dutifully followed them upstairs. There the conversation turned to George and the other young men that Lydia so obviously flirted with. It was decided that everyone would write their own news home. Lizzy resolved that within the week, she would have a serious talk with Lydia about her flirtatious ways, and about George Wickham especially.

Jane and Lydia retired early, and Lizzy, even though exhausted by the day's events, couldn't settle down to sleep. As her sisters readied for bed, she instead retreated to the abandoned parlour to sit alone and think. The extraordinary gesture of rescuing her from gaol and the letter she found in her bag had her mind awhirl with thoughts of Mr Darcy.

She should thank him for his efforts on her behalf, that went without saying. His letter was so frank, yet she could feel him reaching out from it and holding her at arm's length. And why shouldn't he? She made it all too clear to him what her feelings were when he burst forth with that astonishing proposal of marriage... and in the Selfridges window of all places.

A sole lamp was burning on the small writing desk that had once been in their room. She wondered if there might be writing paper and envelopes still in the drawers that she and Jane might have forgotten in their haste to move in a cot for Lydia. That was it. She should write to Mr Darcy and thank him. It was the polite thing to do.

Sitting down at the desk, she indeed found what she needed. She wouldn't be effusive, but she would thank him politely for rescuing her from prison... and she could do him the courtesy of telling him she believed him regarding Mr Wickham. She would not mention her family. He would get no satisfaction from her in that respect. Grasping the fountain pen firmly, she began.

Dear Mr Darcy, (not "my dear," as he began)

I am compelled to write to you and thank you for your extraordinary kindness in extricating me from gaol. I must admit that I was... (What was she? Frightened? Terrified? Incredibly relieved that she was rescued? She would never admit any of that, especially not to him. She picked up the pen again.) *... surprised and pleased that you put forth the effort and money to remedy my difficult situation, despite what had transpired between us. I do not know how I can ever repay you.*

I also appreciate the candour of your letter. I must tell you that I do believe your version of events regarding Mr Wickham. He has revealed himself in many ways since our first acquaintance that aligns with your version of his history. You may also rely on my discretion regarding what transpired between himself and your sister.

She wanted to ask him a thousand questions. Why did he come for her? Why did he care what happened to her? Why bother explaining himself? Did he still harbour affectionate feelings for her? No, he made it clear that he would let that episode rest in peace. If he wished to continue this correspondence, he could do so. She would leave it to him. Yet, something nagged at her. How did she feel about him now? Should she open the door a wee crack and see if he would again step through? She put pen to paper once again.

Again, thank you for your intervention on my behalf. I am most grateful. Your efforts have enabled me to fight another day.

Sincerely,
Elizabeth Bennet
Suffragette

She read the letter once more. Yes, that is what she wanted to say. She thanked him, and that should be enough. She sealed the envelope and would ask Mr Bingley tomorrow for Mr Darcy's address in town. As she rose from the desk and turned off the lamp, she was suddenly overcome with weariness, as if she deliberately snuffed out the small flame of a candle that was lit within.

***

Christmas fast approached when a letter arrived from Longbourn. Her father's handwriting addressed the envelope, and Jane encouraged Elizabeth to read it.

"*Dear Jane, Lizzy, and Lydia,*

I send this letter to all three of you because the news in it affects us all. You may have heard the news already, for Charlotte might have told you, Lizzy."

"Have you heard anything from Charlotte?" Jane asked Lizzy.

"No. Our correspondence has fallen off after the summer. I just attributed that to our lives going in different directions."

"Oh, for goodness's sake, Lizzy, keep reading. I'm all on tenterhooks." Lydia sat on her cot, idly poking a piece of embroidery on which she never seemed to make any progress. Elizabeth continued reading.

"I have bad news for all of you. Charlotte Lucas has married Mr Collins."

Lydia screwed up her face. "Who is Mr Collins?" She stood up and peered over Elizabeth's shoulder at the letter. "And why is that bad news?"

"Honestly, Lydia. Don't you remember? He was that distant cousin, the clergyman, who spent those few days with us at Henley." Jane looked expectantly at her.

Lydia looked pensive for a moment. Then her face was all amusement. "Oh, you mean that dreary man who was looking for a wife among all us Bennets? I think it is capital news that he married Charlotte."

"Mama certainly doesn't think so. He is the means in which all of us will be disinherited. Longbourn goes to him after…" Lizzy shook her head and didn't continue.

"Oh, no matter. You two needn't worry. I will marry a rich man and take care of all of you." Lydia stuck her nose in the air and resumed her seat on the cot. Then picked up The Lady magazine and began perusing the advertisements. Elizabeth sighed and continued reading.

"This is all your fault, Lizzy. You should have been more attentive to him at the regatta. I don't know what you said to him there, but that was the beginning of the end. He sat with the Lucases most of the day and then, off you went to London again, spoiling everything. I am sure he did not approve of your being employed. Now, we will all suffer from your wilfulness."

Elizabeth stopped reading and flipped the page over to read the rest of the letter. Her scowl at her mother's words melted into a smile.

"What does it say, Lizzy?" Jane brushed gently at her arm.

"There is a bit at the end here from Father. I'll read it to you," she said eventually, then began to read.

"I know your mother is angry with you, Lizzy. I suspect that really, she is only anxious for your and your sisters' welfare. I will tell you the truth now, daughter. I am very relieved that you did not encourage Mr Collins. I found him a supercilious, insufferable bore, but if you mention this to your mother, I will deny it. I am quite proud of you girls and your ambition. Of course, I would never tell your mother as it would only result in an attack of nerves. I will address this letter and post it before your mother sees it. All my affection to you, Jane, and Lydia. Papa."

Elizabeth handed the letter Jane, who gave her a knowing smile.

"What does 'supercilious' mean?" Lydia still paged through the magazine.

"It means acting like a snob," Elizabeth said.

"Oh, like that Mr Darcy person."

Elizabeth didn't know why, but that remark cut her to the quick. It was useless to try to explain the difference between Mr Collins and Mr Darcy to Lydia. She did want to say something, though. "So, you remember him, who you've only met once at Henley, but not our cousin, Mr Collins."

Lydia looked up from her magazine for an instant and with an expression on her face that said, "Really, how can you be so stupid?" She sighed. "Of course, I remember him. He was much better looking." With that, she went back to ladies' fashion.

Chapter 21

As Christmas drew closer and closer, Selfridges bulged with people. Lydia acquitted herself well.

***

As a family, they spent a pleasant day putting up a Christmas tree and making loops of paper in chains to hang on it. Elizabeth and Jane bought something for each of them at Selfridges since Mr Selfridge was kind enough to give a discount to his employees on various goods. They spent some of the afternoon wrapping gifts in tissue paper and decorating them with ribbon. Since they were to have a large Christmas dinner at Netherfield the next day, their repasts were moderate for the season, and their mother insisted on the entire family attending Midnight Communion. The preparations during the day, the ebullient spirit in the house, and the arrangements they made for their visit to Netherfield kept Elizabeth's mind busy and lightened her mood. By the time she lay her head on the pillow in the bedroom she shared with Jane, she felt more at peace with herself, and frankly, more at home.

"You've been very quiet during this entire visit." Jane turned out the electric light next to the bed they shared.

"Are you happy, Jane?" A shuffling of bedclothes accompanied Jane's settling into bed.

"Of course. I'm happier now than I have been in a long time. I do hope Mama and the younger girls will behave themselves tomorrow, though." She sighed.

"I think they could burn Netherfield to the ground and Mr Bingley wouldn't care a jot. He loves you, Jane. I could tell from the start."

Jane didn't say anything for a while, and then turned on her back to face the ceiling. "Would you be very angry with me if I left Selfridges to marry?"

Lizzy snapped on the light on her side of the bed. "Look at me." When Jane did, her eyes brimmed with tears. "Jane. Don't worry. If you should marry Mr Bingley, I'd be very happy for you."

"Really?" Jane quickly dabbed her eyes.

"Silly girl. Of course. We women should be free to make our own choices."

Jane gave a quick laugh, and her expression lightened. "You sound as if you are making a speech at the WSPU in Hyde Park."

Elizabeth had to laugh. "I suppose I do. Even if you leave Selfridges, I will make my own way. Is that what you are worried about?"

"I don't want to leave you in a lurch."

Elizabeth turned the light off again and settled looking up at the ceiling. "Oh, don't be silly. After all, I have Lydia…" She smiled to herself at the thought of Lydia being helpful.

"Yes, that worries me too."

"I always can find a way. Now, go to sleep. Perhaps tomorrow Mr Bingley might give you a Christmas present you will never forget."

"Wouldn't that be nice?"

Elizabeth lay awake for a while longer, listening to Jane's gentle breathing. She had put on a brave face for Jane, but she would miss her terribly if she left Selfridges and Mrs Clarke's.

Sleep eluded her for a time. Maybe she wasn't as independent as she thought she was.

Chapter 22

"I don't know what you're so angry about, Darcy."

"I'm not angry." Was he shouting? He was shouting. He needed to get hold of himself. "It's just a surprise, that's all."

"How can it be a surprise when you know that the Bennet family is in the neighbourhood? You, of all people, know how I feel about Jane. It is a perfect time for me to really get acquainted with her family, and you and Miss Elizabeth have had some lively discussions…"

Darcy didn't hear what Bingley said after that. Lively discussions indeed. If he only knew of the lively discussion the two of them had in the shop window at Selfridges. Darcy was so mortified by the incident that he didn't dare speak of it to anyone, not even Charles. Now, the entire Bennet family would be there for Christmas dinner. How was he to go through with it? Her letter of thanks was cordial, but not effusive. It certainly was not encouraging. She might still be resentful about his disclosure of his feelings about her family. It only confirmed what he thought already. He should keep his feelings to himself. No good came of it otherwise.

In any case, it was too late to change plans now. Georgiana was home from Harpenden School for Girls where she was thriving. Only twenty girls were in attendance, and the arts and modern languages were emphasised in the curriculum. There she was able to study piano with the intensity that she desired.

The school was located in Hertfordshire, near Netherfield, and that fact started the entire idea of inviting the two families for Christmas in Caroline Bingley's head. Why should they languish alone at Pemberley when they could celebrate the season at Bingley's new estate? Charles thought Caroline's idea was absolutely brilliant. And although Bingley had not bought Netherfield yet, it seemed likely. He confided in Darcy that he would be married soon, and he needed a permanent place for his wife and future family.

Netherfield was a splendid house, Georgian in architecture, but with many quasi-modern improvements, not the least of which was a large bathhouse and swimming pool installed by the owner during the Victorian craze for bathing pools. The public, of course, wasn't invited to this one. Darcy made use of it every day of his stay. The feeling of the water slipping over his skin as he trained his body gave him a certain solace. The water was cold, but they heated the pool house just for him. He was grateful to Charles for that.

Christmas Day arrived, and the dinner was to take place in early afternoon, sometime after one. Charles had scoured the countryside for a decent cook and found a few young people who were not farmhands nor had left for the city to wait at table. So, once his breakfast had settled comfortably, Darcy set out for the pool house in his new velvet dressing gown that Georgiana had given him for Christmas. It kept him warm enough as he crossed the stone walkway behind the house dressed only in it, his slippers, and the bathing costume he purchased at Selfridges. The tank suit, which had no sleeves, a v neck, and vertical striping, reached midway down his thighs. It was a big improvement over the bulkier suits of the past few years. When he was alone at the lake at Pemberley, he sometimes swam in the altogether if he convinced himself that he was quite alone. Here, he wouldn't dare. The guests were not due for a few hours, but he never knew what Caroline Bingley would get into her head or if his sister might seek him out for some reason.

Plunging off the side into the chilly water gave his body a shock. Kicking his way to the surface, he began the front crawl. This stroke was considered un-European, but it propelled him quickly through the water. Once he warmed up, he would allow himself a half an hour of breaststroke. He then tried to stop thinking… stop thinking of Elizabeth, of his proposal, of her imminent re-entry into his life. He would just swim.

***

"Oh, I do believe there is someone in the pool, Miss Elizabeth. You are quite right. Must be Darcy." Bingley stood at the edge of the pool and craned his head to peer into the rippling water.

"Oh." Elizabeth spent the night tossing and turning, ruminating on the awkwardness of her and Darcy's first meeting after that disastrous proposal of his, and now, here she was and here he was, half naked in a bathing costume. Perhaps he wouldn't come out of the water. He probably didn't even know they were there.

While these thoughts were swirling in her head, a figure of a man—a fine figure of a man—pulled himself up a ladder at the far end of the pool, took a white towel in his hands, and began rubbing it through his black, wavy, dripping hair. He began to speak, the towel draped in front of his face obscuring them from his view. Elizabeth marvelled at his physique. The muscles in his arms flexed and unflexed as he towelled his hair. The rest of his body, the wet bathing costume clinging to his every sinew and muscle—an ideal of young manhood. She had seen him in this state before, at Henley, but only from a distance. Now, here he was, a statue of David come to life.

"Come to swim, Charles? Water's a bit nippy, but… Oh, Miss Bennet."

Taken completely unawares, Darcy lunged for his dressing gown, awkwardly struggling into it and tying the tassels tightly around his waist before facing them again. Elizabeth was mortified. She had no intention of embarrassing Mr Darcy and dreaded their meeting over the Christmas dinner table. This was much worse. It was as if the gods were conspiring against them. Various alternatives flashed in her head. She could follow her first impulse and flee the scene, but that would make their next meeting at dinner so much more difficult. She could brazen it out, but she didn't feel brazen at the moment and didn't want to confirm what she believed was his worst opinions of her. Why did she care? She didn't know, but she *did* care. There was only one thing for it.

"Do you think that I might swim here whenever we are at Longbourn, Mr Bingley? If Mr Darcy can brave the cold water, I do believe I could as well."

"Most certainly, Miss Elizabeth. I would prefer that the pool is enjoyed rather than languish here unused."

Darcy approached them, and a smile crossed his face. The dressing gown was firmly closed around his body and his slippers made a soft flopping sound on the deck of the pool as he walked. He focused on Bingley. "Oh, it will not languish, Bingley. I told you at Henley that I would teach you to swim, and I will. You can count on it."

Bingley joined Elizabeth at the edge of the pool, dipping his hand into it. "Oh, my word. This is colder than the Thames." They both stood and joined Darcy. "You may teach me, but in the summertime. I don't have your fortitude. Come along now and dress. Our guests have arrived, and Georgiana has promised to play carols at the piano so that we might sing. It will be quite jolly. Come along."

Darcy cleared his throat and, with a gesture, he indicated that Elizabeth should lead the way. As soon as they were on the garden path, Charles took off at a trot to play host, no doubt, which left Lizzy and Darcy to head towards the house together.

They walked together in silence for a few moments, but Lizzy couldn't bear it. She had to say something. "I want to thank you again for coming to my aid when I was arrested."

Darcy made a dismissive gesture with his hand but said nothing. Lizzy had dreaded the moment they would first see each other alone, and this was more painfully awkward than she had imagined. The house seemed miles away in the silence. She wracked her brain for something else to say. She refused to mention the weather.

"How is your sister?" she said as he simultaneously asked, "How are your sisters?" Their gazes met, and she gave a laugh. He didn't smile. *Oh dear.* As they reached the house, he opened the door and held it for her.

"Thank you, Mr Darcy." Lizzy looked directly at him. Surely, he would say something.

"If you'll excuse me," was all he could manage as he disappeared up the rear staircase. That didn't go well. He was still angry with her because of her not-too-gentle refusal of his proposal of marriage. Ah, well. They needed to get through this holiday together as best they could, and then they could go their own separate ways. As she neared the drawing room, the merrymaking drifted on through.

***

Bingley was correct. The singing, the Edison lights on the tree (only the drawing room and the kitchen had electricity), the sumptuous dinner, made livelier by her sisters, and the joy of being together settled Lizzy's spirit. The house itself was resplendent with holly branches and yew. Dinner was several courses including roast pork and roast goose, and when the flaming plum pudding made an entrance, Lydia stood and gave it an ovation, which caused everyone to not only burst into laughter, but applaud as well. Thankfully, Mr Darcy made no move to speak to her alone and she didn't seek him out either. Conversation at dinner was pleasant, and with Mary less introspective and Kitty and Lydia less boisterous, all was calm and bright.

Lizzy deduced it was the posh surroundings and the meal fit for Buckingham Palace that brought about this temporary change. Mr

Darcy's attention was frequently engaged by Miss Bingley, but every so often, he'd send a long look her way. The intensity of his gaze sent a thrill through her, which she made an effort to ignore. His sister, Georgiana, stayed very quiet. She certainly did her duty well at the piano before dinner during the singing but seemed shy and reserved whenever conversation was required.

After dinner, they gathered in the drawing room, and Mr Bingley didn't have the gentlemen withdraw. Elizabeth suspected that he didn't want to miss one moment with Jane. They did seem to gaze at each other longingly, and Elizabeth wondered if he might use this festive occasion to ask her to marry him. He did shake himself free of his admiration and play host, however. Cards were brought out, but Elizabeth needed air and a moment to think.

"I hope you don't mind, Mr Bingley, but I would like to take a walk."

"The sun is setting, Miss Bennet. Don't be out too long..." He then offered to accompany her.

"No thank you. I just need some air. I won't be long."

For all the jollity, being in the same house with Mr Darcy was disconcerting, and Lizzy needed to think. He promised in his letter never again to bring up the subject of marriage, but the letter set her back on her heels. Her work at Selfridges, the suffragette movement, and of course, trying to rein in Lydia all occupied her mind, but now that he was there, in the same room with her, it was disconcerting to say the least. Certainly, seeing him at the pool today sent a flood of animal desire coursing through her. He was a fine-looking man. She was also beginning to suspect that he was a fine man—full stop. He certainly was protective of his sister, and of his friends—devoted to his duty as the lord and master of Pemberley—even lowered himself to visit a police station to, and it must be admitted, rescue her.

The cold refreshed her body after the heavy dinner, but her emotions were in tumult. No matter how many times she turned over in her mind the brief encounters she had with him, the words they exchanged, she couldn't deny that he wrenched from her a torrent of raw feeling that no amount of willpower on her part could dissipate. He, no doubt, still harboured some resentment of her, for which she could not fault him. As darkness descended, she returned to the house. She didn't ring the bell, as she wanted to slip in quietly.

A low roar of conversation with occasional squeals and bursts of laughter came from the drawing room. From what Elizabeth could make out, the company had forgone the more complex bridge and whist games for a rowdy game of Bread and Honey. The younger girls must have suggested it. Perhaps they finally drew out Georgiana from her reserve and encouraged her to play. Elizabeth tiptoed past the door. She wasn't quite ready to join in, but… what to do now?

Barely audible above the din, Lizzy heard music. Yes, quite exquisitely rendered piano music. It had to be Georgiana. Elizabeth made her way down the hall. The pocket doors of the music room were partially open, and Elizabeth peered in. From where she stood, she could see the top of Georgiana's head behind the music stand on the grand piano, but other than that, she seemed alone. Darkness had descended outside the nearly floor-length windows and a sole gas light made a silhouette of the piano, sending shadows across the unlit music room. Elizabeth crept in, and slowly approached, not wanting to disturb the melancholy melodies emanating from the instrument. She stood mid-room until the piece was finished. Before she began again, Lizzy moved closer.

"Was that Chopin?"

Georgiana jerked her head towards Elizabeth. "You startled me."

"I am sorry. That was beautiful."

"To answer your question, that *was* Chopin." A masculine voice arose from the shadows. Lizzy started as Mr Darcy stepped into the light of the gas lamp.

"Oh, I didn't see you there. So sorry to disturb the two of you. I'll be…" She turned to escape.

"Don't go." Darcy lit the gas light near the sofa.

Elizabeth turned fully to look at him, and for a moment, neither of them spoke.

Georgina broke the silence. "I'll play a waltz, shall I?"

Darcy raised his eyebrows, then offered his hand to Elizabeth. "May I have this dance?"

Netherfield wasn't fully furnished as it was, after all, a house that was let. Carpets would be left to the new owner, so there was a large expanse of inlaid floor in the middle of the room. Elizabeth took Mr Darcy's hand, and he took her in his arms.

As the notes of Chopin's Waltz in B Minor drifted through the room, Elizabeth floated in Mr Darcy's embrace. She inhaled the scent of him—witch hazel and the fresh scent of pressed linen. The music was poignant and melancholy. Gently locked in Darcy's whirling embrace, she tried hard to keep her eyes from brimming.

Stop it, Lizzy. Stop. Swallowing hard, she dared not look at him. He drew her closer as they glided around the music room, his cheek brushing hers. She yielded to him. It was so easy to yield to him. Was he still in love with her? She resolved to speak to him, once her head was clear. There was so much to say: his proposal, the letter, his timely rescue of her from the police… her change of heart, if that was what this was. Meanwhile, she couldn't think, only turn in gentle arcs with him in this intimate ballroom where only the two of them existed.

"There you all are. We wondered." Bingley broke the spell. Darcy didn't let go of her at once, but softly brought her to a stop and stepped away.

"We want to dance. Lizzy, why don't you play some ragtime music for us?" Kitty led the way as the rest of party rushed into the room.

It felt as if a bucket of cold water had woken her from a dream. At first, she said nothing. Then, glancing over at Georgiana, she balked at the proposal. "Oh, I don't think I'd better."

Georgiana didn't hesitate. "I have some of Scott Joplin's music here, Miss Elizabeth."

"Oh, then *you* play… please."

Kitty bounced on her toes with impatience. "Just play together, for goodness' sake. I want to teach everyone the Grizzly Bear."

"Oh, I know it." Lydia began pushing furniture aside to make the dance floor even larger. Someone lit more gas lamps.

"Here's the music. Why don't you play the right hand and I'll play the left?" Georgiana sent Lizzy an encouraging look as she leapt up from the bench and ran to a small trunk. The girl traveled with her music.

"Oh, no. If we are to attempt this, I will play the left hand, you play the right. I am barely competent at the piano, and you are a genius… I'll play the clunk, clunk part."

Lizzy was flattered but knew her limitations.

Georgiana was smiling broadly and quite animated. "Oh, Miss Bennet. I am sure you are a very good musician."

"Don't say I didn't warn you." And so they began. Elizabeth was correct in her assessment of their relative proficiency. Sometimes, she made such clumsy mistakes that she began to laugh, and so did Georgiana, but they persisted while her sisters taught the animated company The Grizzly Bear. When Lizzy looked up after the first piece was finished, Mr Darcy had left the room.

Chapter 23

"My goodness, Mr Darcy. I am so relieved that is over." Miss Bingley greeted Darcy at the door as he entered the foyer at Netherfield after motoring the Bennets back to Longbourn. "Have you ever witnessed such behaviour, such a hullabaloo?"

She took him by the arm and led him to the drawing room. Before Darcy could answer, Bingley bounded through the front door and called to Darcy and his sister, never slowing his step at he approached. "I do believe that is the best Christmas I have ever had in my life, don't you agree, Darcy?"

Darcy looked from one to the other and said nothing for a moment. "I believe I'll have a brandy." If he was honest with himself, he didn't know if he agreed with Bingley or his sister, or whether his opinion swung nauseatingly between the two. In some respects, seeing Elizabeth again was something of a sharp, delicious pain that permeated his entire being: a sweet torture. He knew he still loved her. How did she feel about him? He'd felt her yield to his embrace when she danced in his arms, but they were never alone to speak about anything, least of all his letter. Could he still hope that she might yet be his? In all probability, he was torturing himself. She made it quite clear he was the last man in the world she would ever marry.

The servants quietly cleared the card tables in the drawing room, and Caroline sent them away, letting them go to bed. Darcy glanced over at Bingley. He sat in a wingback chair near the fire, looking like a figure of bygone Victorian days, his countenance awash in happiness. He was absently swirling a cognac in a snifter.

Darcy took a seat opposite. "You look very pleased with yourself."

"I asked her to marry me. I'll speak to her father tomorrow."

Although Bingley spoke in low tones, his sister cried out from across the room where she had been dealing with the servants. "What? Who?"

Bingley didn't stir nor raise his voice. "You know very well who, Caroline. I asked

Jane Bennet, and she accepted. I love her. I have for ages."

Caroline bustled over to Bingley's chair and peered over the wing. He didn't raise his gaze to look at her. "Oh, Charles. That family. Are you quite sure?"

He didn't speak for a moment, and then raised his gaze to hers. "Quite sure. And I don't know what you mean. I enjoyed her family immensely tonight. Immensely." He grinned at her like the Cheshire Cat.

She sighed and looked heavenward, exasperated. Then, her face darkened, and she looked pointedly at Darcy. "Aren't you going to say anything?"

Darcy studied her scowl for a moment, then directed his attention to his friend. "Congratulations, Charles. I hope you'll be very happy."

Caroline looked from one to the other and, harumphing loudly and muttering to herself, left the room.

***

Elizabeth sat trying to read as she half dozed, waiting for Jane to come to bed. She'd whisked their father off to his study the minute they divested themselves of their coats and hats. It was after midnight, and with all that had happened that day, Lizzy was exhausted. Still, she tried to force herself to stay awake. She suspected that Jane had something exciting to tell her.

Her own situation was much more fraught. The meetings with Mr Darcy throughout the day had been awkward, beginning with surprising him at the pool.

A shudder of desire passed through her.

My god, he looked splendid.

They both were cordial to each other at dinner, and there was so much happy laughter and conversation that she felt at ease in his presence for a time. That waltz, though. The memory of George and the tango flooded back to her. George's animal magnetism and the suggestiveness of the dance couldn't hold a candle to how Mr Darcy made her feel as she floated along in his arms.

These conflicting thoughts flew about in her mind until Jane alighted in the room and slumped happily on the bed. "Oh, Lizzy. He's asked me. He's asked me to marry him."

Lizzy smiled at her, and then the smile vanished. Jane would leave Selfridges and it would be much more difficult to make ends meet, even at Mrs Clarke's. Lizzy would be left to mind Lydia alone, which she didn't relish. And, worst of all, her friend and confidante would be gone.

"Aren't you happy for me?"

Elizabeth slipped out of bed and hugged Jane as she stood. "Of course, I am, silly girl. I know it is what you wanted. I'm just surprised that it took Mr Bingley this long to propose to you."

Jane's face lit up. "I knew you'd understand."

Elizabeth forced herself to sound nonchalant. "So, will the wedding be soon? Young men usually don't want to wait."

Jane sat on the side of the bed and let her hair fall. "He speaks to Father tomorrow, but I have paved the way."

"So, Papa gave his approval?"

"Papa said that if I'm happy, then he's happy. I left it to him to tell Mama. I believe he will leave it until morning so that he can get some sleep." She glowed with happiness. "Oh, you asked about the wedding. We're leaving that until the spring. Charles…" She seemed to let his name roll off her tongue, savouring it for a moment, "… wants to buy Netherfield and have all the modern conveniences installed so that he can bring me to a perfect home."

Lizzy didn't want to appear selfish, but she had to ask. "So, I suppose you will be leaving Selfridges right away, then?"

Jane shook her head. "Oh, no. I couldn't do that to you and Lydia. No, I'll stay on for the time being. What would I do here but wait about? I quite like working. I didn't think I would from the beginning, but I do now. I think I'll miss it when I marry."

That was good news. Lizzy had a reprieve, and she helped Jane undo the clasps on her dress before they tucked up in bed. Lizzy leaned over to turn out the light. "I'm happy for you, Jane. Very happy."

"Thank you." Jane's contented sigh drifted over, and Lizzy tried her best to think only of her sister's happiness and not of herself.

***

After an exciting breakfast where Jane told her younger sisters the news and her mother fluttered about her telling her what a good girl she was, they settled down to a quiet Boxing Day at Longbourn. Since Netherfield didn't yet have a telephone, Mr Bingley came after luncheon unannounced. Lizzy wasn't surprised.

"I do hope I am not disturbing you." He entered the foyer and handed his hat and coat to Kitty and Mary as he shook off the cold. Mrs Bennet left the drawing room at once to greet the visitor.

Their mother clapped her hands together. "Certainly not. Certainly not, Mr Bingley. We are very happy to see you. Come along to the drawing room and sit by the fire."

Jane came in to greet him and he took her by her hands and leaned over and kissed her on the cheek. Jane coloured immediately.

"Did Mr Darcy not come with you?" Elizabeth tried to be casual.

Charles didn't take his gaze off Jane. "Oh, no. He and his sister left for Pemberley this morning. They wanted to spend some of the holiday season at home."

Of course, they did. How stupid of her. She should have spoken to him yesterday when she had the chance. He left without attempting to see her again either. Well, that was that. He was being polite at Christmas and nothing more.

"Come along, girls. Let's have a cup of tea and Mr Bingley can tell us of all his plans for Netherfield." They adjourned to the drawing room, and tea was served. Mr Bingley was animated in describing the home he would prepare for Jane, and all were mesmerised. All except Elizabeth. She sat and smiled and tried to pay attention but her missed opportunity to speak with Mr Darcy nagged at her.

***

"Oh, Fitzwilliam, I do so like Miss Elizabeth. She's such fun. You like her too, I can tell."

Darcy sighed and settled in the back of the Pierce-Arrow. "You are always inventing romances for me, Georgiana. Please cease and desist."

"I am not inventing this one, dear brother. I could see the way you looked at her when you were dancing. You love her. Admit it."

No one would dare to speak to him in such a manner except for his sister. Most of the time, he felt as a father would towards a daughter, but in times like these, she felt like his sister, his annoyingly perceptive little sister. He could feel her looking at him, so he took his gaze off the retreating scenery of Hertfordshire and returned her look. "All right. I do admit it."

"Splendid. Hooray." She clapped her hands. "You must ask her to marry you at once."

Darcy looked away and gazed out the window. "I have. She refused me."

"Oh." Georgiana's voice became very small. "Oh," she said again. They were silent for a time. "I think you should ask her again. She might have changed her mind."

Darcy said nothing as the landscape flew past in a blur on the way to Pemberley and home.

Chapter 24

Mr Selfridge wasted no time and no opportunity. As soon as the Christmas season was over, the windows were changed to reflect the celebration of the New Year. The day fell upon a Sunday, and to celebrate New Year's Eve, Mr Selfridge closed early and arranged a fireworks display on the roof of the store. Elizabeth marvelled again at her luck to work for such a man.

It was the culmination of a demanding week's work for Lizzy and Jane. Wasting no time on sentiment, The Chief wanted all the windows cleared of Christmas displays and filled again with fashions for the new year. Elizabeth was grateful for it. The more she had to concentrate on work, the less she dwelt upon Mr Darcy and the impending departure of her favourite sister.

January turned into a rainy February, and Jane increasingly spent her Sundays at home in Longbourn, which wasn't a great distance by Underground and train. Elizabeth liked to do work for the WSPU on most of those days but needed to keep a close eye on Lydia. Luckily, her youngest sister made friends easily, and a group of them, young men and women, mostly from Selfridges, would call on Lydia to take her to a music hall performance, or even a tango tea. Elizabeth was not terribly concerned about Lydia straying too far as she always came and went with a group. After a long talk with Lydia about the dangers of friendships with older men, and more specifically, with a certain Mr Wickham, Lizzy was pleased to see her youngest sister begin friendships with some of her peers at work.

After all, Lizzy could not watch her every second and Lydia was, surprisingly, making a success of herself at Selfridges. This winter might be a turning point for all of them.

***

George Wickham entered the dining room with a flair: Beef Bourguignon for table five balanced perfectly on his right arm, whilst holding two filets of sole in each hand. Today, to his surprise, he found Matilda Maxwell flipping her menu impatiently, glaring at him. He would attend to her presently, but there were other customers waiting. Every time he stole a look in her direction, he found her staring at him. Now that he safely delivered a pair of a filet of sole and roast partridge to table seven, he was free to wait upon his paramour. She did, as she always did, come straight to the point.

"He's home." She regarded him with hooded lids and a pout. Taken by surprise, he didn't understand at first.

"Who's home?"

"My husband. Henry. Back from Egypt. Home for the New Year." The *maître d'* seated another couple nearby and caught his eye, motioning with his head to the new arrivals.

"Ah, yes, madame. The fish is very fresh today." Wickham let his voice carry a bit louder and more strained than he intended. She didn't take the hint to keep this formal.

"This is the end, George. He can't find out about us."

Wickham couldn't imagine that it would take very long for someone to whisper in his ear about the tango teas and the subsequent late-night goings-on involving his wife and a certain waiter.

"Is he a violent man?" Wickham pointed to something on the menu to continue the charade of waiter and customer. The skin on the back of his neck prickled. He felt that everyone in the restaurant watched them.

Matilda gave a huff. "No, of course not. He spends most of his life with a pick and brush uncovering shards of pottery." She was looked at the menu. "I'll have the cassoulet and a lemonade."

"Excellent choice, madame."

"And, George…" She slowly raised her gaze to meet his. "I am deadly serious. It is over between us. Don't ever speak to me again."

"Very good, madame." He tried to keep his expression neutral, but conflicting emotions ran rampant through him. His pride was hurt. That was certain. On the other hand, he had come away from this entire affair with some very nice gifts: gold cufflinks, a new suit, silk shirts, a gold watch, a nice flat, not to mention the eradication of more than one gambling debt. As he turned to take the order from the newly seated customers, relief flooded him. This parting could have been so much worse. They could have been caught *in flagrante delicto*, followed by a great deal of screaming and perhaps a bit of swordplay, despite Matilda's assurances that her cuckold wasn't a violent man. By the time he reached the kitchen with his order pad, he was positively grinning. He'd done it again. Had his cake and eaten it too. Now, he could concentrate his energies entirely on the enticing young thing from the cosmetics department, little Lydia Bennet.

***

Wickham kept watch from the pub across the street from the music hall. His patience was rewarded only a few minutes later. The gaggle of chattering teenagers approached from the opposite direction. Now was the time for him to move.

"Oh, fancy meeting you here." He arrived at the box office just as Lydia and her compatriots queued up for tickets to the night's performance. They stopped chatting at once and exchanged looks of disbelief. He was ten years the senior of some of them, and he knew they had little or no use for him, with one exception.

"Oh, Mr Wickham, are you here to see the show?" Lydia's eyes shone when she looked at him.

"I thought I might, but as you see, I'm on my own."

"Oh, do join us. The more the merrier." She spoke for all of them, and it didn't escape his notice that many of them, especially the young men, were not of the same opinion.

"Only if you will allow me to sit next to you."

She giggled. "I'm sure that can be arranged." She took his arm. He paid for her ticket. The innocent beginning of the seduction sent chills up his spine. Wickham could hardly contain his grin as he escorted the youngest Miss Bennet into the cavernous and opulent depths of the music hall.

***

With Jane's imminent departure, the aim of Elizabeth's life began to veer away from her girlish dream of being a shopgirl at the most glamorous and exciting store on Oxford Street. The women's suffrage movement took hold of her with a ferocity, and she poured all the energy she had to spare into it. The work she and her fellow suffragettes were doing would change women's lives forever, and with that, the course of history.

March blew in lustily, and the WSPU was again armed and ready for another protest. Standing in her room, Elizabeth read aloud her invitation from Emily Pankhurst herself:

MEN AND WOMEN I INVITE YOU TO COME TO PARLIAMENT SQUARE ON MONDAY, MARCH 4TH 1912 at 8 o'clock to take part in a GREAT PROTEST MEETING against the government's refusal to include women in their reform Bill. SPEECHES will be delivered by well-known Suffragettes, who want to enlist your sympathy and help in the great battle they are fighting for human liberty.

"You can't go." Jane wrung her hands as she came over. "You'll lose your position. Remember what happened last time."

"It must be done. Deeds not words."

"Working at Selfridges is your dream. How can you sacrifice it for… for… for something that may not succeed?" She paused for a moment to collect her thoughts. "You could go to prison."

"I'm in a better position than most. If I do lose my position, I can always go home. I'll not starve in the street… or worse." Her time in the cell had given her some perspective.

Lydia seemed lost in one of her fashion magazines and didn't take her attention from the pictures when she piped up. "What do you mean, *worse*?"

Lizzy scowled at her. "Never mind. There's always something worse in any situation."

"I'd never risk my position for something like that. I think that you are wasting your time." With a yawn, Lydia went back to casually flipping pages.

"You were lucky last time," Jane whispered to Lizzy. "If you're arrested this time, I don't know if Charles can help you… or Mr Darcy. I don't believe he is even in town." Jane's voice broke as she spoke.

"Will Mr Bingley break off your engagement if I am arrested and sent to prison?"

Jane looked at her in astonishment. "Of course not."

"Then there's nothing to stop me. Whatever consequences I incur from my actions, I bring them down on my own head. Not on yours." She took Jane's hand. "I couldn't bear that."

Jane held her gaze. "I should have told you that he would break off the engagement. That might have stopped you."

Elizabeth smiled and hugged her. "I would have known you were lying. You're terrible at it." Drawing back, she studied her sister's worried expression. "This is so important. Don't you see that? We must do whatever it takes to get women the vote. As things stand now, it's as if we don't count at all."

"Whatever I say, you will do what you believe must be done. Do be careful. The police are brutes to the suffragettes."

Elizabeth remained silent. She sat on the edge of the bed. How far was she really prepared to go? How much could she endure? The most important question remained: if she didn't go and do her part, could she live with herself?

***

The first time Wickham suggested that Lydia abandon her friends and accompany him, she balked. They stood under the marquee of the music hall out of the rain.

"Oh, I will return you to this spot before the show is over." He crossed his finger over his chest in an unspoken oath.

Lydia looked back at her friends, who were riveted to the drama unfolding before them.

"I don't think you should go, Lydia. What will your sisters say?" That dreary Constance Maguire always looked daggers at Wickham whenever he joined their jolly little group.

"If you'd rather not, I will understand. After all, I realise that you might be afraid." He baited the trap and waited for Lydia to spring it on herself.

"Afraid? What do I have to be afraid of?" She turned to Constance. "My sisters won't say anything because you won't tell them. Will you?" The last two words were laced with threat.

"Well, Lydia Bennet, then do as you like. See if I care." Constance turned her back on Lydia and Wickham, and the rest of the group wordlessly entered the theatre.

Wickham took Lydia by the arm, and when she raised her gaze to his, trepidation filtered through. He needed to assuage it at once. "Perhaps a bit to eat, m'lady?" He turned on his most charming and least threatening manner.

"That would be lovely, m'lord." Lydia squeezed his arm as he led her down the street to a quiet bistro.

Chapter 25

Darcy returned to Pemberley after taking Georgiana back to school. The grand house stood dreary and empty, so when an invitation to a shooting weekend in Scotland arrived, he accepted. He knew himself and his tendencies well enough: he would collapse into brooding and isolation if left alone in his great house. With the winter season bringing an end to much of the farm activity and fewer visitors to the public rooms of the house, there wasn't much to occupy him or banish his gloomy thoughts. Perhaps he should have waited until after Boxing Day to leave Netherfield. Perhaps he should have paid a call on Elizabeth once more. That dance with her in the music room... he felt a change in her then, or was it merely his fevered imagination? He so wanted her to relent in her opinion of him. Could his letter have awakened her affections? The letter he received from her afterwards did not indicate any profound change. He had the chance to speak to her at Netherfield but couldn't find his tongue. Now he would never know. The time had passed.

The shooting in Scotland did serve to divert him for a time, and he accepted another invitation to Netheravon House near Salisbury. The Duke of Beaufort, Archibald "Archie" Somerset had a lovely house overlooking the River Avon, and the hunting was expected to be excellent. Darcy was in vain hopes that Charles would be there, but he was completely preoccupied with readying Netherfield for his impending nuptials. He was on his own this winter. Ah, well. At least there would be activity, and activity was as good a substitute as any for a life with purpose.

Soon after he arrived, they were shown into a large drawing room filled with overstuffed chairs and other comfortable furniture arranged in small groups. A roaring fire in the hearth warded off the chill. Darcy was surprised and, dare he say it, pleased to see Harry Gordon Selfridge among the weekend guests. As soon as he caught sight of Darcy, he strode over.

"This is such a pleasure. Is Charles here with you?"

Darcy shook the man's hand warmly. "No, I am afraid not. He is preparing his new house for his bride-to-be."

Selfridge's eyebrows popped up in surprise. "Well, well, good for him. A man should be married. Gives him stability, don't you think?"

Darcy didn't reply at once. Harry Selfridge's reputation for chronic infidelity had taken him aback for a moment. Darcy admitted to himself that he was never good at small talk because the first thing that popped into his head was the truth. Therefore, it took him a moment to think of what he was expected to say.

"Yes, I suppose so. Charles is a very solid fellow in any case."

"Yes, he is. Yes, indeed. You know, Darcy, I meant to speak to you."

"Certainly."

Selfridge took Darcy by the elbow and led him to two vacant chairs by the fire, away from the other men, who were now being joined by their wives and, dare he think it, mistresses.

Whatever Selfridge had to say to him, it was no doubt something to do with business. Darcy's endeavours to familiarise himself not only with retail commerce but the flamboyant way that Selfridge organised his business sometimes left him completely flummoxed. It was so different from the life he lived and the life he had been prepared for.

As soon as they were seated, Selfridge leaned in close. "You've taken a greater interest than most of my board members in how I do business."

"Does that worry you in some way?" Whatever was this man getting at?

"No, no, of course not. No... I welcome it. I do..." Selfridge seemed to be searching for words. "I was just thinking... now this would be completely up to you, of course... that perhaps you might visit Marshall Fields in Chicago. It might give you greater insight in why I do the things I do."

"Marshall Fields? Who is he?"

Selfridge gave out a great guffaw, so great that it drew the attention of some of the other men who were now seriously engaged in imbibing. "No, I didn't mean the person. Marshall Field has gone to his reward, but his store is what I am referring to. I think you should visit his store. It is where I started out, and I think you would gain a greater understanding of the workings of my mind and, of course, the way we Americans view commerce."

Darcy blinked at Selfridge in confusion. Had the man actually suggested that he take an ocean voyage and then who knows how long a train journey just to see a store? It was absurd. Since Darcy didn't answer immediately, Selfridge eased back.

"Well, you don't have to make up your mind right away. It was just a suggestion." Swivelling in his seat, he caught sight of someone and called out, "Syrie, what a surprise to find you here." Selfridge was out of his seat like a shot. Darcy sniffed in disgust. A surprise, indeed. Everyone knew of his affair with Syrie Wellcome. Darcy had had enough. It was back to Pemberley for him. Even brooding alone was better than this company. The seed for travel, however, had been planted, and the thought of a journey to America began to turn over in his mind.

***

"My humble abode…" Wickham acted as doorman with a mock bow for Lydia. "I arranged for a small repast for the two of us." A few weeks had passed from the time he first diverted Lydia from her young crowd, and she was now putty in his hands. Still, he would proceed carefully. Who knows what might have been said in Lydia's ear about his past indiscretions. She may be on her guard against him. He would never force her. Never. There were so many fish in the sea, there was no need for drastic measures.

Lydia turned this way and that. "Is this all for you? You don't live with anyone else? My, goodness. It's lovely." She removed her hat and laid it on the table near the entrance. The place was small: a galley kitchen to the right and a small sitting room with two floor-to-ceiling windows at the front. The furniture was of good quality, if sparse, and a sofa and button-backed chair faced the hearth in which a fire burned. He was proud of it. His paramour and patroness, Mrs Maxwell, had provided for him nicely. Next to the kitchen stood the bathroom, complete with a sink, toilet, and tub.

Wickham motioned her inside. "If you would like to refresh yourself, I will make us a cup of tea." She handed him her coat and entered the bathroom. He deliberately didn't show her the bedroom. Experience taught him that any reference in that area, especially to one so young and inexperienced, usually meant immediate flight. No, he would take his time. If things progressed as he imagined they would, the sofa would do just as well.

***

Elizabeth shook Mr Goldsman's hand warmly as she left work on March 4. He had no idea of her plans, but she doubted that she would ever see him again. With almost an hour remaining before Lydia would be dismissed from her class, she wandered the store as the clerks and shopgirls put away merchandise and cleaned their counters for the night. Lizzy would never forget her time here at Selfridges. It opened a whole new world for her, but she was now committed to a more important cause. Her throat constricted at the thought of what might happen to her on the streets tonight. The police had been brutish to the suffragettes, pawing them, reaching up their skirts, pinching their breasts. The women who had been imprisoned and went on hunger strikes were strapped down and force fed. She shuddered. It was one thing to lose one's position; it was quite another to be tortured and violated.

Lizzy sat down in the employees' locker room and watched the bustle of her fellow workers. Tears filled her eyes, and she wiped them away quickly so that no one would notice. She didn't know them all, but she would miss them. Looking at the clock on the wall, she realised it was time to collect Lydia after her class. Would she ever do that again? One thought cheered her: she no longer saw George Wickham hanging about amongst the younger employees. The talk she gave Lydia must have had the desired effect, or George had returned to a rich woman who was keeping him in the style he desired.

"There you are, Lizzy. What's the matter?"

Lizzy took Lydia by the hand. "We'll talk about it at home. Did you have a good day?"

"Everything is just ducky." Lydia launched into the dramas and intrigues of the cosmetics department. Lizzy was grateful for the ebullient chatter. The animation in her younger sister's face momentarily took her mind off the momentous task she was about to undertake. After she delivered Lydia home, she would strike out for the rally.

***

"Don't endanger your position at Selfridges by looking for me tomorrow," Elizabeth said to Jane as she donned her purple, green, and white sash.

"Don't go, Lizzy. Please. Someone else will take your place." Jane hurried over.

"If everyone said that, no one would be there and nothing would ever change. I must go." She threw on her coat and gave Jane a quick hug. "I will contact you if I can. Be of good cheer. Perhaps I won't even be arrested."

Lydia sat watching the exchange, and when Elizabeth let go of Jane and turned towards the door, Lydia grasped her from behind and held her close. "Oh, do be careful, Lizzy."

Elizabeth was moved at the sudden show of emotion from her. "I'll be all right. You'll see. I'm doing this for you, you know? For all of us." With that, she left quickly and ran for the Tube station.

***

All doubts and thoughts for her own safety fled Lizzy's head during the speeches given by the Pankhursts, Millicent Fawcett, and Edith Garrud. They were heroic and unstoppable. As she stood in the crowd, Lizzy felt as if she were standing on the cusp of history. The suffragettes would succeed; she knew it. And she needed to be a part of it. Her actions today would pave the way for women to finally influence the course of the nation. She looked into the expectant faces of her compatriots and surreptitiously accepted a toffee hammer from a woman who passed through the crowd. Before long, they were on their way back to a place Elizabeth knew well, Oxford Street.

After emerging from the familiar Tube station where she and her sisters exited every morning since she began her employment at Selfridges, Lizzy and her sisters-in-arms scattered along the street towards their objective: office and shop windows. It gratified her that they were all given specific instructions to spare Selfridges. Mr Selfridge was an ally, who printed their news leaflets at his own expense. Lizzy and Jane even hung bunting about the store and in the windows in the WSPU's colours of green, purple, and white.

Running along as best she could, considering the confines of her skirts, she took aim at a shop window and swung her hammer. As she turned her face from the glass, the window shattered. Satisfied, she ran on. Women on both sides of the street shattered glass. Elizabeth was gratified as the crowd in their rampage slipped past Selfridges without leaving so much as a scratch on the building. After that, every window within her reach, however, was fair game, and she smashed one after the other without so much as a look back.

Men sprang seemingly out of the very brick and mortar of the buildings. None were dressed as policemen. They quickly outran some of the women and catching them by the arm or by the skirts, they threw them to the ground or bludgeoned them with billy clubs. Lizzy looked about for an escape route, but before she could take a step, nothing but blackness and a shower of stars filled her gaze.

The jostling of the horse-drawn police van awakened her.

"Are you all right, my dear?" A woman's voice cut through the fog. "That's a nasty bump that copper gave you."

Elizabeth gingerly touched the back of her head. She felt as if it was split in two. When she looked at her glove again, blood covered it. "I don't feel very…"

Blackness and stars returned.

Chapter 26

The train gently jostled Elizabeth awake. For a moment, she couldn't remember where she was, then her father gently dozing, head resting on the windowpane, came into focus. Jane sat quietly next to her, reading a book.

She could not remember at once what day it was, but she did remember she was going home in disgrace; her grand experiment in pieces around her feet.

When she'd finally awakened after the attack on Oxford Street, Jane told her how the suffragettes had brought her home. A doctor had been called. She remembered none of it. Her sister warriors were all set free from the police van once Elizabeth had lost consciousness and couldn't be awakened. No doubt, the police wanted to be as far away from all of them as possible if Elizabeth decided to be rude enough to die from the blow. She hadn't died, but she and Jane did lose their positions at Selfridges... Jane for the minor infraction of coming in late on Tuesday after the attack, and she, for not showing up at all. Lydia, however, hung on, and they left her in London in the care of family friends, the Forresters, who promised to look after her. Lizzy was in no condition to object or even remark on these arrangements, because for several days, she was dizzy and nauseous and had to keep to her bed.

They concocted a story among them to tell their mother. Lydia was also sworn to secrecy and seemed to enjoy it immensely. She liked nothing better than intrigue. As for Mr Bingley, Lizzy knew that he wouldn't deliberately betray their confidence, but he was so open and guileless a person that he might let something slip that his sister would pounce upon with hyenalike viciousness. No, better to keep the news to themselves and say that Elizabeth fell down the stairs in the Underground and hit her head.

"Oh, Lizzy, come in. Come in. Your room is all ready for you. You know, I never thought of you as a clumsy child, but here you are. First, a spill in the Thames during the regatta and now this. I don't know what we'll do with you." Her mother prattled on in this vein all the way up the stairs and into Lizzy's and Jane's room as she instructed the servants on where to deposit the bags.

Finally, Lizzy spoke up. "Mama, I am a little tired. I would like to lie down for a while." Her mother smiled weakly and scolded the servants to leave the room at once. After pulling the curtains to darken a brilliant March day, she left Lizzy to her thoughts.

And they were gloomy thoughts indeed.

***

"Darcy... Darcy... I say, what's so fascinating?"

Darcy started at the sound of Bingley's voice. "Oh, do pardon me. I was just reading…" The paper crumpled in his hands.

Bingley took a seat opposite Darcy, set down a small whiskey and relaxed into the leather chair. "…of the latest exploits of the women warriors." Bingley finished his sentence for him.

"Not that I am particularly interested…"

"Oh, no. Of course not." Bingley crinkled his gaze in amusement, and then seriousness set in. "The police are meeting these suffragette actions with increasing violence."

Darcy laid the paper on his lap and met his eye. "Yes, I know. It's worrying."

"If you are concerned for Miss Elizabeth Bennet—"

"I didn't say I was."

"But if you were, you'd have reason to be."

Darcy glared at him. "If that's a joke, it's in very poor taste."

"It is no joke." Bingley broke his gaze and took a deep breath.

"For God's sake, speak up, man. What do you know?"

Bingley leaned into the back of the chair and met his eye. "She's been injured. The police…"

Now Darcy was on his feet. "Injured? The police what?"

"Calm yourself and let me tell you. It appears they hit her in the back of the head with a truncheon. She is recovering but has left London with Jane. They have returned to Longbourn."

Darcy sat back down heavily in his chair. "Are you sure she is all right?"

"I have seen her. She is not fully herself yet, but the doctors believe she will make a full recovery."

Darcy nodded absently and spoke so softly to himself. "Good. Good. Perhaps I should…"

A butler arrived with a silver tray and interrupted the conversation. "This just arrived for you, sir." The butler bent forward and presented the envelope. Darcy picked it up.

"Telegram?"

"My steamer ticket. I'm travelling soon." Darcy was grateful for the change of subject.

"Oh, really? Where?"

"America."

"You will be back for the wedding I hope."

"Of course, Charles. Of course. I'll leave in early April and should be home in plenty of time. You know these new ships. They can make the crossing in less than a week. This one is brand new… White Star Line… reported to be the swiftest of them all."

Bingley took a sip of his whiskey. "And what ship is that?"

"The RMS *Titanic*."

"Ah. Jolly good."

Although they spoke of other things, Elizabeth and her injury preoccupied Darcy. He resolved then and there to see for himself how she fared. Perhaps it was not too late to repair the breach between them.

***

The date for Jane and Charles's wedding was set for early May. Jane fairly hummed joy and excitement. She moved almost suspended off the ground, hovering here, hovering there, and then suddenly flitting to her next task. Many hours were spent at Netherfield as tradesmen arrived with samples of fabric and upholstery and even paint. She tried in vain to induce Lizzy to take an interest.

"Isn't this fabric lovely? I think it will do nicely on the drawing room furniture. Charles dislikes anything too dark. What do you think? Lizzy?"

"Yes. It's very nice. You have wonderful taste." Even to herself, Lizzy's voice sounded half-hearted at best.

Jane put the fabric down on the chair in the drawing room at Longbourn and sat down next to Lizzy on the sofa. She took Lizzy's hands in hers. "Are you in pain? Are the headaches back?"

Elizabeth looked at Jane. Concern etched through her eyes. "No, I'm fine. I think I'm spoiling your happiness by being so gloomy. I'm sorry."

"You want to be back in London, don't you? With the suffragettes."

Lizzy sighed. Jane knew her so well. "I don't want that part of my life to be over. There is so much to do. The fight has just begun."

Jane patted her hand. "If I know you, you will find a way, Elizabeth Bennet. You will. But for now, help me make some decisions." She rose and returned to the samples of fabric lying on chairs about the room.

"Lizzy, telegram." Their mother interrupted them from the door of the drawing room. Lizzy sprang up and took it gingerly from her hand. Charlotte's name scrawled across it, so she tore it open.

Huntsford Westerham

Lizzy come for a visit will meet your train don't say no.

Charlotte Collins

"Something from those Collinses, I suppose," her mother muttered as she tried to peer over Lizzy's shoulder.

"Charlotte wants me to come for a visit."

"You should go. There's no reason for you to mope about here." A clatter of a cup from the kitchen distracted her mother, and she was left with Jane, who looked at her sympathetically.

"You should go, Lizzy. The change will do you good."

Lizzy nodded lamely. "Why not? Perhaps I will recruit Charlotte to the cause."

That remark caused Jane to grin and shake her head. Lizzy smiled for the first time in a long while. A change of scene might be just the thing.

***

The distance from London to Hertfordshire wasn't a long one, and Darcy decided to drive himself. It gave him an opportunity not only to view the countryside, but to compose a myriad of conversations he might have with Elizabeth. The pretext of his visit, of course, was to see Bingley and marvel at the many improvements his friend had made in Netherfield since his last visit at Christmas. Jane would be there. Darcy would be invited to Longbourn. There he would suggest a walk in the garden with Elizabeth and ascertain the state of her health and, hopefully, the state of her heart. If she gave him the slightest encouragement, he would dare to ask her again.

"Darcy, how marvellous to see you. You are just in time for luncheon." Bingley answered his own door as arrangements for servants had not been made, and from what Darcy could see, the house was still in a state.

"Work moves on apace, I see." He handed his hat to Bingley and looked around. Scaffolding lay everywhere, a thin film of dust peppered the floor, and most of the furniture was covered in sheets.

Bingley laughed. "Yes, you see, when we began to install the electrics, it seemed the plumbing was amiss, and one thing led to another. Once they began tearing into the walls, Jane and I decided to redecorate the entire place. Clear out the Victorian gloom and all that, eh?"

Darcy nodded. One style seemed as good as the next to him, but his friend seemed happier than he had ever seen him. Jane arrived in the hall, her dress powdered with plaster, her hair covered in a white cap, a few strands escaping to frame her lovely face. Even in disarray, she looked beautiful. Darcy suddenly felt his stomach clench. What if Elizabeth told her of his role in keeping Bingley away for all those weeks? She smiled sweetly at him and extended her hand.

"Oh, Mr Darcy. How nice of you to visit." She absently brushed a stray strand of hair away from her cheek. "I'm afraid we are in the midst of absolute chaos. The only place we have to receive you is the kitchen, which is hardly the place to receive guests."

Bingley absolutely beamed. He couldn't take his eyes off his bride-to-be. "It's all right, my love. Darcy here is more family than friend, aren't you, old man?"

Darcy was touched by that remark, so much so that he nearly made a spectacle of himself. Clearing his throat, he let Bingley take him by one arm and Jane took the other. When they arrived in the kitchen, Jane began to retrieve some ham from the icebox and soon was engaged in preparing sandwiches for them. Now was the time.

"Do you miss Selfridges, Miss Bennet?"

"Oh, do call me Jane." She sliced the bread carefully, not looking up at Darcy. "I did enjoy working, but I think Lizzy misses it more... London, I mean... and the suffragettes."

"I told Darcy that your sister got quite a nasty blow from the coppers."

Jane stopped her preparations and looked up at Darcy. "We were quite afraid for her at first. She was in and out of consciousness and not herself at all."

It was as Darcy feared. They had broken her.

"But she's quite all right now," Jane added and turned to the stove as the kettle began to boil.

"Do you think she might like a visitor?" Darcy was trying to be as subtle as possible but dared not look at Bingley.

"Oh, she isn't here at the moment. She's gone to Kent to visit her friend Charlotte." Jane set the teapot and sandwiches in the table. "There, all done."

Darcy smiled weakly. All done indeed.

Chapter 27

"Wickham, Mr Caverly would like a word."

Wickham frowned at the *maître d'* as he passed him by. He wasn't late. He was never late. As he made his way through the kitchen to the manager's office, he wracked his brain, wondering why he'd been called in. Perhaps they were promoting him or raising his wages. Wickham grinned. That had to be it.

After a knock at the door, the manager called him in. "Don't bother sitting down. This won't take long. I'm afraid we're going to have to let you go." Mr Caverly didn't raise his eyes from the papers on his desk. "Go and get your things from the employees' locker and collect your wages. Mr Selfridge is giving you a week's severance."

For the first time in his life, Wickham was speechless. "I'm sacked? Why? I thought I always gave good service. I don't understand…"

Mr Caverly sighed and raised his doughy face to Wickham. "I don't understand either. This comes from up top. They gave me no reason, just the order. I'm sorry."

"Can you, at least, provide me with a reference? That at least."

"Yes, about that… we were told to give you this… much good may it do you." He handed Wickham an envelope. He stood at the desk for a moment, opened the envelope, and perused its contents. It was a letter of reference, and a good one. Folding it carefully, and not knowing what else to say or do, he went to collect his things and his pay. He would go this very day and find a new position. The Palm Court Restaurant wasn't the only one in London.

Wickham spent the next three days scouring every posh restaurant in town inquiring after a position. Some made the excuse that they weren't looking for staff at this time. Some refused to see him altogether. He couldn't make head nor tail of it. The recommendation was glowing. Why didn't one of them want to even speak to him?

With hope fading, he made his way to the Boulestin in St. James's. As the manager scrutinised his letter, a wry smile crossed his lips. The smile blossomed into outright mirth. Wickham could endure many things but being laughed at wasn't one of them.

"Have they been leading you in a merry chase, Mr Wickham?" The manager spoke impeccable English through a charming French accent. His pencil-thin moustache twitched.

Wickham was perplexed. "Whatever do you mean?"

"Ah, I see you do not know yet. You have been, how do you say, blacklisted in all the better places in London."

"Blacklisted?" Wickham felt as if someone had knocked the wind out of him.

"Yes, it seems that a rather wealthy patron of this, and many other places of entertainment for the, how shall we say, discerning and well-heeled, has made it his mission to see that you will not find any employment in the better places in town. A word from him here, a word from him there, and we all know your name. We all cannot offer you employment. That is *blacklisted*, no?"

"Yes, yes indeed." Wickham stretched out his hand, wanting the letter back. "I don't suppose you know who has done this to me. It couldn't be Harry Selfridge."

"No, no, his name is not Selfridge. I believe it is Maxwell."

***

Mr Collins met Lizzy at the train, and with every utterance that burbled out of his mouth, Lizzy grew more and more grateful that he was Charlotte's husband and not hers. A horse-drawn cart delivered them to the vicarage, a rather imposing two-story brick building with five large multi-paned windows at the front.

As they pulled up in front, Charlotte ran out and met Lizzy with an embrace. "It is so good to see you. How are you feeling?"

"Right as rain. If they would have me, I would return to Selfridges tomorrow."

Mr Collins joined them and said nothing, but his face betrayed his disapproval. Charlotte didn't seem to share his opinion. "You are such an adventuress. I wish I had such spirit."

"I would not like to see it," Mr Collins commented curtly. "You have the perfect spirit for a parson's wife." With that, he strode ahead of them into the house. Lizzy looked over at Charlotte to gauge her reaction.

Charlotte laughed. "I suppose he's right. Oh, it is good to see you. Let us go in and have tea."

The visit was the change of scene Lizzy needed to shake herself out of her melancholy and set her brain to thinking again. Charlotte seemed contented enough with Mr Collins, although she couldn't see what had prompted her to chain herself to him for life. Of course, she couldn't ask such a question, but knew her face must be betraying her feelings. Charlotte, however, had become masterful at seeing only what she wanted to see and hearing only what she wanted to hear. Lizzy supposed it was a vital skill when married to Mr Collins. After a few days, a dinner invitation at Rosings from Lady Catherine de Bourgh arrived. The village was small and still kept to the old ways of deference to the lord, or in this case, lady of the manor.

They were at breakfast in the dining room of the parsonage. The large windows streamed with morning light. Mr Collins began his morning *sermon*. "You are very privileged, Miss Elizabeth, to have Lady Catherine invite you to dinner. She does not always show such deference to those who do not share her pedigree and class." Lizzy bit her bottom lip. She was about to answer when Mr Collins continued. "Being her clergyman, my dear wife and I have frequently been honoured with her presence." Mr Collins looked at her pointedly for a comment.

Lizzy hesitated. She was in this man's house as a guest. Charlotte was her dearest friend. She swallowed down the words of indignation at the insult that he wrapped so sweetly in what he must have considered a compliment. That man was a dolt.

"How nice." She really wanted to scream but smiled instead. Her eyes must have betrayed her true feelings because Charlotte immediately changed the subject.

"Shall we go for a drive in the pony cart tomorrow, Lizzy? Would you like to see more of the grounds? We are adjacent to Rosings after all."

"You two go, by all means," Mr Collins interrupted, as he frequently did, before Lizzy could answer. "I have work to do tomorrow."

"An outing sounds lovely." But a day without Mr Collins sounded even lovelier.

***

The year 1912 had arrived, yet Elizabeth's most formal gown was last year's fashion: an electric blue with cap sleeves and a rather low-cut bodice, yet it was discreet enough not to excite disapproval in Mr Collins, and hopefully, not in Lady Catherine. The great lady sent her motor over to collect them, and soon they stood in the great house at Rosings.

The stately home had an aura of bygone opulence that didn't bear much scrutiny. Great wealth had once been here, but that era was fading before their eyes.

They met in an ornate drawing room, decorated in the heavy Victorian style: pale green walls with decorative woodwork painted gold. Dark red velvet drapery matched the red and gold carpet. The furniture was also red and gold brocade and the room dominated by a large gold-gilt mirror. On the opposite wall, a portrait of Queen Victoria and Prince Albert. It was a monument to the past. The tour of the room by Mr Collins was interrupted by Lady Catherine's entrance. She appeared to be somewhere near her sixtieth year, but her gown was of a modern cut. She swept the room with a steely gaze, and Mr Collins rushed up to her and began chattering in an extremely obsequious manner. Lizzy glanced over at Charlotte, but Charlotte's attention was on her husband.

"You already know my wife," said Mr Collins, "and this is Miss Elizabeth Bennet."

"So very glad to meet you, Lady Catherine." Lizzy nodded a little. Despite being slightly shorter than Elizabeth, her ladyship appeared to be looking down on her. It was most disconcerting.

"I have heard much about you, Miss Bennet. So glad you could join us this evening. Come, sit here next to me… Mrs Collins over there, and Mr Collins, go sit beside your wife."

Here was a woman used to being obeyed. They all took their places, Lady Catherine and Elizabeth on the sofa, and Charlotte and Mrs Collins in the chairs opposite.

"You have heard much about me, Lady Catherine?" Puzzled, Lizzy shot a quick look at Charlotte to garner a clue.

"You needn't look over at your friend. My information comes from my nephew, Mr Darcy."

Why did the mere mention of his name send shivers through her, even at this late date? They hadn't seen each other since Christmas, and yet, here he was again, in spirit, if not in body.

"Really? I can't imagine why your nephew would be discussing me."

Lady Catherine scrutinised her with the air of a farmer evaluating a prize pig when a pale young woman, her hair neatly done in the bouffant style, entered the drawing room. "So sorry to be late, Mama. I felt a bit dizzy earlier."

"Ah, Anne. Are you feeling better, my dear?"

"Yes, Mama."

"Come and greet our guests. Mr and Mrs Collins you know... and this is Elizabeth Bennet."

Maybe it was Lizzy's imagination, but the young woman scowled at her for a moment. Before she could fathom it out, the butler arrived.

"Dinner is served."

The evening passed much as Elizabeth expected: small talk peppered with proclamations by Lady Catherine and Mr Collins. Lizzy said little, as she disagreed with almost all their opinions, but didn't want to sour the gracious mood of the evening nor create any awkward situations for Charlotte. After a tour of the public rooms after dinner led by Mr Collins, in which he described in detail the art and furnishings accumulated across the generations by Lady Catherine's husband's family, it was time to take their leave, thankfully.

"I'll send the motor round to take you and Mr Collins home." Lady Catherine smiled in Charlotte's direction as they waited in the marble entrance hall.

"That is very kind of you, Lady Catherine." Charlotte smiled sweetly.

"You, Miss Bennet. You shall remain here for a time. I wish to speak to you."

Lizzy exchanged a glance with Charlotte, but neither said anything. As Charlotte took her leave with Mr Collins, Lady Catherine led Elizabeth back to the drawing room. Anne was nowhere to be seen.

"I'll come right to the point, my girl..." Lady Catherine's tone was less than cordial as she took a seat. In fact, it was a bit menacing.

"Yes, Lady Catherine?" Lizzy didn't sit down. She had a feeling she wasn't meant to.

"Are you or are you not engaged to my nephew, Fitzwilliam Darcy?"

Lizzy failed to utter a word, although she tried to. Twice.

"Don't look so surprised, Miss Bennet. I have heard rumours that I am sure must be an exaggeration or untrue altogether."

"If you don't believe them to be true, then why ask me?"

"Don't be impertinent. Has my nephew asked you to marry him?"

Lizzy hesitated a moment. "Yes… yes, he has."

"Then you *are* engaged to him…" She shook her head with disgust. "… a shopgirl."

"My father is a gentleman with an estate in Hertfordshire, but that is neither here nor there. Yes, I have endeavoured to make my own way in the world. I don't see how that—"

"Are you or are you not engaged to him?"

"I am not."

Lady Catherine gave an audible sigh of relief. She then narrowed her eyes at Lizzy. "And will you promise never to enter into such an engagement?"

This poor deluded woman. She obviously didn't know anything firsthand from Mr Darcy, or she would never have asked such an absurd question. Lady Catherine's adversarial attitude did nothing but inflame Lizzy's will. How dare this woman question her on her personal matters? Who did she think she was? "I will not."

"You will not *what*?"

"Lady Catherine, with all due respect, this matter is none of your business… but to answer your question, I will promise you nothing. The matter of my association with your nephew is private and only of concern to Mr Darcy and myself." Lizzy wouldn't give her the satisfaction of explaining anything, least of all that she refused him already.

Before Lady Catherine could recover from the shock of being addressed in such a manner, Lizzy turned to leave. "Don't bother sending the motorcar around for me, I'll walk." With that, she slid open the pocket doors of the drawing room.

"Before you go, Miss Bennet, you should be aware of something." The older woman was not going to let Elizabeth have the last word. She turned to face her. Lady Catherine's gaze glinted with anticipation. "Whether you have designs on my nephew or not, they must surely come to naught. He leaves for America soon."

Lizzy tried to remain impassive, but her head reeled. As she left the drawing room, Lady Catherine called after her. "You didn't know that, did you? Did you?"

The cold night air felt good against the heat rising in Lizzy's body. America? Surely he wouldn't abandon his beloved Pemberley when it seemed the centre of his existence. And what of his sister? Would he leave her in school and emigrate without her? Of course not. He was merely taking a holiday of some sort. That had to be it. Then why did she feel so utter a sense of loss?

When she opened the front door of the vicarage, Charlotte and Mr Collins were standing in the vestibule waiting for her. "What did Lady Catherine want with you, Miss Bennet?" Mr Collins didn't mince his words.

"William." Charlotte flicked Lizzy and apologetic glance. "That information is private, surely. Elizabeth needn't answer unless... unless she wants to." Lizzy could tell from Charlotte's expression that she hoped Elizabeth wanted to.

"Have no fear, Mr Collins. The matter doesn't concern you. It had to do with Mr Darcy and myself..." She walked between them to the staircase. "I would be much obliged if you would arrange for a train ticket for tomorrow morning. I think I'd like to go home."

Chapter 28

"Oh, Wickie. That is terrible. Whatever are you going to do? It's so unfair."

Wickham ran his hand up Lydia's calf, over her knee, and onto the inside of her thigh above her stocking. Even that did not shake him from his foul mood.

"There is only one thing for me to do. Tomorrow I will take a train to Southampton. The place is bustling with ocean liners always looking for staff. I will seek my fortune there." He stood and crossed his arms in a determined fashion.

"Oh, but George. You can't leave. You can't. What will become of me?"

The tears were making their way down her cheeks, which made her look all the more adorable. He could take her with him, and why not? They could make the crossing to America. He could enjoy her on the way, and then? Oh, why think that far ahead?

"Come with me. We'll go together."

"And will we be married then? After all, you promised, and I do love you so."

He cleared his throat. "Of course. We'll be married. We'll be married... in New York. Yes, that's it. New York."

It was then they hatched the plot. She would leave for Selfridges in the morning as usual. She was always the last to leave the house, save the servants. This time, however, her bags would be packed for New York.

***

No sooner had Lizzy arrived home, she began to construct a plan to get back to London to continue her work with the suffragettes. She would again be employed and independent, and lastly she'd find Mr Darcy and talk to him frankly about all that had happened... before he left for America. She confided her idea to no one, including Jane. It was odd, but she felt as though she didn't need anyone, not even her beloved sister, to accompany her this time. The path seemed clear to her, and she felt that she could face anything now.

All this optimism about the future came to a screeching halt when Lizzy descended the stairs for breakfast and saw her father standing in the front hall, holding a telegram.

"Papa?" With shaking hands, he handed the paper to Lizzy.

Knightsbridge, London

Mr Bennet come at once Lydia missing

Mrs K. Forrester

Her father shrugged helplessly at her. "Oh, Lizzy. What are we to do?"

Elizabeth realised then how ineffectual her father had been in rearing them. In fact, he had hardly participated at all, leaving most of the work to their mother.

She could blame her parents, but she had to be honest. This entire situation was her fault. If she hadn't gone on that window smashing campaign, she, Jane, and Lydia would still be at Selfridges, and Lydia would have been under the watchful eye of herself and Jane. As it was, she was left in the care of people of dubious responsibility, and now, this disaster. Elizabeth said a silent prayer that Lydia was still alive. Anything could happen to her in London.

"We'll set off for London at once. I will go with you. Send a wire to Uncle Gardiner and apprise him of the situation. If he can, he will go to the Forresters ahead of us and ascertain what they know. Come, Papa."

***

Bags packed and sitting next to them on the platform, Lizzy and her father waited for the noon train. They had been waiting for nearly an hour, the minutes ticking away slowly, before Kitty pushed her way through the crowd and rushed over.

"A letter, Papa. A letter from Lydia." Kitty sat on the other side of their father and both she and Lizzy peered over his shoulder as he tore open the envelope.

Dear Mama and Papa,

You will be so happy when you hear my news. I am going to America. Mr Wickham, whom Lizzy and Jane know, has got us both jobs on a ship. It is the newest and biggest ship ever built, and they were looking for people to work on board. I have a job as a stewardess, can you believe it? and will be serving the first-class passengers. My dear George will be working as a waiter in first class. We both gave our notice at Selfridges yesterday.

Here is the best news of all. George said that we will be married as soon as we arrive in New York. Won't Jane and Lizzy be jealous when I am married before them? We set sail on April 10, so I must close. Please do not worry about me. I am in good hands with George.

Your daughter,
Lydia

Her father gave Lizzy a desperate look, then turned to Kitty. "Go home. Tell your mother that Lydia is alive and well and we hope to bring her home soon. Go on, now."

Kitty kissed her father's cheek and disappeared into the crowd.

"Who is this Wickham? Lydia said you and Jane know him."

Elizabeth toyed with the idea of not telling him her honest opinion, but the time had passed to spare his feelings. "He won't marry her, Papa. He is a libertine of the worst kind. No doubt he got himself into some difficulty with a jealous husband or gambling debts and had to leave the city, and what better way?"

"You sound like you know him quite well." Her father's eyes narrowed.

"Yes. He courted me for a time before he found a rich, married woman to carry on with. That didn't stop him from preying on the younger, female members of the staff at Selfridges. Lydia is deluding herself if she thinks he will marry her."

"We must stop her, then, but we don't even know what ship she is on."

Lizzy patted her father's hand. "Give me the letter. I think we can determine where she is and rescue her before it is too late. We still have time to wire my uncle. He needs to meet us in Southampton."

***

The SS *New York* and the RMS *Titanic* docked next to each other at the Southampton harbour. When they all arrived at the port, it was only hours from departure for one of the ships.

"She has to be aboard the *Titanic*. The SS *New York* just arrived, and no other ships are scheduled to depart today." Mr Gardiner was poring over the shipping schedule.

"You will never find her on that monstrosity before it departs. She could be anywhere." Mr Bennet wrung his hands as he gazed at the titan docked in the harbour.

Lizzy stood with the two men on the dock, gazing in awe at the ocean liners.

"One of us must sail with her." Her uncle appeared resolute.

Elizabeth had been thinking the same thing but didn't know how that could ever be arranged in so short a time. Her father looked like a frightened rabbit. He could never go. Her uncle had his own family to consider. It would have to be her. Her luggage was hardly enough for an ocean voyage, but it was something, but the ticket? How could they even afford such a thing? And perhaps the ship was fully booked.

As if reading her thoughts, her uncle looked at her. "You'll have to go. It's the only way. I'll see if I can arrange it."

Within the hour, she was walking up the gangplank with the other passengers, a second-class ticket on the RMS *Titanic* in hand. She would have been content with steerage, but her uncle wouldn't hear of it. As a steward showed her to her cabin, a terrifying thought seized her.

What if this was the wrong ship? What if Lydia had laid a trail to divert them and wasn't on board at all? What if she and Wickham were still in London, holed up somewhere, laughing at all of them? And most importantly, what would Lydia's disgrace do to Jane? Would their youngest sister's rash behaviour ruin them all?

***

Darcy settled into his stateroom, allowing his valet to unpack under his supervision. The White Star Line really thought of everything. The four-poster, curtained bed was nearly as large as the one he had at home. Walnut wainscotting rose to nearly halfway up the wall and was met by exquisite wallpaper. The coffered ceiling of ivory and gold leaf was opulent to say the least. A comfortable, overstuffed chair, a small table with two chairs, and an ample wardrobe completed the state room. He usually wasn't impressed by such luxury, having grown up in the midst of it, but this room really was very impressive. He tipped the valet, and then settled down in the chair to think for a moment.

He didn't know if he was doing the right thing. By the time he returned, perhaps Lizzy would have another suitor, and then it would be too late. No, he shouldn't deceive himself. His cause was lost, and he needed to set himself on a different path. Removing himself from painful memories and travelling to America was just the thing.

He resolved to take a turn about the deck to pass the time when a steward brought him a telegram. Darcy took it. It could just be a bon voyage message, or something could be wrong at home. Perhaps Georgiana had met with an accident. Neither of these things were in the message and it couldn't have surprised him more.

Hertfordshire, Meryton

Lydia Bennet run off with Wickham might be on your vessel. Stop see what you can do most urgent

Bingley

What in God's name? A chill ran through him. Wickham was a predator and another young and foolish quarry had been entrapped in his snare. This didn't bode well for Bingley's wedding plans to say the least, and it could bring ruin upon Elizabeth and her sisters. Their marriage prospects were not the best as it was. The girls might have to seek employment in the city as their eldest sisters did or go into service. It certainly wasn't fair, but society had a double standard in regard to the behaviour of men and women.

The idea of a stroll abandoned, Darcy set out to see if Wickham was indeed aboard this vessel. The telegram didn't say if he was a passenger or a crewman or if they were married or not. Married? Surely not. Wickham wouldn't marry unless he could attach himself to money. The first step was to persuade a steward to let him see the roster of male crew members.

When he came on deck, all was a hubbub. Passengers were boarding in great numbers and looking for their accommodations. He didn't see one crewman who wasn't engaged in several activities at once. They would be no help until everyone was aboard and they were safely out to sea. He would look among the passengers then. Knowing that Wickham had almost no money, he never did, Darcy would look first in steerage.

After making his way from the bridge deck where his stateroom was located, and down crowded stairways, he arrived at the shelter deck. He peered into a smoking room in which a few men who were decidedly not first-class passengers lounged about inside with cigars. Wickham was not to be found. The next attempt was a deck lower at the saloon deck. The first-class dining room was empty and rather quiet. None of the dining rooms were populated, but all the hallways, staircases, and decks teamed with people making their way to their accommodations. The crush of passengers and crew made the situation impossible. If Wickham and Lydia were aboard, he would have to find them later. Struggling between the steamer trunks, the bellboys and bedroom stewards, and the seething crowd of passengers, Darcy wrestled his way back to his stateroom. The search would recommence when they were out to sea. He resolved to remain in his cabin until then. After all, there was no one to see him off.

After divesting himself of his celluloid collar and tie, he settled back to *Ethan Frome*. Even if Elizabeth was never to be his wife, she'd changed him in many ways, expanding his horizons. He never would have considered reading an American novel written by a woman before he met her. He opened the book. For a few hours, at least, the Bennets and their troubles would have to wait.

Chapter 29

Lizzy tossed the stream of paper ribbon towards her father and uncle, who stood on the dock, amid the crush of well-wishers. They were clever enough to find and hold on to it while the ship pulled off. She wasn't sure that the ribbon would even reach them, she was so far from the dock. The ship was gigantic, monumental. She felt alone and vulnerable as the paper connection to her family snapped and floated down into the murky sea. She stood for a while on the promenade deck until she could no longer see the dock, her father's face, or the land of her birth. They were proudly steaming towards Cherbourg to collect more passengers. Lizzy made her way back to her cabin, needing to find that first before the search for Lydia could begin.

Knowing that her sister was employed on the ship, she must have quarters somewhere. No doubt the female and male crew were housed separately, so she might yet be in time to save Lydia's honour. After all, she and Jane watched her like two temple dogs while she was living with them at Mrs Clarke's.

A steward passed her by, and she drew him to a stop. "Are the women crew chiefly stewardesses for the first-class passengers?"

"Yes, miss." He smiled stiffly at her. "They are."

"Oh, thank you very much." Lizzy headed towards the first-class staircase, but the steward spun on his heel and came after her.

"Oh no, miss. Can't go there. First-class passengers only."

"You don't understand. I must find my sister."

"Orders is orders, miss. You might try the glory hole later on." He touched the rim of his cap.

"Glory hole? That sounds revolting."

The steward laughed. "It's quite clean now, miss, the ship being so new. It's where we all sleep. I'll show you the entrance to the women's quarters. Crew bunks are forward on the middle deck. You might try your luck there waiting at the entrance. They won't let no passengers in the glory hole. No, sir... I mean... no, miss." He touched his hat once again and gestured for her to follow him.

On the way to the middle deck crew quarters, the steward informed Lizzy that all the stewardesses were busy during the day, and a good place to wait might be near the crew mess hall. After all, they all had to eat. The mess hall was forward near the third-class open space, so Elizabeth resolved to arrive there near four o'clock and wait until Lydia made her appearance, if she ever did.

***

Dressed for dinner, Darcy left his stateroom at seven o'clock when the bugle summoned guests to the reception room for cocktails. As he descended the forward grand staircase, the hum of quiet conversation among the first-class passengers greeted him. There would be no imbibing for him tonight. He needed all his faculties if he were to catch Wickham. The dining room for the first-class passengers was just beginning to fill up, and he realised as he entered that he knew no one on the ship and therefore had no one with whom to dine. Before the voyage, he considered taking his meals alone in his room, but now he was seeking out Wickham, who on further consideration may not be a passenger but working as a waiter here in first class.

After requesting a small table to himself at the far corner of the dining room where he had a view of the entire opulent space, he sat down to keep an eye on who came and went. Everything that would provide comfort and luxury was carefully planned and executed. The dining room was in the centre of the ship where movement and noise from the engines were at a minimum. The portholes were disguised by leaded, stained-glass windows. Carved wood panelling painted a brilliant white lined the walls. Except for a slight movement of the ship, one would never know one was at sea. Darcy redirected his attention from the décor to the staff. Picking up a menu, he perused it, and then peered over it, and strained his eyes for a glimpse of his quarry.

The dinner was top-notch: duck with buttered boiled potatoes and minted peas. There was a squab course, an asparagus salad, a palate-cleansing rum punch, pâté de foie gras with celery, and other delights to tempt his palate and distract him from his mission. After dessert of French ice cream (they really did think of everything), he rose to leave. So far, his mission bore no fruit, but resolving to take as circuitous route as possible through the great salon, he hoped to spy Wickham. Dawdling near the entrance, he watched and waited. Within minutes, the white of a waitstaff tunic caught his eye.

Wickham waited at the captain's table.

Perfect. He would endeavour to be invited to dine with the captain tomorrow. Hopefully, Lydia's honour would stay intact until then.

***

The mild weather followed them as the great behemoth chugged its way towards France. Lizzy began her watch slightly after four when the ship landed in Cherbourg to take more passengers. She found a deck chair and sat down to wait for Lydia, holding a book as a pretext. If anyone approached to begin a conversation, she merely held the book up and gently waved them away. The gusts on deck nearly dislodged her saucer-like hat, but anticipating the sea breeze, she took extra care in anchoring it with pins to her low pompadour. The wind off the ocean was not kind to the puffy swirls of hair piled high on the head, so she wisely chose to dress her hair so that it sat low on her neck.

It neared dinnertime, and a soft rumble of her stomach told Elizabeth she hadn't eaten. She would wait until half past seven to allow for the rush, and if Lydia didn't appear, then she'd postpone her task until tomorrow. The sun had set, and the deck was becoming chilly. Enough was enough. Elizabeth rose from her seat and was just descending the staircase leading to the crew's mess. She had to choose her way carefully as the stairways were streaming with crew hurrying in both directions. Her skirt caught momentarily on the heel of someone's shoe, and as she moved to dislodge it, she nearly crashed headlong into Lydia, who was looking behind her at one of her fellow stewardesses.

"Oh… Oh, my Lord… Lizzy." Lydia jolted and drew back. "Whatever are you doing here?"

Lizzy caught hold of her arm and pulled her up the last step and onto the deck. By the time they reached the railing, Lydia twisted away. She squared her shoulders and narrowed her eyes. "Clever, Lizzy. You worked out which ship I was on. I thought perhaps I said too much in my note."

"Is that all you're worried about? What are you thinking? Have you married Mr Wickham?"

Lydia laughed. "I told you we're to be married in New York." She tried to pull away. "If it is any of your business, we see very little of each other on the ship. The men's and women's quarters are separate, you know."

"Oh, thank goodness." For the first time since seeing that note, the panic roiling around inside Elizabeth subsided. The relief was short-lived when she saw the look in Lydia's eyes. "How ever did you get involved with him? I thought Jane and I stopped that nonsense long ago."

Lydia curled her lips into a sneer. "You two think you are so smart. You know all those times I went to the musicale or the cinema with Johnny and Constance and that bunch? I walked out with them, and then met Georgie. That's how we went out together. Right under your nose. What a laugh we had."

Lizzy stiffened. "And has he taken any liberties with you? Answer truthfully."

Lydia rolled her eyes as a couple passed them by. "Don't be such a child, Lizzy. You can't keep a man like George Wickham unless you give him what he wants."

Elizabeth closed her eyes for a moment and leaned heavily on the railing. "Oh, Lydia." When she opened them again, Lydia was looking out to sea.

"He will marry me in New York. You'll see." She wouldn't meet Elizabeth's eyes, and her voice quavered a bit as she spoke. The little girl in her was not half sure of herself.

"You're coming with me. Go tell the matron that you are leaving your position as of this moment and spending the rest of the voyage with your sister. I have an entire second-class cabin to myself, with two bunk beds, there is plenty of room—"

Lydia stepped back, and her mouth curled into a snarl. "I will do no such thing. I am keeping my position; I am seeing George whenever I can *and* I am getting married in New York. There is *nothing* you can do to stop me. Nothing." She didn't wait for a reply and ran to the crew's mess.

Elizabeth covered her mouth and choked back a sob. All she did was inflame Lydia's will. She failed. Getting a hold of herself and taking a deep breath, she shook it off. This encounter did not go well. So be it. Tomorrow, perhaps she could find Mr Wickham. Maybe there was some hope that he really intended to marry her. It was an unrealistic thought, Lizzy knew, but she would hold on to it until tomorrow. For now, she needed to eat something and clear her head. She might have lost the first battle, but she would win the war.

Chapter 30

When Darcy awoke the next morning, his thoughts turned to Lydia and Elizabeth. His mind must have been working as he slept, for he knew what he must do. Finding Lydia and untangling this fiasco that Wickham had created was his way to undo some of the damage he'd done the Bennets as a whole. He'd injured Jane with his interference regarding Bingley, but now he would restore Lydia to her family, and if circumstances with Wickham had progressed beyond that point, at least deliver her back to them a married woman.

Sipping his coffee and loitering over his two soft-boiled eggs, he pressed the waiter for information about the crew, trying not to arouse suspicion. He discovered a good deal more about how the ship was run than he really needed to know, but he let the crewman speak. During his detailed ramblings, Darcy discovered that Lydia would be somewhere in first class where she worked as a stewardess.

During the morning hours he must have walked ten miles through the corridors of first class. He met several young women carrying elegant lady's clothing in or empty food trays out. None of them looked remotely like Jane or Elizabeth, but he asked them their names, nonetheless. Most of the time, he got a severe look for his trouble. Sometimes he was greeted with more enthusiasm for his inquiry than he required. He conjured a scenario in which he was inquiring in one hallway while Lydia was bustling down another. She also could have been one of the girls who refused to answer him. In any case, the search was fruitless.

At half past eleven, the ship docked off the coast of Ireland. Darcy emerged on the first-class promenade deck and stared out of the enclosed space towards the shore. Small boats were chugging their way to the *Titanic*, no doubt to deliver the last passengers they would take on before they set out for the open ocean tomorrow.

There was only one thing left for him to do. Before they were too far out to sea to receive cables from home, he spent the rest of the afternoon sending inquiries and orders to his solicitor. Arrangements must be made to settle a sizable sum on Wickham to induce him to marry Lydia, and he needed the evidence that such arrangements had been made to show the scoundrel in case he doubted Darcy's word. His time was better spent with such an endeavour. He had the entire voyage to locate the two of them and see to it that the deed was done.

By the time dinner was served, all was in readiness. Tomorrow, after a good meal, a walk about in the open air, and a good night's sleep, Darcy would set things to rights for Lydia.

***

"Oh… oh, it's you. Hello, Elizabeth." Wickham stood on deck, hatless, his waiter's uniform gone and a celluloid collar, tie, woollen suit, and overcoat replacing it.

"Hello, George. Expecting someone else?" She'd spied him just as she exited the double doors of the second-class dining room and breathed in the fresh air on deck.

A fleeting look of dread passed over him, but brashness soon replaced it. "Perhaps I am… Walk with me."

Elizabeth had to admire his coolness. Rather than fumbling for words explaining himself, defending himself, or any normal reaction from a man knocked on his back foot, George brazened it out.

He sauntered along, and Elizabeth walked beside him.

"So, taking an ocean voyage, are we?"

"I'm looking for my sister," Lizzy said coolly. "She's run off, and I believe she is aboard this ship... with you." She awaited his reply, anticipating lies either way if Lydia had found a way to let George know her sister was onboard.

He opened his mouth to no doubt start on the lies, hinting Lydia hadn't managed to get a message to him, but he must have thought better of it. A moment later, he regained his footing. "You know very well that she is aboard, don't you? You've already spoken to her." His eyes narrowed for a moment, and then his face took on that affable expression that he usually wore. "She is in love with me. Can I help it?"

She wanted to slap that smile from his face. "You can help what you do about it." He leaned back into the railing and looked out into the black and starry night. She stepped beside him but he continued to gaze at the sea. "Do you intend to marry her when we reach New York?"

He faced her now. His smile was gone, and he sighed. "Why don't we see what happens when we reach New York."

Elizabeth had no means to cajole or insist that he do the right thing by Lydia. He could do as he pleased, and she could do nothing to change the situation. Her father was an ocean away, Lydia was enamoured of him, and George knew it would be her sister's reputation that would be sullied by their liaison, not his. Men could do as they pleased, and women bore the consequences. She bit her lower lip and glared at him. He dismissed her disapproval.

"This has been a very pleasant chat, Elizabeth. We must do it more often. As for now, I have an appointment and I am already late." He inclined his head in her direction and sprang to the stairwell where he leapt like a gazelle up the spiral towards the boat deck. Elizabeth watched him go, defeated for the second time in one day. She was stymied at every turn, and this voyage was slowly sinking into catastrophe.

***

Darcy climbed the grand staircase towards the boat deck like a water creature swimming against the tide. Most of the other passengers passed him heading in the opposite direction. Having taken their evening constitutional, they retreated from the chilly night air into the first-class surroundings no doubt seeking some evening entertainment.

Grateful to be alone on deck with his thoughts; the rhythmic churning of the engines was just loud enough to allow him to empty his mind of his cares. The sea air grew colder by the minute and he blew into his hands against it. They were well into the North Atlantic, and he shrugged inside the warmth of his woollen overcoat, the velvet collar brushing his cheek. He secured his homburg against the wind and began a brisk stroll around the deck.

Secured all around the edge of the deck, lifeboats hung on gigantic cradles. On his second circuit around the empty space, he stopped to listen. He was sure he heard voices but, swivelling his head this way and that, could see no one near him. Perhaps it was just the wind and his imagination.

After completing the third circuit, tiredness crept in and he began making his way towards the entrance of the grand staircase. Upon passing one of the lifeboats, he heard the voices again, more distinctly this time, and giggling. Yes, that's what it was… giggling. Quietly approaching each lifeboat, he listened attentively. Whispers came from boat number 6, and occasionally it moved against the breeze. Definitely something untoward was happening under that canvas cover, and he decided to ignore his discovery when a familiar voice came through.

"Alone at last, my little dove."

Wickham. He'd know that voice anywhere.

"I don't know…" The other voice was definitely female. Lydia? Darcy couldn't be sure. He hadn't spoken to her much. Whoever it was, Wickham had her in a compromising position, and Darcy would put a stop to the proceedings at once. Mr Wickham would soon to be a married man if he had anything to say about it.

Summoning determination, he stepped up on one of the cradles to where the canvas was no longer secured. With one quick and powerful movement, he tossed back the canvas to expose Wickham and his paramour.

A high-pitched scream erupted from the lower recesses of the boat, and the sound of jostling in the darkness. Wickham bolted upright, clutching his open trousers, vainly trying to do them up while scrambling upwards. He needn't have made the effort. Darcy seized him by the lapels and dragged him over the seats towards him. The two of them fell to the deck. Wickham shuffled to his feet, trying to arrange his clothing, as a young girl peeked over the gunnel.

"Go back to your quarters, Lydia. Right now," Darcy barked, instantly seeing Elizabeth in her young features. Lydia's eyes grew wide as she clutched her coat. While Wickham tried to recover himself and his dishevelled clothing, Darcy lifted Lydia over the edge of the lifeboat and set her on her feet. As soon as she touched the deck, she was off like a frightened hare. Wickham started buttoning his coat and then made the mistake of opening his mouth.

"I say, old man, that was rather rude."

The scene in which Darcy discovered Wickham with Georgiana played instantly in his mind, and Darcy lunged at him in a fury. They landed on the deck, and he dragged Wickham to his feet by his lapels. With a snarl, Wickham twisted from Darcy's grasp and ran towards the stern. Waves crashed in Darcy's ears as he pursued Wickham, sometimes within an inch or two of catching hold of him again. Within seconds, they were at the stern, and Darcy threw himself at Wickham, nearly tipping them both over the side.

Trying to prevent himself from flying backwards off the ship, Wickham clutched the railing as Darcy grabbed him around the throat and lifted him off his feet. The water roiled below, and the propellers of the behemoth churned through the icy black depths. Wickham held on to the railing, gurgling and trying to twist free.

Pitch this blackguard into the sea, and no one would be the wiser. In the moonlight, terror shone in Wickham's eyes. Darcy held him there a moment longer, breathing hard. Then he yanked Wickham forward and set him on the deck.

Wickham rubbed at his throat as he began to cough. When he could regain his speech, he looked at Darcy and balled his fists. "You nearly killed me."

"Nearly." Darcy was calm now, his fury spent.

"I should report you to the captain." Wickham sneered.

Darcy shrugged. "I wish you would. I could then explain to your superiors how it is I came upon you and your dreadful treatment of Lydia Bennet."

Wickham scoffed. "Lydia Bennet. I have had a dozen 'Lydia Bennets'. What is she to me?"

The fury that had subsided in Darcy began to rise in his throat, but he choked it down. It wouldn't serve Elizabeth and the Bennet family at all were he to throw this scoundrel to the sharks or beat him within an inch of his life, however satisfying that might be.

"She'll be your wife."

Wickham looked like he'd laugh, but then drew back his head and that scornful smile that Darcy hated so much returned.

"That is going to be an expensive proposition."

Darcy nodded. "Come to my cabin, room two sixteen, at three o'clock, fifteen hundred hours in your jargon. I have a proposition for you that you will appreciate."

Wickham nodded slightly, then turned on his heel to go, but stopped and faced Darcy. "Why are you doing this? What does this little girl mean to you?"

Darcy stared at him for a minute. "Three o'clock tomorrow. Don't be late."

Wickham rubbed his neck again, hesitated, and then walked away.

Darcy returned to his stateroom and strode immediately to the small cabinet to pour himself a brandy. As liquid spilled over the sides, he swore softly and tried to will his hands to stop shaking. They wouldn't obey him, and he abandoned the effort and sat on the edge of the bed. Still in his coat, he cradled his head in his hands and realised he'd lost his hat… probably on deck.

On deck.

Where he nearly killed Wickham.

He had *wanted* to kill Wickham.

A knock came at the door. "Do you require my services, sir?" The valet who had been assigned to him when they embarked cleared his throat.

"No, thank you, Montgomery." He raised his voice to be heard through the door. He hadn't even the energy to rise from the bed and open it.

"Very good, sir."

"My God, my God." He repeated the phrase over and over to himself. He'd nearly killed a man tonight. It was as if there was someone else in charge of his body. Someone made of years and years of pent-up rage and wrath. Darcy dealt with the incident of Wickham and his sister with the manners of a gentleman. Wickham's disparaging remarks about his character he met with forbearance. Wickham's squandering of the legacy Darcy's own father bestowed on him he bore with quiet dignity. Tonight, though, over a girl he hardly knew, a beast arose inside of him created from unexpressed anger, of swallowed rage. And yet… and yet, something stopped him from strangling Wickham with his bare hands. Was it his honour as a gentleman? No. Honour hadn't crossed his mind in that moment. Was it fear of punishment? He hadn't thought of that either. Perhaps it was the visceral fear in Wickham's eyes… his helplessness. Even as the overwhelming anger and indignation possessed him, that look… that fear… it evoked just enough sympathy in Darcy that enabled him to gain control of himself.

Now he was exhausted. Tomorrow, he would deal with Wickham again. Then there would be legal arrangements, papers to be signed, and witnesses. Tomorrow, there would be a wedding.

Chapter 31

Elizabeth had to admit defeat and resolved to send a message to her father via the Marconi transmitter. It would have to make its way through Newfoundland and then back across the ocean, but she decided not to wait until they landed in New York. She'd let her father and uncle know that there was nothing she could do to control Lydia. She was racing headlong into her fate and wouldn't listen to anyone.

As Lizzy arrived at the radio room, many first-class passengers queued ahead of her, most bubbling with happy conversation. She wanted to shout at them that she had important news to relay, that her family faced social ruin and her sisters were doomed to disgraced spinsterhood, and that their messages were frivolous and silly. Instead, she resolved to return to the radio room in the evening, after dinner. No doubt, the hoi polloi would be otherwise engaged by then.

***

Wickham's celluloid collar seemed determined to choke him this evening, and he tugged at it with his forefinger, which elicited a stern look from Darcy. Time to direct his attention elsewhere, and he turned to look upon his bride. She was so deliciously young and lovely, but he'd had young and lovely before. Many times. Many just like her.

Where Darcy had found an American justice of the peace aboard this vessel in so short a time, he'd never know. But here they all were, Darcy, Lydia, himself, this drawling American officiant, and two crewmates of the RMS *Titanic* as witnesses. The echo of his vows rang in his head as he said them, "for better or for worse, for richer for poorer..." Well, he was richer now by quite a lot. That thought made him smile as he spoke the solemn words. Lydia's eyes as they met his glowed with happiness, and if he was correct, not a little triumph. No doubt his eyes bore the same expression. He knew he'd marry eventually and for money. This little wedding came a bit earlier than he had planned, but it was as good as he could have hoped. No gorgon of an heiress on his arm, but a sweet, young thing. No father keeping an eye on his daughter's fortune, just Darcy. Darcy, who, he hoped, would soon lose interest. With a wife so young and inexperienced, Wickham didn't fear that his adventures among the fairer sex need be curtailed in the slightest.

"I now pronounce you man and wife. You may kiss the bride." A sweet and tender kiss that promised so much more.

"All right, Wickham. Back on duty. You've got to finish your shift." His fellow waiter, and witness, handed him his white jacket.

Wickham shook himself out of his wedding coat and resumed his duty. The wedding night would have to wait a few more hours.

***

An hour later, as Darcy finally laid his head on the pillow, he felt so weary as to verge on collapse. Yet his mind throbbed with the incidents of the day. At least he had repaired the breach that Wickham had torn asunder in the lives of the Bennets. Lydia was married to the rogue and, in the innocence of youth, overjoyed at it. Was it guilt at saddling that young and gullible girl with a husband such as Wickham, or was it joy at snatching back the Bennet family honour? The Bennets. Tomorrow he'd wire Bingley and let him know all was set to rights. The soft churning of the engines faded as he slipped into sleep.

Darcy awoke with a start. Something… something felt different. He flipped on the light, squeezing his eyes shut at the flash. Then, blinking, sitting up in bed, he glanced over the room. Nothing… nothing had changed. He was about to lie back down when he noticed the ticking of the clock, and suddenly realized he'd never heard it before.

Setting his feet on the carpet, it came to him.

Vibration.

The vibration of the engines had gone.

His first impulse was to throw his overcoat over his pyjamas, pull on his shoes, and go on deck in disarray. Sense took over, and he dressed and went on deck. As a steward passed him near one of the smoking saloons, Darcy drew his attention. "Why have we stopped?"

"Dunno, sir, I'm sure. Can't be much."

"I'll go up to the boat deck and see."

"You can, sir, but it is mighty cold up there."

He wasn't wrong. On the top deck and open to the night sky, the temperature plummeted. It was late, and mind-numbingly cold. The first-class quarters, the captain's bridge, and the steerage quarters were all deserted. Finally, he peered over the starboard side. Nothing there but a still and glassy black sea.

Perhaps they had problems with an engine or some such thing. Not that he knew much about seafaring vessels. Just to reassure himself, he took the stairway to the deck below where some men were playing cards in one of the salons. After he enquired of them what they knew of the stoppage, most agreed that they felt a heaving motion some time before, and one claimed to have gone on deck.

"I saw a great iceberg go by at very close quarters, perhaps it was ninety to a hundred feet high."

"Probably just glanced off us," volunteered another. "The captain will have something to answer for if he's scraped the paint of the hull."

A chorus of laughter came from the card players.

Darcy turned to go. He would get no more information from this lot.

"If you come upon some ice on the deck, I wouldn't mind a small piece for my whiskey, wot." A middle-aged card player waved his glass at Darcy. Again, amused laughter. Darcy needed to check the boat deck. There might be more to be learned by now.

Arriving at the top of the staircase, he frowned. A few passengers in various states of dress and undress had wandered out and discovered a large pile of snow that covered a section of the deck. Snowballs flew about to much giggling and guffawing.

"Lydia, Lydia, come away at once. You'll catch your death of cold."

Elizabeth.

What was Elizabeth doing here? It couldn't be. As if Darcy was in a trance, his footsteps took him to the gambolling crowd.

Dressed in her dressing gown, coat, and slippers, Lydia squealed with delight as snowballs disintegrated in midair and showered her with icy shards. Elizabeth caught her by the arm and dragged her away from the merrymakers. Her back to him and thoroughly engaged with restraining her sister, Elizabeth didn't notice him. His heart caught in his mouth.

"Good evening, Mrs Wickham, Miss Bennet."

Elizabeth snapped her head in his direction quickly and then, just as quickly, back to Lydia.

"Mrs Wickham?" She still held her sister fast. "Mrs Wickham?" Then she turned back. "Mr. Darcy? What is going on?"

"Oh, let me go, Lizzy." Lydia grinned. "I am Mrs Wickham, so ha." She twisted herself free and stomped her foot defiantly.

Elizabeth looked from one to the other. "What? How long have you been married?"

Lydia tossed her head. "Oh, I don't know. What time is it?" She pointed at Mr Darcy. "Ask him. He was there."

Elizabeth rounded on Darcy and a plethora of emotions played across her face. She opened her mouth to address Darcy, then turned on Lydia. "If you are Mrs Wickham, where, in heaven's name, is your husband?"

"Oh, as soon as some American magistrate married us, George had to return to duty. The captain was kind enough to give us one of the empty first-class cabins for our honeymoon. He will join me there shortly." Lydia gave Elizabeth a smirk.

"Oh, I don't understand." Elizabeth turned towards Mr Darcy, again eyeing him. "And you knew?" He did not answer immediately. She shook her head. "If you will forgive us, sir, my sister and I have some matters to discuss. You'll excuse us."

"What? Where are we going? Let go." Lydia again attempted to extricate herself from Elizabeth's grasp.

Elizabeth's parting words drifted as she pulled Lydia by the hand. "If you have a cabin, then take me there and explain yourself."

Darcy followed mutely. He would rather explain everything to Elizabeth himself than have a garbled account of the day's proceedings pour out of Lydia.

They made for the stairway, but as they climbed, Darcy seemed not to be able to put his foot right, as if the stairs were twisted or melted. They looked the same but felt odd. The entire evening felt odd.

"Perhaps I should go with you," he said as they reached the first-class deck.

"I don't believe that will be necessary. I would like to hear from my sister what has been happening behind my back."

Darcy had intended to make his involvement in Lydia and Wickham's marriage remain a secret to Elizabeth for one reason and one reason only. He didn't want her to look favourably upon him out of gratitude, but to like him, or really, to love him, for himself alone. His ruminations were cut short as the steward approached them.

"All passengers on deck with life belts on."

"*Life* belts?" Lydia paled.

"I am sure it is just a precaution." Darcy could see no sense of alarm among the other passengers, who were now more numerous and passing them on the deck. "Do you know where yours is?" he inquired of Elizabeth.

"I don't believe so." Her voice quavered slightly. "I thought this ship was unsinkable."

"I am sure it is." He offered a smile. "No one seems alarmed, not even the crew." He indicated the other passengers.

"Lizzy, don't leave me. Where is George?" Lydia began to whimper, and Darcy curbed a desire to tell her to stop acting like a child, which, he realised to his chagrin, was exactly what she was.

"I won't leave you." Elizabeth's tone came softer than before, and she turned to Darcy. "If you do not have anything else pressing, could I ask you to kindly stay with us until this crisis, or whatever it is, is over?

Darcy gave a slight bow. "I am at your service, of course. But come along to first class. We shall retrieve the life belts from both our cabins and, Mrs Wickham, you can change into something more suitable for the night air.

Lydia looked down at her dressing gown peeking beneath her coat and began to giggle.

Chapter 32

Elizabeth would never admit it to him, but she was relieved and grateful for Darcy's presence. It was obvious to her that he was aboard ship on his way to America, just as Lady Catherine had thrown in her face not that long ago. Why he was present at Lydia's wedding and how such a wedding came to be in the first place remained unanswered. She knew for a fact that Mr Wickham intended to enjoy Lydia until they came to New York and then abandon her. None of that mattered now. With their life belts securely fastened, they followed Mr Darcy up to the boat deck. Many people milled about now, some still half in nightclothes. The ship felt solid as a rock. She peeked over the side and the sea remained as still as a pond, black as obsidian.

A great roar blasted steam from the funnels above them, and Lizzy flinched. The noise stopped all conversation. Some passengers laughed nervously; others, along with Lizzy, silently looked up.

"What are they doing?" she shouted at Mr Darcy eventually. He stood, gazing up at the funnels, his expression implacable.

"Relieving steam from the engine, I believe." He frowned. "Why it's making so much noise, I am at a loss." He looked at her. "I don't believe it is anything alarming."

As Lizzy looked about the deck, few seemed the least bit alarmed. The ship stood perfectly still in the ocean as solid and reassuring as could be. She tried to calm her own unease. The staff surely would let them know if it was anything more alarming.

"It's very noisy up here." Lydia covered her ears. "I think I need to go and wait for George in our cabin. Come on, Lizzy. Follow me." She slipped away without looking back and disappeared in the crowd.

Elizabeth glanced at Darcy, and for the first time, apprehension was apparent in his expression. "We can't get separated. We must go after her." He took Elizabeth by the hand. A thought crossed her mind that she should resist this gesture, but she had to admit that it felt comforting. Darcy pulled her through the crowd to the stairwell, and she caught occasional glimpses of Lydia trying to step forward but countered at every turn by the crowd streaming onto the deck.

"Lydia. *Lydia.*" Elizabeth knew she would soon be hoarse if this noise were to continue. Luckily, Lydia heard her before she was swept back to her by the swelling crowd.

"Oh, never mind," she said breathlessly. "Georgie will have to find me here."

Lydia was safely by her side, that was all that mattered, and Lizzy glanced around. The crew calmly but steadily unwrapped the lifeboats, arranged the oars, coiled the ropes that would soon be run through the divets and pulleys to lower those boats into the glassy sea.

Lifeboats? She looked at Lydia, nervously biting her lip while searching the crowd, no doubt, for George. Lizzy's heart sank. She couldn't see them separated. She'd remain here with her sister and Mr Darcy until George came. Although the crew got the boats ready, there was no indication that anything was wrong with the ship: no wind, no churning of the sea, and certainly no icebergs. A bit of snow was kicked about on the deck, but how much harm could that have done to a great ship such as this one?

Darcy still had Elizabeth's hand in his, not such a tight grip as before, but not tenuous either. She left it there as an officer began walking the deck.

"All women and children get down to the deck below and all men stand back from the boats," he shouted above the screaming steam escaping from the funnels.

"This is where I leave you, ladies." Darcy let go of her hand, and Lizzy suddenly felt very vulnerable. Despite the assurance of the crew, the atmosphere had turned suddenly frightful, and perhaps deadly.

When the crew began to fill the lifeboats, some women resisted, some wailed over being forced to leave their husbands. Officers separated them, forcefully pulling the women down the staircase to the deck below. Most of the crowd did as they were told. Mr Darcy had the most placid look on his face.

"I don't think we should be separated," Elizabeth said at last.

"Those are the orders, Miss Bennet. I am sure that it is just a precaution. They will row you all out a bit, and once whatever problem they are having is solved, they will row you back again. Never fear."

"I am not frightened in the least bit." Of course, she was, though she would certainly never betray it to him. She could barely admit it to herself. Lydia's change from biting her lip to dancing from foot to foot *did* betray her anxiety, and Lizzy knew that she had to be strong for her sake. Lizzy looked around for George. Could he be behaving contrary to his nature and attending to his duties? In any case, perhaps Mr Darcy was right, and all these life belts and boats were only a precaution.

Just then, a hiss and a roar assailed them, and Lizzy's gaze turned skyward. A rocket sped up, up, upwards towards the stars and then exploded into a thousand shining fragments.

"Rockets," he said. Mr Darcy reached for Elizabeth's hand once again. She took it. Then another rocket, and then another. Rockets exploded the stillness of the cloudless night and the stillness of the sea. Rockets at sea meant only one thing: they were calling desperately for help from any ship nearby that could see them. They were calling into the still night because they were sinking.

"There's nothing more to be said. Go down to the B deck at once." Darcy pointed at the boats as he found Lizzy's gaze. The crew let the ropes slip through the cleats that allowed them to be lowered down to the deck below.

"Come with us." Elizabeth gripped his hand tightly. He was going to be noble and let others go before him into the lifeboats. At that moment, she knew that she loved him. She had to tell him. It might be her last chance.

Her expression betrayed her because he touched her cheek ever so gently. "I'll accompany you as far as I can, but the boats are for the women and children." The officer overheard his remark, for as they reached the stairwell, he shouted, "Men are being taken off the port side, sir. Upper deck."

Leading the way down the stairwell, Darcy pulled Elizabeth by the hand and she, in turn, led Lydia through the crowd of passengers. When they reached the deck, boat 13 swung level with the railing.

"Lydia—*Lydia*." Out of the crowd, George appeared still dressed in his white waiter's jacket and gloves. His hair was dishevelled, and his coat soiled. Glancing from Elizabeth to Darcy to his wife, he suddenly pulled Lydia to him. "Darling."

"Oh, Georgie. I'm so glad you're here." Lydia threw her arms around his neck and clung to him. "Come along with us. We're leaving."

Darcy turned a cold eye towards George. "Men are boarding on the port side, up top."

"Any more ladies?" came the cry from lifeboat 13.

"Yes, two more here," Darcy shouted.

"You there, waiter, help them aboard." The officer watched Wickham keenly. He was shaking all over.

"Come on, man. Help your wife." Darcy cut through the noise. He hesitated a moment more and then said, "We'll go and see about the men on the port side."

Lizzy guessed he was only reassuring Wickham to get him to pry Lydia loose so that she could be saved. Wickham peeled Lydia's hands from his neck and handed her to the officer in the boat.

"Come along, miss. We must be off." The officer turned to Lizzy.

How could she leave Darcy now? All became clear to her in that moment. George wouldn't marry unless there was money involved, so Darcy must have arranged this marriage between them. He must have paid Wickham off handsomely. That first-class cabin for their honeymoon? That was his doing as well.

He still loved her.

If they died tonight, they'd die together. She couldn't leave him.

"Darcy—"

"Go, go," Darcy shouted above the din of the roaring funnels. His hands were upon her waist, pushing her toward the lifeboat.

"No, no." She tried to twist around. "I want to stay with you."

His eyes met hers, and they softened for a moment. Then determination took over. He hesitated, then smiled. "No need for such heroics, my dear. Wickham and I will be on one of the boats leaving the port side. No need to worry at all." He turned to indicate Wickham, but the rat was nowhere to be found.

"Any more ladies?" The cry went up from the lifeboat crew again.

Lizzy briefly glanced at the chaos around her. "No, I won't leave you." She turned in his arms and kissed him hard on the mouth. He pulled back, and then he kissed her, tenderly, passionately, desperately.

"I love you," he said in her ear as he pulled away.

"I love you. And I'm so sorry, I…"

"Go, go. Look after your sister."

Lydia screamed, tears streaming down her face. "Lizzy, Lizzy, don't leave me."

Darcy kissed Lizzy's cheek. "I will be all right. You'll see. This ship is unsinkable." He kept his voice steady, but in the flash of the rockets she could see the truth in his eyes. He didn't believe his words any more than she did.

She threw her arms around him, pressing her cheek to his, and then took the hand of the officer in lifeboat 13. By the time she had settled next to Lydia, Darcy was gone.

***

Elizabeth gripped the wooden seat as the crew lowered the boat, fearing they might be dumped headlong into the sea. Sixty people packed the boat, most of whom remained oddly silent except for the occasional remark about what a lark this voyage was turning out to be. One woman behind her, clutching her fur collar tightly around her neck, remarked that she would be glad to get aboard again and secure her jewels.

Lizzy gazed heavenward as the crew on deck handled the ropes that lowered their boat down so the great black wall of the ship slipped past them.

"Beware of the condenser exhaust: we don't want to stay long or we shall be swamped. Feel on the floor and be ready to pull up the pin that lets the ropes free as soon as we are afloat."

She shot a glance back into the boat and the crewman who addressed them. There was scarcely enough room to stand, let alone bend over and feel about on the floor of the boat, they were so tightly packed together. Lizzy wiggled her arm free from Lydia, who stayed oddly silent as she felt along the bottom of the boat. There was the pin. Looking up at the crew member at the stern, she nodded to him, and he nodded back. She would pull the pin on his signal. The "condenser exhaust" was a stream of water that perpetually gushed from the ship as they made their way. In days past, when she looked over the side, she marvelled at it. It spewed a forceful rush of water from the side like an artificial crashing wave. The force of it could easily topple the boat and spill all of them into the icy, black sea. The roar of the jet got nearer and louder. Elizabeth forced herself to watch the crewman for a signal.

Abruptly, they plopped into the water, and she pulled the pin. Her fellow passengers must have done the same for the force of the jet pushed them in a tidal wave from the side of the ship directly under boat 15, which lowered above their heads.

"*Stop lowering boat fifteen.*" Panicking cries from Lizzy and everyone in the boat rent the night air. People desperately reached up, trying to stop the descending boat from crushing them.

Passengers from boat 15 joined in the shouts. With the whistling steam escaping from the funnels and the shouting on deck, crew members lowering the boats couldn't hear their cries. Desperate, Elizabeth reached up and instinctively slapped the bottom of the descending boat, trying frantically to push her away. Lydia clung to her skirts like a child and fell silent.

"Move." A crew member from Lizzy's boat pulled out a knife and clambered over people to get to the ropes that still held their boat fast to the *Titanic*. As he started slicing, he kept looking up furiously. "Cut the ropes, cut the ropes."

He cut his rapidly at the stern, and Elizabeth's boat swung away from the side just as the boat above them splashed into the water. The force of the exhaust stream washed them clear of the ship. Some muted applause erupted from their boat, but nothing more. Oddly, everyone seemed calm, so Lizzy patted Lydia's hand. "That seems to be the only excitement we will have for the evening," she said reassuringly. Lizzy hoped and prayed it would be, but her heart sank as she turned to look at the ship.

"Oh, I do hope so. I wonder how Georgie is doing?"

Chapter 33

With great difficulty due to women and children streaming in the opposite direction, Darcy climbed the staircase to the boat deck and thought he would see for himself if men were being taken off the port side. If there were enough lifeboats for everyone, there was no reason he should "stand upon the burning deck" as it were and go down with the ship. Now that Elizabeth and Lydia were safely away, he could think about saving himself, if indeed that was necessary. As he reached the boat deck, the portside boats were away already. By this time, a definite tilt to the bow kept him steadying his stance, and Darcy's worst fears were confirmed. They were sinking and sinking quickly. He might not survive this night.

He returned to the first-class deck, where a crewman blocked the way of a second-class passenger. "No, madame, you may not enter here, but go to a boat on the B deck, in second class." The woman didn't seem to be alarmed and thanked the man for his directions. The scene was worse on the second-class deck. Women and children from both second class and steerage were the only persons allowed on the boats. That was as it should be. If he was to die tonight, then he should make himself useful whilst he still had time.

He approached the B deck lifeboats, where a steward still reassured passengers. "You need to get into the lifeboat only as a precaution, madame. This ship cannot sink."

Most of the women obeyed placidly, many still clad in nightclothes with coats hastily thrown over. Darcy positioned himself near the railing and, extending his hand to a mother carrying an infant, and helped her negotiate the expanse between the ship and the swinging boat.

"Lev... *Lev*," she called as soon as she landed in the boat. Dressed in a worn overcoat and no doubt her husband, a young man stood stock-still on the deck. With a long beard, sidelocks, and a faded muffler about his neck, he kept his expression sedate, but Darcy could see by his trembling lip that he could barely contain himself at their parting.

"You, sir."

Darcy looked about.

"Are you addressing me?" he asked as he helped another woman and her two children into the boat.

"Yes. There's room in the boat for you, sir," he said. All heads turned towards him. He looked down at his clothes momentarily. The silk scarf, the smartly tailored black overcoat with velvet collar. In an instant, he knew he was being given a place because he was a first-class passenger. He swallowed hard. This one moment would test everything he believed in... honour, duty, the unwritten code of a gentleman. He also knew that he now, literally, held his life in his hands. Glancing around at the upturned faces, he spotted the young man, Lev, still rooted to the spot where he let his wife and baby go. Darcy gestured to him. "Go," he said. "They need you."

The young man looked about in disbelief. The sailor made no protest. The boat, fully laden, was already being swung by the divets out over the black water. His overcoat billowing, the young father leapt from a nearly standing position and threw himself into the boat. A cry went up from one or two of the female passengers, upon whom he had landed. As he rose up from the bottom of the boat, he called out to Darcy in a loud voice. "Thank you, thank you. What is your name?"

"Darcy, Fitzwilliam Darcy."

"I am Lev Shklovsky. We will never forget you." The boat began to disappear over the side.

Darcy walked back to the rail and looked over, watching what was probably his last hope of rescue disappear down the great wall of the ship.

Straightening himself, he took a deep breath, and looked down the deck where other boats were being loaded.

Wickham?

At least he thought he saw Wickham rushing down the deck as more women and children were hastily loaded into the straining boats.

Darcy shifted over just as a pink-cheeked lad of perhaps thirteen years of age was dragged from under the seat of lifeboat 14. An officer aimed a pistol in the lad's direction. screaming, "I'll give you just ten seconds to get on that ship before I blow your brains out."

The boy raised his hands. "Please, sir, don't shoot. Let me stay. I won't take up much room. *Please.*"

The officer lowered his weapon. "Be a man."

The boy stood up in the lifeboat, then swung himself back onto the deck of the *Titanic*, where he sat down and wept.

More life-and-death decisions unfolded around Darcy. Men begging their wives to take the children, reassuring them that they would find another boat. Women weeping. For a moment he stood at the rail, breathing in deeply the frigid air. The realisation that he *would* die that night struck him with full force. For a few moments he watched the sobbing boy on the deck. The poor child was asked to be a man. Darcy was a man, and a gentleman, and would act like one to the end. There was no point in doing anything else. Perhaps it would make up for his murderous thoughts of the other night. Was it only yesterday?

The squeaking of the divets swinging lifeboat 14 over the side wrenched him from his reverie and forced his attention back on Wickham. He had seen him. As the boat swung out from the deck on its divets, ready to be lowered, he scanned the faces of the crowd.

Pacing the deck and looking intently at the passengers in the lifeboat, a rather broad-shouldered female shielded her face by looking out into the blackness of the sky and sea. Something about her looked familiar. When someone bumped her and she shifted to retain her balance, Darcy froze.

With all the noise on deck, the screaming funnels, the shouting men, he didn't expect his voice to carry, but— *"Wickham."*

The sailors loosened their ropes to lower the craft on its seven-story journey to the glassy surface of the ocean. As the boat slipped from view, the "woman" turned to look in Darcy's direction and he smirked and gave a feminine sort of four-fingered wave. That was the last Darcy saw of George Wickham.

***

Hope still beat in Lizzy's breast that the rockets that came howling from the deck into the placid night sky might be seen by some other ship that was invisible to them, and at this moment, would be steaming to their rescue. The *Titanic*'s black monolithic size looming above them would last the night, surely. Its great structure dwarfed their tiny boats like an elephant beside an ant. How could such a thing topple and sink into the sea? It couldn't. Everyone said so.

She swore she caught a ship in the distance, one of those tiny points of light that flashed at the razor cut of the black horizon. Not a star, but a ship. It had to be. It would come and take all who were left behind, including Mr Darcy. Take them off the behemoth and scoop their boat up, too, one by one. Then, by morning, all the tearful departures, all the sacrifice, all the high emotion and grief would be gone, and all would be reunited with their loved ones, and she with her beloved.

Why hadn't she told him of her feelings sooner? Darcy was in many ways exactly what she thought of him the first time she met him: proud, moody, ensconced in his upper-class ways. And yet she'd misjudged him so. He wasn't arrogant or cruel. He was capable of deep thought … of altering his first impression and even the beliefs that had been instilled since childhood. And he loved her.

Where was the rescue ship? Why hadn't it come to their aid?

One of the oarsmen who claimed to be one of the engine stokers shivered in his shirt and trousers, having been dressed for the heat of the engine room. Now he was afloat in this windless, icy night. A lady, well dressed in a fur, offered him her coat, but he wouldn't take it. He did avail himself of a rug that that self-same lady brought with her. It was obvious that he couldn't wrap himself in it and keep on rowing, so Elizabeth volunteered to take his place at the oars. No one objected, and she watched him disappear below the stern in an effort to roll himself into a ball, covering himself with the rug in an attempt to prevent himself from freezing to death.

"The water is so still. Isn't it, Lizzy?" Lydia stayed as close to Elizabeth as she dared while she rowed. Elizabeth, preoccupied as she was with rowing their lifeboat away from the great wounded beast of a ship, finally looked at the glossy sea. Except for a slight bobbing motion, almost indiscernible from stillness, her oar cut into what looked like a great pond of oil, it was so without ripple or wave.

"Let us heave and move to more open water, for if she does go down, she's such a size that she'd suck us all into a watery grave with her," the crewman who captained the lifeboat ordered. They rowed out into the frigid night, at one with the glittering stars and the lifeless sea.

"Never seen the stars so bright in all me life," said someone. It was true. There wasn't a hint of mist nor cloud and the brilliant swath of the Milky Way shown like a wispy tapestry across the sky.

From her position at the oar, Elizabeth watched the lights of the portholes in the *Titanic*, reflected in the still ocean. Slowly, they lost their parallel position to the sea's surface, and the lights met their counterpart reflections in an arrow pointing to their destruction.

"She's sinking for certain, and quickly." A disembodied male voice broke over the quiet conversation. There was no denying it.

The tip of the bow was already under water. Elizabeth was grateful for the physical exertion and the pain of the burgeoning blisters on her hands. It kept her from bursting into sobs.

"I wonder where Georgie is. Am I to be a widow so young?" Lydia asked mournfully. *And, Darcy, where are you? Are you safe?*

***

At two in the morning, Darcy remained on the boat deck as the last four collapsible lifeboats were filled. Exhausted, he witnessed Ida Straus, the wife of the Macy's department store magnate, refuse to leave her husband. A string quartet stayed on deck, playing their final dirges into the night as the ship listed toward the starboard bow. Everything seemed dreamlike. Women were thrown by their husbands into sailors' arms and forcibly taken into the last lifeboats. Darcy scanned the horizon. The light was so deceptive. If all had been well, this would have been a most glorious night. The sea was as still as a millpond, the stars blazing, unveiled in their magnificence. And yet, here they all were, hundreds of them, about to be swept under the freezing, black water by the death throes of this monstrous vessel.

Still, there was a slight chance. It crept upon him as he helped load the lifeboats and looked down into the black abyss of the ocean. Matthew Webb swam the English Channel, which was cold, but certainly not as hellish as this icy ship's graveyard. He was in the water over twenty hours because of the grease he slathered over his body. The kitchens were on the saloon deck between first and second-class dining saloons. Certainly, there would be grease there. Fighting his way through the increasingly panicked crowd, Darcy descended the listing staircase and made his way through the nearly abandoned dining rooms.

Strangely, some people lounged about there.

"Have a drink, friend." A very drunken man beckoned Darcy over. "We're all going to die, anyway," he slurred. "Might as well be drunk."

Darcy sped past him and his other nearly unconscious companions and flung open the kitchen doors. The place was deserted. Stoves creaked against the bolts that held them to the floor and wouldn't stay in place long. In desperation and scouring the place for a bucket of discarded fat, he even considered looking in the refrigerated compartment on the port side and coating himself with that French ice cream. It couldn't be any colder than the water into which he was about to plunge.

Only a minute or two into his search, he found what he was looking for. Stripping off his coat, shirt, trousers, socks, and shoes, he stood in his underclothes and then, looking about, stripped those off as well. Taking handfuls of stinking grease from the buckets, he began with his head, and as quickly as he could, slathered himself in grease. His back. What would he do about his back? Thinking quickly, he dipped his underclothes in the grease and put them back on. The long sleeves and leggings that reached his ankles might afford him extra protection. The ship's heavy appliances groaned and strained as the ship listed. He needed to leave before he was crushed as their bolts tore loose from the floor and hurled themselves toward the bow of the ship. He put on his coat and his shoes and climbed the leaning stairwell to the deck.

The last of the lifeboats were gone. The passengers who remained were crowding, foolishly and hopelessly, to the stern of the ship, screaming and clinging to the railings. All was madness.

Darcy knew that it meant almost certain death were he to attempt to swim in the iceberg-laden, glacial water. Still, it seemed a better end to freeze to death whilst swimming than to lie in a dark cabin as it slowly filled with water, or cling to this wounded titan as it sucked him down into the dark depths. He shuddered. After moving to the stern of the ship that was crowding with increasingly panicking people, he looked down into the impenetrable blackness. The walls of the vessel seemed higher now than ever they were. It was now or never. The stern of the ship was nearly out of the water. Soon the *Titanic* would plunge headlong into its watery grave, taking all of them with her.

If he jumped from this position, he might break his legs as he landed. Although it seemed counterintuitive, he moved toward the bow, which was now almost completely submerged. He needed to move immediately, or the death throes of the *Titanic* would suck him under with the rest of these poor unfortunates. After a few shallow breaths, he sat down on the sloping deck and removed his shoes and his coat. After standing only in his underclothes, he climbed over the rail.

"He's going to jump," a woman screamed.

The next second, he plummeted toward the icy water.

Chapter 34

A terrific roar echoed across the empty blackness towards Lizzy: metal rent in half, explosions from red-hot boilers meeting the cold, impassive sea. Lydia covered her ears. The stern of the *Titanic*, still fully lit, tilted up nearly vertical in the air, and looked almost as if a huge building suddenly jutted out from the bottom of the sea. Lydia hid, burying her face in Lizzy's shoulder. They had stopped rowing, and gazed out onto the perfect night, the still calm waters, the blazing stars, and the death agonies of their unsinkable ship. Tiny figures at the end of the upright stern clung to railings, then those who could not cling on slid down the deck and plunged into the sea. Cries went up from their small boat.

A steady hum almost like bees buzzing or locusts humming drifted over.

Lydia stared out at the horrific spectacle of the dying vessel. "What is that?" she asked, to no one in particular.

"Everyone is screaming," Lizzy said simply.

They cried out for mercy and rescue.

None came.

None was offered.

An explosion lit up the night from somewhere deep in the ship, and the lights that had shone so brightly and steadily blinked, blazed, and finally went out. With one final, terrific, shrieking roar, the ship tore itself asunder and plunged into the sea toward the bottom of the ocean.

Nothing but a calm, frigid starlit night remained. The world was suddenly still.

***

Darcy kicked his way to the surface, a thousand icy knives plunging into his body. Forcing himself to take a breath, he looked up, but saw nothing but the black sea meeting the starry night at the horizon. He began swimming the Australian crawl, thinking that would get him the farthest distance from the ship in the quickest amount of time. As his head came out of the water, a steady buzzing sound assailed his ears. At first, he thought the screaming cold had frozen his mind, but then he realized it was voices... voices of the damned going down with the ship.

He never knew that cold could be so painful. He began to count, *one-Piccadilly, two-Piccadilly, three-Piccadilly...* When they rescued him, he could then tell them how long he survived in the water. If they rescued him.

A terrific sound of an explosion rent the air, and twisting around, he watched the *Titanic*'s stern, now vertical and black against the starry sky, quickly plummet straight into the sea. He swam in earnest away from the ship, forgetting to count. A solitary wave rolled under him and swept him outward from where he determined the ship had sunk. It didn't crash over him, or swamp him, but pushed him gently on as if a friendly dolphin had let him ride for a moment on its back.

A sudden weariness overtook him, and he changed his stroke to the breaststroke he learned as a child. His eyes closed for a moment, and he forced them open. "*Help. Help.* Can anyone hear me?"

The night was silent and sleepiness enveloped him again. Fighting to remain conscious, he realised he was freezing to death. It wasn't unpleasant, almost welcoming...

He sputtered.

No, if he continued with breaststroke, he would surely drown. Much better to lie on his back and freeze to death. Rolling over, he stretched out his arms. It seemed as if he stretched them. They were too numb to tell. Looking up into the starry sky, he blinked hard and fast. "Can anyone hear me? I'm over here. Please help."

He watched as a rose petal fell on grass. He sat in a garden with Georgiana. Was she four or five? She played close by in the pond with their father, a pond their father had stocked with exotic fish after one of his travels to the east.

"Georgiana, come away. You'll fall in and spoil your pinafore… Georgiana."

She turned to Darcy, holding a wriggling fish in her chubby hand. She tried to give it to him. He extended his hand and the fish dropped in.

"It is so slippery, slippery. I can't seem to get a hold."

***

Elizabeth strained against the darkness, searching the night. Surely, some ship had seen the barrage of rockets they had set off. There was nothing they could do now but wait. The night was so frigid she was afraid some of her fellow passengers might have escaped drowning only to die of the cold. Attempting to keep both her herself and Lydia from freezing to death, she opened her coat as did Lydia and they huddled together. They would survive, perhaps minus some fingers or toes, but they would survive if any ship was close enough to see their fiery cries for help.

Through the fog of her grief-stricken brain and her frozen limbs, the lights of a ship inched onto the horizon, but the darkness of the early morning made her question herself. When the ship finally loomed above them, her legs were so stiff from cold and inactivity that she and Lydia had to be hoisted aboard in a sling. All around the ship the sunrise caught shining monolithic icebergs floating like tall golden buildings catching the sun's rays as they rose from the sea. A beautiful, unforgettable sight, but one accompanied by the music of the sobbing and wailing of the women survivors.

Lizzy was swung onto the deck and deposited near one of the rescue ship's lifeboats. *Carpathia*. As their rescue ship pulled to its bosom the floating survivors of the unsinkable *Titanic,* Lizzy tried to shake off the numbness that had overtaken her.

"Come along, my dears. Let's get some hot food into you." Someone was speaking to Elizabeth. She had a kind face. Lydia was still clinging to her like a lost child. They followed the woman into a crowded dining hall and were served a bowl of hot porridge.

"I don't think I'm hungry." Lizzy looked up at her.

"It doesn't matter. Eat anyway," she said gently. "It will make you feel better."

Lizzy dipped her spoon into the porridge. It smelled like her mother's kitchen, and she burst into tears.

***

As soon as Wickham boarded the *Carpathia*, he sought to divest himself of a lady's accoutrements. With frosty air biting into his fingers, he reluctantly removed the black woollen coat with its fur collar and the velvet hat that did so well in hiding his face. The lifeboat he was on was crowded and the occupants so immersed in their own misery that no one noticed him. After rolling down his trousers to cover the long stockings on his legs, he sought shelter inside the dining salon, out of the cold morning air.

The crew of the *Carpathia* was doling out a meagre breakfast, but he was famished. After taking it to a secluded corner away from the rest of the survivors and the prying eyes of the *Carpathia*'s passengers, he slid down the wall and sat on the carpeted floor.

Spooning the porridge into his mouth, he finally had time to take stock of his position. He had survived, while many didn't. An image of Darcy standing on the deck watching him as he escaped suddenly surfaced and closed his throat. He dropped his spoon into the bowl. He fought to swallow down unusual guilt, but it kept resurfacing like a corpse. He laid the bowl down and shut his eyes. The image of the great vessel, upright in the still, black water, issuing the wailing of a thousand voices as they clung to her doomed deck, wouldn't leave him be. He'd survived. That was a good thing, wasn't it?

Again he could see Darcy's face as it receded with the descending lifeboat. He'd left Darcy there to die. *Darcy...Darcy... stupid man.* He could have escaped if he'd wanted to. He was so bloody-minded, full of duty and noblesse oblige. What if he, Wickham, had stayed on board? He too would be at the bottom of the ocean or floating, blue and lifeless, on the sparkling surface of the now transfigured sea. What good could that possibly have done?

He stared at his breakfast. Although still hungry, he couldn't eat anymore. Life must go on whether one had regrets or not. He should search for Lydia and Elizabeth. Lydia, the key to his fortune, and oddly, a comfort. At least one person in this world cared whether he lived or died. George fought to banish his maudlin thoughts, but they wouldn't leave him be. Maybe he really cared for Lydia. She was his wife now and the thought of her began to banish the cold that not only ate at his bones but gripped his heart. He resolved then and there, he would try to be a better man, whatever that meant.

He reached inside his waiter's jacket and felt for the papers. From the moment of his marriage, he had not parted with them. They could now be at the bottom of the sea, with the man who arranged for his fortune dead and unable to vouch for the wedding that had taken place on the bridge of the *Titanic*. His fingers brushed over them, and he patted them to reassure himself. As he rose, he began to concoct a reason for his survival that didn't include a fur-collared coat and a lady's hat.

***

By the time Elizabeth and Lydia finished choking down their rations, all the lifeboats that could be found had been hauled aboard. Hoping against hope, Lizzy walked up and down the decks of the *Carpathia* with Lydia, in and out of the public rooms, searching for Darcy and

Wickham. Trying desperately to think clearly, Elizabeth tried to be systematic in her search, and came upon the idea of asking any groups of men that she found together to see if there was a chance that either Darcy or Wickham were among them, or if they heard any news.

"Have you seen either of these men? A Mr Wickham, he's a waiter from the *Titanic*, or a man called Darcy, Fitzwilliam Darcy? He has dark hair and dark eyes and was in first class."

Men looked at her hollow-eyed and shook their heads. Many had wives clinging to them, but some were crew members who had manned the boats. Lydia wouldn't leave Elizabeth's side and held her hand like a small child afraid of losing her mother. Even when she had to visit the water closet, Lydia would stand outside the door and insist on Elizabeth talking to her.

"How long do you think it will take until we get to New York, Lizzy? Do you think George might have been saved?" Whenever she mentioned Wickham, her voice would waver and break. There was nothing Elizabeth could do. Her voice was wavering as well.

Grateful that she was dressed for the cold weather, she pulled up the collar of her woollen coat and straightened the turban-like hat that had kept her warm during the long night on the lifeboat. She was grateful that morning for things that never entered her mind before. A warm coat, feet that were not frozen, a velvet hat that kept out the wind. Seeing another group of people huddled on deck, she stopped and asked again.

"I am looking for a man named Darcy. He is a first-class passenger—"

Before she could finish, a man close by in another group called out to her. His coat was tattered and a woman she assumed was his wife clung to his hand as he stood. She cradled an infant asleep in her arms.

Many people sat around him on the deck, so he made no move to climb over them, but stood gazing at her. When he did not speak further, she spoke to him. "Have you seen Mr Darcy? Does he live?" She clutched her mouth and tried to regain her composure.

"Was it a man called Fitzwilliam Darcy?" When she nodded, the tears began to course down his cheeks. He made no move to wipe them away but blinked at her and swallowed hard a few times as if the words were choking him. She didn't move, nor encourage him, for she didn't want to hear his words.

Finally, he managed to regain his composure. "The crew of the lifeboat had one more place. They offered it to this fine gentleman, Mr Darcy. My wife and baby were already in the boat. He gave me his place. He saved me for them." At that, he could no longer speak but covered his face while his wife squeezed his free hand.

"Were there other boats? Perhaps he got another boat?" Elizabeth knew the answer to her question before these poor people had a chance to utter it, but she forced herself to listen, nonetheless. She had to know.

This time, his wife spoke. "It was one of the last boats, a collapsible they said. Your Mr Darcy saved my family. We will never forget him."

Elizabeth stood motionless for a moment, staring at the three of them. The poor man was beside himself with grief. She had to say something. "Thank you for telling me." She turned to go, but then turned back to look at the young man who had been spared by Darcy. "Don't feel guilty that he gave his life for yours. I believe if it wasn't you, it would have been someone else. That was the sort of man he was."

The young man nodded, closed his eyes, and sat down next to his wife once again, putting his arm protectively around her.

"Come along, Lizzy." Lydia stood by her side. "Let's find a place to sit and rest." She took Lizzy by the hand and found a deck chair. Lizzy sat down as Lydia knelt beside her. Neither of them spoke.

A deckhand looked their way, then came over and handed them a pair of blankets to help ward off the frigid wind coming off the sea.

All Lizzy could think about was Darcy. She refused a man who gave his life for another... someone he didn't even know. There were so many times that she could have mended the breach between them but didn't. Now, it was too late.

She looked down at Lydia, who rested her head on Elizabeth's knee, and laid her hand on her head. So much loss... for both of them. She laid her head back on the canvas and wrapped the blanket tightly around her. The world seemed grey and lifeless. All hope was lost.

"Lydia?"

Lydia suddenly jerked away as Lizzy opened her eyes.

"George, Georgie. Oh, thank goodness. I thought you were drowned. Oh, Georgie." Lydia ran and threw her arms around Wickham.

Lizzy gaped open-mouthed at Wickham. How could he have survived? He pulled a blanket around his shoulders, hair dishevelled, waiter's coat crushed and wrinkled, linen trousers rumpled below the knee. Elizabeth looked at his unshaven face and felt weighted down with bags of sand. She couldn't move from her seat.

"Goerge, she's just found out that Mr Darcy has been lost," whispered Lydia.

Wickham said nothing, but after he disentangled himself from Lydia, he knelt beside Lizzy.

Was it Elizabeth's imagination or did he look genuinely distressed at the news?

Wickham made his best rendition of a sympathetic expression. "Oh, bad luck. Bad news. So much bad news on this ship this morning." He tut-tutted and shook his head.

"I hear congratulations are in order." Lizzy managed to say something.

He cocked a brow and managed a strained smile. "Oh, thank you so much. Yes, we were married last night."

"I thought you were to be married in New York." It felt her words were spoken through fog.

"Ah, yes… that was the original plan, but then we thought why wait?"

"Yes, why wait?" Lydia clung to Wickham's arm and chirped cheerfully. "Won't Mama and Papa be surprised?"

Elizabeth shot her a look, but it seemed to bounce off into the morning air. "I believe that they will be waiting to hear if we survived. No doubt, the news of the sinking will reach England before we land in New York."

Lydia's smile faded. "I didn't think of that." She looked down at the deck for a moment, then her head popped up again. "No matter. They will know soon enough that we are alive and that I am Mrs George Wickham." Lydia made a little pout. "Do you think you will be all right for a while, Lizzy? I'd like to take a walk with… my husband." She was bursting with joy.

Elizabeth couldn't wait for her to leave.

"Yes, please do. Go, but try to be discreet. There are so many in pain on this vessel." Lydia nodded solemnly, but then wrapped her hand around her husband's arm and, smiling ear to ear, trotted off with him. All Elizabeth wanted at that moment was to be alone with her grief, to weep, to cry out at the unfairness of life, but the ship was overcrowded and many of her fellow passengers were on deck with her. She sat back and looked out over the cloudless sky, thinking of all she had lost.

Chapter 35

In three days, they reached New York. The *Carpathia* steamed into the harbour under a foggy, weeping sky. As they docked, Lizzy heard the bells tolling from everywhere in the city, marking how she and the survivors had arrived spectres from a ghost ship. Photographers came in close, flash powder igniting in their faces as they disembarked. On the dock, they were instructed to enter partitions alphabetically arranged according to their last names. Of course, no one was there to meet them, but Elizabeth insisted on standing about in the D partition, hoping against hope that somehow they had neglected to find Mr Darcy on the crowded *Carpathia,* but he would be there, waiting for her. She sent her sister and Wickham to the B partition in case Mr Darcy would look for her there. The reasonable part of her mind told her that he was dead at the bottom of the sea, but like so many of the wailing widows around her, she hoped against hope that he still walked among the living. After nearly all of the crowd had dispersed, most in despair, Lydia persuaded Elizabeth to abandon her vigil.

Lydia no longer clung to her once Wickham was found. Why he was alive was cruelty to Elizabeth. If Mr Darcy had arranged for him to "do right" by Lydia, no doubt he would see none of the money he was promised if he abandoned her. Even if Mr Darcy himself wasn't there to oversee the arrangement, he likely had solicitors who would.

To those like Lizzy who'd washed up on their shore in the midst of the horror, the citizens of the great City of New York took care of them and ushered them into a waiting room on the dock.

The Red Cross sorted through the survivors who had lost everything and had no one to meet them on friendly shore, mostly the ones who had no means of housing or feeding themselves for the foreseeable future.

Wickham pushed through the crowd; his brow furrowed.

"We are being sent back tomorrow," he said out of breath, "Lydia and me."

"What do you mean, George?" Lydia glanced at Lizzy. "Just you and me? What about Lizzy?"

"The shipping line will house the crew for the night and are sending us home on the *Lapland* tomorrow." He looked at Lizzy with more concern than she had ever seen in his face. "I can see if I can find a place for you too, Elizabeth."

Lizzy couldn't think. What would she do in New York alone? What if Mr Darcy was still alive, perhaps in another boat and was rescued by another ship? She couldn't just go back to England not knowing. She knew it was illogical, even hopelessly ridiculous. Here she was in a strange land, with only the clothes on her back and in the care of strangers, but she couldn't go.

"No, it's all right. You two go. Go back. I will follow shortly."

"I don't think it's wise, Elizabeth. Let me see what can be done."

"All right, George. See what you can do."

Lydia gazed wide-eyed at Wickham, and he patted her arm. After walking briskly to the area where the Red Cross was processing passengers, he disappeared into the crowd.

"You can't stay here alone, Lizzy," Lydia said quietly. "You can't. Come with us."

"It may not be possible. You know that. I will sort something out."

"But why? Why stay? There is nothing for you here."

What could she tell her? That she was nursing a fantasy in which she waited for a lover who would never return? That was the truth of it, although something created out of the pure stubbornness of denial made her resist running back home.

Wickham came back over and had in tow a middle-aged woman, her face creased with kindness. She wore a long white dress and a rather oddly shaped head covering that looked somewhat like a nun's veil. Wickham sighed. "I'm sorry, Elizabeth, but there's no room on the *Lapland* for you."

The woman came over and patted her hand. "I'm Sister Mary Harris. We can find lodgings for you and provisions while you book your return voyage, if that is what you want. Come along. We'll make arrangements."

Lizzy rose from her seat, and embracing Lydia, she held her for longer than she intended. "Go on. Your place is with your husband. Tell everyone I will see them soon."

After a moment, Wickham took Lydia's arm and led her away, and as she looked back at Lizzy, tears streaked her face. They disappeared into the evening shadows.

Within the hour, Elizabeth was introduced to a Red Cross volunteer, a woman called Marjorie, who, with carpetbag in hand and a business-like manner, took her on the streetcar through the streets of New York. Lizzy stared out the window, seeing but not seeing, as images flashed by.

Lizzy received temporary shelter near a place called Columbus Circle. The streets were numbered instead of having names, and she and her companion made their way to 58th Street. For a moment, she stood on a pathway in front of a group of row houses her companion called brownstones. A large stone stairway with six steps led to the house proper, but Marjorie took her to a stairway that dipped downward from the street.

"Here you are, my dear, and here's the key." She pressed five dollars into Lizzy's hand and set down a carpetbag that held clothing and some toiletries. Another bag held groceries. A single streetlight glowed by the sidewalk, but shadows shrouded the doorway. After fumbling with the key, she turned the lock. Her companion reached for a light, and a yellow glow lit up the place. The apartment was small: a sitting room, a bedroom, and a kitchen. Elizabeth was impressed that here in America, a bathroom with a toilet, sink, and bathtub were here for her exclusive use.

"I know it's not much, but..." Marjorie began. She was a well-dressed woman, near her age, who surveyed each room they entered with a sceptical cock of her brow. She had the oddest regional accent, not at all like Mr Selfridge's, that Elizabeth found charming.

"It is lovely. It will do nicely until I can..." She wanted to say more, but her throat closed, and her eyes began to water. Marjorie laid her hand on Elizabeth's arm. Her tone softened.

"Would you like me to stay a while?"

Elizabeth shook her head. "I am rather tired, if you don't mind. I'd like to just take a bath and go to bed."

"I'll look in on you tomorrow." With that, she left, closing the door behind her. Elizabeth sat on the tufted red velvet sofa and gave way to tears. After hiccupping from sobbing, she shook her head, wiped her eyes and stood up.

"Enough of this. Time for a cup of tea." With a determined air, she grasped the bag of groceries and headed into the kitchen. Unpacking bread, eggs, and a bit of butter, she found not tea—but coffee. "Well, old girl. You are really in America now."

***

Lizzy spent two days walking between the telegraph office and the bank, trying to arrange for funds to be sent from home. Her new friend from the Red Cross arrived the next day to help familiarise her with the shops and neighbourhood. The New York subway was easy for her to navigate, as she had taken the Tube so many times whilst living in London. The constant errands between the White Star Line offices, the Western Union, the bank, the shops to buy necessities, and the exploration of her new, albeit temporary, neighbourhood gave her little time to think of the horrors of the last few days. Her second day in New York she'd seen Wickham and Lydia off at the dock on the *Lapland*. She hoped that Lydia would be all right. Just thinking about getting on another ship so soon after the tragedy made her blood run cold.

But, for good or ill, she had her passage booked for the following week and retreated to her garden apartment in the brownstone she now called home. A massive park stood a short walk from her house, and she spent her second afternoon exploring there. Elizabeth resolved to spend every afternoon here before her ship left for home. It gave her comfort to be out amongst the grass and trees. The first of the spring flowers were also in bloom. Towards evening, she returned to her dark little apartment, grateful to have shelter and food, but alone in the great city.

She sat in solitude there at night, a single bulb illuminating the kitchen table as she pored over the *New York Times*, reading every word about the *Titanic*'s colossal loss of life. Every day the numbers of the dead were revised and grew larger until she could read no more, and tumbling the papers into the rubbish bin, she gave up every hope that Mr Darcy was still amongst the living.

Chapter 36

"Elizabeth."

Darcy heard the croaking sound of his own voice as his eyes fluttered open. Clutching the sheets, he braced for movement of a ship, but none came, and he let out a shaky breath as he tried to twist his head and look around.

"Doctor, he's awake."

Doctor? He was in hospital? Darcy tried to sit up, but gave up as his head swam. He closed his eyes again as someone reached around him and helped him sit up.

Wincing, he opened his eyes.

A woman in a white cap and a long-sleeved grey gown smiled in her struggle to get him upright. With all the strength he could muster, the two of them managed it, and before he could ask, she set a glass of water between his lips.

"Take it easy… take it easy… slowly…"

He finally took a breath. "Thank you, sister. I was quite thirsty." She smiled kindly at him and retreated before a balding man in a brown gaberdine suit, stethoscope about his neck, took her place, scrutinizing him.

"You are a miracle, you are." The doctor probed under Darcy's jaw and then proceeded to open the white gown Darcy wore and apply the cold, tiny horn of the stethoscope to his chest.

Darcy shivered as his thoughts began to clear. "*Titanic*. Did it sink?" He couldn't remember. "Miss Elizabeth Bennet. Did she survive?"

"Shush. Take a deep breath." After listening attentively, the doctor turned to the nurse. "No sign of pneumonia… heart sounds good…" Then directing his attention to Darcy, he said, "You are a very lucky man. You seem to have come out of this unscathed."

"But the *Titanic*—"

"At the bottom of the ocean taking more than fifteen hundred souls with her."

"Oh."

The doctor turned to the nurse again. "Call the Red Cross and see if they can send someone over. I'm sure Mr… Mr…" He shot an inquisitive glance towards Darcy.

"Darcy. Fitzwilliam Darcy of Pemberley."

"Yes, Mr Darcy… see to it that you get some food into him. Start with broth—"

"But the ship… I need to find someone… I—"

The doctor moved on to the patient in the next bed, ignoring him. Fluffing his pillow, the nurse nodded to him. "I'll get you something to eat and then I'll answer all your questions. Just rest now."

"No, wait. I have to know…" But she bustled off.

A mass of confused thoughts hit Darcy all at once. *What of Georgiana, his Aunt Catherine, even Bingley? Did they all think he was dead?* How did he get here? Was Elizabeth rescued? If she was, why wasn't she here?

The questions swirled about as sleep overtook him once again.

***

Entering the subway, Elizabeth knew that she wasn't seeing sense, but she needed to get to the Red Cross building to inquire if any more survivors had been rescued after the *Carpathia* left. Logically, her efforts were futile. Word reached New York that the body of

John Jacob Astor was found along with other corpses, floating in the freezing, iceberg-infested waters where the *Titanic* lay in its watery grave. At least the Astors knew for certain that their loved one was lost. Darcy *was* lost. She knew and yet she didn't know.

Unsure of where to go, she walked over to an attendant. "Could you tell me how to get to 49th Street and 10th Avenue, please?"

He looked her up and down and shook his head. "Hell's Kitchen…. That's no place for a lady."

The response made her even more determined, and she took a map instead. She'd have to walk a few city blocks from the subway to reach it, and she'd have to walk unaccompanied. Arriving at her destination and stepping out into the sunlight, she understood now why the attendant tried to discourage her.

Newspapers floated by in the breeze as piles of rotting vegetables and horse excrement littered the pathways. Squalling infants sat in the laps of filthy children on tenement stairways. Men who passed her mumbled obscenities. She wanted to run but knew that would be a mistake. Instead, she walked at a steady pace, head held high, not speaking to anyone.

It was nearly two o'clock in the afternoon when she reached the Red Cross building. For the second day in a row, she scanned the list of survivors of the *Titanic* that was now displayed in the window. It hadn't changed. Mr Fitzwilliam Darcy was still numbered amongst the lost.

Biting her bottom lip, she resolved not to give way to tears as so many of the women did who stood by her shoulder to shoulder, gazing up and down the lists. No, she would not give up hope. Tomorrow, she would return and look again. She would look again and again, up until the day her ship left for home.

***

Darcy finally set foot on the New York pavement. Five days…. Five days from the night of his plunge into the frigid, inky blackness of the Atlantic. A volunteer from Bellevue Hospital finally found the time to tell Darcy his remarkable tale. Someone in one of the *Titanic*'s lifeboats pulled him from the water just as the screaming aft hull of the *Titanic* plummeted to its grave. He nearly drowned. They'd had a difficult time taking hold of him, covered in grease as he was. These brave and heroic folk aboard the lifeboat kept him from freezing to death while they waited for the rescue ship, the *Carpathia,* to arrive. He remembered none of it. He'd left the *Carpathia* unconscious on a stretcher. He awoke in Bellevue Hospital three days after the sinking. His rescuers must have brought him here. No one knew who he was. He arrived in America in the state in which he arrived in the world as an infant. As soon as he was strong enough to move about, he obtained a list of survivors of the tragedy.

Elizabeth, Lydia, and even that coward Wickham were all listed as survivors, but Darcy knew no more than that. His only hope in finding Elizabeth was to visit the Red Cross headquarters in a place called Hell's Kitchen. He didn't like the sound of the place, but there was nothing to be done. The doctor gave him five dollars of his own, as Darcy refused to wait another minute at the hospital. No doubt, his hotel reservation had been cancelled and he hoped against hope that the money he had arranged for at the Security Bank of New York was waiting for him there. Of course, would anyone believe that he was Fitzwilliam Darcy? According to all the records of the tragedy, Fitzwilliam Darcy was dead... and then there was his current attire.

Someone else's underclothes, a shirt without a collar, a brown woollen suitcoat, gaberdine trousers held up with braces, but still puddling around scuffed shoes that were a trifle too small for him... he was dressed in clothes donated to the indigent at the hospital. They had no proper hat to give him, so he wore a flat cap that threatened repeatedly to fall down over his eyes. Thusly attired, he walked up First Avenue in search of a Western Union office where he spent most of the five American dollars he was given by the Red Cross.

WESTERN UNION
CABLEGRAM

Harpenden, Hertfordshire

   I survived sinking Titanic stop Telephone Bingley Aunt Catherine and Huntley. Elizabeth Bennet?

Fitzwilliam Darcy

The telegram cost more than he expected, and he thought ruefully that this was the first time in his life he was seriously worried about money. He fingered the meagre bills and coins in his pocket. He was quite weak from not having eaten in the three days he was unconscious aboard the *Carpathia* and refused to stay in the hospital past a day to regain his strength. He had to find Elizabeth.

Armed with a map of the New York subway, the address of his bank, the Red Cross, and the White Star Line, he set out first to retrieve his funds at the bank. Once he had money, he could reach the Red Cross office and get further information on the *Titanic* survivors.

The bespectacled clerk at the window squinted with beady eyes and a look of general distaste at Darcy. "Do you have any proof you are who you say you are?"

"It is at the bottom of the ocean, my good man." Darcy attempted to remain calm. It was fortunate for the clerk that there were bars across the teller window or Darcy would have lunged through it and taken the little martinet by the collar and shaken him until his teeth rattled.

The two men glared at each other like two fighting cocks, when the clerk sighed. "A moment please."

He walked to a desk at the back of the bank where sat an impeccably dressed clean-shaven gentleman with white hair, wearing a rather expensive-looking grey suit and an air of authority. The clerk kept gesturing towards Darcy and after some moments returned to the window with a clipboard and a paper.

"Did you say your name is Darcy?"

"Yes, I told you… Fitzwilliam Darcy."

The clerk surveyed the paper in his hand, running his finger down the page. Stopping at one spot, he twisted the paper towards Darcy. "Fitzwilliam Darcy is listed as one of the lost. Shame on you for trying to withdraw his funds. Have you no respect for the dead?" Raising one eyebrow, he directed his gaze to the cap in Darcy's hand and surveyed his ragtag appearance once again. "Get out of here before I call the police."

Darcy wouldn't be put off so easily. "Let me speak to the manager. I can explain everything."

"Do you have anything to prove that you are this Mr Darcy?"

Darcy sighed. "No, I lost everything when I swam away from the ship."

The clerk's eyes crinkled, and he looked from one side to the other at his fellow tellers. "Did you hear that, boys? This jolly good fellow went swimming with the icebergs." He shook his head in disbelief, and casting his eye over Darcy's head, he gestured to someone on the other side of the bank.

Within moments, two burly bank guards threw Darcy out into the street.

He lost his footing and splayed across the sidewalk. The bustling crowd parted like the Red Sea around him as he struggled to his feet. Casting about for a safe haven, he spied a small gap between the bank and the building next to it and made for it. Leaning against the solidness of the building, he tried to take stock of his situation. He was furious at the teller, judging him by his clothes and his reduced circumstances and giving him no chance to explain himself. Gaining access to his funds would have to wait. Unfolding his small map, he decided on his next destination. His sartorial expression might in fact be an asset for where he was going. There it was, Hell's Kitchen. After dusting off his trouser legs and his jacket, he made for the subway.

***

Seated at a desk overflowing with ragged papers arranged haphazardly in piles that overflowed onto the floor, the young man scrutinised Darcy.

"You were taken aboard the *Carpathia,* you say."

"I assume so. I was unconscious when I was brought aboard. Whoever pulled me from the water kept me alive until the rescue ship came upon the scene. I'm told the *Titanic* had already sunk by that time."

"You were in the water?" The young man adjusted owl-like eyeglasses that threatened to slip down his nose.

"The lifeboats were all gone."

"Amazing… amazing… Yes, of course, Mr Darcy. We will amend the lists of survivors to include you. It will be posted and distributed tomorrow. I'm sure your family will be relieved to hear that you are still with us… so many were lost…"

This was Darcy's opportunity. "Yes, regarding that… I am looking for my… fiancée…a Miss Elizabeth Bennet. She was rescued. She had to be. I put her in a lifeboat myself… I was wondering if you might know her whereabouts…"

A rustle of paper came from behind the piles of documents that separated him from the Red Cross officer. "Hmm…. Miss Elizabeth… Bennet did you say? Hmmm…." After some minutes of fruitless search, the young officer looked up at Darcy with a sheepish grin. "I'm afraid I don't have her exact whereabouts. You see, we don't have everything collected in a central location… the swiftness of the accident and the great need, you know… If you could come back tomorrow."

Darcy planted both hands on the piles of papers on the desk as he stood. "Can't you tell me anything? By tomorrow, she may have left for England."

"Now, now, sir, don't get excited..." He shuffled through more papers and retrieved one. "I can tell you that many of the survivors are temporarily housed in some brownstones on 58th and 59th Street near Central Park... but if you come back tomorrow..."

Darcy was already out the door. Here was something... something he could finally hold on to. It would be a matter of minutes or perhaps hours and he would see Elizabeth again. How difficult would it be to find her? He still had some hours of daylight left. By the clock in the clerk's office, it was nearing three. He would find her soon. How big could this Central Park be?

***

Elizabeth needed to clear her head. Even though it looked like it might rain at any moment, she stopped at her temporary domicile for a quick bite of lunch and walked to Central Park. How marvellous it was to have this gigantic green space in the heart of a bustling city. The Red Cross was kind enough to provide her with an umbrella, and being English, she was no stranger to rain. In fact, if truth be told, she preferred it when out for her strolls. It enveloped her in kind of a hush that left her alone with her thoughts.

Elizabeth made her way around Columbus Circle and entered the park near 59th Street. She had only been in the city two days and had already visited the park twice. She made her way toward the centre of the park, where she had learned from the grocer that a Literary Walk existed. He suggested that she might want to visit a statue of Shakespeare there to make her feel more at home. He couldn't know how she longed for home. Although this great metropolis welcomed the survivors with open arms, she couldn't help but feel that the memory of their ordeal was already fading from the public consciousness. Only she and the weeping widows of the *Titanic* would carry that night inside themselves forever.

Small paths and large avenues split the park into a picturesque mosaic, and many well-dressed men in bowler hats and tailored suits walked along with their wives or sweethearts on their arms. Children ran about, and she stopped to give a penny to an organ grinder's monkey who made the children giggle as it danced about on the sidewalk with its tiny hat in its hand.

As she neared the leafy avenue, a gentle drizzle began to splash on the path. Many around her began to hurry away at the first sign of rain, but she dreaded returning to her dark, lonely abode, and so walked on. The wind intensified and threatened to puff her umbrella inside out, so she leaned it against the wind and, turning about, made for home.

***

Darcy rattled along in the electric streetcar, elbows on his thighs, and stared at the rubbery floor. He'd never even considered this mode of transportation in his native London, and now, this was his second journey on such a conveyance in this strange city. His compatriots spoke myriad of languages, some of which he never heard even though he'd travelled extensively. Many of the men were dressed as he was, labourers, no doubt, come to seek their fortune in the Land of Opportunity. From the looks of them, many hadn't found it. Etched in their faces was the grinding work of the factory or mill, relentless, back-breaking labour with little pay. How many men, just like this, were at the bottom of the Atlantic?

The wooden car was strewn with lights that illuminated the map he retrieved from his pocket. The nearest he could reckon, he should take the streetcar to Columbus Circle and begin walking there. The car rattled to a stop. He gave a lady his seat and hung one-handed from a strap. No one met another's eye unless they were travelling together. He focused his attention out the window on the bustling inhabitants as he rattled past.

With Christopher Columbus presiding from a monolith in the centre of the great traffic circle, he leapt off the streetcar, finding that the April weather wasn't on his side. A sharp gust of wind hit him. He missed his woollen overcoat, now at the bottom of the sea, and turned up the collar on his patched jacket, pulling his cap low over his eyes so as not to lose it.

The park stood on his right, and streets radiated out from every direction. He found he was already on 59th Street and began walking along. The buildings in America were of a tremendous size and girth. How he would find Elizabeth in this mass of brick and mortar was anyone's guess. The skies darkened with every step, and gusts of wind drove shards of cold rain into his eyes. This wouldn't do at all. A row of massive brick and stone buildings, more than ten stories high, lined the street, and he ran up some stone steps and ducked under the white archway of the nearest building to save himself from the onslaught. Shivering, he leaned his head against the cold, ungiving stone, and gave way to despair. What was he thinking? He should have sorted himself out before trying to find Elizabeth. The man said "tomorrow". Could he not wait until then?

When the rain stopped, he would return to Hell's Kitchen and find a bed for ten cents a night. He would find Elizabeth tomorrow.

From his perch at the entrance to an apartment building, Darcy watched people rushing down the street, newspapers over their heads, umbrellas in their hands. The rain spattered the pavement, making small, rapid splashes as it poured down. A young woman, her face hidden beneath an umbrella, struggled against the wind. A man running in the opposite direction was trying to hail a taxi, and they looked to collide at any moment.

"Look out. *Look out,*" Darcy cried.

The man looked up and splashed off the curb into the street, cursing. The woman lowered her umbrella and stopped dead in her tracks, looking about frantically.

Elizabeth? His heart pounded in his chest. *"Elizabeth."*

Elizabeth's umbrella slipped from her fingers and somersaulted down the street with a gust of wind. Rain pelleted her cloche hat and ran in rivulets down her upturned face. She began to walk against the crowd as if in a trance, pedestrians jumping out of her way or pushing past her.

Darcy couldn't move, then shaking off the shock, he ran to the bottom of the stairs and pulled her into the shelter of the stone archway.

"D-Darcy?"

A buttery, soft light emanated through the windows of the apartment house lobby, bathing Elizabeth's rain-splashed face in a supernatural glow. She didn't speak, but touched his face with both hands, examining it as if she were blind. Then she patted his chest and ran her hands down his shoulders as if trying to convince herself that he was real.

"Darcy?" she whispered again. "I... I thought... How...? How did you..." She staggered backward slightly, and he caught her in his arms.

He swallowed, eyes filling, and he opened his mouth to speak, but not a word would escape. Instead, he kissed her cool, wet cheek and then her lips, softly, gently at first, and then with an urgency met equally by hers. She broke away, and clasping the back of his neck, she pulled his head into the nape of her neck, winding her other arm around his waist and pulling him against her with all her strength.

"Thank God. Thank God. Thank God."

Darcy began to pepper her neck with soft kisses when a sharp jab with an elbow hit him just below the kidney.

"For Christ's sake, take the lady upstairs. Doncha have any class?"

Darcy turned his head as the man by the doorway unlocked the door of the building and slammed it behind him with a hard look back at Darcy.

All he could do was laugh, and laugh and laugh, almost to the point of hysteria. He fought to gain control of himself. Finding Elizabeth this way pulled every nerve from his body and exposed them to the air.

Elizabeth laughed softly with him and touched his cheek. "Come. Let's go home."

She took him by the hand and led him down the stairs into the dark street.

Chapter 37

They reached the steps of her temporary dwelling, and she led him down from the street level to her garden apartment. Closing the door behind them, she let the light flicker on, then ran a look over him in wonder. Hair tussled from the rain, he raked his hands through it. His chin bore the signs of a day's growth of dark whisker, and as he removed his coat, he looked a bit thinner than he did when she saw him step from the pool at Netherfield. A million questions still danced in her mind, but she couldn't snatch one long enough to ask it. She wanted to tell him over and over again that she loved him, but all she could find to say was, "Are you hungry? I have some stew in the ice box."

Darcy smiled. "That sounds marvellous. I don't think I've eaten since this morning at the hospital."

Lizzy was already in the small kitchen by the time he finished his sentence, and she peered around the corner at him. "Hospital? Why were you in hospital? Tell me everything."

He drew up behind her and gingerly placed his hands on her waist. She moved to the stove. "I don't suppose you could make us a cup of tea…" he asked. Of course. Tea.

She leaned against him and closed her eyes a moment. "In the pantry. I found some tea at the grocer's this morning. There's milk in the icebox."

They felt awkward together, the passion of their meeting lost back in that shelter from the rain. Getting them both something to eat. That's what she would do… and just look at him.

They sat down to two bowls of stew, bread from the Russian bakery and butter, and a pot of tea. She ate slowly, watching him. He was ravenous. By the second bowl, he'd told her of his swim in the iceberg-strewn Atlantic, of his resignation to death as his limbs slowly froze, and his awakening at Bellevue Hospital.

A pensive look crossed his face as he settled into silence for a moment. "You didn't, by any chance, find a person on board called Lev… Lev… something with a "ski" at the end of it?"

"Lev Shklovsky."

His dark eyes sparkled. "Yes, that was his name. He was rescued, then?"

Lizzy nodded. "He was, and his wife and child…" She blinked slowly, the scene aboard the *Carpathia* instantly before her eyes—Darcy was dead. He'd given his place to another, then he disappeared as their lifeboat was lowered… rowing through the black night… rending metal, the strange keening of a thousand voices as they desperately clawed as the near vertical deck of the great vessel dragged them to their deaths.

Darcy spoke, but she couldn't hear him. His face was the perfect image of joy unburdened of suffering. But her throat closed with sorrow, a paralysis of grief.

He stopped talking for a moment to finish his meal, and she felt herself floating away. In panic, she reached over and grabbed his forearm to anchor herself, and for no reason that she could fathom, the tears came. Not just coursing down her cheeks, but a great silent howl that she tried desperately to release. No sound came, then as she sucked in a breath, the great wracking sobs gushed forth in wave after wave. She had no control over them. They vomited out of her like a long-suppressed infection that his presence had finally lanced.

Darcy abandoned his chair and lifted her from her seat. He didn't speak, or if he did, she didn't hear him. He drew her down on the sofa, wrapping her in his arms. He rested his cheek upon her head, holding her tight against him. She trembled, the cold, merciless water of the Atlantic finally seeping into her bones, freezing her. The memory of the dark water lapping against the sides of the lifeboat, the shrieking of the thousand voices of the doomed, the monolith disappearing into the depths, all kept at bay for so long, now flooded over her. She wept and coughed and wept again. How long he held her, she didn't know, but after a time, the crying stopped, and she was breathing hard as she did as a girl when she ran from Longbourn to Meryton. This time, there was no joy in it. She was suddenly very tired.

***

The unmitigated relief Darcy felt when he'd first laid eyes on Elizabeth took a sudden turn into desperation. Until he held her, her shaking fragility in his arms, he had no idea of the toll the events of the last week had taken on her strength and independence. She shifted from his embrace and got shakily to her feet. He held out his hand to her, and she took it to steady herself and then let it go. She straightened her hair and walked back to the table. With trembling hands, she shakily finished the tea that had gone cold in her cup. Taking a deep breath, she excused herself to the water closet. Darcy sat, staring after her.

After a few moments, she came back out and leaned against the doorjamb, shivering, her body the essence of exhaustion.

"Come." He stood and waited. "Let's get you to bed."

He thought perhaps she'd have a teasing retort for such a notion, but her eyes were dull and full of suffering.

She took his hand this time, and after leading her to the bedroom, she sat heavily on the edge of the bed. He knelt down and unbuttoned her shoes, then slid them off. Leaning over, she attempted to roll down her stockings, but wobbled and then caught herself before she fell back.

A thousand times he had envisioned such a scene in his fevered imagination, but never under such heartrending circumstances.

He shifted her skirt slightly, exposing her thighs, and one by one, he rolled her stockings down as she attempted to undo the bodice of her dress. Her hands shook and wouldn't obey her, so he undid the clasps and eased it over her head. Her hair spiked in utter disarray, and he painstakingly removed all the pins until it fell lifelessly to her shoulders. Still restrained in her corset, he divested her of it. Dressed now only in her chemise and drawers, she put a hand to her head, looking more and more unsteady, and he eased her back to rest upon the pillow. She curled herself in a ball, and even though the room was warm, she shivered.

"Cold," she said.

He stood there for a moment, battling with himself. They weren't married. Everything he ever learned about what society allowed, about what he felt was right, warred with his inclination. As a gentleman, he should keep his distance, now, especially. But there she was, his Elizabeth, shivering and shaking with torment. She needed him. He needed to hold her, comfort her. Could that be wrong? What did it matter, right or wrong, acceptable or unsuitable? Here they were in a strange land, among strangers, having survived a monumental tragedy. So why did he still hesitate?

"C-cold," she whispered.

He hesitated no longer. After taking down his braces, he slipped out of his trousers and laid them on the foot of the bed, then undid the buttons of his shirt. Clad only in his underclothes, he lay down next to her, the mattress springs squeaking slightly as he pulled her close. Within seconds, she turned in to him, nestling her head on his shoulder, her breathing ragged from sobbing. Pulling the blanket to cover her back, he rested his cheek in her hair and his own reserve began to splinter.

Elizabeth didn't speak or attempt to look at him. He couldn't think anymore, only feel. Was it unmanly of him to weep with her? Grateful she couldn't see his face, tears slipped from his eyes. He rubbed her back and shoulder as she nestled into him, her body unwinding from its protective curl. He wanted to wail and cry out, just as she did, to add his voice to the great screaming howl of the lost ship that he so fortunately escaped. Instead, he gulped the warm air of the room, and let his silent tears spill into her hair. He could not bring himself to release her, even to wipe them away. Her breathing eventually slowed into the pattern of slumber, and kissing the crown of her head, he gave way to sleep.

***

The tolling of the noon bells roused Lizzy. She turned over and ran her hand over the bed. Empty save herself. For a moment, she tried to recollect the events of the previous evening. Of one thing she was sure—Darcy had spent the night in her bed.

"Darcy?" She called out his name once, twice, thrice. No answer. Pulling the blanket over her shoulders, she peered through the open door of the bedroom into the sitting room. The dishes from the previous night were gone, and a folded piece of paper leaned against the sugar bowl.

She went over and picked it up. In pencil the words *Dearest Elizabeth* were scrawled. She opened it.

My Darling Elizabeth,
I have gone back to the bank in search of my money, and failing that, to the Western Union to send a telegram to my solicitor. Those two activities will probably bankrupt me for the moment, so you will be my sole means of support.

She crinkled her eyes in amusement before a sudden wave of panic overtook her.

What if he never came back?

She had no doubt that he would never abandon her through his own volition, but what if he was struck by a streetcar or an automobile? These Americans insisted on driving on the wrong side of the road. If he forgot that for a moment, then....

Sitting heavily, she leaned her elbows on the table and rested her head in her hands. *Stop it, Lizzy. Stop it this instant.* She'd never felt this way in her life. It was as if every ounce of strength she possessed had drained. Forcing herself to read on, she spread the letter on the table.

I will be back as soon as I can. I hope you can forgive me for leaving you alone this morning, but you were sleeping so peacefully, I didn't want to wake you. Say a prayer that the bank is more understanding this morning. We can make our plans after that.

Yours Always,
Darcy

She rose from the table and stood for a moment. A lightness of spirit filled her for the first time since... since that waltz at Netherfield. He was hers. She read the words again... *Yours Always, Darcy*. She wondered if her cheeks would begin to ache from smiling so much. Taking a breath, she marched back into the bedroom. There were things to do, not the least of which was to bathe and dress. Darcy would be back.

Chapter 38

Mr Huntley, of Huntley and Associates, was a shrewd man, and never, ever again would Darcy entertain the thought that he paid his honoured solicitor too much money. Reentering the Security Bank of New York for the second time, Darcy looked even more bedraggled than he did the previous day. The rain did nothing for the cut of his oversize suit, his shirt was a bit worse for wear, and although he'd bathed that morning, his underclothes had not.

Unfortunately, the clerk who had him ejected the previous day wasn't at the window. The new lad, on hearing his name, immediately reported to his grey-haired superior, and Darcy was escorted to a wood panelled office in the back where he was given tea and courtesy.

"We are so sorry for your inconvenience of yesterday, Mr Darcy." The bank manager wouldn't meet Darcy's eye but kept his attention on the papers on his desk. A telegram sat atop his documents. He waved it in Darcy's direction. "Your solicitor in London sent us information that you had, indeed, survived the sinking of the *Titanic*, and that your funds should be released to you posthaste." When Darcy didn't reply, he continued, sputtering a bit. "You can understand our scepticism, Mr Darcy, surely. I mean, the way you are dressed…"

"As I explained to your clerk yesterday, my clothes are at the bottom of the sea, under an iceberg."

"Yes, yes, of course. So sorry…"

"Perhaps, in future, you should not be so quick to judge people merely by their appearance." He curled his mouth into a half smile. Did those words really come out of his mouth?

"Yes, yes of course. How stupid of me. I hope this won't affect any business dealings we may have in the future…"

Within minutes, Darcy cashed a sizable bank note and, hailing a taxi, headed off to the nearest department store.

***

21 April 1912

Dear Papa, Mama, Kitty, and Mary,

By the time you read this letter, I may already be back in England. Due to the quick thinking and persistence of Mr Darcy, both Lydia and I survived the sinking of the Titanic. *I'm sure you know by now that Lydia is married to Mr Wickham. They should arrive back on your shores before this post. Please be gentle with Lydia. She has been through a great deal.*

The Carpathia *plucked us from the sea just as the sun was rising and we were brought to New York. The Red Cross has been very helpful. They found me some clothes, a place to live, food, and even some money for post and such things. I am near a large, lovely park in the heart of the city called Central Park. I wish you could see it. Just like everything here, it is much larger than any park back home.*

Mr Darcy, although he did not come along with us in our boat, and gave his place to another, somehow survived the sinking by swimming away from the ship. The sea was full of ice and so cold that one could freeze within minutes, but he managed to get away and was rescued by another lifeboat. We found each other yesterday.

Seated at the table, Elizabeth stopped writing for a moment and fluffed her fingers through her hair. Bathing, dealing with her coiffure, and dressing had taken up much of the afternoon. Darcy still hadn't returned, and she fought down this roiling ball of panic that seethed in her belly. Writing to her parents was helping somewhat, but she could never reveal to them what she really felt. After putting the pencil down, she reread what she had written, and resting her elbows on the table, she knit her fingers together and pressed them to her lips. What else could she tell them?

Startling her, a knock came at the door.

"Elizabeth… Lizzy… open the door."

Darcy.

Releasing her breath and smiling, she quickly got up and headed over.

When she opened the door, Darcy stood there so laden with boxes, Elizabeth could barely see his face.

Carefully dodging her, he eased past, followed by a dapper-looking chap with black hair parted in the middle and slicked down so extremely as to appear painted on. He carried a towel over the arm of his cutaway jacket and pushed in a tray covered in a white tablecloth and dinner plates.

"That's right. Bring it in here. Very good." From beside the door, Darcy cocked his head and waved him in.

As Lizzy eased aside, she didn't know where to look first. The waiter snapped a white tablecloth in the air, and it settled like a landing dove on their table. With practiced efficiency, he began to lay out the place settings, dishes, and the like. Darcy deposited the boxes he carried on a small table near the door and removed his hat and coat. He was much changed from the morning. His labourer's cap was replaced by a smart homburg, his inadequate sodden coat, by a navy-blue ulster. His suit was grey with hints of navy striping, and peeking from it a new shirt, collar, and tie. He was also clean-shaven. When he'd dismissed the waiter, he took her hands in his and pulled her towards him. The fragrance of clean wool and witch hazel drifted over.

The minute the door closed, leaving them alone, Lizzy threw her arms around his neck and pressed her cheek to his. As she leaned back to look at him, a look of concern crossed his face.

"Are you all right?"

"Of course." Her reply gurgled out of her mouth as her voice broke slightly. She was angry at her body for betraying her. She let go of him and turned toward the table. "It looks like quite a feast." Again, her voice trembled ever so slightly. She cleared her throat and wouldn't look at him.

"I'm a stupid fellow. I should never have left you." He stepped up behind her and put his arms around her waist.

"Don't be silly..." When she turned to face him, her eyes filled again. After breaking from his embrace, she clutched the back of the chair. "I don't know what the matter is with me. I really don't." She walked to the two front windows and drew the curtains as dusk approached.

"There's nothing the matter with you that isn't also the matter with me."

Of any words of comfort he could have said, those were the most surprising. Now she could look him in the eye. He held his hands out to her.

"What are you talking about? Look at you. You're a tower of strength." His gaze was directed at the floor

"Do you want to know a secret?" He met her eyes again and offered a rueful smile back.

She gulped slightly, her tangled emotions rising to the surface. "What?"

"I've had nightmares almost every night since the sinking. I even had them after the two of us dove into the river after Bingley."

"Oh, Darcy..."

He hesitated, then spoke. "I wept with you last night. You just didn't know it."

She quickly wiped her eyes and then threw her arms around him, burying her head in his shoulder. He rested his head in her hair.

When she finally pulled away, his eyes were as full as hers. "I don't suppose you thought to buy a handkerchief."

He laughed, and after pulling his pocket square out of his suit breast pocket, he gently dabbed her eyes. He did the same for himself.

She kissed him gently. "What a pair we are."

A fleeting smile crossed his countenance. "I think I could use a drink." She hadn't noticed before, but along with whatever comestibles arrived in those covered dishes, a bucket of ice with a bottle of champagne arrived with them. He deftly popped the cork and poured each of them a glass. She held it, watching the bubbles detach themselves and rise to the surface.

"What shall we drink to?" she asked, and his smile disappeared. Darcy set his glass on the surface of the table.

"Sit down a moment, Elizabeth."

The table was small and round, and he motioned her to a seat next to him. He took one of her hands in his. "I was thinking..." He studied her, then began again. "I was thinking that tomorrow, we should...book a voyage home."

He was very confusing. After all that had just passed between them, he was now talking of travel arrangements. "I am already booked—"

"Yes, yes... I had assumed that a booking had been made for you. It's just that I was thinking..." The set of his jaw was determined, his breathing like that of a fighter about to enter the ring. She tried to encourage him to continue with as open an expression as she could muster.

"Perhaps we should sell back that ticket and book one stateroom in first class."

Elizabeth raised a brow. "What are you suggesting?"

He ran his fingers through his hair and shook his head. "I... I'm making a botch of this. I knew I would." He looked away; his attention directed anywhere but at her.

Finally, she caught his eye and smiled at him. "Do go on. I am listening…"

He reached into his suit coat pocket and produced a small box, which he placed in front of her on the table. "Open it, please."

Elizabeth's heart began to pound in her chest and she picked up the box.

"Dare I ask you again, Elizabeth?"

Lizzy caught her breath and opened it. Inside the box a gold ring sat sedately, a rather large, square-cut ruby in the centre flanked by two smaller diamonds. Lizzy stared at it for a few moments, long enough for Darcy to speak again. His voice was a whisper now. "Will you marry me, Elizabeth?"

***

Darcy held his breath. Maybe it was too soon to ask her. She seemed so vulnerable and fragile. Was it fair of him to push her so? But what else could he do? They would be going back to England in a few days, or, perhaps, if she refused him, he'd be travelling on to Chicago alone as he intended. Why didn't she speak?

He couldn't see her expression clearly, only the topknot of her chestnut bouffant as she gazed at the ring. Finally, she spoke, "I suppose you only want to marry me out of duty since you spent the night in my bed."

My God. Darcy stiffened. But as she lifted her head to look at him, her eyes crinkled and she smiled from ear to ear.

Darcy let out a breath in sweet relief. She ran her fingers along his cheek and kissed him once, twice, and slipped her arms around him. Catching her breath, she gently pulled him in to the base of her neck and whispered in his ear, "I love you. Of course, I'll marry you."

He kissed her, deeply, hungrily. He wanted to devour her.

Eventually he broke the embrace and reached for the ring before slipping it on her finger. "I wanted to give you my mother's ring, but this one will have to do until we return to Pemberley…"

Before he could finish, she kissed him again. She worked her way to his jaw, his neck, then drawing him to her again, she kissed his lips, this time opening her mouth to his. His tongue flicked hers, then he deepened the kiss, drawing her into him, mingling tongue and lips. Pleasure swirled and rose between his thighs, a most dangerous reaction, and he gently broke from her embrace and stepped away.

"We must stop, Elizabeth. Now." He breathed hard. His manhood strained at his underclothes, and he quickly turned away from her to hide his physical reaction.

"Take me to bed, Darcy."

Darcy turned, startled. "But we're not married… I—"

"If today is all we have, all we will ever have, I don't care if we're married. I don't care about the honourable thing. All I care about is that you and I are here, and we are alive, and we love each other." She stroked his cheek. "Do you love me, Darcy?"

***

Darcy stared at her incredulously. "How can you doubt it?"

Lizzy arched an eyebrow. "I don't. I don't doubt it for a minute. That's why I will ask you again. Will you come to bed with me?"

A myriad of expressions flew across his face: desire, struggle, resistance, then finally, his dark eyes burned with passion.

He didn't speak but removed his jacket. She hooked her fingers in his waistcoat and pulled him into the bedroom.

The bed was turned down, the sheets clean and fresh. She had no idea that morning that he would ask her to marry him, but she wanted him, all of him, and prepared this bed for tonight. He stood, his eyes hooded, whilst she undid his waistcoat, button by button. She loosened his tie, and he, in his impatience, tore it off. Her movements must have been too slow for him now as he struggled out of his shirt and sat on the edge of the bed to remove his shoes and socks. She sat next to him to do the same, but he stayed her hand. "Allow me."

As he had yesterday, he knelt before her and undid the buttons of her shoes, one by one. Without a hint of shyness, he ran his hands over her knee, and then reaching a little higher, he took hold of the stocking and slowly unrolled it. As he ministered to the other leg, a desire she had never felt so intensely before stirred between her thighs. She stood and turned her back, and he started untying the fastenings of her dress. After she pulled it over her head, she watched in the mirror how he took down the braces from each shoulder.

She faced him. "Now, allow me." Standing only in her corset, gown, and drawers, she brushed his hands aside and with great concentration began to undo the buttons of his trouser front. A groan escaped him. As his trousers puddled around his ankles, his member strained against his underclothes.

It was something she'd never seen before, but she heard talk of in great detail by some of the working-class women she'd met at her suffragette meetings. It occurred to her that she'd learned about more than women's rights at those gatherings. When she smiled at the thought, he bent his head and searched her face.

"Are you sure? We can stop now... I don't want to take advantage..."

She didn't let him finish. After pulling the pins from her hair, she let the tresses cascade to her shoulders with a shake. Then, gently stroking his cheeks, she drew him into a kiss. He kissed her tenderly and tentatively as he wrapped his arms around her and pulled her hard against him. His arousal pressed into her, but her corset remained a barrier between them.

As he pulled back, breathing hard, his eyes bored into hers. "I love you very much, Elizabeth. And I want you. If you are sure..."

She had never been surer of anything in her life. "Anything can happen. Anything. I won't lose you again—"

"No matter what happens now, you'll never lose me. Never." He stepped back from her, never taking his gaze off her.

My God, always the gentleman.

"Help me out of this corset."

Darcy coaxed her mouth to his, and she opened herself to his passion before he leaned his forehead against hers, breathless, and with a look of determination, he began to undo the clasps of her corset. Hands shaking, she helped him. Soon it lay on the floor like a discarded suit of armour along with her undergarments until she stood only in her chemise, her breasts covered in white ruffles.

He touched her cheek with such tenderness, and she turned into it, brushing her cheek against his fingertips. The soft black curls of his chest hair peeked above the opening in his underclothes, and she began in earnest to undo the buttons as he let his hand fall to his side. When she reached the bulge below his waist, she looked up at him. Every breath of his came slowly. She undid the buttons below his waist.

Darcy pulled her against him, and in one swift movement, he eased her chemise over her head. His engorged member rubbed against her belly, and she went liquid with desire.

Warmth filled the apartment so unlike the damp cold of England, and yet her skin prickled under his gaze. They stood there, as nature made them. Then she gently reached for his hands, entwining her fingers through his, and placed them on her breasts. He caressed her, teased her—teased his lips where his fingers had been. She sighed… groaned.

He took her by the hand, and with equal tenderness, gave her leave to touch him in his most intimate spot. She marvelled at the softness of his skin and caressed him, stroked him as his breath began to come in short bursts. "Wait."

"Am I doing something wrong?"

His black, sparkling gaze flooded with tenderness. "No, no… on the contrary." He kissed her mouth lightly and led her to bed. As she lay there, he gazed at her from the foot of the bed. "How perfect you are."

Her gaze swept over his body, his perfect swimmer's body, a sleek, taut sea animal. *No, you are perfect, my love.* He stood there, so unabashed, able to say to her what was in his heart when the words stuck in her throat. *My prince, my Adonis.* No, it sounded too silly, even in her head. She wanted him to cover her with his body, to touch her everywhere. She wanted to feel all of him, to explore him with her eyes, her hands, her mouth.

"Come to me." She offered her hand, and he took it, entwining his body with hers, warmth on warmth. A film of sweet perspiration coated her skin, mingling with his as they gave way to desire to know one another completely.

Lizzy lost all inhibition, running her fingers from the backs of his legs up to his shoulders and round to his chest, entangling them in the black curls. He touched her everywhere, and she opened herself to him, nearly crying out the first time his fingers explored the tender folds of her. She wanted to pull him inside, to keep him with her always. Their mouths met, and with light and feathery kisses, he scattered them on her neck, her shoulders, and then met the softness of her breasts.

"Oh, Darcy. *Darcy.*"

He raised his head at the sound of his name, and he searched her face, his expression changing like the sky during an English summer shower. Passion… desire… tenderness—love.

She undulated under him, her desire almost painful.

"Guide me," he whispered. Still locked in his embrace, she did as he asked and let him become one with her. He plunged into her like a perfect dive into a placid pool. She wasn't sure if she should move with him, but her body knew. Exquisite sensations rippled through her. Her love for him unbound.

She wrapped herself around him, pulling him over her, cradling his head in the crook of her neck, then they lost themselves in one another, crashing like waves against a shoreline until they spent themselves and lay tangled together, still touching.

Soon sleep overtook them both.

Chapter 39

Darcy awoke early and, not wanting to disturb Elizabeth, drew himself a bath and got dressed. He realised as he sat down at the table, he'd never so much as made himself a cup of tea in his entire life, nor had he ever shaved himself. He so wanted to awaken Elizabeth and make love to her again, but today they needed to sort themselves out. They'd book passage back to England, and then, before the day was through, they'd marry. Was it possible to do things so quickly in New York?

Her hair wild, eyes half open, Elizabeth opened the bedroom door, dressed only in her chemise, the bedsheet wrapped protectively around her. She pushed up at her auburn mane in a vain attempt to set it to rights. "I must look a sight."

"A wonderful sight." Darcy got up and took her in his arms. She pulled back from him, a mischievous smile on her face.

"Well, Mr Darcy. Now you'll have to marry me."

He laughed. "I suppose I will."

He could see his life unfolding clearly before him for the first time. This woman, this headstrong, determined, brilliant, passionate young woman, would be his helpmeet, his lover, his partner for the rest of his life. He could see them as an old couple, like the Astors on the deck of the *Titanic*, not able to bear being apart, even if it meant certain death.

"Whatever are you thinking?" Elizabeth knitted her brows, a look of concern creeping into her eyes.

"You see it, then. This is what you will have to put up with married to me. I am deliriously happy and then—"

"And then a thousand thoughts enter your head on how that happiness could be taken from you." There it was. She was a mind reader too. He kissed her beautiful, smiling lips. Then, kissed her again.

"All right, Mr Darcy. That's quite enough. If we continue this way, we'll never get anything done today."

"I don't mind." He kissed her again, and then began a trail down her jawline to her neck.

She laughed, then looked at him with a frown. "Do you want me to call you Fitzwilliam, or William, or Will or Willie or … not Fitz, surely."

He pulled a face. "Surely not." She smiled. He let go his embrace and entwined his fingers with hers. "Fitzwilliam is so cumbersome, don't you think?" He led her to the sofa and drew her down next to him.

"It doesn't matter. It is your name."

"So it is. Georgiana calls me Fitzwilliam, as did my mother and father. I never liked it much. Darcy is best, I think… I like it best."

"And I like Lizzy best."

"My wonderful Lizzy." She kissed him on the cheek.

"And I shall call you Mr Fitzwilliam Darcy only when we quarrel."

"Quarrel? We shall never quarrel."

"Oh, I'm sure we shall, once we are used to each other… but we shall always make it up… always."

He took both her hands. She looked so soft and drowsy from sleep, so ready to yield again to him. "I'd like to go back to bed." He kissed the nape of her neck as he sought the soft pillows of her breasts.

"Oh, so would I." She clasped his wandering hands. "But we have much to do today. You must make an honest woman of me." She stood up and left him on the sofa to gain control of himself. "And I will make an honest man of you." She threw a smile back his way.

***

While Elizabeth bathed, Darcy took a walk to find the barbershop he had passed off Columbus Circle yesterday. He returned clean-shaven to a breakfast of tea and the dinner they'd neglected the previous night. Somehow everything was warm and ready. Weren't women wonderful? They could do all these tasks that just eluded men completely. For a brief moment, he wondered why men ruled the world.

His life had much improved now that he had access to his money. They left together, a yellow taxicab hired for the day. In the White Star Line office, they were treated with the utmost care and courtesy by the ticket agent, who trembled a little holding the list of survivors in his hand. The clerk opened the timetable for the crossings and, spinning it upside down from himself, presented it to Darcy.

He glanced at it and became quite thoughtful. "Could you give us a moment?"

"Of course." The clerk excused himself.

"What's the matter?".

"Nothing, it's just that…"

Elizabeth squinted at him, and then reared back. "You think I won't be able to cope with another ocean voyage, is that it?"

"No, no, that's not it at all."

"What, then?" Her face flushed and her eyes burned fiery. She was correct. They would have their quarrels, but not today.

"I was thinking that perhaps we could postpone our voyage and complete my original plan to visit Chicago. After all, I would like to see this Marshall Fields store where Mr Selfridge began and learn more about the business since I am to be on the board."

"Really?" She cocked her head. "Chicago…. It sounds so exotic, in… an American sort of way." He watched her ruminate over the idea momentarily. "Oh, but what of my family, and Georgiana? They will want to see us right away, don't you think?"

"They know we are safe, and soon they will know that we are married. After all, we are living in a modern age and can send them a wire as to our plans. I don't think they would begrudge us a short honeymoon." Darcy tried to sound certain, but he wasn't at all. Truth be told, it wasn't the lure of Chicago. It was he who didn't relish another ocean voyage so soon.

Elizabeth hesitated a moment. "Would you be very disappointed if I said I'd like to go home right away… as soon as possible? I'd like to be back in plenty of time for Jane and Charles's wedding."

Darcy was taken aback momentarily. "My word, I'd forgotten about the wedding until just this minute." He laughed ruefully. "I had a return booking on the *Titanic* for the first of May just for that purpose." Elizabeth shuddered as the clerk knocked on the door and came through at Darcy's request.

"Have we made a decision, Mr Darcy?"

They had indeed. "We'd like to book first-class passage on the *Olympic* as soon as possible, or even something on the Cunard line, it is of no consequence which."

The clerk peered over the top of his glasses at various papers and timetables as he sat down. "Well, let's see here… the *Ascania,* which is a Cunard ship, sailed today and won't be back for a couple of weeks. We could book you in first class, let's see, for the return voyage… the first week in May." He ran his finger down the one page and then another. "That would get you to Southampton by May 8. Okay?"

He gave Darcy a self-satisfied grin. It wasn't, as it he put it, okay. Elizabeth's expression told him that it was not *okay*.

"What about the *Olympic*? Can it get us home sooner?"

The clerk squinted at Darcy and screwed up his face. "Yes, the *Olympic* leaves the day after tomorrow, but first class is fully booked. You'd have to travel second class."

Darcy opened his mouth to speak but Elizabeth's touch on his sleeve stopped him. "I already have a second-class cabin on the *Olympic* for that day." She shot a glance at Darcy and then the clerk. "For a Miss Elizabeth Bennet…"

More paper shuffling ensued, and the clerk confirmed her reservation. Raising an eyebrow, he looked askance at Darcy. "Well, sir?"

What was it about these minor officials? Why did this tiny modicum of power give them such a self-righteous attitude? He knew what the ticket agent was thinking… a *Miss* Bennet and a Mr Darcy, alone on an ocean voyage. He suddenly thought of Wickham.

"Would it be so terrible to travel second class?" Elizabeth interrupted his thoughts. "We already have the booking."

"And there are two beds in the cabin," the clerk said with a smirk.

The slimy little toad. Of course, he would acquiesce to Elizabeth's wishes and have the added satisfaction of putting the clerk in his place.

"Change the booking to Mr and Mrs Fitzwilliam Darcy. I'll pay for the extra ticket now."

"Oh, no. No charge, sir… You've paid already for your return on the *Titanic*."

Yes, the *Titanic*. Darcy swallowed hard and tried to put that night out of his mind. After all, today he was to be married.

***

Elizabeth had waited as Darcy borrowed the city directory and looked up a registrar's office and two Episcopal churches. He'd muttered surely one of them would do for a marriage ceremony. As they settled back in their taxicab, Darcy fiddled in his waistcoat pocket and produced a wedding band. "Our next stop, Lizzy. Unless you'd like to shop for a trousseau first. After all, it is customary."

Elizabeth inspected her outfit. It was one of the two sets of clothes the Red Cross had given her only a few days ago. They were presentable enough, but certainly not elegant. "Are you ashamed to be seen with me?" She teased, but Darcy flinched.

"Certainly not. How could you say such a thing?" He took her hands in his. "I—"

"I don't want to wait, Darcy. I really don't."

Darcy nodded, then gave the registrar's address to the driver. Within half an hour, they left the office—an incomplete marriage license in Darcy's hand. His jaw was set and his eyes alight. "Damn and blast. Oh, I do beg your pardon, Elizabeth."

"Damn and blast, indeed," she repeated as harshly and nearly burst into a laugh when she saw the expression on his face.

He had to smile back at her. "Why does one need a birth record or naturalization record? We don't want to live here—"

"It's all right. We can try the churches. He said it might be easier there…" She patted his arm.

He let out a deep sigh and shook himself as if he were shaking off all his frustrations. "You're right, of course. Let's get something to eat and continue our quest."

A quest it was, all right. The driver proved to be a font of information, not the least of which was a thorough knowledge of the eateries in lower Manhattan. After an interesting lunch of food she had never tasted before, something called spaghetti, which was delicious if difficult to eat, they arrived at a church that was approximately the same denomination as the one they both attended at home. The front doors were unlocked, so they entered there into the soft darkness of the cathedral. The sun attempted to peek through the stained glass onto the dark wooden pews. It reminded her of every church she had ever entered back home. They soon found the rector.

"I'm afraid that we'll have to publish the banns before we can proceed. That should only take about three weeks," said the rector.

"Three weeks?" Darcy's voice echoed in the empty nave. Elizabeth laid her hand on his arm as she watched the thundercloud descend on his countenance. Before he could speak, she intervened. "Sir, we are from England. We have just survived the sinking of the *Titanic*..."

The rector jerked back, his mouth gaping in surprise. "My word. God has protected you—"

"And God would like us to marry as well, so if you please..." Darcy said.

The rector raised his hand and briefly shut his eyes. His pose reminded Elizabeth of the statue she once beheld called *The Infant Jesus of Prague*. "I'm afraid that is not possible. Surely, you can wait the proper time..."

"I'm afraid we cannot," said Darcy. "We leave very shortly for England, and in the name of all that is holy, what possible use is publishing the banns? Who would object to our marriage? We are here alone in a foreign country."

The rector shook his head, then tilted it to once side. "I am sorry..."

Elizabeth slipped her arm through Darcy's. The muscles tightened beneath his suit coat. Ignoring him, she whispered to Darcy. "We could try another church...?"

"I'm afraid you will get the same response from all the churches in the city. Rules are rules, you know. Good day to you." The rector turned away with quiet steps and made for the sanctuary.

Darcy hardened his expression. Elizabeth knew of his gentlemanly restraint, but this rector was sorely trying his patience. On impulse, she whispered to him, "Ah well. We'll just have to live in sin a while longer."

Darcy didn't appear amused, having been thwarted for the second time in one day. They were both silent as they exited the cathedral and made themselves comfortable in the back of the cab. Darcy sighed.

"Where to, sir?"

"I have no idea. The vicar was quite adamant that he could not marry us today… and made it clear we would find no other church in the city that would do so. The banns and all that…"

The driver turned in his seat, wrapping his arm around the seat back. He squinted at Darcy. "If you are not too particular about which church is which, you could try the Unitarians on Lexington Avenue and East 80th. They are a little off the beaten path religion wise, if you know what I mean."

Elizabeth didn't know what he meant, and Darcy looked at her sceptically. "Is that all right with you, my dear?"

"God works in strange and mysterious ways, don't you think?" she said, and they drove on.

***

Mr William Sullivan answered the door of the church house when Darcy and Elizabeth called. He seemed singularly nonplussed about identity documents, banns, or even the fact that neither Darcy nor Elizabeth were members of his denomination.

While Mr Sullivan left to find his housekeeper and the groundskeeper for witnesses, Darcy and Elizabeth waited near the nave of the church. The interior was all white and ivory, its curved ceiling like a bridal veil on a wedding day. Even the pews were white with their bit of walnut trim. No stained glass intervened with the morning light streaming through the windows. The place shone in the April sunlight like the entrance to heaven. They sat in the front pew to wait.

Darcy stared down at their clasped hands. "Are you very disappointed?" He didn't look at her at first, then raised his gaze to meet hers.

"Whatever are you talking about?"

"I thought, perhaps, that you would like to have had a double wedding with your sister and Bingley... dressed in white, me in white tie and tails, your family all about..."

Elizabeth sighed. "I am not shedding any tears for anything today. A month ago, all that pomp and ceremony would have meant the world to me. Today...." She sighed and contemplated her white and shining surroundings, sweeping her eye over all. "Today, I'm grateful to be alive—that you are alive...." She squeezed his hand and swallowed the lump in her throat. "I feel nothing but gratitude and love and happiness." Her heart was so full that it threatened to spill again.

The echo of a door shutting cut off anything Darcy had to say, and the two of them stood as Reverend Sullivan appeared from the side of the altar and descended the steps to the floor at the front of the church. He was followed by a middle-aged woman in a dark dress and white apron, tucking the errant strands of hair that escaped her white cap.

"This is Mrs O'Brien. She'll stand as witness."

Elizabeth took her hand. "Thank you." Mrs O'Brien beamed, her rosy cheeks colouring.

"The grace o' God on ye," she said in a broad Irish brogue and clasped Elizabeth's hand momentarily, giving a quick nod to Darcy.

"Now where is Mr Moretti? I just spoke to him." Mr Sullivan bounced on his heels.

The boom of a heavy door drew all their attention to the back of the church, where a shortish man, whisps of gray hair fluttering, rushed up the aisle. He sheepishly handed Elizabeth a makeshift bouquet.

"Dis for a-you... for you a-wedding day. April flowers. Beautiful, no?" Mr Moretti's accent betrayed his Sicilian origins. What a lovely thought from the stranger: yellow daffodils, tulips in shades of pink and red, and a cluster of blue goblets Elizabeth had never seen before. As she touched them, he continued. "Ver-geenea bluebell." His lips creased into a smile. *Virginia bluebells, lovely.*

"Thank you." She kissed his cheek. He stepped back, abashed, and stood next to the housekeeper.

"Are we ready?" The Reverend opened his prayer book, and Darcy stepped up next to Elizabeth, squaring his shoulders.

"I am ready." He expression told her everything. "More than ready."

Elizabeth brushed Darcy's fingers, and the ceremony began.

Chapter 40

The rest of the day passed by in a whirl, but Lizzy loved every moment. She and Darcy sent announcement telegrams home. The rest of the day she let him buy her new clothes and the luggage and trunks to carry them aboard ship. When they finally reached their brownstone flat on 58th, Elizabeth was done in. Divesting herself of her hat, she sighed and sat down at their little table.

"Would you like a cup of tea, Mr Darcy?"

"Thank you very much, *Mrs Darcy*." He crossed the room and knelt at her knee. "That sounds nice, doesn't it?" After touching her cheek, he drew her to him and kissed her. Any touch from him rippled through her body like electricity. She wondered if that would always be so.

"I'll get the tea." She rose and went into the small galley kitchen, where she lit the stove.

He followed her and stood leaning on the small ice box. "I meant to ask you: would you like to move to a hotel for the next few days before our trip? We could have room service… breakfast in bed…"

She should have expected this. A small wave of panic washed over her. "I can bring you breakfast in bed here." She spoke without looking at him. How peculiar. She had only been in this little, dark flat for a few days, and yet it seemed like home to her, and she was reluctant to leave. Lizzy looked over her shoulder. "Do you mind staying here? I…"

Darcy closed the few steps between them and took her hands in his. "I don't mind at all. This place is… our little refuge, isn't it?"

She was so grateful that he understood. Elizabeth wrapped her arms around him, pinning his arms to his side, and leaned her head against his chest. He smelled of witch hazel and wool, and something indistinct that was him and only him. Inhaling slowly, she filled herself with his essence. "I'm glad you understand. I'll be sad to leave this place. Isn't that funny?"

"No, I don't think it is. I feel the same. What is funny is that I find I can be happy with so little. All I really need is food, shelter… and you."

How does he think of these wonderful little things to say? She let him go as the kettle began to whistle.

With tea, sandwiches, and a bit of cake set on the table, they ate and talked of their trip before Lizzy said, "Oh, I'd really like to finish my letter home. Would you mind very much?"

"No, of course not. I did buy the evening paper. We can sit about like an old married couple."

His presence instilled a comfort Elizabeth didn't expect to find. She knew that there was a sort of terrible love that bound her to him. She was helpless in the face of it. The more he revealed himself to her—his character, his kindness, his ability to sacrifice his own needs for another—the more she loved him. What she didn't expect was this warm blanket on a cold and damp night, a contentment that washed over her.

She cleared the dishes and sat again at their little table. Darcy sprawled on the sofa, the newspaper lying about him like fallen leaves. He'd removed his tie and suit jacket and sat with waistcoat unbuttoned, collar and shoes off, intently reading. She stared at him for some moments, and as if he could feel her gaze, he suddenly folded the sheet he was reading and caught her eye.

"By Jove, I forgot to ask. How did Lydia fare? Did Wickham stick by her?"

"They left on the *Lapland* the day after the *Carpathia* docked. The White Star Line sent all the surviving crew back to Southampton."

"And left you here to survive on your own?" His voice squeaked a bit as he spoke, which she found endearing.

"They couldn't take me with them, and they had a chance to return. I don't think Lydia was too eager to get on board a ship so soon."

"So, he was with her, then?"

"Yes, most definitely." She hesitated and then asked, "What did you do to persuade George to marry her?" His expression told her that she caught him out. He'd have to tell her and confirm what she suspected: that he was instrumental in restoring Lydia's honour. "Now, don't try to think up something to say other than the truth—"

"I would do no such thing." He smiled. "Yes, I arranged for the scoundrel to receive regular payments each quarter if he would do the right thing. How did you know?"

"You just told me. I merely suspected it before."

He slapped the sheet of newspaper on his lap. "You are far too clever for your own good, Elizabeth Ben... Darcy. There won't be anything I can keep from you." He laid the newspaper down. "I expect I'll be receiving communication from my solicitor any day now asking for further instructions. I'm sure that Wickham was anxious to return to England with Lydia to prove to Mr Huntley that the marriage indeed took place on the *Titanic,* and there he'll be, his wife in tow."

Elizabeth's smile faded. She took no joy in the fact that her sister was saddled with that contemptable Wickham. "Do you think he has any affection for her?"

"I don't know, Lizzy. I really don't. I expect he'll stick by her, though. Otherwise, the money will dry up."

She fell quiet for a moment. "We're very lucky, aren't we?"

"Very..." He moved as if to rouse from the sofa, but she held up her hand.

"Don't disturb yourself." Amid the rustle of papers, she eased away from the table and kissed his eager mouth, savouring the feel of him, wanting to pull him inside of her. She laid a hand on his chest and broke away. "I really must finish that letter and post it tomorrow. Otherwise, we will arrive before it does."

He brushed the papers aside and stood, shaking himself rather like a puppy that had just come in out of the rain. "Now you've made me feel guilty. I should write to Georgiana."

The two of them sat across the table from one another. Lizzy handed Darcy paper and pen, and she continued the letter she had started only a day ago.

20 April 1912

Everything is happening so fast. You know this already because I sent you a telegram, but I love writing it again. Mr Darcy and I were married today. Due to the intransigence of the New York Registrar's Office and the Episcopal Church (Church of England over here), we were married in a Unitarian Church in New York City. The reverend was very kind, and his housekeeper and groundskeeper stood as witness. The groundskeeper, Mr Moretti, even picked me a bouquet of spring flowers. The church was lovely, all in white. I couldn't be happier.

We will arrive in Southampton on the Olympic *on the 25th or the 28th and will come immediately to see you. I can't say that I look forward to another ocean voyage, but since I cannot walk home, it can't be helped.*

I hope Lydia is settling into married life. I can only wish that she is as happy with Mr Wickham as I am with Mr Darcy. I miss you all. I will be home soon.

Yours,
Lizzy

***

Two days later, as Darcy supervised the packing of their suitcases into the Yellow Cab that would take them to the pier, he observed Elizabeth as she stood on the sidewalk, gazing at the brownstone. He placed his hand gently on the small of her back and she started.

"I could buy it for you, if you like."

She crooked her neck to shoot him a quizzical look. "Buy what?"

"This building, then we'd have it forever."

She shook her head. "No, no. That would never do. This place should be filled with life. If we had it, that flat would sit empty. It shouldn't be a memorial. It should be someone else's little refuge."

"Perhaps you're right." He sighed and took her hand. After opening the door to the taxi, he handed her in, taking one last, wistful look at their temporary home on 58th Street. They sat in silence on their brief ride to the pier, and Darcy stole a glance at her from time to time. He wished he knew what she was thinking. His letter to Georgiana remained unfinished, for as soon as Lizzy laid down her pen to beckon to him with her smouldering gaze, they commenced their wedding night. There was nothing tentative about their union this time. He couldn't get enough of her, and in the morning, he commenced again, exhausting his passion in her tender folds. Perhaps it was too much. After all, she and her delicate body were new to carnal delights, and perhaps he shouldn't demand so much of her. Yet as he commenced his rhythm, she matched his movement with her own, grasping him, caressing him, and with such a look of ecstasy that he couldn't help but believe she ached for him as much as he did for her.

There was no one to see them off, of course, so they proceeded to what was to be Elizabeth's cabin where she'd planned to return home alone. The steward unlocked the door, and the porters moved past with suitcases and a steamer trunk. He and Lizzy had been busy in the city, filling their bags with necessities, since everything they brought from England slept at the bottom of the Atlantic. After tipping the porter, Darcy stepped in behind Elizabeth. The cabin was much smaller than he had expected, and his eye immediately went to the bunk beds on the far wall. A padded bench seat sat against the opposite wall. Their trunks were piled on it, and a small desk resided at the left of the bench, whilst a wash basin took the right.

"How lovely," Elizabeth exclaimed.

Lovely? Certainly not. Having grown up with every comfort, expecting every comfort, expecting deference in fact, despite all the loss, it didn't take long to fall back into his old attitudes. He instinctively reached into his breast pocket to assure himself that his funds were still there. Being ignored and treated with suspicion as he'd spent the day in a workman's cap hit him hard. After all, it had only been a few days before.

"Is everything all right, dearest?" Elizabeth cut through the fog of his reverie.

"I suppose you'll have to get used to my moods, Lizzy. If there is a silver lining, I will always find the cloud."

She held out her hand, and he took it.

As soon as they were settled, Darcy escorted Lizzy topside as the ship pulled away from land and made for the open ocean. Elizabeth had a stillness about her as she leaned against the stern rail, watching the grey buildings of New York fade into the mist.

They ate dinner in the second-class salon, sharing a long table with many other guests. The room had a certain understated elegance: a pressed tin ceiling painted white to match the linen tablecloths, polished oak pillars modestly carved at the top, and comfortable, stylishly carved chairs. Elizabeth kept up a chatter at dinner to all and sundry about her, but Darcy's head swam with doubts. If he should ask her if he was being too demanding of her, she would be honest with him, wouldn't she? And if she told him to cool his ardour for a time, what would that mean? Did she not enjoy his attentions, or did she just need some time to, well, recover from their exertions? Or would she say anything to please him because she loved him so?

"My goodness, you've gone quiet." Elizabeth slipped her arm in his as they walked the deck after dinner.

"Have I? I suppose I have. Can we go back to our cabin now, Lizzy? I'd like to talk to you."

A look of concern crossed her face. "That sounds ominous."

"No, no, not really. I…" He looked around at the other passengers strolling about the deck. "I just don't want to discuss it here."

***

There was no doubt in Lizzy's mind that she loved Darcy, but he did seem to take sharp turns into the darkness just as things were going well. What could he possibly want to talk about that warranted such a grim expression? Was he regretting their whirlwind marriage already? No, that couldn't be it. He offered her a seat and then sat down across from her, leaning his elbows on his thighs and looking down at the floor.

"Whatever is the matter?"

He turned his head side to side, still not meeting her gaze. Finally, he slapped his legs with the palms of his hands and looked her in the eye.

"Am I demanding too much of you, Lizzy? You can be honest with me."

She had no idea what he was talking about. "Demands?"

He intertwined his fingers and tapped them against his mouth. "We have only been together for a short time, and you are new to… how can I say it… our *being together*." He nodded towards her expectantly as if she was party to what he was thinking, and she searched for some meaning to all this. "Lizzy, I don't ever want to hurt you for any reason, especially physically hurt you…" He raised his eyebrows again.

It suddenly became clear to her. "Oh… *oh*. No, no, I'm quite all right in that regard. You're right, it does take a bit of getting used to, all this… *togetherness*. But I will tell you right away if I need to rest a while. I suppose all this fervour will wear off eventually anyway…"

He looked rather alarmed. "Do you really think so?"

"Oh, I expect so, once we begin to live our real lives again. I think we should enjoy this time while we can, don't you?" She smiled at him all this time, but then a surge of emotion welled up. "I do love you, Darcy.

He stood and took her in his arms, kissing her urgently. "Come along, then. Let's go to bed."

He perused the top bunk and then the bottom and then the top again.

"It's all right. We can begin the evening together here." She patted the bottom bed.

Lizzy had fewer inhibitions each time they were together. He caressed and kissed her, eliciting responses from her body she'd never felt before. Tonight, she was wild for his union with her, and as she wrapped her legs around him, the movement of the ship rocked them.

"Just hold me… let the ocean do the rest," she whispered in his ear. He moved slightly so that they were as one, and she let the slight pitching of the ship and its surging back and forth bring them to the brink of ecstasy, holding them there for miles and miles.

Lizzy had never experienced anything like this before. Darcy's body seemed to fit with hers so perfectly, the heightened pleasure his skin, his warmth, the taut contour of his muscles emptying her mind of thought and filling her only with feeling. She felt him… not only his body, but the essence of him, entwined with all that was her. The slow surges of pleasure rippled over the tenderest part. The moonlight penetrated the porthole window, illuminating his face, his dark eyes, exposing his naked soul as he joined with her. How long they lay together in this exquisite agony she didn't know, but eventually he lay sleeping next to her, propped up on his side in their tiny berth, his soft breaths coming in regular rhythm along her neck.

What she didn't tell him during his awkward and completely endearing questioning of her earlier in the evening was that, each time they lay together and he was asleep, she would explore the concave contours of his body: the little indentation behind his ear, the valley between his neck and his collarbone, the squarish curves of his chest muscles. Moonlight outlined the ripples of his abdomen, and the L-shaped ridge where his leg and his torso met. His beauty was almost more than she could bear.

The morning after their wedding, she'd awakened him with a touch that ran along his hip and nestled in the curls on his chest. She would confess to him that he need never worry that the pleasures of the flesh were too much for her. In fact, her carnal desires could equal or perhaps surpass his.

She kissed him gently and his eyelids fluttered. A dreamy smile crossed his lips. "Shall I go up top so you can sleep, my love?" Part of her wanted him there with her and part of her was so tired that the thought of this little bunk all to herself overrode her desire for closeness. Before she could speak, he nudged her slightly, and she let him go. He pulled his nightshirt over his head and climbed the ladder to the bed above.

Chapter 41

As dusk settled over the horizon on the third day at sea, Darcy sat at their table in the dining hall, quietly eating dinner and passing looks to Lizzy. They'd found that moment, where comfort in silence passed between them with only a glance, as though they'd lived through a lifetime in just a few short days. Darcy hid a private smile. Everything felt so… right. The moment passed and his usual thoughts assailed him. He knew that when contentment beckoned, inadvertently, his mind would catastrophize. The worrisome idea that he couldn't possibly remain this happy must have shown on his face because Lizzy shot him a quizzical look. "I—" he began.

A loud cry jerked his attention away as the shout of "Iceberg" rang out, startling many of their fellow diners. Some eased up from their seats and gaped out of the walnut-framed windows of the dining salon. Others even left their tables to peer out at the blueish behemoths that shone eerily in the moonlight.

The warning was heeded this time, but Elizabeth dropped her fork with a clatter on the china plate. Darcy held on to the sides of the table as he felt the ship steer off to the side.

"Oh my dear." A motherly woman, Mrs Hampton, who had shared their table with them yesterday alongside her husband, placed her napkin on her dinnerplate and rushed over. "Are you quite all right?" She touched Elizabeth's arm.

Lizzy stayed pale and silent. They'd mentioned nothing to anyone aboard about what they'd faced, trying so hard to keep focus on all the good. From the tightness of her lips and her failure to meet his eye, Darcy knew Elizabeth was trying to maintain her composure. He took her hand from across the table.

"Good heavens, whatever is the matter?" asked Mrs Hampton.

Elizabeth gave Darcy a tight nod.

"We're travelling home after escaping with our lives from the *Titanic*," he said simply. "If you'll excuse us."

Taking Elizabeth by the arm, he rose from the table with her, and Mrs Hampton gracefully stepped aside before hurrying off to whisper to her husband.

As they made it out of the hall, Lizzy stopped for a moment and shook her head. "Let's get our coats." She pulled him forward towards the second-class staterooms. "I want to stand on deck."

"What? Wait." He tried to pull her to a stop. "Are you sure that's a good idea? I—"

"I want to watch those things all night if need be. I can't bear to be belowdecks. Not now." She trembled against him as he protectively pulled her close.

"All right. I'll stand watch with you."

Once they stood at the rail, a field of icebergs drifted all around like a silent, deadly army.

Lizzy sheltered against Darcy, her arm around his waist, both of his enclosing her. The air was frigid but unmoving, the sea still as glass. An echo of the night they nearly lost their lives. She shivered in his arms.

"Are you sure you don't want to go inside? It's a brutal night." He shifted stance against the frost. They'd stood there for more than an hour as the ship inched its way between the icy sentries. "Perhaps a cup of tea in the reception room, and then we can resume our watch. All right?"

She said nothing, only loosened her grip on him, and they retreated to a nicely appointed lounge with red and gold upholstered chairs and paned windows set into oak-panelled walls. It looked like a drawing room one would see on land, and only the sway of the ship as it slowly and meticulously made its way betrayed that they were at sea.

Darcy became aware that he was staring at Lizzy as if she were an explosive that could detonate at any minute, so raised his gaze from time to time to admire the beamed and coffered ceiling. She didn't speak, and he didn't press her. He knew himself how irritating it could be when someone attempted to jolly him out of his dark moods. Best let it run its course and let it pass. If he was honest, he had to admit that with the sea strewn with treacherous mountains of ice, he much preferred to be awake and on deck to observe the *Olympic*'s passage through the maze.

"Would you mind very much if I left for a moment to enquire as to our progress through the ice field?"

The sound of his voice startled her as she jumped slightly, her teacup rattling in the saucer. She shakily navigated it back to the table. "Oh, I think that's a very good idea. I'll stay here and warm up a bit."

He drew his coat on again and went out to seek an officer. When he returned, Elizabeth stood at the window, and for a moment she didn't turn back to acknowledge he was there.

"Lizzy," he said gently. "The captain said that they might lose as much as six hours in the ice field, but he doesn't want to take any chances."

Her eyes widened. "You spoke with the captain?"

He nodded. "Who would know better than he? I mentioned that we had survived the *Titanic* and he assured me that his instructions were clear from the shipping line: he was to take no risks for the sake of speed; he was to keep in constant communication with all ships within radio distance. I have confidence in him. I really do." He was also doing his best to be reassuring, but her expressions changed chameleon-like as he spoke, and he couldn't read her.

"I'm warm now," she said eventually. "I'd like to go back on deck. You needn't stay with me."

"I am at your service, Mrs Darcy... always."

That last word seemed to settle her a little. Donning their coats, hats, and mufflers, they headed back on deck and stood watch until the wee hours and the icebergs finally left them in peace.

***

The evening before they were to dock at Southampton, Elizabeth stood at the rail in the moonlight, watching the sea clouds sail across the sky, dusted with silver. She felt calmer, not entirely at ease. A strong hand on the small of her back let her know that Darcy joined her.

"I'd like to kiss you... but this hat." He brushed a thumb along the rim. Prodigious ostrich feathers fluffed all around the cap, and a wide brim kept all and sundry at arm's length.

"You bought it for me, Mr Darcy, to my objections, as I recall." She reached and ran her fingertips along his cheekbone. "You'll just have to wait until we are alone, and I remove it: the waiting will enflame your ardour." She returned to her watch.

"My ardour doesn't need inflaming." He chuckled and leaned next to her.

"Besides, there are people about..." Then in her best New York accent, she said, "What's a madder wich ya, doncha have any class?" She snickered at her own joke, and then tilted her head as he laughed with her.

He then pulled her hat off and kissed her—not the chaste kiss, but the urgent and passionate kiss they exchanged only when alone together, away from prying eyes.

"*Mr* Darcy." She gave him a slight push and put on her best mock-indignation.

"Is this guy bothering you, miss?" A gruff voice sounded over Darcy's shoulder.

He glanced back then had to look up slightly to a man with a face like a pie dish with a nose that seemed hammered flat by someone. The man was massive.

"Oh." Elizabeth quickly stepped in. "It's all right, thank you sir. This man is my husband."

"Oh." The giant grunted and turned away.

Elizabeth couldn't contain herself a moment longer and laughed until tears ran down her cheeks.

"So you think that was humorous." He was trying mightily to remain serious, which made her laugh all the more. Taking her in his arms, still clutching that silly hat, he kissed her again.

"I don't think I've ever been so happy in all my life." Her merriment spilled out of her and he gave her a huge grin. She threw her arms around him.

"I know I haven't," he whispered into her hair, and then when she raised her head, he kissed her forehead. "Come along. One more turn 'round the deck and then to bed. Tomorrow, we see family."

Oh, yes. Family... *the* families.

***

The *Olympic* docked safely in Southampton, and Lizzy watched the crew finally let down the gangplanks with maddening slowness. Tears threatened again, but this time she had a handkerchief of her own at the ready.

"All ready?" Darcy slipped his arm around her waist. He tried to look serene and nonplussed, but from the high colour in his cheeks and the softness around his eyes, he was as excited as she to set foot again on British soil.

From the top of the gangplank, Lizzy scanned the crowd. She thought she caught Kitty leaping in the air and waving a handkerchief, but it was too great a distance, and she wasn't sure.

They made their way to the pier, towards the shore, and through the crowds.

A sudden flash blinded her, then another, then voices assailed them from every direction.

"Is it true, Mr Darcy, that you gave your place to another and then swam away from the *Titanic*?"

"Did you two marry in New York? Did you meet on the *Titanic*?"

Lizzy couldn't even tell which direction the questions came from as she raised a hand to shield against the blinding lights.

"What lifeboat were you in, Mrs Darcy?"

"Is it true that you are a suffragette?"

Elizabeth clutched Darcy's arm and tried to get her bearings as blobs of blue light floated in her gaze. The acrid smoke from flash powder sullied the air. Journalists. They surrounded them. How utterly peculiar.

"Gentlemen, I don't see how any of this is your business. Now leave us alone." Darcy cut through the chaos.

"Oh, come along, sir." Another voice rose above the tumult. "All you survivors are of national interest. You need to give us some sort of a statement."

Darcy waved the journalists away to no avail, and he kept Lizzy close to his side as they persisted in following them as they approached the crowd waiting for the passengers.

Elizabeth turned this way and that, more annoyed now at the wall of reporters separating her from her family.

But at the back of the crowd, elbowing her way through, a female journalist called her name. Elizabeth stopped and Darcy stopped as well.

The woman seemed familiar. "Don't I know you?"

"We went to some of the same suffragette meetings together. I'm Nellie Winston, *Morning Chronicle*. Here's my card." The young woman was all business, even down to her smallish bicorn hat, which enabled her to navigate through this sea of men without losing it.

"I'll telephone you as soon as we get settled and give you an interview if that suits?" She looked up at Darcy, who wore an expression of pure scepticism, and then turning to Miss Winston, she was greeted with a quiet nod and a knowing grin. The rest of the journalists fell away as they reached the gate that separated the passengers from the welcoming crowd.

They were barely through it before Lizzy spied Kitty, hopping about and waving. It had been her. She had to relinquish Darcy to Georgiana, who had her arms around his waist, hugging him close. Lizzy was immediately surrounded by Jane, her mother, and Kitty. Everyone began to talk at once. Lizzy felt quite overcome, and the tears that threatened were unrestrained the minute she saw the same running down Jane's cheeks.

"Oh, you don't know what it did to my poor nerves, not knowing what had become of you," her mother blubbered, snorting into her handkerchief.

"Did you bring me anything from America?" Kitty was given a stern look from her mother for asking.

"I'm so glad you are home, Lizzy… grateful… grateful you have been spared." Jane's words started a flow of tears again as her father stepped up. He gave her a tender smile, a quick embrace, then immediately coughed and stepped back.

"Now, now, children. Enough of that. We must all hear the tale that you have to tell, Lizzy, and you must properly introduce us to your Mr Darcy. We've only met him briefly, you know…"

Lizzy peered through her throng of relatives to Darcy, who presently wiped tears from Georgiana's cheek. Surreptitiously, he wiped away a few of his own.

***

Darcy detested emotional scenes such as this one, especially in public. He was grateful to Elizabeth for scattering the jackals of London's yellow journalism but was not best pleased that the price of their freedom was bought with what they called in the trade as an "exclusive interview."

The onslaught of Lizzy's family temporarily separated them, but Georgiana instantly swooped him up in her embrace, one he welcomed more than he realised.

"Thank God you're alive. I thought I lost you…" She wept and it touched him to the core. It was times like these, of high emotion, that he could admit to himself just how much he loved his only sister.

"I'm sorry I worried you."

"It doesn't matter now—you're home." She clung to him, squeezing him hard, then leaned back to study him. "And you brought Elizabeth. Your wife…." She grinned as she wiped away a tear. "I always wanted a sister."

"Now you have five… all the Bennet sisters."

She laughed and threw her arms around his neck. "I'm so glad you're home. So glad."

"Darcy… *Darcy*…" An imperious tone cut its way through the crowd. Most people, including Darcy, turned to see his aunt scanning the crowd. Lady Catherine's imposing presence brought silence as she stood like a great bird of prey, complete with a crown of feathers thanks to her resplendent hat.

"Aunt," was all he said and took a few running steps towards her. She stood a good head shorter than he, but was so commanding a presence, she always seemed monumental. Now, despite her gruff manner, she appeared tiny and fragile, as if she might shatter if he touched her.

Lady Catherine looked almost alarmed as he reached her. He knew that he shouldn't hesitate and threw his arms about her, kissing her quickly on the cheek, and her bird-like hands fluttered against his back. She stepped away quickly. "For goodness's sake, Darcy, what a display… in public, no less." Her face bore a tender aspect that she remedied the second she realised he had seen it.

"Ladies and gentlemen," said Mr Bennet. "You are all invited to join us at the Dolphin Hotel. Mrs Bennet and I invite you to dine with us in celebration of the homecoming of our dear daughter and son-in-law." There was a moment of silence. Before Lady Catherine gathered her wits again to speak, Darcy intervened.

"Splendid. On behalf of my wife, my aunt, my sister, and myself, I thank you for your gracious hospitality."

There was nothing Lady Catherine could do. She thanked Mr Bennet for the kind invitation, but it amused Darcy to see her arch her brow at him, as she took her chauffeur's arm. As he watched her go, a hand touched his shoulder.

"Didn't think I'd get a chance to welcome you home myself, old boy."

Darcy spun around.

"Bingley."

Giving him a wide a grin, Bingley offered his hand and Darcy took it.

"Gave us all quite a fright." Bingley didn't let go for a long moment, but neither did Darcy.

"I'll endeavour not to do so in the future," Darcy said playfully, but Bingley's jovial expression slipped.

Bingley rubbed his eyes and shook is his head. "Must be the fog got in my eyes."

Good old Bingley. Darcy had missed him so much and endeavoured to lighten the mood. "I hear you are to be married soon."

Bingley took a breath and the lighthearted aspect that so characterised his friend returned to him immediately. "Yes, next week. You'll stand up with me, won't you...? Best man and all that?"

"I'd be honoured." Darcy offered his hand again, and Bingley shook it. He rather wanted to embrace him, but... no, that wouldn't do.

The Bennets began to move down the pier, and Elizabeth and Jane smiled at each other as they remained behind. "Gentlemen..." Elizabeth took Darcy's arm, and Jane took Bingley's.

"I don't know about you, but I'm famished," Bingley said. It was just the right thing to say. Darcy could see the rosy tint about Elizabeth's eyes and knew this reunion was an emotional time for all of them.

As they walked along, arm in arm, he laid his free hand upon hers. "Glad to be home?"

"So glad to be home."

Chapter 42

Lizzy tucked away the errant strands of her coif with a sigh. In the reflection of the mirror, Darcy observed her from the lounge. The bride and groom, Jane and Bingley, were gone from Netherfield and off to Paris. Lizzy and Darcy were alone at Netherfield, save the servants, for at least for a few more days. It was oddly empty and silent after the hubbub of the wedding. Lizzy smiled at her husband, who met her gaze, but had that pensive look that usually meant a storm was brewing.

"Beautiful wedding, don't you think?" Lizzy attempted to break the silence. She laid her hat on the dressing table, and its brim nearly covered it. She turned to Darcy, who didn't reply.

"Hm?" He seemed so lost to thought. "What? Oh yes, of course. Beautiful."

"It was a shame Lydia couldn't be here." She continued talking, needing to draw him out. He was brooding again. "Imagine going back to America so soon. Still, Jane looked so lovely. Stunning even. That train… it must have been ten yards of silk, her sleeves covered in lace… and the flowers. When she handed me that bouquet, I thought I might not be able to lift it, it was so heavy…"

Finally, he spoke. "Not like that puny bouquet you held in New York."

So that was it. His pride in his ability to give her only the best was pricked by this lavish ceremony of his best friend and her sister. Darcy and she had only been married a few weeks, but this was not the first time his mood shifted from day to night unexpectedly. It appeared to her to occur especially when he seemed to be the most content. He looked miserable.

"It wasn't puny," she said gently. "I loved it. The fact that Mr Moretti thought to pick those flowers for me, a stranger…"

"Really?" He lifted his gaze to hers. "Really, Lizzy? Be honest. We can hold a wedding just like that one, better if you like—"

"Were you unhappy with ours?"

He got to his feet and took her hands in his. "No, no, of course not. That was the most, I don't know, beautiful day of my life: the white church streaming with sunlight…"

"…that kind Mr Sullivan taking in the lost travellers. I wouldn't trade that day for ten weddings just like this one. It was perfect for Jane and Charles… but not for us."

"No, not for us…" He kissed her, and she leaned against him, her cheek upon the crisp starch of his white shirt. It was all right. Everything was going to be all right.

"I'd like to leave for Pemberley tomorrow. There is nothing keeping us here. I'd like to finally take you home."

She smiled and closed her eyes briefly. "Of course." Home. Pemberley in all its grandness was now to be her home.

***

Darcy's chauffeur met them at the station, and Lizzy sat in the rear seat of the Pierce-Arrow for the short ride to the manor house. She knew Darcy well enough by now. His calm and nearly immobile aspect didn't fool her. He needed to be home, and to show his legacy: his grand estate.

The Pierce-Arrow moved through a stand of trees onto open fields and beyond that, anchored in the manicured lawns, stood a fine Georgian manor house. To Lizzy it looked rather like a painting, standing on a slope, its white stone set off by the greenery of the trees behind it.

"That, my love… is Pemberley." Darcy pointed out the window. "There used to be a stream running in front, but we dammed it up and diverted it to the farmland some years ago. There is a small lake not far from the house…" She was listening, but not listening as it suddenly occurred to her that she could have teased him over how, if he'd shown her this magnificent manor with all its lands, he might have persuaded her to marry him sooner. Listening to the earnestness in his voice that matched the glow of pride in his eyes, she thought better of it. He was a brooder by nature, and some stupid, casual remark made only in jest might weigh on him for all their married life.

"What are you smiling about?"

"Oh… I'm just happy." She squeezed his arm.

They reached the circular drive and stopped before the stone steps that led to the front door of Pemberley. After they exited the motor, she held him back while she drank in the splendour of this place. He took her hand.

"Welcome home, Mrs Darcy."

Epilogue

It didn't take long for Elizabeth to master the role of mistress of Pemberley, but her duties there didn't reduce her commitment to the cause of women's suffrage. By the summer of 1913, she'd marched with the suffragettes, this time with the National Union of Women's Suffrage Societies, a nonviolent branch of the movement. She helped organise one branch of the Suffrage Pilgrimage consisting of six routes, each originating in different places in England. Although she didn't participate in the entire five weeks (her first born, Charlie, was only a few months old at the time), she did march in the route that originated in Manchester.

Mr Darcy wouldn't let her travel alone, so often found himself at odds with the crowds at various stopping points, and even at odds with the police, who didn't seem to care whether the marchers were protected or not. Eventually, she and Darcy, and fifty thousand other supporters of votes for women, rallied in Hyde Park on 26 July, 1913. Lizzy emerged from the experience with even greater enthusiasm for the cause and renewed hope for an act of Parliament. After all, such a showing of support from the British public must have proven to the powers that be that the country was ready for women to have the vote.

George and Lydia returned to America where George was determined to go west to California. George's resolve to lead a better life after his rescue from the *Titanic* soon faded. Ironically, the couple made it as far as Chicago, where, during an overnight train stop, George won a tavern in a card game. He was quite pleased with himself as his business afforded him an opportunity to gamble, as well as ample drink. Lydia, however, proved quite formidable once the scales fell from her eyes and she kept a close eye on their money, if not on George's infidelity.

The rest of the Bennet clan remained at Longbourn except for Mary. She decided to attend Goldsmith's College at the University of London and become a teacher. Mrs Bennet thought that much more suitable than being a shopgirl, though she had to admit, Jane and Elizabeth had done rather well for themselves. Kitty, much tamed by the outrageousness of her younger sister's exploits, remained at home, resolving to marry a steady young man with prospects.

Jane and Bingley were blessed with a child a few months after Charlie's birth. They continued to live at Netherfield. After the great rally, Darcy, Elizabeth, and Charlie returned to Netherfield from town for a time where, finally, Mr Darcy taught Mr Bingley how to swim.

ABOUT THE AUTHOR

Maggie began her career by writing a Star Trek novel called A Free Radical. She got an agent who took it to the Powers-That- Be and they told her they wouldn't read anything by anyone but the authors they already hired.

Next, she turned to screenwriting. Working with her mentor, Madeline DiMaggio, she was a semi-finalist in the Prime-Time Television division of the Heart of Film Screenwriting Contest at the Austin Film Festival for her script "X-Files Mananangal" and won a screenwriting contest sponsored by Square Magazine in New York. All of these and subsequent screenplays and teleplays remain stubbornly unproduced.

Taking a different tack, she began work on Elizabeth in the New World. After finally finishing it, she set out to answer that question "Will anyone think this is good enough to publish?" One year and one large spreadsheet later filled with "No, no, no, no, thank you, but no, we are not looking for that type of manuscript at this time," it happened. The rest is history, or really, historical fiction, which is what she writes.

Maggie also climbed Kilimanjaro, stood on The Great Wall of China, visited Eiffel's office on the famous tower in Paris, and stood with Solidarity as they called an end to a strike in Warsaw.

She has a grown son, a very old dog, and likes to cook, and play the piano.

But can she write?

Well, read some of her stuff and you decide.

Get in touch with Maggie:
Website - moohabooks.com
FB – Author Maggie Mooha
Twitter- @mmooha
IG - maggiemoohabooks

www.BOROUGHSPUBLISHINGGROUP.com

If you enjoyed this book, please write a review. Our authors appreciate the feedback, and it helps future readers find books they love. We welcome your comments and invite you to send them to info@boroughspublishinggroup.com.

Follow us on Facebook, Twitter and Instagram, and be sure to sign up for our newsletter for surprises and new releases from your favorite authors.

Are you an aspiring writer? Check out www.boroughspublishinggroup.com/submit and see if we can help you make your dreams come true.

Love podcasts? Enjoy ours at www.boroughspublishinggroup.com/podcast